Weyward

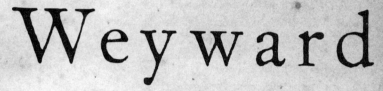

Weyward

A Novel

Emilia Hart

ST. MARTIN'S PRESS
NEW YORK

For my family

First published in the United States by St. Martin's Press, an imprint of St. Martin's Publishing Group

WEYWARD. Copyright © 2023 by Emilia Hart Limited. All rights reserved. Printed in the United States of America. For information, address St. Martin's Publishing Group, 120 Broadway, New York, NY 10271.

On Lies, Secrets, and Silence: Selected Prose 1966–1978 by Adrienne Rich, W.W. Norton & Company, Inc.

The Collected Poems by Sylvia Plath, HarperCollins Publishers.

www.stmartins.com

Designed by Jen Edwards

The Library of Congress Cataloging-in-Publication Data is available upon request.

ISBN 978-1-250-28080-0 (hardcover)
ISBN 978-1-250-28081-7 (ebook)
ISBN: 978-1-250-28897-4 (Canada & international)

Our books may be purchased in bulk for promotional, educational, or business use. Please contact your local bookseller or the Macmillan Corporate and Premium Sales Department at 1-800-221-7945, extension 5442, or by email at MacmillanSpecialMarkets@macmillan.com.

First U.S. Edition: 2023

First International Edition: 2023

10 9 8 7 6 5

PROLOGUE

ALTHA
1619

Ten days they'd held me there. Ten days, with only the stink of my own flesh for company. Not even a rat graced me with its presence. There was nothing to attract it; they had brought me no food. Only ale.

Footsteps. Then, the wrench of metal on metal as the bolt was drawn back. The light hurt my eyes. For a moment, the men in the doorway shimmered as if they were not of this world and had come to take me away from it.

The prosecutor's men.

They had come to take me to trial.

CHAPTER ONE

KATE

2019

Kate is staring into the mirror when she hears it.

The key, scraping in the lock.

Her fingers shake as she hurries to fix her makeup, dark threads of mascara spidering onto her lower lids.

In the yellow light, she watches her pulse jump at her throat, beneath the necklace he gave her for their last anniversary. The chain is silver and thick, cold against her skin. She doesn't wear it during the day, when he's at work.

The front door clicks shut. The slap of his shoes on the floorboards. Wine, gurgling into a glass.

Panic flutters in her, like a bird. She takes a deep breath, touches the ribbon of scar on her left arm. Smiles one last time into the bathroom mirror. She can't let him see that anything is different. That anything is wrong.

Simon leans against the kitchen counter, wine glass in hand. Her blood pounds at the sight. The long, dark lines of him in his suit, the cut of his cheekbones. His golden hair.

He watches her walk towards him in the dress she knows he likes. Stiff fabric, taut across her hips. Red. The same color as her underwear. Lace with little bows. As if Kate herself is something to be unwrapped, to be torn open.

She looks for clues. His tie is gone, three buttons of his shirt open to reveal fine curls. The whites of his eyes glow pink. He hands her a glass of wine and she catches the alcohol on his breath, sweet and pungent. Perspiration beads her back, under her arms.

The wine is chardonnay, usually her favorite. But now the smell turns her stomach, makes her think of rot. She presses the glass to her lips without taking a sip.

"Hi, babe," she says in a bright voice, polished just for him. "How was work?"

But the words catch in her throat.

His eyes narrow. He moves quickly, despite the alcohol: his fingers digging into the soft flesh of her bicep.

"Where did you go today?"

She knows better than to twist out of his grasp, though every cell of her wants to. Instead, she places her hand on his chest.

"Nowhere," she says, trying to keep her voice steady. "I've been home all day." She'd been careful to leave her iPhone at the apartment when she walked to the pharmacy, to take only cash with her. She smiles, leans in to kiss him.

His cheek is rough with stubble. Another smell mingles with the alcohol, something heady and floral. Perfume, maybe. It wouldn't be the first time. A tiny flare of hope in her gut. It could work to her advantage, if there's someone else.

But she's miscalculated. He shifts away from her and then—

"Liar."

Kate barely hears the word as Simon's hand connects with her cheek, the pain dizzying like a bright light. At the edges of her vision, the colors of the room slide together: the gold-lit floorboards, the white leather couch, the kaleidoscope of the London skyline through the window.

A distant crashing sound: she has dropped her glass of wine.

She grips the counter, her breath coming out of her in ragged bursts, blood pulsing in her cheek. Simon is putting on his coat, picking up his keys from the dining table.

"Stay here," he says. "I'll know if you don't."

His shoes ring out across the floorboards. The door slams. She doesn't move until she hears the creak of the elevator down the shaft.

He's gone.

The floor glitters with broken glass. Wine hangs sour in the air.

A copper taste in her mouth brings her back to herself. Her lip is bleeding, caught against her teeth by the force of his hand.

Something switches in her brain. *I'll know if you don't.*

It hadn't been enough, leaving her phone at home. He's found another way. Another way to track her. She remembers how the doorman eyed her in the lobby: had Simon slipped him a wad of crisp notes to spy on her? Her blood freezes at the thought.

If he finds out where she went—what she did—earlier today, who knows what else he might do. Install cameras, take away her keys.

And all her plans will come to nothing. She'll never get out.

But no. She's ready enough, isn't she?

If she leaves now, she could get there by morning. The drive will take seven hours. She's plotted it carefully on her second phone, the one he doesn't know about. Tracing the blue line on the screen, curling up the country like a ribbon. She's practically memorized it.

Yes, she'll go now. She *has* to go now. Before he returns, before she loses her nerve.

She retrieves the Motorola from its hiding place, an envelope taped to the back of her bedside table. Takes a duffel bag from the top shelf of the wardrobe, fills it with clothes. From the en suite, she grabs her toiletries, the box she hid in the cupboard earlier that day.

Quickly, she changes out of her red dress into dark jeans and a tight pink top. Her fingers tremble as she unclasps the necklace. She leaves it on the bed, coiled like a noose. Next to her iPhone with its gold case: the one Simon pays for, knows the passcode to. The one he can track.

She rummages through the jewelry box on her bedside table, fingers closing around the gold bee-shaped brooch she's had since childhood. She pockets it and pauses, looking around the bedroom: the cream duvet and curtains, the sharp angles of the Scandi-style furniture. There should be other things to pack, shouldn't there? She had loads of stuff, once—piles

The Weyward Sisters, hand in hand,
Posters of the sea and land,
Thus do go, about, about,
Thrice to thine, thrice to mine,
And thrice again to make up nine.
Peace, the charm's wound up.

—*Macbeth*

Weyward is used in the First Folio edition of *Macbeth*.
In later versions, *Weyward* was replaced by *Weird*.

PART ONE

and piles of dog-eared books, art prints, mugs. Now, everything belongs to him.

In the elevator, adrenaline crackles in her blood. What if he comes back, intercepts her as she's leaving? She presses the button for the basement garage but the elevator jerks to a stop at the ground floor, the doors creaking open. Her heart pounds. The doorman's broad back is turned: he's talking to another resident. Barely breathing, Kate presses herself small into the elevator, exhaling only when no one else appears and the doors jerk shut.

In the garage, she unlocks the Honda, which she bought before they met and is registered in her name. He can't—surely—ask the police to put a call out if she's driving her own car? She's watched enough crime shows. *Left of her own volition*, they'll say.

Volition is a nice word. It makes her think of flying.

She turns the key in the ignition, then taps her great-aunt's address into Google Maps. For months, she's repeated the words in her head like a mantra.

Weyward Cottage, Crows Beck. Cumbria.

CHAPTER TWO

VIOLET
1942

Violet hated Graham. She absolutely loathed him. Why did he get to study interesting things all day, like science and Latin and someone called Pythagoras, while she was supposed to be content sticking needles through a canvas? The worst part, she reflected as her wool skirt itched against her legs, was that he got to do all this in *trousers*.

She ran down the main staircase as quietly as she could, to avoid the wrath of Father, who thoroughly disapproved of female exertion (and, it often seemed, of Violet). She stifled a giggle at the sound of Graham puffing behind her. Even in her stuffy clothes she could outrun him easily.

And to think that only last night he'd boasted about wanting to go to war! Pigs had a greater chance of flying. And anyway, he was only fifteen—a year younger than Violet—and therefore far too young. It was for the best, really. Nearly all the men in the village had gone, and half of them had died (or so Violet had overheard), along with the butler, the footman, and the gardener's apprentice. Besides, Graham was her brother. She didn't want him to *die*. She supposed.

"Give it here!" Graham hissed.

Turning around, she saw that his round face was pink with effort and fury. He was angry because she'd stolen his Latin workbook and told him that he'd declined all his feminine nouns incorrectly.

"Shan't," she hissed back, clutching the workbook to her chest. "You don't deserve it. You've put *amor* instead of *arbor*, for heaven's sake."

At the bottom of the staircase, she scowled at one of the many portraits of Father that hung in the hall, then turned left, weaving through the wood-paneled corridors before bursting into the kitchens.

"What are ye playing at?" barked Mrs. Kirkby, gripping a meat cleaver in one hand and the pearly carcass of a rabbit in the other. "Could've chopped me finger off!"

"Sorry!" Violet shouted as she wrenched open the French windows, Graham panting behind her. They ran through the kitchen gardens, heady with the scent of mint and rosemary, and then they were in her favorite place in the world: the grounds. She turned around and grinned at Graham. Now that they were outside, he had no chance of catching up with her if she didn't want him to. He opened his mouth and sneezed. He had terrible hay fever.

"Aw," she said. "Do you need a hanky?"

"Shut *up*," he said, reaching for the book. She skipped neatly away. He stood there for a moment, heaving. It was a particularly warm day: a layer of gauzy cloud had trapped the heat and stiffened the air. Sweat trickled in Violet's armpits, and the skirt itched dreadfully, but she no longer cared.

She had reached her special tree: a silver beech that Dinsdale, the gardener, said was hundreds of years old. Violet could hear it humming with life behind her: the weevils searching for its cool sap; the ladybug trembling on its leaves; the damselflies, moths, and finches flitting through its branches. She held out her hand and a damselfly came to rest on her palm, its wings glittering in the sunlight. Golden warmth spread through her.

"Ugh," said Graham, who had finally caught up to her. "How can you let that *thing* touch you like that? Squash it!"

"I'm not going to *squash* it, Graham," said Violet. "It has as much right to exist as you or I do. And look, it's so pretty. The wings are rather like crystals, don't you think?"

"You're . . . not normal," said Graham, backing away. "With your insect obsession. Father doesn't think so, either."

"I don't care a fig what Father thinks," Violet lied. "And I certainly don't care what *you* think, though judging by your workbook, you should spend less time thinking about my *insect obsession* and more time thinking about Latin nouns."

He lumbered forward, nostrils flaring. Before he could make it within five paces of her, she flung the book at him—a little harder than she intended—and swung herself into the tree.

Graham swore and turned back towards the Hall, muttering.

She felt a pang of guilt as she watched the angry retreat of his back. Things hadn't always been like this between them. Once, Graham had been her constant shadow. She remembered the way he used to crawl into her bed in the nursery to hide from a nightmare or a thunderstorm, burrowing against her until his breath was loud in her ears. They'd had all sorts of japes—ripping across the grounds until their knees were black with mud, marveling at the tiny silver fish in the beck, the red-breasted flutter of a robin.

Until that awful summer's day—a day not unlike this one, in fact, with the same honey-colored light on the hills and the trees. She remembered the two of them lying on the grass behind the beech tree, breathing in meadow thistle and dandelions. She had been eight, Graham only seven. There were bees somewhere—calling out to her, beckoning. She had wandered over to the tree and found the hive, hanging from a branch like a nugget of gold. The bees glimmering, circling. She drew closer, stretched out her arms and grinned as she felt them land, the tickle of their tiny legs against her skin.

She had turned to Graham, laughing at the wonder that shone from his face.

"Can I've a go?" he'd said, eyes wide.

She hadn't known what would happen, she'd sobbed to her father later, as his cane flashed through the air towards her. She didn't hear what he said, didn't see the dark fury of his face. She saw only Graham, screaming as Nanny Metcalfe rushed him inside, the stings on his arm glowing pink. Father's cane split her palm open, and Violet felt it was less than she deserved.

After that, Father sent Graham to boarding school. Now he only came home for holidays, and grew more and more unfamiliar. She knew, deep down, that she shouldn't taunt him so. She was only doing it because as much as she couldn't forgive herself for the day of the bees, she couldn't forgive Graham, either.

He'd made her different.

Violet shook the memory away and looked at her wristwatch. It was only 3 P.M. She had finished her lessons for the day—or rather, her governess, Miss Poole, had admitted defeat. Hoping she wouldn't be missed for at least another hour, Violet climbed higher, enjoying the rough warmth of bark under her palms.

In the hollow between two branches, she found the hairy seed of a beechnut. It would be perfect for her collection—the windowsill of her bedroom was lined with such treasures: the gold spiral of a snail's shell, the silken remains of a butterfly's cocoon. Grinning, she stowed the beechnut in the pocket of her skirt and kept climbing.

Soon she was high enough to see the whole of Orton Hall, which with its sprawling stone buildings rather reminded her of a majestic spider, lurking on the hillside. Higher still, and she could see the village, Crows Beck, on the other side of the fells. It was beautiful. But something about it made her feel sad. It was like looking out over a prison. A green, beautiful prison, with birdsong and damselflies and the glowing, amber waters of the beck, but a prison nonetheless.

For Violet had never left Orton Hall. She'd never even been to Crows Beck.

"But *why* can't I go?" she used to ask Nanny Metcalfe when she was younger, as the nurse set off for her Sunday walks with Mrs. Kirkby.

"You know the rule," Nanny Metcalfe would murmur, a glint of pity in her eyes. "Your father's orders."

But, as Violet reflected, knowing a rule was not the same as understanding it. For years, she assumed the village was rife with danger— she imagined pickpockets and cutthroats lurking behind thatched cottages. (This only enhanced its allure.)

Last year, she'd badgered Graham into giving her details. "I don't know what you're getting so worked up about," he'd grimaced. "The village is dull as anything—there isn't even a pub!" Sometimes, Violet wondered whether Father wasn't trying to protect her from the village. Whether it was, in fact, the other way around.

In any case, her seclusion would soon come to an end—of sorts. In two years, when she turned eighteen, Father planned to throw a big party for her "coming out." Then—he hoped—she would catch the eye of some eligible young man, a lord-to-be, perhaps, and swap this prison for another one.

"You'll soon meet some dashing gentleman who'll whisk you off your feet," Nanny Metcalfe was always saying.

Violet didn't want to be whisked. What she actually wanted was to see the world, the way Father had when he was a young man. She had found all sorts of geography books and atlases in the library—books about the Orient, full of steaming rain forests and moths the size of dinner plates ("ghastly things," according to Father), and about Africa, where scorpions glittered like jewels in the sand.

Yes, one day she would leave Orton Hall and travel the world—as a scientist.

A biologist, she hoped, or maybe an entomologist? Something to do with animals, anyway, which in her experience were far preferable to humans. Nanny Metcalfe often spoke of the terrible fright Violet had given her when she was little: she had walked into the nursery one night to find a weasel, of all things, in Violet's cot.

"I screamed blue murder," Nanny Metcalfe would say, "but there you were, right as rain, and that weasel curled up next to you, purring like a kitten."

It was just as well that Father never learned of this incident. As far as he was concerned, animals belonged on one's plate or mounted on one's wall. The only exception to this rule was Cecil, his Rhodesian ridgeback: a fearsome beast he had beaten into viciousness over the years. Violet was forever rescuing all manner of small creatures from his slobbering jaws. Most recently, a jumping spider that now resided in a hatbox under her bed, lined with an old petticoat. She had named him—or her, it was rather hard to tell—Goldie, for the colorful stripes on his legs.

Nanny Metcalfe was sworn to secrecy.

Though there were lots of things Nanny Metcalfe hadn't told *her* either, Violet reflected later, as she dressed for dinner. After she'd changed into a soft linen frock—the offending wool skirt discarded on the floor—she turned to the looking glass. Her eyes were deep and dark, quite unlike Father and Graham's watery blue ones. Violet thought her face quite strange-looking, what with the unsightly red mole on her forehead, but she was proud of those eyes. And of her hair, which was dark, too, with an opalescent sheen not unlike the feathers of the crows that lived in the trees surrounding the Hall.

"Do I look like my mother?" Violet had been asking for as long as she could remember. There were no pictures of her mother. All she had of her was an old necklace with a dented oval pendant. The pendant had a *W* engraved on it, and she asked anyone who'd listen if her mother's name had been Winifred or Wilhelmina. ("Was she called Wallis?" she had asked Father once, having seen the name on the front page of his newspaper. He sent a bewildered Violet to her room without any dinner.)

Nanny Metcalfe was just as unhelpful.

"Can't quite recall your ma," she'd say. "I was not long arrived when she passed."

"They met at the May Day Festival in 1925," Mrs. Kirkby would offer, nodding sagely. "She were the May Queen, being so pretty. They were very much in love. But don't ask your father about it again, or you'll get a right whipping."

These crumbs of information were hardly satisfactory. As a child, Violet wanted to know so much more— Where did her parents marry? Did her mother wear a veil, a flower crown (she pictured white stars of hawthorn, to match a delicate lace dress)? And did Father blink away tears as he promised to have and to hold, until death did them part?

In the absence of any real facts, Violet clung to this image until she became certain that it had really happened. Yes—her father *had* loved her mother desperately, and death *had* done them part (she had a shadowy idea that her mother had died giving birth to Graham). *That* was why he couldn't bear to talk about it.

But occasionally, something would blur the image in Violet's head, like a ripple disturbing the surface of a pond.

One night, when she was twelve, she'd been foraging for jam and bread in the pantry when Nanny Metcalfe and Mrs. Kirkby walked into the kitchens with the newly employed Miss Poole.

She'd heard the scraping of chairs on stone and the great creak of the ancient kitchen table as they sat down, then the pop and clink of Mrs. Kirkby opening a bottle of sherry and filling their glasses. Violet had frozen mid-chew.

"How are you finding it so far, dear?" Nanny Metcalfe had asked Miss Poole.

"Well—Lord knows I'm trying, but she seems such a difficult child," Miss Poole had said. "I spend half the day looking for her as she tears around the grounds, getting grass stains all over her clothes. And she—she . . ."

Here, Miss Poole took an audibly deep breath.

"She *talks* to the animals! Even the insects!"

There was a pause.

"I suppose you think I'm ridiculous," Miss Poole had said.

"Oh, no, dear," said Mrs. Kirkby. "Well, we'd be the first to tell you that there's something different about the child. She's quite . . . how did you put it, Ruth?"

"Uncanny," Nanny Metcalfe said.

"No wonder," Mrs. Kirkby continued, "what with the mother, being how she was."

"The mother?" Miss Poole asked. "She died, didn't she?"

"Yes. Awful business," said Nanny Metcalfe. "Just after I arrived. Didn't have much chance to know her before that, though."

"She were a local lass," Mrs. Kirkby said. "From Crows Beck way. The master's parents would've been furious . . . but they'd passed, just the month before the wedding. His older brother, too. Coach accident, it was. Very sudden."

There was a sharp intake of breath from Miss Poole.

"What—and they still went ahead with the wedding? Was Lady Ayres . . . in the family way?"

Mrs. Kirkby made a noncommittal noise before continuing.

"He was very taken with her, I'll say that much. At first, anyway. A rare beauty, she were. And so much like the young lady, not just in looks."

"How do you mean?"

Another pause.

"Well, she were—what Ruth said. Uncanny. Strange."

CHAPTER THREE

ALTHA

The men took me from the gaol through the village square. I tried to twist my body away, to hide my face, but one of them pinned my arms behind my back and pushed me forward. My hair swung in front of me, as loose and soiled as a whore's.

I looked at the ground, to avoid the stares of the villagers. I felt their eyes on my body as if they were hands. Shame throbbed in my cheeks.

My stomach turned at the smell of bread and I realized that we were walking past the bakers' stall. I wondered if the bakers, the Dinsdales, were watching. Just last winter I had nursed their daughter back from fever. I wondered who else bore witness, who else was happy to leave me to this fate. I wondered if Grace was there or if she was already in Lancaster.

They bundled me into the cart as easily as if I weighed nothing. The mule was a poor beast—it looked almost as starved as I was, its ribs jutting out beneath its dull coat. I wanted to reach out and touch it, to feel the beat of its blood beneath its skin, but I didn't dare.

As we set off, one of the men gave me a sip of water and a heel of stale bread. I crumbled it into my mouth with my fingers, before leaning over the side of the cart to vomit it up. The shorter man laughed, his breath rancid in my face. I lay back against the seat and tilted my head so that I could look out at the passing countryside.

We were on the road that runs alongside the beck. My eyes were still weak, and the beck was just a blur of sunlight and water. But I could hear its music and smell its clean, iron scent.

The same beck that curved bright around my cottage. Where my mother had pointed out the minnows shooting out from under pebbles, the tight buds of angelica growing along the banks.

A dark shadow passed over me, and I thought I heard the beat of wings. The sound reminded me of my mother's crow. Of that night under the oak tree.

The memory turned in me like a knife.

My last thought before I drifted into darkness was that I was glad Jennet Weyward did not live to see her daughter thus.

I lost count of the number of times the sun rose and fell in the sky before we reached Lancaster. I had never been to such a place, had never even left the valley. The smell of a thousand people and animals was so strong that I narrowed my eyes to squint, in case I could see it hanging in the air. And the sound. Loud enough that I couldn't hear a single note of birdsong.

I sat up in the cart to look around. There were so many people: men, women, and children thronged the streets, the women hitching up their skirts as they stepped over mounds of horse dung. A man cooked chestnuts over a fire; the smell of their golden flesh made me dizzy. It was a bright afternoon but I was shivering. I looked down at my fingernails; they were blue.

We stopped outside a great stone building. I knew without needing to ask that it was the castle, where they held the assizes. It had the look of a place where lives were weighed up.

They pulled me from the cart and took me in, shutting the doors behind me so that I was swallowed whole.

The courtroom was like nothing I'd ever seen before. The sun flared through the windows, lighting on stone pillars that reminded me of trees curving towards the sky. But such beauty did nowt to quell my fear.

The two judges were seated on a high bench, as if they were heavenly beings, rather than meat and bone like the rest of us. They put me in mind of two fat beetles, with their black gowns, fur-trimmed mantles, and curious dark caps. To the side sat the jury. Twelve men. They did not look me in the eye—none bar a square-jawed man with a kink in his nose. His eyes were soft—with pity, perhaps. I could not bear the sight of it. I turned my face away.

The prosecuting magistrate entered the room. He was a tall man, and above his sober gown, his face had the raw, pitted sign of the pox. I gripped the wooden seat of the dock to steady myself as he took his place across from me. His eyes were pale blue, like a jackdaw's, but cold.

One of the judges looked at me.

"Altha Weyward," he began, frowning as though my name might sully his mouth. "You stand accused of practicing the wicked and devilish arts called witchcraft, and by said witchcraft, feloniously causing the death of John Milburn. How do you plead?"

I wet my lips. My tongue seemed to have swollen and I worried that I would choke on the words before I got them out. But when I spoke, my voice was clear.

"Not guilty," I said.

CHAPTER FOUR

KATE

Kate's stomach is still oily with fear, even though she's on the A66 now, near enough to Crows Beck. Just over two hundred miles from London. Two hundred miles from him.

She's driven through the night. She's used to getting by without much sleep, but even so, she's surprised at how alert she is, the fatigue only beginning to show itself now in a cottony feeling behind her eyeballs, a thudding at her temples. She switches on the radio, for voices, company.

A jaunty pop song fills the silence, and she grimaces before switching it off.

She winds down the car window. The dawn air floods in, clean and grassy, with a tang of dung. So different to the damp, sulfuric smell of the city. Unfamiliar.

It's been over twenty years since she was last in Crows Beck, where her great-aunt lived. Her grandfather's sister—Kate barely remembers her—died last August, leaving her entire estate to Kate. Though *estate* seems the wrong word for the small cottage. Barely bigger than two rooms, if she remembers correctly.

Outside, the rising sun turns the hills pink. Her phone tells her that she's five minutes away from Crows Beck. *Five minutes away from sleep*, she thinks. *Five minutes away from safety.*

She turns off the main road down a lane thick with trees. In the distance, she sees turrets gleam in the morning light. Could this be the Hall, she wonders, where her family once had their seat? Her grandfather and his sister grew up there—but then they were disinherited. She doesn't know why. And now, there's no one left to ask.

The turrets disappear, and then she glimpses something else. Something that makes her heart thud sharply in her chest.

A row of animals—rats, she thinks, or maybe moles—strung up on a fence, tied by their tails. The car rolls on and they slip mercifully from view. Just some harmless Cumbrian custom. She shudders and shakes her head, but she can't forget the image. The little bodies, twisting in the breeze.

The cottage is slung low to the ground, like an anxious animal. The stone walls are blurred with age, ivy-covered. Ornate letters carved into the lintel spell its name: *Weyward*. A strange name for a house. The familiar word with the odd spelling, as if it's been twisted away from itself.

The front door looks done in, the dark-green paint peeling from the bottom in ribbons. The old-fashioned lock is large and cobwebbed. She fumbles for the keys in her handbag. The jangling sound cuts through the morning quiet and something rustles in the shrubbery next to the house, making her jump. Kate hasn't set foot inside since she was a child— way back, when her father was still alive. Her memories of the cottage— and her great-aunt—are dim, shadowy. Still, she's surprised by the fear in her gut. It's just a house, after all. And she's got nowhere else to go.

She takes a breath, goes inside.

The hallway is narrow and low-ceilinged. A cloud of dust rises from the floor with each step, as if in greeting. The walls are lined with pale-green wallpaper, almost hidden by framed sketches of insects and animals. She flinches at a particularly lifelike rendition of a giant hornet. Her great-aunt had been an entomologist. Kate can't quite see the appeal, herself—she's not exactly fond of insects, or anything that flies. Not anymore.

She finds, at the back of the house, a threadbare living room, a wall of which comprises the kitchen. Blackened copper pots and twists of dried herbs hang above a range that looks centuries old. The furniture is handsome but weathered: a buckling green sofa, an oak table surrounded by a motley of mismatched chairs. Above a crumbling fireplace, the mantelpiece is littered with strange artifacts: a withered husk of honeycomb; the jeweled wings of a butterfly, preserved in glass. One corner of the ceiling is shrouded in cobwebs so thick they look intentionally cultivated.

She fills the rusted kettle with water and puts it on the stove top while she searches through the cupboards for supplies. Behind tinned beans and jars of pale, pickled mysteries, she finds some tea bags and an unopened packet of chocolate bourbons. She eats over the sink, looking out of the window to the bottom of the garden, where the beck glints gold in the dawn. The kettle sings. Clutching her mug of tea, she tracks back up the corridor to the bedroom, floorboards creaking underfoot.

The ceiling is even lower here than in the rest of the house: Kate needs to stoop. Through the window she can see the hills that ring the valley, dappled by clouds. The room is crowded with bookcases and furniture. A four-poster bed, piled high with ancient cushions. It occurs to her that this is probably the bed her great-aunt died in. She passed away in her sleep, the lawyer said—found by a local girl the next day. Briefly, she wonders if the bedding has been changed since, considers sleeping on the sagging sofa in the other room. But fatigue pulls at her, and she collapses on top of the covers.

When she wakes, she is confused by the unfamiliar shapes in the room. For a moment, she thinks she is back in the sterile bedroom of their London apartment, that any minute Simon will be on top of her, inside her . . . then she remembers. Her pulse settles. The windows are blue with dusk. She checks the time on the Motorola: 6:33 P.M.

She thinks, with an acid wave of fear, of the iPhone she left behind. He could be looking through it right now . . . but she'd had no choice. And anyway, he'll find nothing he hasn't already seen before.

She isn't sure when he started monitoring her phone. Perhaps he's been doing it for years, without her realizing. He'd always known the passcode, and she offered it up to him to inspect whenever he asked. But even so, last year, he'd become convinced she was having an affair.

21

"You're meeting someone, aren't you?" he'd snarled as he took her from behind, his fingers tight in her hair. "At the fucking *library*."

At first, she thought he'd hired a private investigator to follow her, but that didn't make sense. Because then he would know that she wasn't meeting anyone—she just went to the library to read, to escape into other people's imaginations. Often, she reread books she'd loved as a child, their familiarity a balm—*Grimms' Fairy Tales*, *The Chronicles of Narnia*, and her favorite, *The Secret Garden*. Sometimes, she would close her eyes and find herself not in bed with Simon, but amongst the tangled plants at Misselthwaite Manor, watching roses nod in the breeze.

Perhaps that was what he really had a problem with. That he could control her body but not her mind.

Then there were other signs—like the row they'd had before Christmas. He knew, somehow, that she'd been looking at flights to Toronto, to see her mother. She realized that he'd installed spyware on her iPhone, something that allowed him to track not only her whereabouts, but her search history, her emails, and texts. So when the lawyer called her last August about the cottage—her inheritance—she'd deleted the call log from her history and resolved to somehow get a second phone. A secret phone that Simon would never know about.

It had taken her weeks to scrounge enough cash—Simon gave her an allowance, but she was only supposed to spend this on makeup and lingerie—to buy the Motorola. Only then had she been able to start planning. She'd had the lawyer deliver the keys to a PO box in Islington. Began hiding her allowance in the lining of her handbag, depositing it weekly into the bank account she'd opened in secret.

Even then, she wasn't sure whether she'd go through with it, whether she deserved it. Freedom.

Until Simon announced that he wanted a child. He was expecting a lucrative promotion at work—starting a family was the natural next step.

"You're not getting any younger," he'd said. And then, with a sneer, "Besides, it's not as if you have anything better to do."

A chill had spread through her as she listened to him speak. It was one thing for *her* to endure this—to endure him. Spittle flying in her face, the burn of his hand against her skin. The ceaseless, brutal nights.

But a child?

She couldn't—wouldn't—be responsible for that.

For a while, she'd kept taking contraception, hiding the sheath of pink tablets inside a balled-up sock in her bedside table. Until Simon found it. He made her watch as he popped each pill from its blister pack, one by one, before flushing them down the toilet.

After that, it became more difficult. Waiting until he had fallen asleep to slip from the bed, crouching silent in the bathroom over the blue glow of her secret phone, she researched the old methods. The ones he wouldn't suspect. Lemon juice, which she stored in an old perfume bottle. The sting of it was almost pleasurable; it left her feeling clean. Pure.

As she planned her escape, greeting the monthly petals of blood in her underwear with relief, his rule tightened. He interrogated her endlessly about her daily movements and activities: had she taken a detour, spoken to anyone else when she collected his shirts from the dry cleaner? Had she flirted with the man who delivered their groceries? He even monitored what she ate, stocking the kitchen with kale and supplements, as if she were a prize ewe being fattened up for lambing.

It didn't stop him from hurting her, though—from twisting her hair around his knuckles, from biting her breasts. She doubted he wanted a baby for its own sake. His need to possess her had grown so insatiable that it was no longer enough to mark her body on the outside.

Swelling her womb with his seed would be the ultimate form of dominance. The ultimate control.

And so she found a grim satisfaction in watching a green swirl of kale disappear down the toilet, the same way her birth control pills had. In smiling slyly at a delivery man. But these small acts of rebellion were dangerous. He tried to catch her in a deceit, laying verbal traps as deftly as if he were a lawyer questioning a witness in court.

"You said you would collect the dry cleaning at 2 P.M.," he'd say, his breath hot on her face. "But the receipt is time-stamped for 3 P.M. Why did you lie to me?"

Sometimes his cross-examinations lasted an hour, sometimes even longer.

Lately, he'd threatened to confiscate her keys, declaring that she couldn't be trusted during the long hours when she was alone in the gleaming prison of their apartment.

The net was closing. And a baby would bind her to him forever.

Which was why yesterday, the future—with its distant promise of freedom—seemed to drain away as she huddled in the bathroom, watching dye spread across a pregnancy test. The tiles were cold against her skin. The whirr of a fly batting itself against the window mingled with her own ragged breaths to form an unreal music. "This can't be happening," she said out loud. There was no one to answer.

Twenty minutes later, she ripped a second test from its packaging, but the result was the same.

Positive.

Don't think about that now, she tells herself. But she still can't believe it—the whole drive up, she itched to pull over and open the cardboard box she'd stowed in her bag, just to check that she hadn't imagined those two blurred lines.

She had tried so hard. But in the end, none of it mattered. He had got his way.

Nausea roils in her, furs the roof of her mouth. She shivers, swallows. Tries to focus on the here and now. She's safe. That's all that matters. Safe, but freezing. She heads for the other room, wondering if the fireplace is functional. There's a stack of firewood next to it and a box of matches on the mantelpiece. The first match refuses to light. So does the second. Even though she's hundreds of miles away from him, his voice is loud in her head: *Pathetic. Can't do anything right*. Her fingers tremble, but she tries again. She grins at the sight of the small blue flame, the orange sparks.

The sparks grow into flames, and Kate stretches out her hands to warm them, before thick smoke billows into the room. Chest heaving, she grabs the kettle from the stove and flings water on top of the fire. Once it is out, her insides grow cold. Perhaps the voice is right. Perhaps she *is* pathetic.

But she's come this far, hasn't she? She can do this. Rationally, she knows, now that her breathing has slowed, that something must be blocking the chimney. A poker leans against the fireplace. Perfect. On all fours, eyes stinging from smoke, she shoves the poker up the chimney and feels it connect with something, something soft . . .

She screams when the dark bundle tumbles down, screams again when she sees it's the body of a bird. Ash quivers on feathers the color of onyx. A crow. The bright bead of its eye follows her as she recoils. She doesn't like birds, with their flapping wings and sharp beaks. Has avoided them since childhood. For a moment, she resents her great-aunt for having lived in—of all the places on God's green earth—*Crows Beck*.

But this crow is dead. It can't hurt her. She needs a bag, some newspaper or something, to dispose of it. She's almost out of the door when she feels a shiver of movement in the room. Turning, she watches in horror as the bird takes flight, risen like some sort of corvine Lazarus. Kate opens the window and frantically brandishes the poker at the crow until it flies out. She slams the window shut and runs from the room. The sound of its beak tapping on the windowpane follows her down the corridor.

CHAPTER FIVE

VIOLET

Violet straightened her green dress as she followed Father and Cecil out of the dining room. She'd barely been able to eat a thing, and not just because Mrs. Kirkby had made rabbit pie (she had tried not to think of silky ears and delicate pink noses as she chewed). Father had asked her to accompany him to the drawing room after dinner. The drawing room—furnished in oppressive dark tartans—was where Father enjoyed his postprandial glass of port and silence, observed by the stuffed head of an ibex that hung over the chimneypiece. Women were forbidden (apart from Mrs. Kirkby, who had lit an unseasonable fire in the grate).

"Close the door," Father said once they were inside. As she swung the door shut, Violet saw Graham glower at her from the corridor. *He* had never been invited to the drawing room. Though perhaps that was a good thing. Violet turned back to Father and saw that his face had taken on the ashen hue that usually signaled grave displeasure. Her stomach flipped.

Father stalked over to the drinks trolley, where crystal decanters sparkled in the firelight. He poured himself a generous glass of port before sinking into an armchair. The leather squeaked as he crossed his legs. He did not invite her to sit down (though the only other chair in the room, an austere wing-back, was rather too close to the fire—and Cecil—to be inviting).

"Violet," Father said, crinkling his nose as though her name offended him in some way.

"Yes, Father?" Violet hated how thin her voice sounded. She swallowed, wondering what she had done wrong. He normally only bothered to discipline her when Graham was around. Otherwise, she largely escaped his notice. For the second time that day, she thought of the incident with the bees and winced.

He leaned over to stoke the fire violently, so that it spat pale ash onto the richly patterned Turkish carpet. Cecil yelped, then began to growl in Violet's direction, deducing that she must be the cause of his master's displeasure. A vein jumped at Father's temple. He was silent for so long that Violet was beginning to wonder whether she could just creep out of the drawing room without him noticing.

"We need to discuss your behavior," he said, finally.

Her cheeks grew hot with panic.

"My behavior?"

"Yes," Father said. "Miss Poole tells me that you have been . . . *climbing trees.*" He spoke the last two words slowly and clearly, as if he couldn't quite believe what he was saying. "Apparently, you ripped your skirt. I'm told it is . . . ruined."

He stared into the fire, frowning.

Violet twisted her hands, which were by now slick with sweat. She hadn't even noticed the tear—snaking the full length of the wool skirt—until Nanny Metcalfe had collected it for the wash. The skirt was ancient, anyway, and far too long, with horridly prissy pleats. Secretly, she was glad to be rid of it.

"I'm . . . I'm sorry, Father."

His frown deepened, creasing his forehead. Violet looked to the window, forgetting that the black-out curtains were drawn. A fly buffeted its tiny body against the fabric in desperate search of the outside world. The whirr of its wings filled Violet's ears and she didn't hear what Father said next.

"What?" she said.

"*'I beg your pardon, Father.'*"

"I beg your pardon, Father?" she repeated, still watching the fly.

"I was saying that you have one last chance to conduct yourself appropriately, as befits my daughter. Your cousin Frederick is coming to stay with us next month, on leave from the front." He paused and Violet braced herself for a sermon.

Father often talked about his time fighting in the Great War. Every November he made Graham polish his medals in preparation for Armistice Day, when he had the entire household gather in the first sitting room for the minute of silence. Afterwards, he gave a repetitive speech about valor and sacrifice that seemed to get longer every year.

"Knows naught about real fighting," Violet had heard Dinsdale, the gardener, mutter to Mrs. Kirkby once after a particularly long address. "Spent most of his time in the officers' mess with a bottle of port, I'd wager." Father had seemed almost gleeful when war was again declared in 1939. He had immediately commanded that Graham and Violet set about gathering conkers from the horse chestnut trees that lined the drive. Apparently, the round seeds, glossy as rubies, were bound to be indispensable in the production of the bombs that would explode all over Germany and "send the Boche to kingdom come." Graham collected hundreds of the things, but Violet couldn't bear to think of the beautiful seeds coming to such a grisly end. She secretly buried them in the garden, hoping that they would grow anew. Fortunately, Father soon lost enthusiasm for the war—kept from enlisting by a lame knee and "duties to the estate"—and forgot all about this assignment.

But there was no martial sermon tonight. "I expect you to be on your best behavior around Frederick," Father continued instead. Violet thought this was all very odd. She couldn't remember ever hearing about a cousin called Frederick—or any cousin at all, for that matter. Father never spoke of any relations—not even his parents and older brother, who had died in an accident before she was born. This subject, too, was forbidden—she had once received three stinging raps on the hand for asking about it. "Consider it . . . a test. If you fail to conduct yourself appropriately during his visit, then . . . I'll have no choice but to send you away. For your own good."

"Away?"

"To finishing school. You'll need to learn to behave properly if you're to have any chance of making a match. If you can't show me that you're capable of comporting yourself like the young lady you are, there are several institutions that may be suitable for the task. And where none of this gallivanting around outdoors, collecting grubby leaves and twigs like some sort of *savage* will be permitted." He lowered his voice. "Perhaps they can stop you from turning out like . . . *her.*"

"Her?" Violet's heart fluttered. Did he mean her mother?

But Father ignored her question. "That's all," he said, looking up at her for the first time. "Good night."

There was a strange expression on his face. As if he were looking at her but seeing someone else.

Violet waited until she was safely alone in her bedroom before she let the tears fall. She wept quietly as she changed into her nightdress and got into bed. After a while, she tried to steady her breathing, but it was no good. The air in her little room tasted stale, and—not for the first time—she had the feeling that she was as out of place in the Hall as a fish would be in the clouds. She longed for the sturdy embrace of the beech tree, for the night breeze on her skin.

The snippet of conversation she'd overheard when she was younger rang in her ears.

So much like the young lady, not just in looks.

Had her mother been like this, too? Had nature pulled at her heart the same way it pulled at Violet's now?

And what could possibly be so wrong with that?

Sighing, she kicked off the coverlet. After turning out the lamp, she crept over to the window, pushed aside the horrid black-out curtain and opened the sash.

The moon shone like a pearl in the dusky sky, lighting up the cragged hills. There was a gentle wind, and Violet heard the trees shift and murmur. She closed her eyes, listening to the hoot of an owl, the flap of a bat's wings, a badger rustling on the way to its burrow.

This was home. Not the Hall, with its dingy corridors and endless tartan and the threat of Father hulking around every corner.

But if she were sent away . . . she might never see any of it again. The owls, the bats, the badgers. The old beech that she loved, and its village of insects.

Instead, she'd be cloistered indoors and forced to learn all manner of useless conversational skills and rules of etiquette. All so that Father could offer her up to some grizzled old baron or another—as if she were something to be bartered with for favors.

Or something to be rid of.

But no—he *wouldn't* send her away. She wouldn't let him. When she left Orton Hall—she imagined herself moving deftly through a jungle, brushing against ferns dripping with beetles—it would be on her own terms. Not Father's, nor anyone else's.

She'd be here, she vowed to herself, not at some horrible finishing school, when winter came to take the leaves from the trees. She would even stay inside, if that was what it took. Just until the visit from the dullard relative was over. That would show Father how well behaved she could be.

CHAPTER SIX

KATE

K ate burrows under the duvet to muffle the *clink* of beak on glass, waiting for the crow to give up its assault on the window. She takes deep, shuddering breaths, gagging on the musty scent of the bedding. Eventually, the sound fades, and she imagines that she can hear the cut of wings through air as the crow flies away. Her breathing settles, the thrum of her pulse slows.

She lifts her head and looks about the room: the stooped ceiling, the green-painted walls that are almost convex with age, closing in. Framed photographs stare down at her, along with sketches—all of animals, insects, birds. One image looks three-dimensional, sculptural almost: a tawny snake, gleaming beneath its glass frame. Struck by its russet glimmer, she takes a closer look. It isn't a snake at all, she sees, but the preserved body of a centipede: shining wetly in thick segments, caught forever in glass.

She shudders as she reads aloud the curling script on the frame, the words strange as a spell.

"*Scolopendra gigantea.*"

The thick silence makes her dizzy. Sick, almost, with the unfamiliar feeling of freedom. It sits uneasily, like rough cloth against her skin. It needs adjusting to.

This is the longest she's gone without speaking to Simon since they

31

met six years ago, when she was twenty-three. Thinking of that first night makes something in her stomach hurt. She can see herself clearly: impossibly young and shy, standing with her friends in a pub in London. Though she wonders now if *friends* was ever the right word for the women she met at university. She never managed to match her speech to the cadence of theirs, never quite correctly timed a joke or a laugh. It's a feeling she's had since childhood: that she is somehow separate, closed off from everyone else.

The feeling of separateness had been particularly strong that night, because her mother had just moved to Canada with her new husband, leaving Kate all alone. It was no more than she deserved, but it still hurt. She remembers looking down into her pint glass, full of the heavy, sour ale she pretended to like, trying to think of an excuse for leaving early.

She'd looked up, with the idea of heading to the restroom for a reprieve, when she'd seen him. It was his posture she'd first admired. The easy, leonine grace with which he leaned against the bar as he surveyed the room. Flushing with surprise and pleasure, she had realized that he was looking at her. A deep, primal part of her had recognized something in his slow, sensuous smile when their eyes met. Had known what would happen, even then.

There's a rushing sensation inside her skull, and Kate shuts her eyes.

She breathes deeply and listens. If she were in the apartment, she'd be able to hear traffic, the laughter of the post-work crowd drinking outside the pub on the corner, a plane rumbling overhead. The double glazing on their trendy Hoxton high-rise was no match for the soundscape of London, for the hum of eight million lives.

But here there are no cars, no planes roaring overhead, no distant drone from a neighbor's television. Here there is just . . . silence. She can't tell if she likes it or finds it eerie. If she strains, she thinks she can hear the distant babble of the beck, vegetation rustling with the local nightlife. Caterpillars, stoats, owls. Though of course that isn't possible. She draws back the faded curtains from the window and sees that it is securely shut. There's no way her hearing is that good. She's imagining things, like she used to as a child. "Come down from those clouds," her parents used to say, catching her in one of her reveries. "And while you're here, do your homework!"

But she never listened.

No matter where they were, she was always letting things distract her . . . a worm, glimmering pink in the sand at the playground; a squirrel, streaking up a tree on Hampstead Heath. The birds, nesting in the eaves of their house.

If only she'd listened.

She was nine the day it happened. Her father was walking her to school—a summer morning, hazy with heat. They took their usual route, a road shaded with lush oak trees, their leaves dappling the light green. Her father held her hand as they approached the pedestrian crossing, reminding her to look both ways, to pay special attention to the blind corner on the left, where the road curved away in a sharp bend.

They were halfway across the road when a birdcall tugged her back, pulling at some strange, secret part of her. A crow, she thought, from its husky caw—she had already learned to recognize most of the birds that sang in her parents' garden, and crows were her favorite. There was something intelligent—almost human—about their sly voices and dark, luminous eyes.

Kate turned, scanning the trees that lined the road behind them. And there it was: a velvet flash of black, shocking against the lurid green and blue of the June day. A crow, just as she'd thought. Pulling her hand free of her father's, she ran towards it, watching as it took flight.

A shadow fell across the road. There was a distant roar, and then a monster—the kind that she pretended she was too old to believe in, with red scales and silver teeth—appeared around the corner, bearing down on her.

Her father reached her just in time. He shoved her, hard, onto the grassy verge. There was a sound like paper ripping, like the air tearing in two. She watched, stunned, as the monster plowed into him.

Slow, then fast, he fell.

Later, when the emergency services had arrived—two ambulances and a police car, a convoy of death—Kate saw something gold on the asphalt.

It was her bee brooch, the one she always carried in her pocket. It must have fallen out when her father shoved her away, saving her from the monster—the monster that she now knew was really just a car, with chipped red paint and a rusted grille. She looked around and saw the driver, a thin-shouldered man, sobbing in the back of one of the ambulances.

A stretcher bearing something black and shiny was being loaded into the other ambulance. It took her a moment to realize that the thing on the stretcher was her father; that she would never again see his smile, the crinkles around his eyes. He was gone.

I killed my father, she thought. *I am the monster.*

She picked up the brooch and turned it over in her hand. There were ugly gaps like missing teeth where it had lost some of its crystals. One wing was dented.

She put it back in her pocket as a reminder of what she had done.

From that day on, she kept away from the squirrels and the worms, from the forest and the gardens. Birds in particular were to be avoided. Nature—and the glow of fascination it had always sparked in her—was too dangerous.

She was too dangerous.

As her fascination turned to fear, she stayed inside, putting herself behind glass. Just like her great-aunt's framed centipede. And she didn't let anyone in.

Until she met Simon.

In the cottage, she chokes down tears. Her throat feels parched and narrow. She can't remember when she last had a drink: she needs some water, something. Vodka would be better, but her aunt's spirits collection—crammed into the kitchen cupboard along with jars of instant coffee and Ovaltine—hasn't yielded anything so pedestrian, only unfamiliar words curled on yellowed labels: *arak, slivovitz, soju*. Languages Kate doesn't even recognize. And anyway—she's not sure it's a good idea. She remembers the chardonnay, with its stink of rot. The decision she has to make, about the baby, sits heavy inside her.

The shadowy shapes of the kitchen loom out at her in the second before she switches on the light. She averts her eyes from the pale rope of cobwebs hanging from the ceiling and turns to the chipped enamel sink.

Taking a mug from the rack on the windowsill, her knuckles brush against something: a jam jar full of feathers. White and delicate, tawny red. The largest is glossy and black—almost blue with iridescence. Looking closer, she sees that it is speckled with white, as though it has been dipped in snow. Just like the crow from the fireplace, which, she realizes now, was flecked not with ash but with similar white marks. Perhaps it is some sort of disease that afflicts the crows around here? The thought spikes the hairs on the back of her neck. She turns on the tap, gulps the water down as if it could cleanse her, from the inside out.

Afterwards, she takes a moment to look out of the window. She can see the moon clearly, so full that she can make out the dips and ridges of its craters. It casts its yellow light on the ramshackle garden, landing on the leaves of the plants, on the branches of the oaks and sycamores. She is looking at the trees, wondering how old they are, when she sees them . . . move.

She can feel her heart beating in her ears. Her breathing grows shallow, the panic washing over her like a tide. Then, as she watches, dark shapes— hundreds of them, it seems—rise from the trees in unison, as if pulled by a puppeteer's string. Silhouetted against the moon.

Birds.

CHAPTER SEVEN

ALTHA

The guards took me down a cramped stone staircase to the dungeon. If the castle had swallowed me, now it had me in its bowels; for here it was even darker than where they'd held me in the village.

My gut churned between hunger and sickness, thirst clawing at my throat. My heart hammered at the sight of the heavy wooden door. I was already so weak. I did not know how much longer I would last.

But they gave me provisions, this time, before they locked me away—a thin blanket, a pot, and a pitcher of water. And an old hunk of bread, which I ate slowly, biting off tiny amounts and chewing until the saliva flooded my mouth.

I only took note of my surroundings once I had eaten my fill, my shrunken stomach cramping. They had given me no candle, but there was a small grate set high in the wall, letting in the last embers of the day.

The stone walls felt cold to the touch, and when I took my fingers away, they were damp. A dripping sound came from somewhere, echoing like a warning.

The straw beneath my feet was sodden, moldering; the sweet rot mingling with the reek of old piss. There was another smell, too. I thought of all who had been held there before me, growing pale as mushrooms in the dark, awaiting their fate. It was their fear I could smell, as if it had bled into the air, seeped into the stone.

The fear hummed within me, gave me strength for what I had to do.

I pulled up my shift so that my belly met with the chill air. Then, gritting my teeth I began to scratch, fingernails tearing at the tiny bauble of flesh below my rib cage. Below my heart.

Just when I was sure that I could bear the pain no longer, I felt flesh come away, then the thick wetness of blood, its sweet tang filling the air. I wished that I had honey, or some thyme, to make a poultice for the wound; instead, I made do with some water from the pitcher. When I had cleaned it as best I could, I lay down and drew the blanket over me. The straw did little against the stone floor, and my bones rang with the cold.

Only then did I allow myself to think of home: my little rooms, neat and bright with jars and vials; the moths that danced round my candles at night. And outside, my garden. My heart ached at the thought of my plants and flowers, my dear nanny goat who kept me in milk and comfort, the sycamore that sheltered me with its boughs. For the first time since they'd torn me from my pallet, I let myself sob. I wondered if I would die of the loneliness before they had the chance to hang me. But at that moment, something brushed my skin, as delicate as a kiss. It was a spider, its legs and pincers blue with moonlight. My new friend crawled into the hollow between my neck and shoulder, clinging to my hair. I thanked it for its presence, which did more to lift my spirit than even the bread and water.

As I watched a moonbeam dance through the grate, I wondered who would give testimony against me the next day. Then I thought of Grace.

I was sure I would never sleep. But it seemed the thought had barely left my mind when I was woken by the creak of the door swinging open. The spider scuttled away at the burn of torchlight, and my heart lurched at the sight of a man in Lancaster livery. Court would begin shortly, he said. I was to make myself presentable.

He gave me a kirtle, spun of rough cloth and smelling of sweat. I did not like to think who had worn it before me, where they were now. I winced at the feel of the cloth against my wound, but when the man returned, I was glad that I had on a proper dress, even if it was crudely made. I wished I had a cap, or something to neaten my hair with, for it hung about my face in rags. Adding to my shame.

My mother always taught me that cleanliness commands respect, and that respect was worth more than all the king's gold—to us, especially, seeing as we often had little of either. We had washed every week. No smell of curdled sweat hung around the Weyward women, not even in high summer. Instead, we smelled of lavender, for protection. I wished I had some lavender now. But all I had were my wits, dulled as they were by lack of proper food and sleep.

The man shackled me for the short walk from the dungeon to the courtroom. I stopped myself from flinching at the shock of the cold metal on my skin and held my head high as we walked up the stairs and into the courtroom.

The prosecutor rose from his seat and walked towards the bench, where the judges sat. His footsteps on the boards drove fear into my heart, and I shook in the awful silence before his speech.

Still, I was unprepared for the horror of his words. His pale eyes burned as he denounced me as a dangerous, malicious witch, in thrall to Satan himself. I had, he said, engaged in the most hellish practice of witchcraft and sorcery, to take the life of Master John Milburn, him being an innocent and God-fearing yeoman. His voice grew louder as he spoke, until it rang like a death knell in my skull.

He turned and spat the closing words at me. "I have confidence," he said, "that the gentlemen of this jury of life and death shall find you as you are. Guilty."

And then, to the court:

"I call the first examinate to give evidence against the accused."

The blood rushed in my ears when I saw who the guards escorted to the box.

Grace Milburn.

CHAPTER EIGHT

VIOLET

Violet was on her best behavior.

All week, she had been focused and diligent in her lessons. Miss Poole was thrilled that she had finally grasped the French pluperfect tense and said that her drawing of a vase of irises was *exquisite*. Violet thought that the blue flowers looked like corpses, with their wilting heads and drooping leaves. Miss Poole had picked them. Violet didn't believe in picking flowers, in snapping their stems for no reason other than to look at them. But she kept her mouth shut and drew their likeness as best she could.

She even made some crooked progress on the silk slip that Miss Poole insisted she sew for her "trousseau." (She couldn't for the life of her think why such a thing was necessary. Nanny Metcalfe was the only person who had ever seen her in her "combinations"—as the nursemaid rather archaically called them—and Violet intended for matters to stay that way.)

Determined to avoid the purgatory of finishing school, she had stayed inside for two weeks now. Two weeks since she had felt the kiss of an insect's wings against her skin. Two weeks since she'd climbed her beloved beech, since she'd removed her treasures—the snail's shell, the butterfly cocoon, the beech nut with its spiky fronds—from the windowsill and hidden them under her bed. She'd taken to asking Miss Poole to shut the windows, even though it was getting so warm that sweat shone on their upper lips, because she couldn't bear the sounds of the valley. The drone of a bee was a torment; a chattering squirrel pierced her heart.

But gradually, the sounds faded away. She was glad of it.

Even Goldie seemed to lose interest in her. Normally, she could hear the faint *click* of his legs as he climbed out of the hatbox and scuttled about the room at night—sometimes she even woke to find him nestled safe in her hair—but now there was just silence. She worried that he'd died but couldn't bring herself to look.

Most days, when she wasn't attending to what Miss Poole dubbed her "improvements," Violet lay on her bed with the curtains drawn, sweating in the dark heat. Mrs. Kirkby began bringing trays to her room: first, elaborate fruit pies and cakes, towering with cream, and when those went untouched, bowls of bland nursery food. Nanny Metcalfe even came in one afternoon and asked if she wouldn't like her to read aloud, something she hadn't done since Violet was small.

"There was that book of tales you loved," she said. "Brothers Slim, or summat—"

"Grimm. The Brothers Grimm," Violet said. She had loved them, it was true, even if Nanny Metcalfe had pronounced half the words wrong. "I'm much too old for that now, Nanny." She turned to face the wall. She could see a chink of golden light on the floral wallpaper.

She heard the rustle of Nanny Metcalfe's dress as she bent over Violet's bed.

"Do you need—"

"Can you draw the curtains more closely together, please, Nanny?" she asked, cutting the nurse's questions off.

"All right, Miss Violet," she said. "If you're sure."

Violet bit her lip. She just had to get through this visit from Father's relative. She had to show him that he didn't need to send her away to some stuffy old school. Then she could go outside again. Until then, all she needed was to be left alone.

That evening, as Violet drifted between sleep and wakefulness, she heard Nanny Metcalfe and Mrs. Kirkby muttering outside her door. Mrs. Kirkby had come to collect another tray of uneaten food.

"I've never seen a person take to their bed like this, without being ill," Nanny Metcalfe said. "But there's naught wrong with her that I can find. No fever, no rash . . ."

"I have," said Mrs. Kirkby. "The late mistress took to her bed, not long before the end."

"Why? Nerves?"

"That's what Doctor Radcliffe said. The master had him come out, the first time, on condition of secrecy."

"Could he say what triggered it?"

"He didn't need to. We all knew the reason. Especially after what happened next."

Perhaps they can stop you from turning out like her.

The next afternoon, while Violet sat limp in the schoolroom, embroidering with Miss Poole, Nanny Metcalfe burst through the door.

"The Master wants Miss Violet to take the air," she said.

Miss Poole looked at the clock, a frown accentuating her reptilian features.

"But we've only just started our needlepoint lesson," she said.

"Master's orders," said Nanny Metcalfe.

"I'd rather stay inside," said Violet, looking down at her fingers on the canvas. Her hands, like the rest of her, had grown pale from lack of sun. Her fingernails were speckled and thin, as if they might peel away. *Could you die,* Violet wondered, *from longing?*

"Well, Violet, if your father wants you to, perhaps you should," said Miss Poole. "But you can continue with your needlepoint after dinner. I'm so very pleased with your enthusiasm. Where has *this* Violet been hiding?"

Nanny Metcalfe offered Violet her arm as they made their way around the grounds. The gardens were bright with flowers—blue spikes of hyacinth, fleshy whorls of rhododendrons—so bright that she averted her eyes and looked down at her feet in their leather brogues.

"Isn't it lovely to be outside, listening to the birds?" Nanny Metcalfe said.

"Yes," she said. "Lovely."

But she couldn't hear the birds. In fact, she could barely hear anything at all, other than Nanny Metcalfe's voice. It was as if her ears were wrapped in wool.

A butterfly passed them. Out of habit, Violet lifted her hand, but instead of coming to rest on her palm, it flew on, like she wasn't even there.

"Your father would like you to take your tea downstairs this evening, in the dining room with himself and Graham," said Nanny Metcalfe.

"Very well," said Violet faintly, watching the butterfly until it was no more than a white flash in the corner of her vision.

"Nanny," she said, pausing as she tried to word the question that had worried at her for days. "Was there something wrong with my mother?"

"Your mother? Don't know where that's come from. Violet, I've said it before and I'll say it again: I barely knew her ladyship, rest her soul."

But Violet saw that Nanny Metcalfe's cheeks had reddened.

"And . . . what about me? Is there something wrong with me?"

"Here, pet," Nanny Metcalfe said, turning to look at her. "Wherever would you get an idea like that?"

"Just something Father said. And I'm not allowed in the village, but Graham is. And—until this cousin—no one has ever come to call."

People were always calling on each other in novels, Violet had learned. And it wasn't as if there was a shortage of nearby families of similar status, who might be disposed to friendship. Why, Baron Seymour lived only thirty miles from Orton Hall *and* had a son and a daughter of equivalent ages to Graham and Violet. She had once looked them up in Father's battered copy of *Burke's Peerage*.

"Och, your father's just overprotective, that's all. Don't you pay him any mind. Here, we'd better be getting back so you can have your bath." Her words made Violet feel very small, as if she were six instead of sixteen.

Violet didn't brush her hair before supper, and wore her least favorite dress, an ill-fitting orange gingham. She knew it made her look sallow and drawn, but she didn't care.

Mrs. Kirkby set a shrunken joint of roast mutton on the table. Violet hated mutton, though she knew from Father's lectures that they were rather lucky to have it at all. Still, she tried not to picture the gentle, cloud-soft sheep that had given its life for their meal.

She looked at her plate. The meat was gray and lumpish, the sort of thing Father would never have eaten before the war. Watery blood leaked from its flesh, staining her potatoes pink. She felt as if she might be sick.

She put her knife and fork down, before realizing that Father was watching her. A fleck of gravy quivered at the corner of his frown.

"Eat up, girl," he said. "Follow your brother's example."

Graham, whose plate was already nearly empty, flushed. Father helped himself to more gravy.

"You will recall," he began, "that your cousin Frederick is coming to stay with us tomorrow. He's an officer in the Eighth Army, taking leave from the fighting in Tobruk. Do you know where Tobruk is, Graham?"

"No, Father," said Graham.

"It's in Libya," said Father between mouthfuls. Violet could see strings of meat in his teeth when he talked. The urge to vomit returned. She trained her eyes on the painting hanging on the wall behind him—the portrait of some long-dead viscount, looking on imperiously from the eighteenth century.

"Godforsaken place," Father continued. "Full of savages." He shook his head. Violet flinched as she felt something brush against her leg. Pretending to drop her napkin, she peered under the table in time to see Father deliver Cecil a swift kick to the rump. "Those wops haven't a clue what they're doing out there. They couldn't govern a sandbar."

The maid, Penny, began clearing the plates to make room for pudding.

Eton mess, a favorite of Father's, who never lost an opportunity to remind Graham that he had expected him to follow in his Etonian footsteps.
(Graham had not got into Eton. He was on summer break from Harrow.)

"Your cousin," said Father, "is risking his life every day, fighting for his
country. I expect you to treat him with the utmost respect when he arrives.
Is that clear, children?"

"Yes, Father," said Graham.

"Yes," she said.

"Violet," Father said, "you will not hide in your bedroom. Such laziness
disrespects the soldiers fighting hard for King and country and is unbe-
coming of a woman. I expect you to maintain a cheerful presence around
the Hall and be gracious towards your cousin. Understood?"

"Yes," she said.

"You will recall what we discussed," he said.

"Yes, Father."

After supper, Violet finished her needlepoint lesson with Miss Poole. When
they were done, she sat for a while, looking longingly out of the window.
It was very bright for seven o'clock. Normally, she'd spend an evening like
this outdoors, sitting under her beech tree with a book, perhaps, or down
by the beck, sketching the frothy white plumes of angelica that grew there.

But with her voluntary confinement still in effect, there was not much
for Violet to do other than to go up to bed. On her way to the staircase,
she passed the library. Perhaps she would try to read in her room. She
went inside, and from the very bottom shelf in the corner, she picked up a
book with a red leather jacket, the front cover embossed with gold script:
Children's and Household Tales by The Brothers Grimm.

She tucked it under one arm and continued upstairs to her bedroom,
where she saw there was a little glass jar on her coverlet, glinting in the
evening sun. Something was moving inside it.

It was a damselfly. Whoever had put it there had poked holes in the lid
of the jar. A note had been fastened to the lid with a green ribbon tied in
a clumsy bow. Violet opened the note and saw that it was from Graham.

Dear Violet, he had written in neat, Harrovian script. *Get well soon. Best wishes, your brother Graham.* She smiled to herself. It was like something the old Graham would have done.

She opened the jar, hoping the insect would come to rest on her hand. Instead, it flew towards the window, fast, like it was afraid of her. It seemed to Violet to make barely a sound. She opened the window to let it out, quickly shutting it again. The fleeting happiness brought by Graham's gift evaporated.

She drew the black-out curtains, blocking out the view of the pink setting sun, turned on the bedside lamp and got into bed.

Dust fell from the pages when she opened them, at random, at the story of "The Robber Bridegroom."

It was a grisly story—much grislier than she had remembered. A man was so desperate to marry off his daughter that he had her betrothed to a murderer. The only saving grace was that the girl managed to outsmart him, with the help of an old witch. In the end, the bridegroom was put to death, along with his band of robbers. *Serves them right,* she thought.

Abandoning the book, she took off her necklace, reaching over to put it on the bedside table. She sighed at the clink and rustle of it slipping onto the floor. Violet peered over the edge of the bed but couldn't see its gold glint; perhaps it had rolled underneath. Cursing, she climbed out from the covers and crouched on the floor, groping for the necklace. Her fingers came away empty, grimed with dust. Had it fallen behind the bedside table, somehow? She should have been paying closer attention. A chill gripped her heart at the thought of losing the necklace. It was true—as Nanny Metcalfe had commented more than once—that it was ugly, misshapen, and blackened with age. But it was all she had of her mother.

Violet grunted with effort as she moved the bedside table, wincing at the sound of it scraping across the floorboards. Her pulse slowed when she spotted the necklace, the links of its chain threaded through with great ropes of dust. She couldn't recall the last time her room had been properly cleaned: Penny, the maid, only seemed to give it a cursory mop once a week. Guilt tugged at her stomach. She knew Penny was a little afraid of her, ever since Violet had convinced her to peer into Goldie's hatbox.

She'd only wanted to show Penny the pretty gold stripes on his legs. She couldn't have known that the maid—who, it transpired, had a horror of spiders—would faint clean away.

Violet bent down to retrieve the necklace and was just about to move the bedside table back again when she noticed something. There was a letter, scratched into the white paint of the wainscoting, half hidden by a spool of fluff. It was a *W*—the same letter engraved on the pendant she gripped in her hand. Gently brushing away the dust, she uncovered more letters, which looked as if they had been painstakingly etched with a pin, or—she shuddered—a fingernail. Together, the letters formed a word, which was somehow familiar, like a long-lost friend, though she had no recollection of ever seeing it before.

Weyward.

CHAPTER NINE

KATE

K ate grabs her bag and runs to the car.

In the rearview mirror, she sees that the birds—crows, she thinks—are still ascending, higher than the bone-yellow moon, the night shimmering with their cries.

"Don't look, don't look," she says to herself, her breath misting in the chill air of the car. Her palms are slippery with sweat and she wipes them on her jeans so that she can turn the key in the ignition. The engine jolts into life and she reverses onto the road, heart pounding.

There are no streetlights, and she flicks on the high beams as she speeds down the winding lanes. Her breathing is shallow, her fingers tense as claws on the steering wheel. She half expects the headlights to reveal something menacing and otherworldly lurking around each corner.

She makes it to the slip road. If she keeps driving, she could be back in London by morning. But then, where would she go? Back to the apartment? Staring down the barrel of the highway, she remembers what happened the first time.

The first time she tried to leave.

It had been soon after they'd started living together. Another argument about her job in children's publishing—he'd wanted her to quit, said she couldn't deal with the stress. She'd had a panic attack at work, during the weekly acquisition meeting. Simon had picked her up and brought her home, then sat across from her in their living room with its glittering view, haloed by the sun like some terrible angel. His words crashed over her—she couldn't cope, he didn't have time to deal with this, there was no point in her working when he earned so much. It was a useless job, anyway—what was the value in a bunch of women nattering about made-up stories for children? Besides, she obviously wasn't very good at it—after all, she barely brought home a quarter of his salary.

It was this last statement that did it—that sparked some forgotten fire in her. And so she looked him in the eye and said what she hadn't been able to tell the kindly colleagues who'd brought her tissues and a cup of tea as she'd recovered at her desk.

Work wasn't the problem; Simon was. His face darkened. For a moment he was still, and Kate's breath caught in her throat. Without a word, he threw his cup of coffee at her. She turned her face away just in time, but the boiling liquid splashed her left arm, leaving a pink line of scalded skin.

It was the first time he had hurt her. Later, it would scar.

That night, he'd begged her not to go as she'd packed her things, telling her he was sorry, it would never happen again, he couldn't live without her. She had wavered, even then.

But when the taxi arrived, she got in. It was the thing to do, wasn't it? She was, supposedly, an educated, self-respecting woman. She couldn't possibly stay.

The hotel—in Camden, she remembered; it had been all she'd been able to find (and afford) at such short notice—had been cold, with the musty stink of mice. The room overlooked the street and the window shook with every car that drove past. She lay sleepless until morning, watching the ceiling glow with the passing headlights, her phone vibrating with pleading texts, the burn on her arm throbbing.

She'd called in sick to work the next morning, spent the day wandering the markets, staring into the oily depths of the canal. Searching for resolve.

By the second night, she'd decided to leave him. But then came the voicemail.

"Kate," he'd said, voice heavy with tears. "I am so, so sorry that we fought. Please, come back. I can't live without you—I can't . . . I need you, Kate. Please. I—I've taken some pills . . ."

And just like that, her resolve evaporated. She couldn't do it. She couldn't let someone else die.

She phoned 999. As soon as she knew the paramedics were on their way, she called a taxi. On the drive back, she stared blankly out of the window as the neat terraced houses, gleaming dark in the rain, gave way to the images from her childhood nightmares. Black wings, beating the air. The road glossy with blood.

I am the monster.

What if she was too late?

The yellow ambulance was parked on their street by the time she got there. She'd barely been able to breathe in the elevator, had hated it for delaying her as it cranked slowly up the building.

The front door of their apartment was open. Simon sat on the couch in his pajamas, flanked by two female paramedics, pill bottles glinting on the coffee table in front of them. Unopened. Ice formed in her gut.

He hadn't taken them at all. He'd lied.

She stared. He looked up at her and the tears fell freely down his face.

"I'm so sorry, Kate," he said, shoulders shaking. "I was just . . . I was so scared that you would never come back."

The paramedics didn't notice the blistered skin on Kate's arm. She walked them to the front door, promising she'd call 999 again if Simon displayed any more signs of suicidal ideation, agreeing not to leave him alone, to follow up on a referral to the local psychology team. Then she shut the door behind them carefully.

Simon got off the couch and walked towards her, until she felt his breath on the back of her neck. Together, they listened to the elevator going down the shaft.

"I'm so sorry that I left," said Kate, without turning around. "Please promise me you'll never hurt yourself or do anything stupid again."

Stupid.

She knew as soon as the word left her mouth that she'd made a mistake.

"Stupid?" Simon asked, keeping his voice low. He gripped the back of her neck tightly, before shoving her against the wall.

She resigned from the publishing house the next day. Surrendering not just her paycheck and her sense of self, but her strongest link to the outside world. To the women who had made her feel valued, intelligent—like she was more than just his girlfriend, his plaything.

Kate switches off the indicator. She thinks of the cells knitting together inside her and is hit with a wave of nausea. If she goes back . . . if he finds out about the baby . . . he'll never let her leave.

She turns the car around.

The next morning, Kate walks to the village for supplies.

The early spring air is cool against her skin, with a smell of damp leaves and things growing. Kate shuts the front door and swallows burst from the old oak in the front garden. She flinches, then watches them pinwheel through the blue sky while she collects herself. The village is just two miles away. The walk will be invigorating, she tells herself. Maybe she'll even enjoy it.

She sets off down the lane, which is bordered by hedgerows fringed with unfamiliar white flowers that remind her of sea-foam. There's the squawk of a crow, and her heart quickens. She looks up, craning her neck until she grows dizzy. Nothing. Just branches patterning an empty sky, their tiny green leaves quivering in the breeze. She walks on, passing an old farmhouse with a sunken roof. Sheep bleat in the surrounding fields.

Crows Beck looks as though it's barely changed for centuries: the only signs of modernization are a BT phone box and a bus shelter. She passes the green, with its ancient well and another stone structure, a small hut with a heavy iron door. Perhaps it was the village jail, once upon a time. She shudders at the thought of being confined in such a small space, doom closing in.

Beyond the green is a cobbled square, hemmed in by buildings—a mishmash of stone and timber, some hunched beneath jutting Tudor gables. A few of them are shops: there's a greengrocer and a butcher, a post office. A medical center, too. In the distance she sees the spire of the church, glowing red in the sun.

She hesitates in front of the greengrocer. Nerves jostle in her stomach: she hasn't been grocery shopping alone since . . . she can't remember when. Simon had arranged for their food to be delivered by a high-end grocery supplier on Sunday evenings. She tries to calm her rapid breathing with the thought that this time, she can buy anything she likes.

The trestle tables out the front of the shop heave with fresh produce. Rows and rows of apples, the air thick with their woody scent. Carrots, half hidden beneath great green fronds, pale mounds of cabbages.

Inside, the only other customer is a woman—middle-aged and flame-haired, a pink sweater clashing luridly. Kate smiles as she shuffles past her, stifles a cough at the strong smell of patchouli oil. She smiles back and Kate turns quickly, scrutinizing a box of cereal. She is relieved when the woman leaves the shop, singing out a cheery goodbye to the cashier.

Kate pulls things from the shelves: bread, butter, coffee. She looks down at her basket. Automatically, she has selected Simon's favorite brand of coffee. She puts it back on the shelf, swaps it for another.

She mumbles hello to the raw-boned cashier. This, she knows, is an interaction she can't avoid.

"Not seen you here before," the woman says as she scans the jar of instant coffee. Kate sees that there is a single hair sprouting from her chin and suddenly doesn't know where to look. Her skin prickles. She feels horribly conscious of what she's wearing: her top and trousers too tight, too revealing. Simon had liked her to be on display like this. Exposed.

"Um—I've just moved," says Kate. "From London."

The woman frowns, so Kate explains that she's inherited a cottage from a relative. "Oh, you mean Weyward Cottage? Violet Ayres's place?"

"Yes—I'm her great-niece."

"Didn't know she had any family living," the cashier says. "Thought all the Ayreses and Weywards were gone. Save the old viscount of course, losing his marbles up at the Big House."

"Not me," says Kate, offering a tight smile. "I'm an Ayres. Sorry—

Weywards, did you say? I didn't realize it was a family name. I thought it was just the name of the cottage."

"It was, and an old one, too," she says, inspecting the carton of milk. "Went back centuries, that name did."

The cashier seems to think the Ayreses and the Weywards are related in some way. She must have it wrong. Aunt Violet had been an Ayres, too, and born in Orton Hall. She would have bought Weyward Cottage after she left home. After she'd been disowned.

"Card or cash?"

"Cash." Kate feels the woman's eyes on her as she pulls notes from a hole in the lining of her handbag. Again, she has the feeling of being exposed. She flushes, wondering if it's obvious. That she's running away from something. Someone.

"You'll be all right, pet," says the cashier now, as if she has seen Kate's thoughts through her skull. She hands over the change. "It's in your blood, after all."

Walking back to the cottage, Kate wonders what she meant.

Kate looks everywhere for Violet's papers, for some connection to the Weywards. In the drawers of the bedside table, inside the cavernous wardrobe. There, she pauses for a moment, inhaling the scent of mothballs and lavender. Her great-aunt's clothes are odd, the sorts of things one might find in a charity shop—kaftans, linen tunics, a beaded cape with the gunmetal sheen of a beetle's shell. Chunky necklaces cascade down the inside of the door, clinking against an age-spotted mirror.

She can't stop looking at the cape, at the way it catches the light. Tentatively she brushes it with her fingertips, the glass beads cool against her skin. She plucks it from its hanger and slips it around her shoulders. In the mirror she looks different: the cape's dark glitter brings out something in her eyes, a hardness she doesn't recognize.

Shame flushes her cheeks. She's acting like a child playing dress-up. She takes off the cape, hurriedly shoving it back on its hanger. Shutting the wardrobe doors, she catches another glimpse of herself in the mirror. There she is: clad in the clothes he has chosen. Her hair, bleached and perfectly layered, just the way he likes. The woman with the hardness in her eyes is gone.

She looks under Aunt Violet's bed. Battered hatboxes yield sketchbooks, their mottled pages filled with annotated drawings of butterflies, beetles, and—she grimaces—tarantulas. A heavy, square object wrapped in muslin turns out not to be a photo album, as she suspected, but a crumbling flank of stone. Turning it over, she sees the striated red imprint of a scorpion.

A folder pokes out from under one of the boxes. Grunting, she yanks it free.

The cover is faded and furred with dust, but the papers inside are neatly ordered: bank statements, utility bills. There are several old passports, their yellowed pages crowded with stamps. She flips through one from the 1960s, recording visits to Costa Rica, Nepal, Morocco.

There's something familiar about the sepia-colored photograph on the first page; about the young woman with dark waves of hair and wide-spaced eyes, the smudge of a birthmark on her forehead. She's never seen any pictures of her great-aunt as a young woman before, and she shivers as she places the feeling of recognition. In the picture, Aunt Violet looks like . . . her. Kate.

CHAPTER TEN

ALTHA

Grace looked very young and small on the witness stand. Her skin was pale under her cap, her brown eyes wide. In that moment, I found it hard to believe that she was a grown woman of one and twenty.

It seemed like barely any time had passed since we were girls, chasing each other through the sunlight. The summer when we were thirteen was sharp in my memory as I looked at her.

It had been a hot summer: the hottest in decades, my mother said. We had roamed all over the village and splashed through the beck, and, once we tired of that, stolen away to the cooler air of the fells. There we'd found slopes and crags wreathed with heather and mist. We'd climbed so high that Grace said she could see all the way to France. I remember laughing, telling Grace that France was very far away, and across the sea, besides. One day, we'd go and look for it, I said. Together.

At that moment, an osprey screamed overhead. I looked up to watch it fly, the sun tipping its wings with silver. Grace took my hand in hers, and a feeling of lightness spread through me, as though I, too, was soaring through the clouds.

Even then, some of the villagers feared our touch, as if my mother and I carried some pestilence, some plague. But Grace was never afraid. She knew—then, at least—that I would never bring her harm.

On our way down, I lost my boot to a bog. I remember being so nervous about telling my mother that I barely said a word to Grace as we walked back. She wouldn't understand, I thought. A yeoman's daughter, she'd had new boots every twelvemonth. My mother had sold cheese and damson jam from dawn till dusk, and tended each sick villager who came to our door to pay the cobbler to repair mine.

But Grace had come in with me, when we'd got to the cottage, and had told my mother it was her fault the boot had been lost to the mud. She'd insisted on giving me her spare pair.

I'd worn them for years after, until they pinched my toes purple. I'd been saving them, thinking I'd give them to my own daughter one day.

There was another reason that this summer, of our thirteenth year, was so strong in my mind when I looked at her across the courtroom. It was the last of our friendship.

And the last of my innocence.

In the autumn, as the leaves fell from the beech trees, Grace's mother fell sick.

My mother woke me well before dawn, candlelight chasing shadows from her face.

"Grace is coming here. Something is wrong," she told me.

"How do you know?" I asked.

She said nothing, but stroked the crow that perched on her shoulder, its feathers sparkling with rain.

It was the scarlatina, Grace said, as she sat at our table not long after, still trying to catch her breath. She'd run the whole two miles from the Metcalfe farm. Her mother had lain, pink-cheeked and sweating, in her bed for three days and two nights, she said. When she was awake, which was rare, she cried out for her long-dead babies.

Grace told us that her father had called for the doctor, who'd said that the patient had too much blood in her body. All that blood was boiling her from the inside out. I watched my mother's face, her mouth set in a grim line, as Grace went on. The doctor had put leeches on her mother, Grace said, only it wasn't helping. The leeches were growing fatter while she grew weaker.

My mother stood. I watched as she filled her basket with clean cloths, and jars of honey and elderberry tincture.

"Altha, fetch our cloaks," she said. "We must make haste, girls. If the physician keeps bleeding her, I fear she will not last the night."

The moon was obscured by cloud and drizzle, so that I could barely see as we walked. My mother strode on determined, gripping my hand tight. I could hear Grace breathing hard next to me.

In the darkness and the wet, I could not see my mother's crow, but I knew that she flew on ahead through the trees, and that this gave my mother strength.

We were halfway there when the rain grew heavier. Water dripped from my hood into my eyes. In the rush to leave I had forgotten my gloves, and my hands were numb with cold. It seemed like an age until I saw the squat, sunken shape of the Metcalfe farmhouse in the distance, the windows yellow with candlelight.

We found William Metcalfe slumped over his wife's sickbed. There was no sign of the physician. The bedchamber was filled with candles, a score of them at least: more than my mother and I used in a month.

"Mama does not care for the dark," Grace whispered.

In the bed, Grace's mother looked like she was asleep. Only, it was no kind of sleep that I had ever seen before. Anna Metcalfe's chest rose and fell rapidly under her nightgown. In the leaping candlelight, I could see her eyelids flickering with movement. Then her eyes opened and she half rose from the bed, screaming and tearing at a leech at her temple, before sinking back down again.

"Holy Mary, Mother of God," William Metcalfe murmured over his wife's crumpled form, "pray for us sinners . . ."

He turned suddenly, having heard us come in at that moment.

I saw he clutched a string of crimson beads to his lips: these he quickly stowed in the pouch of his breeches.

"What the devil are you doing here?" he asked. He looked hollowed out by exhaustion, his face almost as pale as his wife's.

"I brought them, Papa," said Grace. "Goodwife Weyward can help. She knows things . . ."

"Naïve child," he spat. "Those things she knows won't save your mother. They'll condemn her soul. Is that what you want for her?"

"Please, William. Be reasonable," said my mother in a tight voice. "You can see that the leeches are just making her worse. Your wife is frightened and in pain. She needs cool cloths, and honey and elderberry, to soothe her."

As she spoke, Anna let out a moan. Grace began to cry.

"Please, Papa, please," she said.

William Metcalfe looked at his wife, then at his daughter. A vein throbbed at his temple.

"Aye," he said. "But you must stop if I say so. And if she dies, it will be on your head."

My mother nodded. She set about removing the leeches from Anna's skin, asked Grace to fetch a jug of water and a cup. When these arrived, she knelt by the bedside and tried to get Anna to drink, but the liquid just dribbled down her chin. She laid a damp cloth over her forehead. Anna muttered, and I saw her fists clenching and unclenching beneath the bedclothes.

I sat down next to my mother.

"Will you try the elderberry tincture?" I asked.

"She is very far gone," my mother said, keeping her voice low. "I am not sure she will be able to take it in. We may be too late."

She took the small bottle of purple liquid from her basket and un-stopped it. She held the dropper over Anna's mouth and squeezed. A dark splash fell on her lips, staining them.

As I watched, Anna's whole body began to shake. Her eyes opened, flashing white. Foam collected at the corners of her mouth.

"Anna!" William rushed forward, pushing us out of the way. He tried to hold his wife's body still. I turned around and saw Grace standing in the far corner of the room, her hands over her mouth.

"Grace, do not watch," I said, crossing the room. I put my hands over her eyes. "Do not watch," I said again, my lips so close to her face that I could smell the sweetness of her skin.

The room was filled with the terrible sounds of the bed frame shaking, of William Metcalfe saying his wife's name over and over.

Then it grew quiet.

I did not need to turn around to know that Anna Metcalfe was dead.

"Why did you not save her?" I asked my mother as we walked home. It was still raining. Cold mud seeped into my boots. The boots that Grace had given me.

"I tried," my mother said. "She was too weak. If Grace had come to us sooner . . ."

We did not speak for the rest of the journey home. Once we arrived, my mother started the fire. Then we sat looking into the flames for hours, my mother with her crow at her shoulder, until the rain eased and we could hear the birds singing outside.

In the days that followed, I longed for Grace; longed to hold her close and comfort her for her loss. But my mother kept me inside, away from the square, the fields. Where I might hear the rumors that tore like flames through the village. It did not matter: I could guess at them, from the pale set of my mother's face, the dark rings under her eyes. Later, I learned William Metcalfe had forbade his daughter from seeing me.

We did not speak again for seven years.

CHAPTER ELEVEN

VIOLET

Violet woke the next day exhausted from lack of sleep. But she got straight out of bed, even though it was a Saturday, and she had no lessons.

She couldn't get her discovery out of her head. That strange word, scratched into the wainscoting behind her bedside cabinet. *Weyward*.

She touched the gold pendant that hung from her neck, tracing her fingers over the *W*. What if the initial didn't stand for her mother's first name, as she'd thought for all these years? What if it stood for her *last* name, before she married Father and became Lady Ayres?

Longing swelled in Violet's rib cage. She was struck with a sudden desire to push the bedside table aside again and run her fingers over the etchings, to feel something her mother might have touched. But why would her mother have put her own name there? Had she meant for Violet to discover it one day?

She threw back the covers, but quickly drew them up again when Mrs. Kirkby knocked on her door with a tray of tea and porridge.

The housekeeper had a distracted look clouding her broad features, and a faint, meaty aroma. Her knuckles were dusted white with flour, and there was a dark smear of what looked to be gravy across her apron.

Violet supposed she was busy preparing for the impending arrival of this mysterious cousin Frederick. Violet imagined Mrs. Kirkby rather had her work cut out for her, given that they never had guests at Orton Hall. Perhaps she could catch her off guard.

"Mrs. Kirkby," she said in between sips of tea, taking care to keep her tone indifferent. "What was my mother's last name?"

"Big questions for so early in the morning, pet," said Mrs. Kirkby, stooping to inspect a stain on the coverlet. "Is this chocolate? I'll have to get Penny to put it in to soak."

Violet frowned. She had the distinct impression that Mrs. Kirkby was reluctant to look her in the eye.

"Was it Weyward?"

Mrs. Kirkby stiffened. She was still for a moment, then hurriedly removed the tray from Violet's lap, even though she'd yet to finish her porridge.

"Can't recall," she huffed. "But it doesn't do to go ferreting around in the past, Violet. Plenty of children don't have mothers. Still more don't have mothers *or* fathers. You should count yourself lucky and leave it at that."

"Of course, Mrs. Kirkby," Violet said, quickly formulating a plan. "I say—speaking of fathers, do you know what mine has planned for the day?"

"He left early this morning," she said, "to meet your young cousin off his train at Lancaster."

This was excellent news. But she had to hurry, or she would miss her chance.

Violet dressed quickly. She was quite sure that Mrs. Kirkby had been lying when she said she couldn't recall if Weyward had been her mother's last name. What was less certain was how it had come to be scratched onto the wainscoting of Violet's bedroom.

She crept down the main staircase to the second floor. It was a brilliant day outside, and the multicolored light flooding in through the stained-glass window made the Hall look ethereal.

As she turned down the corridor, she passed Graham, carrying an algebra textbook with a look of despair. She remembered the gift he had left for her.

"Um—thank you for the present," she said quietly. It occurred to her that it must have been quite an ordeal for him to coax the damselfly into a jar, given his fear of insects. The bees shimmered in her mind.

"That's all right," he said. "Do you feel better now? You look a bit more—normal. Well—normal for you, anyway."

He pulled a face and she laughed.

"Yes, thanks."

"That's good," he said. "Well, ah—better get on with this." He motioned to the textbook and sighed.

"Graham, wait," she said. "Um—you wouldn't be a brick and do me a favor, would you?"

She saw him hesitate. It had been a long time since she'd asked him for a favor.

"Of course," he said.

"Father's gone to get cousin what's-his-name from Lancaster," she said.

"Ah," said Graham, rolling his eyes. "The feted Frederick."

"Anyway, I've got to look for something in Father's study," she said, hoping she could trust him. "Could you tell me if he comes back?"

Graham's ginger eyebrows shot up.

"Father's study? Why on earth would you go in there? He'll skin you alive if he finds out," he said.

"I know," she said. "Which is why I need you to be my lookout. You can have my share of pudding for a week if you say yes."

Violet watched Graham mull it over, hoping that the lure of extra custard would be too great for him to resist.

"Fine," he said. "I'll knock on the door three times, as a signal. But if you renege on the pudding promise, I'll tell Father."

"Deal," she said.

She turned towards the study.

"Are you going to tell me what it is you're looking for?"

"The fewer people know," said Violet, adopting a low voice, "the better."

Graham rolled his eyes again and kept walking.

Violet felt a rush of nerves as she came upon the study. Normally, Cecil could be found growling at the threshold, as if he were Cerberus guarding the entrance to the underworld. Thank heavens he had gone with Father to Lancaster.

She pushed open the heavy door. Violet tended to avoid the study—

and not just because of Cecil. This was where Father had caned her after the incident with the bees.

The room was no less unsettling now that she was older. It looked as if it belonged to a different era. A different *season*, even—Father had the curtains pulled, and the air felt chilly and stale. She turned on the light, flinching as she made eye contact with the painting that hung behind the desk. It was yet another portrait of Father, and so realistically done—even down to the gleam of his bald pate—that for a moment she thought that he had been there all along, waiting to catch her out.

Pulse thudding, she crept inside, inhaling the scent of pipe tobacco. There had to be some record of her mother in here. How could a person have lived and died in a house yet leave only a necklace and a stash of letters behind? It was as if Father had scrubbed her from the face of the earth.

She scanned the shelves, with their ancient spines labeled in faded blue ink. Ledgers. Dozens of them. She pulled out one marked *1925* and flipped through it. Could there be something in here about the May Day Festival where her parents had met? But no—it was just pages and pages of numbers, transcribed in Father's cramped, terse hand (it took skill, Violet thought, to make even your handwriting look angry). She slammed the ledger shut in frustration.

She looked around the room. Father's mahogany desk hulked beneath his portrait. Strange objects littered the surface. Some of them were interesting—like the faded globe that showed the countries of the British Empire in delicate pink—but others gave her the willies. Especially the yellowed ivory tusk mounted in brass, which spanned almost the entire length of the desk. It conjured images of Babar and Celeste, heroes of her favorite childhood books (which, like all the other nursery volumes, had originally been given to Graham), tuskless and bleeding.

It made her feel sad for another reason. As a child, Violet had assumed that Father's "curios" (as he called them) were signs that he shared her love of the natural world. But it was when Father was telling her and Graham the story of how he came to possess the tusk—on the same hunting trip to Southern Rhodesia that he'd acquired Cecil, skinny and cowering as a puppy—that she realized how wrong she was. Father didn't care that elephants formed close-knit, matriarchal groups; that they mourned their dead like humans. Nor did he consider that the elephant he had killed—for the mere sake of an ornament on his desk—would have been bewildered by fear and pain at the moment of its death.

For Father, the tusk—and everything else in the Hall like it—was just a trophy. These noble creatures weren't to be studied or venerated, but conquered.

They would never understand each other.

But there wasn't time to dwell on such things now, she told herself. After all, she had a mission to accomplish.

She was sure that the desk drawer would be locked but—to her delight—it slid open easily.

Violet riffled through the contents quickly. Father's leather writing-case, with the Ayres insignia (an osprey, picked out in gold); an old pocket watch with a broken face; letters from the bank, his pipe . . . she was just beginning to think that Father hadn't bothered locking his desk because it held nothing important when she saw the feather.

It was large enough to have come from a crow, Violet thought. Or perhaps a jackdaw?

Carefully, she took it from the drawer. It was black as obsidian, shimmering blue where it caught the light. She saw that it was streaked with white—or rather with queer absences of color, like an unfinished painting. The feather appeared to have come loose from a soft wad of material. On closer inspection, Violet saw that it was a handkerchief, fashioned from a delicate linen that had been eaten away by moths. There was a monogram in the corner of the handkerchief, the letters *E.W.* picked out in bottle-green silk.

Violet's heart fluttered in her chest. *E.W.*

W for Weyward?

Underneath the layer of dust, Violet detected the faintest whiff of something light and floral coming from the handkerchief. Lavender. It was barely there, the ghost of a scent, but it was enough. The memories instantly flooded her brain, as if she had tapped into a hidden spring. The feeling of warm arms around her, a thick, fragrant curtain of hair tickling her face. The low melody of a lullaby, the sound of a heart beating next to her ear.

The feather, the handkerchief.

They were her mother's.

And Father had been keeping them in his desk drawer, as if they were something important. Special.

The old fantasy of her parents' wedding day hovered before her. Father looking almost handsome, in a morning suit of soft gray. Her mother—Violet imagined a woman with a heart-shaped face and a dark river of hair—smiling as she took his hand. Their faces golden with sunshine, petals swirling overhead.

Violet sometimes wondered if Father was capable of loving anything—apart from hunting, and the empire—but she also knew that he had defied tradition and his dead parents' wishes to marry her mother. And he had held on to these keepsakes, things that reminded him of her, for all these years. She imagined him sitting at his desk, pressing the handkerchief to his nose the way Violet was doing now.

Could she have misunderstood, that night in the study? *Perhaps they can stop you from turning out like her.* The very words had seemed to drip with hatred.

But perhaps she'd been wrong, confused somehow? Her heart leaped at the thought. Perhaps he *had* loved her mother, very much. And then she had died.

Violet began to feel almost sorry for him.

She wasn't sure how long she stood there with the little bundle in her hand, but after a while she became aware of something strange.

She could *hear*. Properly, this time. It was as if the heavy curtains, the thick glass of the window and the ancient stone walls had fallen away. She could hear the beat of a sparrow's wings as it took flight from a sycamore. The throaty yell of a buzzard, calling to its mate as it circled in the sky. A field mouse, chittering as it foraged in the bushes beneath the window.

Violet stared at the items in her hand in wonder. Then, there were three knocks: Graham's signal. How could Father be back already? Violet looked at her watch: it had just gone ten o'clock. He must have set off earlier than she'd realized.

She wanted to take the feather and the handkerchief with her, but what if Father noticed they were missing? Then he would know she had been inside his study. Perhaps—her heart thudded with the thought, with what she was about to do—he wouldn't miss the feather. She could just keep it, for a little while, and put it back later. After all, Father had had it all to himself for years and years . . .

"Violet?" Graham hissed through the door. "Are you in there? He's back! Hurry!"

Her blood humming with excitement, Violet put the handkerchief back in the drawer, then shoved the feather into the pocket of her dress. She shut the door of Father's study quietly and crept back up the stairs.

As a test, Violet crouched on the floor and pulled the hatbox out from underneath her bed.

The inside of the box was filmy with spider silk. Goldie was alive and well, and judging from the dead flies and ants that speckled his lair, possessed of his usual appetite. He reared up on his legs and blinked his eight beady eyes at her, before leaping into the air in a tawny flash. He came to rest on Violet's shoulder, and she smiled as he nestled against her. Warmth unfurled in her chest, fizzing through her veins.

It was like taking off a blindfold. She hadn't realized how deadened to the world she had become; now, her nerves seemed to bristle with electricity. Colors looked brighter than they had before—through her window, the outside world flared with sunshine—and the *click* of Goldie's pincers was miraculous to her ears.

She was herself again.

Violet smoothed her hair and clothes, checking in the looking glass that she was presentable before going downstairs. She remembered what Father had said after supper the other night. He expected her to be a *cheerful, gracious presence* around her cousin Frederick. Ugh.

As she walked down the stairs, she heard Father talking loudly in the entrance hall. A boorish laugh echoed through the house. It was so loud that Violet heard the family of blue tits that lived in the roof chirrup in fright. She disliked cousin Frederick already.

When she reached the hall, she saw that the owner of the boorish laugh was a straight-backed young man in a sand-colored uniform. He smiled when she drew near, revealing white, even teeth. Below his officer's cap, his eyes were green. Her favorite color. Father, who had just finished telling some dull story, clapped him on the back. Graham stood awkwardly off to one side, looking as if he didn't know what to do with his hands.

"Frederick," said Father, "I'd like to introduce you to my daughter, your cousin. Miss Violet Elizabeth Ayres."

"Hello," said Frederick, extending his hand towards her. "How do you do?"

"Hello," said Violet. His hand felt warm and callused. Close up, he smelled of a spicy sort of cologne. She wasn't sure why, but she felt suddenly light-headed. Was this, she wondered, a normal response to the young adult male? She had never known any apart from Graham, and the gardener's apprentice, Neil—a bucktoothed, wan-faced lad who had perished at the Battle of Boulogne.

"Violet," said Father. "Have you forgotten your manners?"

"Sorry," she said. "How do you do?"

Frederick grinned.

Father rang for Penny, who flushed and almost forgot to curtsy when she saw Frederick. Father asked Penny to show Frederick to his room. Dinner would be at eight, he said.

"Don't be late," said Father, looking at Violet.

Violet wore her favorite dress to dinner—green serge with a full skirt and a Peter Pan collar. It had no pockets, so she had stowed the feather safely between the yellowed pages of the Brothers Grimm. She sat across from Frederick and stole glances at him. She was heady with looking—at the sharp line of his jaw; the square, golden hands with their dark smattering of hair across the knuckles. He was so unlike Father—whose own hands recalled joints of ham—that he might have been a different species. He repelled and fascinated her in equal measure.

She was trying to work out the exact shade of his eyes—the same color as the enchanter's nightshade that grew beneath the beech tree, she decided—when he turned his gaze to her. She flinched.

"How are your parents, Frederick?" Father was asking. Apparently, Frederick's father was Father's younger brother Charles—whom Violet and Graham had never met. It seemed, from the familiarity with which they spoke to each other, that Father and Frederick had kept up a rather involved written correspondence for many years. Knowing this made Violet feel a little smaller in her chair. Why hadn't Father wanted her to meet her only cousin until now? She thought again of the lack of callers, the prohibition on leaving the estate.

"As well as can be expected, I suppose," said Frederick. "Mother's nerves are still a bit frayed, after the Blitz. I keep telling them to leave London— too many reminders—but they won't hear of it. I'll go down and see them before I head back. But I wanted to get some country air first."

"Did you grow up in London?" Violet asked, finding her voice. The prospect horrified her. Everything she knew of London came from newspaper articles and Dickens. In her mind, it was soot-choked and sunless, with no animals except mangy foxes foraging in alleyways. "What was it like?"

"Well, I spent most of the year at school," said Frederick. "Eton, of course." Graham stiffened and looked at his plate. "But it's a wonderful city. Full of life and color. Or, it was, before the war."

"But . . . are there any trees?" Violet asked. "I couldn't imagine living without *trees*."

Frederick laughed and took a sip of wine. The bright green flash of his gaze landed on her again, like sunlight in a forest.

"Oh, yes," he said. "In fact, my parents live in Richmond, just next to the park. Have you heard of it?"

"No," said Violet.

"It's beautiful. Over two thousand acres of woodland, just on the outskirts of London. You even see deer there sometimes."

"Have you thought about what you'd like to do once the war ends, Frederick?" Father interrupted.

"Well, I was planning to move back to London and rent somewhere for a while; maybe in Kensington—if it's still standing, that is . . . my allowance would cover it. I thought I might write a book about the war. But now . . ."

"Yes! Didn't you have a title? *Torment in Tobruk*? You mentioned it in your last letter. Sounded like stirring stuff. You've changed your mind?"

"Well, I'm not sure yet," Frederick began. "I thought of going to medical school, perhaps. One sees things in a war . . . so much death." He was watching Violet. "But miracles, too. Chaps brought back from the brink. In a field hospital, doctors are like . . . God."

There was an awkward pause. Father cleared his throat.

"I think what I am trying to say," Frederick added quickly, "is that I just would like to contribute somehow, when all this is over, to making people's lives better."

"A noble aspiration," said Father, nodding his approval.

"So, would you get to see inside a body?" Violet asked. "Learn how it works? If you went to medical school, I mean."

"Violet," Father frowned. "Hardly appropriate table conversation from a young lady."

Frederick laughed.

"I don't mind, Uncle," he said. "The young lady is right, anyway. To become a doctor, I'd first need to be acquainted with how the human body works. Intimately acquainted."

He was still watching her.

CHAPTER TWELVE

KATE

Kate holds her breath as she dials the number.

Beams of afternoon sunshine pour into the bedroom, catching dust motes. Out of the window, she can see the mountains that ring the valley, purple and distant.

The phone is still ringing. Canada is—she tries to think—five hours behind, so it will be midday there. Her mother will be busy, at her job as a medical receptionist. Perhaps she won't answer. Kate almost wills it.

Don't pick up.

"Hello?"

Her heart sinks.

"Hi, Mum, it's me."

"Kate? Oh, thank God." Her mother's voice is urgent, harried. She can hear the trill of office phones in the background, faint conversation. "Hold on a second."

A door opens, shuts.

"Sorry, just had to find somewhere quieter. Where are you calling from? What's going on?"

"I've got a new phone."

"Jesus, Kate, I've been going out of my mind. Simon phoned me about an hour ago. He said you'd taken off, left your phone behind."

Guilt pulls at her.

"Sorry, I should have called earlier. But listen, I'm fine. I just . . . had to get away."

She pauses. Blood rushes in her ears. Part of Kate does want to tell her the truth. About Simon, about the baby. But she can't seem to shape the words in her mouth, to force them through her lips. To break the glass.

He abused me.

She has already caused her mother so much pain. Even the sound of her voice brings it back—those long days after the accident, when her mother barely left her parents' bedroom. Coming home from school and finding her gray-faced and sobbing, the bed strewn with her father's clothes.

"They still smell like him," she had said, before disappearing back into her grief. In that moment, Kate wished she had never been born.

Years later, when her mother married Keith, a Canadian doctor, she had asked Kate to move with them to Toronto. They could start again, she'd said. Together.

Kate had said no, insisted that she wanted to stay in England for university. But really, she just didn't want to ruin her mother's second chance at happiness. Their infrequent conversations—eventually dwindling from weekly to monthly—felt stilted, awkward. It was for the best, Kate told herself. Her mother was better off without her.

"Away from what?" her mother is asking now. "Please, Kate—I'm your mum. Just tell me what's going on."

He abused me.

"It's—complicated. It just . . . wasn't working. So I wanted to get away for a bit."

"Right. OK, darling." Kate hears the resignation in her voice. "So where have you gone, then? Are you staying with a friend?"

"No—do you remember Dad's Aunt Violet? The one who lived up in Cumbria, near Orton Hall?"

"Oh, yes, vaguely. A bit eccentric, I always thought . . . I didn't know you'd become close."

"We weren't," says Kate. "Close, I mean. She's—dead, actually. She died last year, left me her house. I guess she didn't have any other family."

"You never told me that." She hears the wound in her mother's voice. "I should have stayed in touch with her, your dad would have liked that."

Kate's insides clench with guilt. This is why it's better that they don't speak. She has hurt her mother again, like she always does.

"Sorry, Mum . . . I should have said something."

"It's OK. Anyway, how long are you planning to stay up there? You can always come here, you know. Or—maybe I could come there?"

"You don't have to do that," Kate says quickly. "It's OK. I'm OK. Anyway—sorry again, about Aunt Violet. I should go, Mum. I'll call you in a few days, OK?"

"OK, darling."

"Wait—Mum?"

"Yes?"

"Don't tell him. Simon. Don't tell him where I am. Please."

She hangs up quickly, cutting off her mother's questions.

Tears blur her vision. She gropes blindly for the box of tissues on the bedside table—perched precariously atop a towering stack of *New Scientist* magazines—and knocks it over. Items topple onto the floor.

"Fuck," she says, bending down to pick them up. She needs to pull herself together.

Something else has been knocked to the ground—an enamel jewelry box, patterned with butterflies. Its contents are splayed out on the floorboards, glowing in the sun. Mismatched earrings, a couple of rusted rings, a dirty necklace with a battered-looking pendant. Flustered, she puts them back in the box, tidies the surface of the bedside table.

There's a photograph of her grandfather Graham, behind the stack of magazines. Younger than she's ever seen him: his hair still red, wisps of it lifting in a breeze. He died when she was six and her memories of him are shadowy, fragmented. He used to read to her—*Grimms' Fairy Tales*, mainly, the rich resonance of his voice transporting her into another world.

Though now, as she looks at the photograph, another memory flickers at the edge of her brain. His funeral, here in Crows Beck.

Gripping her mother's hand, looking up at the clouds that hung low in the sky. Thinking that it was going to rain. The graveyard was all moss and stone and trees, full of birds and insects, and Kate remembers it being *loud*. So loud she'd barely been able to hear the minister talking.

Afterwards, she and her parents had gone back to Weyward Cottage for afternoon tea. The only other time she has set foot inside the house. The only time she met Aunt Violet.

She has a vague impression of green. The green door, the green wall-paper inside the house, Aunt Violet wearing an odd, flowing outfit. She remembers the smell of her perfume—lavender, the scent that still lingers in the bedroom. She tries to conjure more details but she can't; the memory is too hazy, as though its edges are frayed.

Really, she'd half forgotten that she *had* a great-aunt, until the call from the lawyer.

Not for the first time, she wonders why Violet left her cottage to a great-niece she hadn't seen for over twenty years.

"You're her only living relative," the lawyer had said when she'd asked him that same question, his northern accent gravelly on the phone. But this sparked more questions than it answered. For instance: why had her great-aunt never contacted her while she was still alive?

Later, Kate decides to explore the garden, while it's still light.

It is overgrown and heavy with the scent of plants she doesn't recognize. Green, furred leaves brush her shoes, trailing silvery lines of sap. Ferns rustle in the breeze.

She hesitates when she comes to the ancient sycamore tree, remembering the crows from her first night. She looks skyward, at the reaching branches, red with the setting sun. The tree must be hundreds of years old. She imagines it standing sentinel for generations, keeping the little cottage safe in its shadow. She reaches out her hand and presses her palm against the bark.

It feels warm. Alive.

The air shifts. Suddenly, she wants to go back inside. There's something about the garden that feels crowded, overwhelming. It's as if there is no longer any barrier between the outside world and her nerves.

She reminds herself she is safe. She won't go back inside. Not yet.

She walks deeper into the garden, listening to the hum of insects, water running over pebbles. The beck glimmers below. She climbs down to its banks, holding the twisted roots of the sycamore to steady herself. The water is so clear that she can see tiny fish, their little bodies shimmering in the light. An insect hovers nearby. She can't remember what it's called: smaller than a dragonfly, with delicate mother-of-pearl wings. It skims the surface of the beck. She stays like that for a long time, listening to the birds, the water, the insects. She shuts her eyes, opening them again when she feels something brush her hand. The dragonfly-like creature with the iridescent wings. The word swims up from the depths of her brain: a damselfly.

Tears well in her eyes, surprising her.

She was fascinated by insects as a child. She remembers begging her mother to spare the moths that fluttered out from wardrobes, the gauzy spider's webs that clung to the ceiling. She'd collected vividly illustrated books about them. About birds, too. She would hide under the covers reading, in the small, silent hours of the morning while her parents slept in the next room. It hurts now, to think of that little girl, her innocent wonder: flashlight in hand, turning the glossy pages and marveling at the wild and wonderful creatures. Butterflies with eyes on their wings, parrots in candy-colored plumage.

After her father died, Kate had collected the books into a shiny, color-ful stack and put them on the pavement outside the house. She'd woken in the night, heart swollen with regret, and crept outside to retrieve them. But they were already gone.

Kate took this to be a sign, confirmation of what she already knew. It was too dangerous for her to be around the insects, animals, and birds she loved. She'd already caused her father's death. What if she hurt her mother, too?

She kept her other books—*Grimms' Fairy Tales*, *The Secret Garden*—the stories that became a salve during those long nights when the only sign of life from her mother's bedroom was the neon glow of the television under the door. Fiction became a friend as well as a safe harbor; a cocoon to protect her from the outside world and its dangers. She could read about Robin Redbreast but she must avoid at all costs the robins that tittered in the back garden.

And she kept the brooch, tucked safe in her pocket through compulsory netball matches, exams, even her first kiss. As if it were a good-luck charm rather than a reminder of what she'd done, who she was. A monster.

The brooch is worn now, the gold dull and black with age. It was beautiful, once—she remembers playing with it when she was very young, the crystals sparkling in the sun so that the wings almost looked as if they were moving. She doesn't remember when she got it. Perhaps that awful moment—holding it tight in her hand while her father's corpse was driven away—has blotted out all other associations, like a harsh light.

Kate shivers. It's getting colder, the warmth leaving with the sun. She stands up, looks around. Then she notices something.

A wooden cross, weathered and green with lichen, is nestled amongst the roots of the sycamore.

There is no name, no date. But, leaning closer, she sees the faint outline of jagged letters. *RIP.*

The sun has disappeared behind dark clouds, and her skin smarts with the first pinpricks of rain.

As she stands before the cross, the garden seems to swell with sound. Her skin feels raw and open, like a newborn animal's. There's a feeling, in her stomach and in her veins, of something wanting to get in. Or wanting to get out.

She runs, then; the strange, grasping plants leaving smears of red and green on her clothes. She shuts the door behind her, drawing the curtains on the windows so that she can't see the garden, the sycamore tree. The cross. The green-mottled wood, the way that it juts out from the roots of the sycamore.

It couldn't be a person's grave, could it? The cottage is so old, after all . . . she remembers what the cashier said. *Went back centuries.* Could it be one of the Weywards?

She'd hoped to learn more in Aunt Violet's papers. But the folder she found under the bed contained nothing earlier than 1942, and nothing about the cottage itself or anyone who might have lived there before Aunt Violet.

Then she remembers that there's an attic. She saw a trapdoor, didn't she? Set into the ceiling of the corridor. Perhaps there'll be something up there.

The top rung of the ladder creaks as Kate steps on it. God knows how old it is: she found it rusting against the back of the house, half covered in creeping ivy. Ignoring the ladder's protest, she pushes the trapdoor open.

Aunt Violet's attic is enormous—big enough that she can almost stand up. She switches on the flashlight on her phone, and the dark shapes take form.

Shelves line the walls, sparkling with insects, preserved in specimen jars. The space is dominated by a hulking bureau. Even under the beam of the flashlight, it looks scratched and very old, possibly even older than the furniture in the rest of the cottage. There are two drawers.

She opens the first drawer of the bureau. It's empty. Then tries the second, which is locked.

She feels around in the recesses of the first drawer again, just in case she's missed something, some clue. She breathes in sharply as her fingers connect with a package. Pulling it out, she sees that it is wrapped in fraying cloth. She won't open it here, in the dark, she decides. Something skitters on the roof and her heart rises into her throat.

She lowers herself down into the yellow oblong of light, the package tight in her hand, its dust working itself into the tread of her skin.

She'll start the fire, make a cup of tea, turn on as many lights as possible. Then she'll look at it. Strange, that the other drawer would be locked. Almost as if Aunt Violet was hiding something.

CHAPTER THIRTEEN

ALTHA

I watched as Grace swore on the Bible, to tell the whole truth and nothing but. The prosecutor rose from his seat and walked slowly towards her. I could see her eyes searching for mine.

I wanted to look away, to hide my face in my hands and curl myself up small, but I couldn't. There were too many people watching. I was Lancaster's greatest attraction. In the gallery, men pointed me out to their wives; mothers shushed their grubby children. There was a low and constant hiss. "Witch," I heard them say. "Hang the witch."

The prosecutor began.

"Please state your full name for the court," he said.

"Grace Charlotte Milburn," she said, too quietly. So quietly that he had to ask her to repeat herself.

"And where do you reside, Mistress Milburn?"

"Milburn Farm, near Crows Beck," she said.

"And who did you live there with?"

"My husband. John Milburn."

"And do you have any children?"

She paused. One hand went to her waist: she wore a kirtle of dark gray wool, thick enough to hide her shape. I willed her not to look at me.

"No."

"Could you tell the court what is raised at Milburn Farm? Crops or livestock?"

"Livestock," she said.

"Which animals?"

"Cows," she whispered. "Dairy cows."

"And how did your husband come by Milburn Farm?"

"He inherited it, sir. From his father."

"So he lived there from birth."

"Yes."

One of the judges cleared his throat. The prosecutor looked up at him.

"Bear with me, your honor, this has relevance to the charges laid upon the accused."

The judge nodded. "You may continue."

The prosecutor turned back towards Grace.

"Mistress Milburn. Would you say that your husband was familiar with cows? With the patterns and habits of these beasts?"

She hesitated.

"Yes, of course, sir. Dairy farming was in his blood."

"And the particular cows at the farm were familiar with him?"

"He took them from barn to field and back every day, sir."

"I see. Thank you, Mistress Milburn. Now, mistress, could you describe for the court the events of New Year's Day, in this, the year of our Lord 1619?"

"Yes, sir. I woke up, at dawn as usual, sir, to feed the chickens and put the pottage on. John had already got up, to milk the cows and then take them from the barn."

"And was John alone in doing this, or did he have assistance?"

"He had help, sir. The Kirkby lad comes to help—came to help—John on Tuesdays and Thursdays."

"And this was a Thursday?"

"Yes."

"What happened next?"

"I was getting ready to get water from the well, to wash the clothes, sir. I had picked up the basin and I was looking out of the window. I wanted to see how thick the snow was, sir, to see if I needed my gloves."

"And what did you see, Mistress Milburn, when you were looking out of the window?"

"I saw the cows, sir, coming out of the barn and into the field, and John and the Kirkby lad."

"And how did the cows seem to you?" Did they seem—agitated? Aggressive, in any way?"

"No, sir," she said.

I knew what was coming next. I felt giddy with dread, as if I might swoon. I was grateful that no one could see my shackled hands, how they shone with sweat. I wiped them on the skirt of my dress.

"Please, go on, Mistress Milburn."

"Well, I had been looking at the window, but then I dropped my basin, sir. It made an almighty clang, loud enough that God himself could've heard, I thought. I bent down to pick it up. While I was crouched on the floor, there was sound from outside, like thunder. I thought maybe a storm was coming. Then I heard the Kirkby lad yelling."

"Yelling? What was he saying?"

"Nothing that made much sense, at first. Just sounds, like. But then he started saying my husband's name, over and over again."

"What did you do next?"

My heart drummed in my ears. The edges of my vision grew hazy. I wished for some water. I wished that none of this had ever happened. That I was safe in childhood, climbing trees with Grace. Pointing out the finches, the shining beetles; her laughing wonder in my ears.

"I went outside, sir."

"And what did you see?"

"The cows were all scattered in the field. Some of them had heaving flanks, wild eyes, as if they'd been running. The Kirkby lad was still yelling, bent over something on the ground. At first I couldn't see John. But then I saw that he . . . my John . . . he was the thing on the ground."

Grace's voice grew thick with tears. She took a handkerchief and wiped her eyes. The gallery murmured with sympathy. I felt their eyes on me; heard the hiss again. *Witch. Whore.*

"And can you describe to the court your husband's condition at this point, Mistress Milburn?"

"He was—he was not recognizable as himself, sir." She paused and licked her lips, steadied herself.

"In what manner?"

"His arms and legs were all twisted, sir. And his face. It . . . weren't there no more."

A memory rose up, like vomit in my throat. That face, bruised and pulped as damson jam. The teeth gone. One eye split and oozing.

"My John was dead, sir. He was gone."

Her voice broke on the last word. She cried prettily, the head bowed in its white cap, the slight shoulders hunched with pain.

She had the courtroom rapt. In the gallery, men comforted their wives who wiped away tears in sympathy. To the jurors, she presented a perfect picture of grief. Even the judges looked softened.

The prosecutor—mindful of this, no doubt—went on gently.

"Could you tell me what happened next, please, Mistress Milburn?"

"It was then that I saw her, running towards me from the trees."

"Who?" he asked.

"Altha," she said softly.

"Please, Mistress Milburn, would you point her out to the court-room."

She looked at me, raising one hand slowly. Even from where I was sitting, I saw the delicate fingers were shaking. She pointed at me.

The gallery erupted.

One of the judges called for order. Gradually, the shouts fell away.

The prosecutor continued.

"Were you surprised to see Altha Weyward standing there?" he asked.

"It was all a blur, sir. I can't remember what I felt when I saw her. I was—overcome."

"But it would have been an unusual occurrence, I assume, to see the accused standing on the edge of your field, not so long after daybreak?"

"Not so unusual, sir. She is known for taking early walks."

"So you had seen her before, then? Taking walks of a morning, near your farm?"

"Yes, sir."

"Regularly?"

"I wouldn't call it regular, sir." I saw Grace's tongue dart out to moisten her lips. "But once or twice I'd seen her, yes."

The prosecutor frowned.

"Would you continue, please, Mistress Milburn. What happened after you saw the accused standing on the edge of the field?"

"She rushed towards me, sir. She asked me what had happened. I can't remember what I said all too well, sir. I was just so—shocked, you see. But I remember, she took off her cloak and threw it over his body, and then she bade the Kirkby lad to fetch the physician, Doctor Smythson. She took me inside to wait."

"And when did the doctor and the Kirkby boy arrive?"

"Not long after, sir."

"Did the doctor say anything to you?"

"Just told me what I already knew, sir. My John were gone. There were no bringing him back."

The little head bowed again. The shoulders quivered.

"Thank you, Mistress Milburn. I can see that having to relive this grave tragedy has been wearing on your spirits. I thank you for your courage and assistance in this matter. I have only a few more questions to ask before I can release you."

He paced back and forth before the bar, before speaking again.

"Mistress Milburn, how long have you known the accused, Altha Weyward?"

"All my life, sir. Same as with most others in the village."

"And what has been the nature of your relationship with her, during your acquaintance?"

"We were—friends, sir. As children, that is."

"But no longer?"

"No, sir. Not since we were thirteen, sir."

"And what happened, when you and the accused were thirteen, that caused the friendship to abate, Mistress Milburn?"

"To—what, sir?"

"To end. What caused the friendship to end?"

Grace looked at her hands.

"My mother fell ill, sir. With the scarlatina."

"And what did that have to do with the accused?"

"She and her mother—"

"Jennet Weyward?"

"Yes—she and Jennet, they came to treat my mother."

"And could you tell the court, please, the outcome of that treatment?"

Grace looked at me before she spoke, so quietly that I had to strain to hear her.

"My mother died, sir."

CHAPTER FOURTEEN

VIOLET

Violet was looking for something to wear.

Father had said that they were going to go clay pigeon shooting with Frederick after breakfast. Violet wasn't fond of shooting. She'd never shoot *real* pigeons, of course (even Father knew better than to ask her to do that), but she still didn't like the way that the gunshots startled the birds in the trees. Besides, she always worried that a bullet intended for a clay pigeon would find a real one instead. She loved wood pigeons, with their pretty plumage and gentle songs. She could hear them now, cheering the morning.

She wondered if Frederick liked birds and animals as much as she did. The thought of Frederick—the heat of his eyes on her—made her stomach flip. She both dreaded and longed to see him. The previous year, she had read about magnetic fields in one of Graham's schoolbooks, and it seemed to Violet that Frederick had his own such field; that it pulled at her like a tide.

She could speak to him today. Over breakfast or while they were shooting. But would *he* want to talk to her? She may have been sixteen, but Violet still felt—and, worse, looked—like a child. She frowned at the looking glass. She had put on a scratchy tweed skirt and jacket, with her stiff brogues. The jacket and skirt were slightly too large for her (Nanny Metcalfe ordered everything a size too big, promising that Violet would "grow into it"), which made her seem even smaller than she was.

Her hair fell past her shoulders in shiny dark waves. She wished she knew how to put it into an elegant chignon—or even pin curls, like the modern-looking women who smiled from the advertisements in Father's newspapers—but the best she could manage was a clumsy plait. She could have passed for twelve.

Before giving up and going downstairs, she made sure her mother's necklace was tucked securely beneath her blouse. Father didn't even know she still had the necklace. He'd made Nanny Metcalfe confiscate it when Violet was six (fortunately, the nursemaid had taken pity on her sobbing charge and returned it). Had it pained him to see it, she wondered now?

She had almost put the feather in her pocket again but thought better of it. What if Father saw? It was too risky. Instead, she'd briefly pressed it to her nose, inhaling its dark, oily scent, the sweet hint of lavender, before tucking it back into its hiding place inside the Brothers Grimm.

Violet still hadn't figured out why that word—*Weyward*—had been scratched into the wainscoting. She'd stayed up until almost one in the morning hunting for more clues in her room, but had found nothing apart from dust and a scattering of mouse droppings. If Weyward was her mother's last name, and if she really *had* been the one to score it into the paint, Violet couldn't for the life of her work out why. Could the room have once belonged to her mother? Violet assumed she would have shared Father's room . . . though the thought of a woman in that draughty, tartan-draped space was somehow wrong, like a robin singing out of season.

Violet had slept in the nursery while her mother was alive and had been too young to remember now what her current room was used for back then. She could still recall the ache she'd felt when she was moved from the nursery, just after the incident with the bees. She had missed its enormous sash windows and the gentle rhythms of Graham snoring at night. Her new room was the smallest in the Hall, with walls painted a greasy yellow that reminded her of fried kippers.

Over time, though, it had become as familiar to her as part of her own body, with its slanting ceiling, chipped enamel washstand, and frayed curtains (these, too, were yellow). She'd thought that she knew every inch of it. She couldn't quite believe it had been keeping secrets from her for all these years. It felt almost like a betrayal.

Perhaps she could ask one of the servants about her room? But then she remembered the way that Mrs. Kirkby had evaded her question about her mother's last name. They were keeping something from her.

Violet felt sure of it.

Mrs. Kirkby had outdone herself for breakfast: the serving table was piled high with an almost prewar quantity of food—silver dishes of baked beans, scrambled eggs, kidneys, and even bacon. (She had an awful feeling that the latter had been procured from one of their sows, a fleshy-nosed, clever animal that she'd taught to respond to the name Jemima.)

From the way *The Times* was folded at his usual chair, Violet could tell that Father had already had his breakfast. Graham was nowhere to be seen: she'd never known him to rise before 9 A.M. (much to Father's consternation).

Frederick was sitting at the table. He wasn't wearing his uniform to-day; instead, he'd donned casual trousers and a pale shirt, which made his dark hair and green eyes stand out. The first three buttons of the shirt were undone, and Violet flushed to see tiny curls of hair on his chest. She filled her plate with beans and eggs—leaving the kidneys and bacon well alone—and sat down opposite him.

"Good morning," she said, looking at her plate.

"Good morning, Violet," he said. She heard the grin in his voice and looked up. She smiled at him shyly. "Did you sleep well?"

"Um—very well, thanks," she said. She had barely slept at all; instead she'd stared at the ceiling, listening to the rustle of bats in the attic and thinking about her mother.

They ate in silence for a while, Violet taking care to eat very neatly. Eventually Frederick put down his knife and fork.

"Your father tells me you're to come clay pigeon shooting with us today," he said. "I expect you're jolly sharp with a rifle, country girl like you."

She quickly wiped away any stray bean sauce from her mouth before answering him.

"Oh—not really, actually," she said. "I don't much like the idea of killing things."

Her cheeks burned as she realized what she'd said.

"Sorry," she said. "I didn't mean that you—"

"That I kill things?" He leaned back in his chair. "Well, it's part of the job description, really. What I signed up for."

Violet looked down at the smears of bean and egg on her plate. The colors seemed very lurid on the white Wedgwood (Penny had laid out the best breakfast service in honor of Frederick's presence). She wasn't sure she wanted to eat any more. When she looked up, he was watching her, waiting.

"Yes, of course," she said, the words rushing out. "You're defending your country." She opened her mouth again, then bit her lip.

"Go on," he said. "Ask what you wanted to ask. I don't bite."

"Well, I suppose I just wondered whether you had . . . whether you had actually ever killed anyone."

He laughed.

"You know, you do seem *much* younger than sixteen," he said. "But in answer to your question—yes, I have. More than one." He stopped. There was a new, dark look in his eyes when he continued.

"You can't imagine what it's like. The Libyan heat sticking to you, day in, day out. Nothing but sand and rock for miles. Not a bit of green. All day, crawling in the dust, shooting and being shot at. Men dying around you. You realize, when you see a person die, that there's nothing *special* about humans. We're just flesh and blood and organs, no different to the pig that gave us this bacon.

"So, all day, dust, death, everywhere. I went to sleep each night with dust in my mouth and the smell of blood in my nose. Even here—I'm still finding dust on me. Under my nails, in my hair, caked into the soles of my shoes. And I can still smell the blood. All so that some English girl, sitting pretty in her father's manor house, can ask me if I ever *killed anyone*."

He stopped talking. The sun was streaming through the windows onto the back of Violet's neck. She felt prickly and hot. She was so stupid. What had possessed her to ask him a question like that? No wonder he'd got upset. She didn't dare look at him. She kept her eyes on her hands, knotted in her lap. Then, fighting back tears, she looked to the ceiling.

She heard a sigh and then the clatter of china as he picked up his cup of tea and put it down again.

"Ah, listen. I've been a brute. Sorry, Violet. Still tired from the journey, I expect."

She had opened her mouth to say something when Father walked into the dining room, wearing his tweeds and cap and carrying his rifle bag, Cecil snarling behind him.

"Good morning," he said, beaming at them. "Marvelous to see you two getting along so well!"

It was a beautiful day outside, and Violet hoped that Frederick would brighten at the sight of the valley. As Frederick and Father instructed Graham on how to throw the clay pigeons in high arcs, she sat on the lawn and looked out at the soft green hills. A bee buzzed nearby, hopping from dandelion to dandelion. She thought of poor Frederick stuck in Libya, without so much as a scrap of green or anything nice to look at. Seeing all those horrible things. Having to *do* all those horrible things.

She tried to imagine killing another person. She had no sense of what a battlefield really looked like: Would you be able to see the person you'd shot? Would you have to . . . watch them die?

Violet had seen animals die. The weasel she'd kept as a pet when she was small; a rose-breasted bullfinch grievously injured by Cecil. She had watched the light go from their eyes; their little bodies slacken. She had felt how afraid they were of whatever came after: the dark unknown, yawning ahead. Violet couldn't imagine condemning another human being to that fate.

But poor Frederick had been given no choice.

They were ready to start shooting now, Father first. She hung back and watched Graham, who was sweating and puffing already, throw the clay pigeons high in the air. Blackbirds flew from the trees at the first shot. Father missed.

"Throw them higher, boy!" he yelled to Graham.

Frederick stepped forward to take his shot. He lifted the rifle as easily as if it were an extension of his body. The clay pigeon shattered, shards drifting to the ground like snow. Father clapped Frederick on the back. They talked for a while—Violet couldn't hear what they were saying—before Frederick walked over to her.

"Your father wants you to have a go," he said. "Come on, I'll show you—it's easier than it looks."

Violet didn't say anything. She'd never shot a rifle before—normally Father just let her sit on the grass and watch.

He handed her the rifle and stepped behind her.

"Put it on your shoulder, that's it," he said.

The rifle was impossibly heavy; Violet's arms shook with the effort of lifting it. The metal felt cool under her hands, and slightly damp from Frederick's sweat. Out of the corner of her eye, she saw Graham watching.

"I'll help you," she heard Frederick say behind her, so close that his breath tickled her ear.

"Here," he said. "Like this."

Frederick put his hands on her waist. When the gun went off, Violet fell backwards into his arms.

CHAPTER FIFTEEN

KATE

K ate takes a long sip of tea before she opens the package. There is
a sweet, cloying scent as she unwraps the cloth, which is spotted
white with mold. Inside, a stack of letters. The ink has faded to a dull
brown, and the paper is creased and yellowed. The date on the first letter
reads *20 July 1925*.

My darling Lizzie,

I have not slept this week for thoughts of you.

*Outside, the world is bright and green with summer, and even
young Rainham has a spring in his step. But I cannot bear the long
days. In fact, I hate them. I hate each and every day that stands
between now and when I shall see you again.*

*I cannot settle to anything—even hunting brings me no comfort.
All I can do is mope about, like a man tormented.*

*I long for you to come and join me, here at the Hall. I truly be-
lieve, my darling, that you will be happy here—much happier than
in that dank little cottage. As I write this, I am looking out through
my study window at the gardens. The roses are in bloom and their
delicate beauty is unmatched in this world, other than by your face.*

Trust me when I say this, for I have seen the world. The world, and every specimen of woman it contains. Oriental girls with coal-black hair and obsidian eyes. African princesses, their swan necks looped with gold. So many faces I have seen and admired.

But none compare to yours.

Oh, your face. I dream of it each night. Your ivory skin. Your lips, as red as fresh-spilled blood. Those dark, wild eyes. Each night I fall deeper into dreams, like a man drowning.

I must have you.

My darling. I have spoken to the vicar and he can perform the ceremony in two weeks' time. But we must ensure that everything is in order before we can proceed, as we discussed. My parents and my brother are due to return from Carlisle on Thursday. I expect them home by sundown.

We are closer than ever now. You must not falter but be brave, for the sake of our union. For our future. It is as Macbeth said:

"Who could refrain, that had a heart to love, and in that heart courage to make love known?"

I enclose, as a symbol of our promise, a gift. It is a handkerchief. I sent to Lancaster for it, demanded only the finest quality for my love. My bride.

I count the days until you are mine.

Yours forever
Rupert

Who are Rupert and Elizabeth? Previous inhabitants of the cottage, perhaps. But, no—Rupert had written of "the Hall." Did he mean Orton Hall—her family's old seat?

Could they be related?

She searches through the other letters, hunting for more details. Rupert writes of first setting eyes on Elizabeth at a May Day Festival in the village. He had—in his words—been "transfixed by her ivory skin and raven locks."

Some of the letters are about arrangements to meet—always at dawn or dusk, where the lovers won't be seen. There's a dark undercurrent to Rupert's words, as though danger stalks the couple, their stars conspiring against them. What did Elizabeth need such courage to face?

She can't figure it out. Nor can she confirm the identities of the correspondents—Rupert never signs his last name, and there are no further references to the Hall.

Sadness wells up in her. Something in Rupert's tone reminds her of early texts from Simon.

I can't stop thinking about you, he'd texted, after their third date. *I feel like I'm sixteen again.*

He had taken her to a little sushi place in Shoreditch. She had felt out of place amongst the other female diners, with their sleek hair and expensive jewelry. She had agonized over what to wear, texting pictures of different outfit options to her university friends. She'd wanted to wear something simple, a plain navy dress she'd had for years, but one of the girls, Becky, had talked her into borrowing a slinky red top. It was so low-cut that it exposed a mole on her breastbone, a dark pink smudge she'd hated since childhood.

She had felt incredibly self-conscious as she walked into the restaurant and scanned the tables, looking for Simon. He stood up when he saw her and smiled, his perfect teeth dazzling. Later, she'd convinced herself that she imagined it, but at the time she thought that a hush fell over the room, as the other diners looked between her and Simon and thought: *Her? Really?*

But Simon had poured her a glass of wine and smiled at her again, in that slow, sensuous way he had. Gradually, her nerves had fallen away, replaced by butterflies of excitement. They had talked about everything, the conversation flowing as easily as the wine that Simon poured into her glass, until quickly they'd had one bottle, then two.

They'd talked about their families—Simon was an only child, just like her. He wasn't really in touch with his parents, he'd admitted—there'd been some kind of argument, when he was younger. Later, she'd realize he wasn't in contact with most people from his childhood, or from university. He had a talent for moving on and starting over, extricating himself as seamlessly as a snake shedding its skin.

But she didn't know any of this that night, as she looked into his eyes—so blue—and opened herself up to him in a way she couldn't remember doing with anyone before. The glass wall she'd built around herself was disintegrating—she could almost see it happening; the fragments winking in the light like tiny mirrors.

Really, it was just that the glass wall was being replaced with another kind of cage. One that Simon spun from charm and flattery, as binding and delicate as spider silk.

Now, she wonders if she'd known this, even then. Perhaps it had been part of the allure—the thought that, after all those exhausting years of locking herself away, here was someone who could do it for her.

Their jobs couldn't have been more different—he seemed to relish the challenge of private equity, telling her of the electric thrill when he acquired a floundering company. It was like hunting, he said, but instead of shooting deer or foxes he was seizing assets and balance sheets, stripping a company of its deadweight like flesh from a carcass.

His world—with its own set of bewildering rules and jargon—couldn't have been more foreign to her. And yet he'd listened attentively as she'd gushed about her job in children's publishing. About the thrill of reading manuscripts, of immersing herself in a story that no one else had yet experienced. She'd even told him how reading had been such a comfort—a life raft, really—after her father's death.

"I love your passion," he'd said, placing his hand on hers, the fine hairs of his arm gold in the candlelight. And then, with a tenderness that made tears prick her eyes, "Your father would be very proud of you."

Other images from that night haunt her, too. Simon helping her into a taxi, asking her to his apartment for a nightcap. Sinking down into his soft leather couch, brain muddled from too much wine . . .

"You're so much prettier when you smile," he'd said, as she laughed at one of his jokes. He had leaned over, brushed the hair from her face and kissed her for the first time. He touched her gently at first, as if she were a wild animal he might spook away. Then the kiss deepened, and his fingers were firm on her jaw.

I must have you.

It was romantic, she told herself the next morning, the way he undid her trousers, pulled down her underwear, pushed himself inside her. The strength of his need.

In the early days of their relationship, she returned to that memory again and again, smoothing its rough edges into a lie she almost believed. It would be years before she remembered the word she had whispered, mind and body dulled by alcohol, as his face blurred over hers.

Wait.

Suddenly, she can't bear the sight of the letters anymore. She folds them up and puts them aside.

She clutches her mug of tea tightly, letting it warm her hands. Outside, it is raining in earnest now; the windows are jeweled with it. She can't see the garden, but she thinks she can hear the branches of the sycamore, scraping across the roof in the wind.

Nausea grips her stomach. The only sign of the baby, other than a new heaviness to her breasts. She wonders if it is normal, this feeling that her guts are pushing up into her throat, if it indicates how far along she is. Almost two months since her last period, since the familiar twist of pain in her womb, the smear of blood on her underwear. Always the color of silt, of soil, on the first day. Looking more like something from the earth than from her own body.

Simon didn't care for blood, unless he'd been the one to draw it. He collected the bruises that bloomed across her skin as if they were trophies, fingering them with pride. But her menstrual blood flowed from her body with its own rhythm, one that he didn't care for and couldn't control. He hated the feel of it, slimy and fibrous. The smell. Like an animal, he said. Or something dead. So, Kate had one week a month when her body was her own.

And now she is sharing it.

She pictures the clump of cells, clinging to her insides. Even now, splitting and reforming, growing. Into their child.

Will it be a boy, she wonders, and grow up to be like Simon? Or a girl, and grow up to be like her?

She isn't sure what would be worse.

CHAPTER SIXTEEN

ALTHA

It had been strange, seeing Grace again. Strange to think of how we'd started off together, side by side, and had ended up with a courtroom yawning between us. She in her neat gown and me in my shackles. A prisoner.

The dungeons were silent, but for a distant wail that might have been the wind, or the souls of those already condemned. I searched for the spider, looking under the matted straw, and my heart ached at the thought that it had gone, had left me to my fate. But just as I had given up hope and curled myself into a ball on the ground, I felt it brush against my earlobe. I wished I could see it—the glitter of its eyes and pincers—but the night was too dark, with not even a sliver of moonlight coming through the grate. So dark that I felt as if I were in my grave already.

If I were to have a grave, that was. I didn't know what happened to witches after they were hanged. I wondered whether anyone buried them. Whether anyone would bury me.

I wanted to be buried. If I must depart this life, I thought, let me live on in the soil: let me feed the earthworms, nourish the roots of the trees, like my mother and her mother before her.

Really, it wasn't death I feared. It was dying. The process of it, the pain. Death had always sounded so peaceful, when it was spoken of in church: a gathering of lambs to the bosom, a return to the kingdom. But I had seen it too many times to believe that. The sweep of the reaper's shadow over an old man, a woman, a child. The face contorting, the limbs flailing, the desperate gasp for air. There was no peace in any death I had seen. I would find no peace in mine.

When I did sleep, I saw the noose, tight around my neck. I saw the breath choked out of me in a white vapor. I saw my body, twisting in the breeze.

They had finished with Grace, it seemed. But I saw her there in the gallery when they took me into the dock the next morning. As of course one would expect. What woman would not want to know the fate of her husband's accused murderer?

We rose when the judges entered the courtroom. I saw one of them look at me, eyes narrowed, as if I were the rot at the center of the apple, a canker to be cut away.

The prosecutor called the physician, Doctor Smythson, to the stand. As I knew he would.

They had brought him to see me at the village gaol. Before they brought me to Lancaster. Though I was mad with hunger and exhaustion, I had not yielded to their questions. They asked if I had ever attended a witches' sabbath, had ever suckled a familiar or lain with a beast. If I had given myself to Satan, as his bride.

If I had killed John Milburn.

No, I said, though my throat was caked with thirst and my stomach groaned with want. *No.* It took all my strength to force the word from my body. To protest my innocence.

I had, until then, held on to hope as if it were a stone in my hand.

But when they brought Doctor Smythson to the gaol I feared it was over.

Now I watched him take his oath on the Bible. He was an old man, and his veins made red patterns on his cheeks. That'll be the drink, my mother would say, if she were here. He'd indulged in it as much as he'd prescribed it. Though that was by far his least dangerous method of treatment. As I looked at him, I remembered Grace's mother, Anna Metcalfe: her milk-white face, the color sucked out of her by leeches.

The prosecutor began his questioning.

"Doctor Smythson, you recall the events of New Year's Day, in this, the year of our Lord 1619?"

"Yes."

"Are you able to relate them for the court?"

The physician spoke with confidence. He was a man, after all. He had no reason to think he would not be believed.

"I began the day at dawn, as is my custom. I'd been up late, the night before, with a patient. The family had given me some eggs. I remember I ate them with my wife that morning. We had not long broken our fast when there was a hammering at the door."

"Who was at the door?"

"It was Daniel Kirkby."

"And what did Daniel Kirkby want?"

"I remember thinking he looked very pale. At first I thought he might have taken ill himself but then he told me there'd been some sort of incident, at the Milburn farm. Involving John Milburn. From his face, I knew it was not good. I collected my coat and my bag and set off to the farm with the boy."

"And what did you find when you got there?"

"Milburn was on the ground. His injuries were very grave. I knew at once that he was dead."

"Can you describe those injuries to the court, please, Doctor?"

"A large portion of the skull had been crushed. One eye was badly damaged. The bones of the neck had been broken, as had those of the arms and legs."

"And what, in your opinion, would have caused the injuries, Doctor?"

"Trampling by animals. Daniel Kirkby told me that Master Milburn had been stampeded by his cows."

"Thank you. And have you ever seen such injuries, in your career as a physician?"

"I have. I am regularly called upon to attend the aftermath of farm accidents, which are common in these parts."

The prosecutor frowned, as if the physician had not given him the answer he wanted.

"Are you able to tell the court what happened next, after you viewed Master Milburn's body?"

"I went inside the farmhouse, to speak to the widow."

"And was she alone?"

"No. She was with the accused, Altha Weyward."

"Can you describe for the court the demeanor of the widow, Grace Milburn, and that of the accused, Altha Weyward?"

"Mistress Milburn looked very pale and shaken, as you would expect."

The prosecutor nodded, paused.

"Are you able to tell the court," he said, "your opinion of Altha Weyward?"

"My opinion? In what respect?"

"To put it another way. Are you able to tell the court the nature of your acquaintance with her, over the years?"

"I would say that she—and her mother before her—has been something of a nuisance."

"A nuisance?"

"On several occasions, I've had reports that she's attended to villagers, patients who were already under my regimen."

"Are you able to provide an example, sir?"

The physician paused.

"Not two months ago, I was treating a patient for fever. Baker's daughter, girl of ten. She had an imbalance of humors: too much of the sanguine. This led to an excess of heat in the body, hence the fever. As a consequence, she needed to be bled."

"Go on."

"I administered the treatment. Advised that the leeches should remain for one night and one day. When I returned the next day, the parents had removed the leeches prematurely."

"Did they say why?"

"They'd had a visit from Altha Weyward in the night. She'd recommended the girl take quantities of broth instead."

"And how did the child fare?"

"She lived. Fortunately, the leeches had been left on for long enough that most of the excess humor was removed."

"And has this sort of thing happened before?"

"Several times before. There was a very similar case when the accused was still a child. She and her mother treated a patient of mine suffering scarlatina. John Milburn's late mother-in-law, actually. Anna Metcalfe. Sadly, Mistress Metcalfe passed away."

"In your opinion, what caused her death?"

"The accused's mother. Whether through malice or not, I cannot say."

"And, in your view," said the prosecutor, "what role did the accused play in Mistress Metcalfe's death?"

"I could not say for certain," the physician replied. "She was but a child at the time."

I could hear the hum of whispers again. I looked at Grace, sitting at the back of the gallery. She was too far away for me to make out her expression.

"Doctor Smythson," the prosecutor continued, "are you familiar with the characteristics of witches, as laid out by His Royal Highness in his work, *Daemonologie*?"

"Of course, sir. I am familiar with the work."

"Are you aware," said the prosecutor, "of whether Altha and Jennet Weyward possessed animal familiars? Familiars," he spat, turning to face the court, "are evidence of a witch's pact with the devil. They invite these monstrous imps—who wear the likeness of God's own creatures—to suckle at their bosom. Thus they sustain Satan himself with their milk."

At this question my heart hammered in my chest, so loud that I wondered that the prosecutor himself could not hear it. Doctor Smythson had never been inside the cottage.

But so many others had. So many others might have seen the crow that perched, dark and sleek on my mother's shoulder, the bees and damselflies I wore in my hair when I was small.

Had someone told him?

The courtroom was still, all eyes trained on Doctor Smythson for his answer. The physician shifted in his seat, mopped his brow with a white handkerchief.

"No, sir," he said, finally. "I have not seen such a thing."

Relief flooded my veins, sweet and heady. But in the very next moment, a cold dread took its place. For I knew what question would follow.

The prosecutor paused.

"Very well," he said. "And have you, in the course of your acquaintance with the accused, had the opportunity to examine her for a witch's mark? An unnatural teat, from which she may give suck to the devil and his servants?"

"Yes, sir. I made the examination at Crows Beck gaol, in the presence of your men. The mark is on her rib cage, below the heart."

"Your honors," said the prosecutor. "I would like to ask the court's permission to make an exhibit of the accused's body, to demonstrate that she shows the witch's mark."

The stouter judge spoke: "Your request is granted."

One of the guards strode towards me. I was hauled, still shackled, to the boards in front of the jury. I stood queasy with fear, until I felt harsh fingers tug at the bindings of my gown before pulling it over my head.

I quivered in my filthy shift, shamed that all and sundry could see me thus. Then the fingers were back, and the shift was gone. My skin met with the clammy air. The gallery roared, and I shut my eyes. The prosecutor circled my body, looking at my exposed flesh the way a farmer looks at his cattle.

I would have prayed, if I had believed in God.

"Doctor," called the prosecutor, "can you point out the mark?"

"I can no longer see it," said Doctor Smythson, his features furrowed. "Alas—what I took to be the witch's mark in the dim of the gaol appears to be but a sore. A flea bite, perhaps. Or some sort of pox."

The prosecutor stood still for a moment, his cold eyes blazing with fury. Rage gave his scarred cheeks a purple hue.

"Very well," he said, after a time. "You may clothe her."

CHAPTER SEVENTEEN

VIOLET

Violet fancied that she could still smell Frederick's cologne in her hair from when he had caught her in his arms.

Father had given them an odd look, as if he had come upon Frederick borrowing something of his without permission. Then the look passed, like a cloud going over the sun, and he had merely nodded at them. The shooting had wrapped up fairly quickly after that, with Frederick declaring that his shoulder ached ("thanks to Jerry") and suggesting an afternoon nap before a walk through the grounds.

Violet decided she would walk next to Frederick. She would show him all of her favorite spots in the grounds, including the beech tree. Perhaps he'd like to climb it with her? She caught herself. She was being ridiculous. She must be *ladylike*. Father would have a fit if she climbed a tree in front of a guest. Anyway, she didn't want Frederick to think she was . . . well, a child.

In the afternoon, when the sun had dipped in the sky to cast long shadows over the valley, she made her way downstairs to meet the others. Father and Graham hadn't come down yet, but Frederick was waiting in the entrance hall. He looked up as she walked down the stairs, and the feel of his eyes on her body made her giddy. A wave of heat rose up her neck. He extended a hand as she approached the bottom step, as if he were helping her down from a horse-drawn carriage in a romance novel.

"M'lady," he said, kissing her hand. The brush of his lips against her skin was like an electric shock. She couldn't tell if she liked it or not.

"Aha," Father's voice boomed down the stairs. Violet looked up to see a reluctant Graham trailing him. "Raring to go, I see."

Outside, the valley was hazy with the afternoon sun. Midges shimmered in the sweet-smelling air.

"Ugh," said Frederick, swatting at his face. "Don't care much for midges, I must say. Not quite sure there's any point to them, the blasted things."

"Oh, but there is," Violet said, excitedly. "A point to them, I mean. They're a very important food source for toads and swallows, actually. You could say the whole valley depends on them, in the summer. And I think they're rather pretty—they look a bit like fairy dust, in this light, don't you think?"

Fairy dust? She chided herself. She was trying to seem grown up in front of Frederick. She hadn't got off to a very good start.

"Hmm. I'm not sure I'd go that far," he said, frowning. "Though they're a damn sight better than Libyan mosquitoes. If I have to be bitten to death by insects, I'd rather they were bloody English ones."

Violet flushed at the swear word. Father hadn't heard: he was walking ahead with Graham, Cecil loping alongside. The occasional burst of their conversation floated back to them and it sounded to Violet as though Graham was getting a lecture about his shooting.

"Terribly sorry," said Frederick. "Not used to keeping fine company these days."

"Are there no girls in Libya?"

"None such as yourself," Frederick said. Violet flushed again. They walked in silence for a while. They were approaching the beech tree now. It looked rather majestic, Violet thought, with the sun dappling the green leaves and painting the branches gold. She waited for Frederick to comment on it, but he didn't. They walked on.

"I say," she began, "how is it that we're cousins, and yet we have never met before?"

"Oh, but we have," said Frederick. "I came to visit with my parents when I was a child. Though I expect you won't remember—you couldn't have been more than a toddler, then."

"Well, why did you come only the once?" Violet asked. "I'd have loved to have a cousin around, growing up. It's just me and Graham, and we . . . aren't close, not anymore. Then, when he goes to school, I'm all alone."

"It's all a bit fuzzy, to be honest," said Frederick. "But—and I don't want to offend you—I think it was something to do with your mother."

"My mother? I barely remember her."

"You look like her," said Frederick. "She had the same dark hair. She was sort of—curious. Spoke like the servants. Mummy told me she was a local girl, from the village. Daddy was a bit put out by the whole thing, I think. Kept saying his parents would never have allowed it, if they'd been alive. Anyway. Sorry, I don't want to offend you any more than I have already today."

"No—please," said Violet, grasping at his words. "Please, tell me more about her. Father never tells us anything. You said she was curious? What did you mean?"

"Well, she . . . wasn't quite well, I don't think. For one, she was always going around with this ratty old bird on her shoulder. Some sort of raven—or maybe it was a crow, I don't remember, but it was obviously diseased: there were these ghastly white streaks on its feathers. Anyway, she called it . . . what was it? Oh yes—*Morg*. Odd name. Mummy was rather scandalized."

Here, Frederick paused and looked over at Violet. She kept her face neutral—afraid that if he could see the effect his words were having on her, he would stop.

A crow with white streaks. Could the feather she found have belonged to Morg? Violet's heart sang. *Her mother.* So she had loved animals, too—just as Violet had suspected.

"She couldn't take meals with us," Frederick continued. "She'd start off but then she'd begin to make strange comments, out of nowhere . . . 'I'll tell them,' she'd say, as if it were a threat. None of us had the faintest idea what she was on about, though perhaps she didn't either, the poor thing. Anyway, your father would have to take her back to her room. Then she'd be ranting and raving, shouting . . . often, he had no choice but to lock her in."

Violet started. "Lock her in?"

"It was for her own safety, you see," said Frederick. "Just until the doctor came. She was—a danger to herself. And the baby."

Violet shivered.

She had never met a mad person. She had an image of a waifish figure draped in white, speaking gibberish, like Ophelia from *Hamlet*.

Perhaps *this* was why Father never spoke of her mother? Because he didn't want Violet to know that she had been mad. Perhaps he was trying to protect her memory. She frowned, then turned to Frederick again.

"Well—can you tell me anything else about her? Was she . . . was she kind?"

Frederick snorted.

"Not to me. Though she didn't like me much—that was evident. I used to catch her staring at me and muttering to herself. And—well, the visit ended rather abruptly."

"What happened?"

"One night, I found a toad in my bed. A live one. I remember touching it with my foot. It was cold and slimy. Horrible," he shuddered at the memory. "They probably heard me scream back in London. Anyway, then Mummy came, and saw the toad . . . and she got it into her head that your mother had put it there. She was hysterical. Your father kept telling her to calm down, that it had to be one of the servants—that your mother had been in her room the whole evening, with the door bolted, but both my parents got quite worked up really. They packed the car—we had a little green Bentley, I remember, new that year—and we left in the middle of the night."

"Oh," said Violet.

"On the way home, my mother kept saying your father hadn't been right in the head since the Great War . . . then our grandparents and Uncle Edward dying in that horrible accident . . . And then my father said . . ." He paused to flick a midge from his shoulder.

"What did your father say?" Violet asked, scarcely breathing.

"That Uncle Rupert had been bewitched."

She didn't know whether or not to believe Frederick's story. She couldn't imagine why he would lie. And yet . . . it was hard to believe the horrible things he said about her mother. It was awful to think of her mother ranting and raving, needing to be locked in a room—and, worst of all, being unkind to Frederick. Perhaps she hadn't meant to scare him with the toad? Violet wouldn't particularly mind finding a toad in her bed. In fact, she was rather fond of them.

But then she remembered Father's words.

Perhaps they can stop you from turning out like her.

Was that why she had this sick, wrong feeling in her stomach?

The air was growing colder now. Violet could hear crickets calling for their mates. She looked at Frederick, walking next to her. In the dim light, his dark features and long strides made her think of a panther.

They hadn't spoken for a few minutes. Violet wondered if he thought she was "curious," too, like her mother. She would need to take care that he didn't catch her staring at him. She wished he would say something. He hadn't commented on the beauty of the sun setting slowly over the valley at all, even though it had put more colors in the sky than she knew the names for.

"Do you hear that?" she asked. "It's such a lovely sound."

"What is?"

"The crickets."

"Oh. Yes, I suppose it is." She heard his laugh, rich and deep.

"What's so funny?" she asked.

"You're an unusual girl. First the midges, now the crickets . . . never known a girl—or a chap, for that matter—to be so fond of insects."

"I just find them so very interesting," she said. "Beautiful, too. It's sad, though—they have such short lives. For instance, did you know that the mayfly only lives for one day?"

She had seen a swarm of mayflies, once, down at the beck. A great, glittering cloud of them, pulsing above the surface of the water. They looked to Violet as if they were dancing—she had been quite disturbed when she learned from Dinsdale, the gardener, that they had in fact been *mating*. Now her cheeks flushed at the image. Would Frederick be able to tell she was having such unseemly thoughts? She wished she hadn't brought them up.

"Imagine," she continued, anxious to change the subject, "having only one day left on Earth. I don't think I'd be able to decide between catching a train to London to see the Natural History Museum, or . . . lounging by the beck all day. One last afternoon with the birds, the insects, and the flowers . . ."

"I know what I would do," said Frederick. They were passing by a briar bush now. Violet realized that she didn't know where Father and Graham had got to: perhaps they were already back at the house. The sound of Father lecturing Graham ("You must *aim* the rifle, boy") had long since faded.

"And what would that be, Frederick?" she asked, blushing at the sound of his name on her lips. A strange, quivery feeling bubbled inside her.

He laughed and moved closer; his arm brushed hers and her heart quivered.

"I'll show you, but only if you close your eyes."

Violet did as she was told. Suddenly, there was a hand on her waist, large and rough through the fabric of her skirt. Opening her eyes a fraction, she saw that the pink glimmer of dusk was blocked out by Frederick's face in front of hers. She could feel his breath tickling her nose. It felt hot and smelled of coffee and something else, a sour note that made Violet think—oddly, unseasonably—of Christmas pudding. Violet tried to remember the word for the thing that Mrs. Kirkby soaked the pudding in before setting it alight, but then—

He was kissing her. Or, Violet supposed that was what he was doing. She knew that people kissed, from reading books ("to smooth that rough touch with a tender kiss"—that was Shakespeare, wasn't it?) and because she had once seen Penny kissing Neil, the ill-fated gardener's apprentice. They had been pressed up against the stable, clinging onto each other as if they were drowning. It had looked rather unpleasant.

Violet was surprised that she was still thinking so much, even though her lips had been completely enveloped in his—rather wet—ones. She was finding it quite difficult to breathe. She wasn't sure *how* she was supposed to breathe, with her mouth covered by his (the taste of his mouth was very adult, as though he had seen things, been to places she couldn't compre-hend . . . again she was reminded of Christmas pudding; why was that?).

She was breathing through her nose now, Violet wondered if he could hear it, if she sounded like a cow . . . Her brain was a whirlpool. She thought of drowning, again. He was kissing her more fiercely now, press-ing her against the briar bush; she felt twigs poking into her back and her hair—she would have to get them out before Father saw . . . Then he did something that made her almost stop thinking. He pushed something wet and slimy into her mouth—Violet thought of the toad—and she realized it was his tongue. She spluttered, and he pulled away. She took a deep breath, gulping at the clean evening air.

"Sorry," he said. "Got rather carried away there." He reached out a hand and traced the chain of her necklace with one finger.

She shivered. It was almost nicer than the kiss.

"Best be getting back for dinner," he said. "We should do this again, though—same time tomorrow evening?"

She nodded, struck dumb. He turned to go, heading towards the Hall, which, with its yellow windows and high turrets, looked to Violet like a scene from a book—a ship on a stormy sea, perhaps. She stayed for a while, waiting for her breathing to slow and picking out the twigs from her hair. As she walked back to the Hall (she tripped a couple of times, still reeling from the feel of his mouth on hers) she wondered if she looked changed, if anyone would be able to tell what had happened just by glancing at her. She certainly felt different. Her heart was beating as hard in her chest as if she had been running.

It wasn't until she shut her bedroom door and her racing mind had settled that something Frederick had said, before he had kissed her so suddenly, returned to her.

She was a danger to herself. And the baby.

Violet had always believed that her mother died giving birth to Graham. But Frederick had made it sound as though he had already been born.

CHAPTER EIGHTEEN

KATE

Kate has been at the cottage for three weeks now. It's late spring, and the year is ripening. It rained last night—hard enough that she feared the roof would buckle—but today the sky is low and blue, the air hot. Hot and thick to match her blood, which seems, in these last weeks, to have slowed its pace through her veins.

On the walk into the village this morning, she passes another row of moles, tied by their tails to a rusted gate. Flies hover about them, flitting between their damp fur and the clumps of dog violet that grow alongside the road. She's learned that it's a local tradition—the cashier at the green-grocer looked bemused when Kate shyly asked about it, explained that was how the mole-catcher proved his worth. But the shriveled bodies still feel like a warning, especially for her.

By the time she reaches the medical center, her shirt is sticky with exertion and anxiety. She was instructed to arrive with a full bladder, and her lower abdomen is tight and painful, straining against the waistband of her skirt. She checks her watch: ten past nine. She's five minutes early.

Perhaps she won't go in. Perhaps she'll turn and walk back to the cottage without even knocking on the door, the same way she repeatedly dialed the number and hung up before anyone could answer. She did this five times before her nerve held and she managed to speak to the receptionist, to actually book this appointment.

She looks around her. This early, the square is empty and quiet, save for a cow's distant lowing. There is no one to see her go in. She looks down at her feet, watching ants serpentine across the cobbles.

Taking a breath, Kate opens the door and is hit by the smell of disinfectant. The waiting room is cold and whitewashed, the plastic chairs and tired noticeboard a stark contrast to the building's Tudor exterior. The space is dominated by a large desk, behind which a woman sits tapping away at a computer. The muffled sounds of conversation come from behind a heavy door: the consulting room, according to a gleaming brass plate.

"Name?" asks the receptionist, a thin woman with a vulpine face.

"Kate," she says. "Kate Ayres."

The receptionist's eyebrows lift as she looks at Kate properly for the first time.

"The niece," she says. It isn't a question.

"Um—yes. Did you know my great-aunt? Violet?"

But the woman is looking back at her computer screen.

"If you could take a seat, please. The doctor will be with you in a minute."

Kate sits heavily on one of the plastic chairs. She wishes she had some water; her stomach roils, and there is a strange taste in her mouth. Metallic, like blood, or even dirt. She's been waking up with it. It reminds her of something, a childhood memory that she can't quite hold on to.

The door of the consulting room opens.

"Miss Ayres?"

The doctor is male—in his late sixties, perhaps; weathered cheeks shaded by white stubble. A stethoscope around his neck. Panic bubbles up in her.

She'd asked for a female doctor, hadn't she? Yes—she's sure of it. The receptionist—likely the same woman staring at her now—had assured her that there would be a female doctor. "Dr. Collins is only available Tuesdays and Thursdays," she'd said on the phone. "So you'll have to come in on one of those days if you want to see a woman, otherwise it's Dr. Radcliffe."

"Ah—sorry," she says now as she rises from the seat, wincing at the feel of her thighs unsticking from the plastic. "I think I was booked in to see Dr. Collins?"

"Couldn't make it in," says the male doctor, gesturing for her to follow him into the consulting room. "Sick child. Always the way with that one, I'm afraid."

She hesitates. Part of her wants to leave; to ask for an appointment with the female doctor another day. But she's here now. And she's not sure she trusts herself to come back.

She follows the doctor into the consulting room.

The gel is cold on her skin. Dr. Radcliffe has already drawn volumes of blood from her arm, prodding and sticking her like a laboratory specimen.

"Just relax," he says, running the ultrasound wand over her stomach. He moves closer and she smells his breath, stale with coffee. "Your husband couldn't make it?"

She has an image of Simon's face over hers, his hand resting on the base of her throat as he moves inside her. His cells traveling up into her body, ready to tether her to him forever.

"I'm not married," she says, blinking the memory away.

"Your boyfriend, then. He didn't want to come?" There is a strange whooshing sound in the room, almost like the beating of wings.

"No, I don't . . . what's that noise?"

The doctor smiles, pressing the wand harder into her stomach.

"That," he says, "is the heartbeat. Your baby's heartbeat."

There is a plummeting sensation inside her.

"Heartbeat? I thought it was . . . too early for that."

"Hmm, you're between ten and twelve weeks along, I'd say. Here, take a look."

He gestures to the blinking monitor, where her womb undulates in gray and white. For a moment she can't make sense of the image, it's like static. Then she sees it: a pearly glimmer, pupa-shaped, almost. The fetus.

Her mouth is so dry that it's hard to get the words out.

"Can you tell it . . . the baby's sex?"

The doctor chuckles.

"A bit too soon for that, I'm afraid. You'll have to come back in a few weeks."

There is something else she wanted—planned—to ask. But now, with the doctor's liver-flecked hands on her stomach, the room filled with the sound of the baby's heartbeat, it feels . . . impossible.

The question shrivels inside her.

The doctor looks at her strangely, as if he has read her thoughts.

"All done," he says abruptly, handing her a piece of paper towel. "You can clean yourself up."

He is silent as he enters information on a computer, carefully labels the ruby-red vials of her blood.

"You look a bit like her," he says after a while. "Your great-aunt, I mean. Violet. Similar sort of eyes—just the hair that's different. Hers was dark when she was younger."

"It's dyed."

"You'll have to stop doing that. Bad for the baby." He goes back to his labeling.

"Did you treat her, then? My aunt."

The doctor pauses, fiddles with the stethoscope around his neck.

"Once or twice, when Dr. Collins wasn't in—she was her patient, really. Only in recent years, though. Before that I think she went to a surgery out of town—she only started coming here when my father died. The first Dr. Radcliffe. He started the practice."

Finished with his labeling, the doctor gets up to usher her out of the consulting room.

"See Mrs. Dinsdale on your way out, please, so you can book in for the next appointment. We'll want you back in eight weeks."

Back in the waiting room, Kate looks at the noticeboard again, at the pamphlets on display at the receptionist's desk. But there's none of the information she is looking for.

"Will you book in for the next appointment today?" asks the receptionist.

"Um. Actually, I was wondering," Kate lowers her voice, glancing over at an elderly woman in the waiting room, "if you have any information about . . . termination services."

The receptionist slides a leaflet across the counter, her eyes narrowed.

"Thank you," says Kate. She pauses. She wants to leave, to get away from the woman's cold stare, but her bladder is tugging at her painfully. "Is there a toilet I can use?"

A nod at the corridor to the left.

She washes her hands, grimacing at the chemical smell of the soap. As she cups water from the tap and drinks, snatches of conversation from the waiting room float back to her.

"Did she ask for what I think she did?" An unfamiliar voice—the elderly female patient.

Kate freezes. She doesn't want to hear this. Her cheeks sting with shame.

"Can't say I'm surprised," the receptionist is saying. "Being from that family."

"Who is she?"

"That's Violet's great-niece."

"Really?" says the old woman. "Didn't know Violet had any family, save for himself up at the Big House. Though not sure he counts for much."

"I wonder if she has it, too."

"They all do, don't they? That Weyward lot. Ever since the first one."

Then the receptionist says something else—a word so unexpected that Kate is sure she must have misheard.

Witch.

Outside, Kate takes deep, gulping breaths. Her brain feels disordered, fogged.

She can still hear it: the strange thrumming of her baby's heartbeat. The way it filled the room. It was hard to believe that it had come from her own body. It sounded like something from the sky—a bird taking to the air. Or something not of this world at all.

It is 2 A.M. but Kate is awake, watching bats flutter past the window, dark against a pale slice of moon.

Her thoughts feel scattered, panicked—flitting away from her as though they, too, have wings. She rests a hand on her stomach, feeling the smooth heat of her own flesh. It seems impossible that, even now, the larval creature she saw onscreen floats inside her. Growing into a child.

Those things the women were saying about her family—they made it sound as though Kate was carrying some sort of faulty gene, an error code lurking in her cells, plotting her demise. Like the crow she found in the fireplace with the strange white pattern across its glossy feathers—a sign of leucism, she'd read, a genetic trait handed down over generations.

She remembers what the greengrocer said, about the viscount. How he'd lost his marbles.

Perhaps they were referring to some kind of mental health issue, running in the family? That wouldn't surprise her. All those panic attacks she'd experienced over the years—the clawing in her chest, her throat tightening.

The feeling of something trying to get out.

After another hour of trying and failing to sleep, she gives up, pushing the bedcovers aside.

Switching on the light, she drags the hatboxes out from under the bed. There has to be something in here—something she missed the first time she looked.

Again, she riffles through the folder with its faded, dusty cover. But there's nothing—nothing she hasn't already seen before. Not a single mention of the Weywards.

Sighing in frustration, she picks up Violet's old passport and opens it to the photo page, staring into the dark eyes that are so like Kate's own. There's a determination there that Kate didn't notice before—the firm set of the mouth, the jut of the chin. As if Violet has fought something and won. She would never have ended up like Kate: soft and malleable, yielding as easily to Simon's fingers as if she were clay.

Suddenly she wishes her great-aunt were still alive, that she could talk to her. That she could talk to someone. Anyone.

She is about to put the passport back when a slip of yellowed paper falls out of it.

It's a birth certificate. Violet's birth certificate.

```
Name: Violet Elizabeth Ayres
Date of Birth: 5 February 1926
Place of Birth: Orton Hall, near Crows Beck,
   Cumbria, England
Father's occupation: Peer
Father's name: Rupert William Ayres, Ninth
   Viscount Kendall
Mother's name: Elizabeth Ayres, née Weyward
```

She remembers the letters. Rupert and Elizabeth—they are Violet's parents, Kate's great-grandparents.

Which means that Kate—Kate is a Weyward.

When she does sleep, Kate has the same nightmare that haunted her throughout her childhood—her father's large hand over her small one; the dark shadow of the crow in the trees. Wings thrashing the air; the shriek of rubber on tarmac. The wet thump of her father's body hitting the ground.

Except that at the cottage, the dream is longer—the flapping of wings morphing into the gallop of her baby's heartbeat. She sees the fetus: growing and growing, like a moon rising into the sky. Growing into a child. But not a boy, blond and blue-eyed like Simon. A girl, with dark hair, dark eyes. A child that looks like Aunt Violet. That looks like Kate.

A Weyward child.

In the morning, she takes the crumpled brochure from the bedside table and unfurls it. But she doesn't dial the number. She can't bring herself to. Every time she picks up the phone, she remembers the sound of the baby's heartbeat, remembers the way it looked inside her, glimmering like a pearl. Remembers that dream-child, with hair and eyes the color of jet, of richest earth.

She is still for a moment, thinking of what Simon would do if he knew she was pregnant. How he would treat their child.

Things will be different, this time. *She* will be different. She will be strong.

She remembers the way she appeared in the mirror, when she tried on Aunt Violet's cape. That dark glitter in her eyes. For a second, she felt almost powerful.

She will keep her baby, her Weyward child. She knows, somehow, that she is carrying a girl.

She will keep her safe.

CHAPTER NINETEEN

ALTHA

Even though they'd let me dress, I felt the pressure of a hundred eyes on my flesh as if I were still unclothed. The men stared with hunger, like I was a sweetmeat they wanted to devour. All except the man with the pitying eyes, who turned his gaze away.

After a time, I could not look at them: not the public sitting in the gallery, nor the judges, the prosecutor, or the doctor. Grace, in her white cap. I had wanted to bring the spider from the dungeons, a friend amidst foes. But I knew it was not safe, that it would only darken the cloud of suspicion that hung over me. Now, a sparkle caught my eye, and I saw that the spider had followed me, that it was spinning its web in the corner of the dock. Tears filled my eyes as I watched its legs dance over the shimmering strands of silk. I wished I could shrink myself as small, and scuttle away from this place.

I was born with the mole. The one I had scratched away, my first night in the castle. I should have thought to do it sooner, before they brought Doctor Smythson to the gaol, back in Crows Beck. But my wits were deadened, from lack of food and light, from resisting the questions of the prosecutor's men. And it was a gamble, in any case: the wound is crusting over now, weeping and angry. Doctor Smythson might have seen it for what it was.

The witch's mark, they call it. Or the devil's. It serves as instant proof of guilt.

My mother had one, too, in near enough the same place.

"Matching," she used to say. "As befits a mother and daughter."

It wasn't the only thing we'd had in common. Everyone said I was the spitting image of her, with my oval face and shocking dark hair.

I used to be proud of this, especially after she first died. I would stare at my reflection on the surface of the beck, desperate for a trace of her in my features. The rippling water blurred my face so that it was just a pale moon. I imagined it was my mother, looking at me through the veil that separates this world from the next.

I wondered what she'd make of it. Of her only daughter, stripped naked in a courtroom, while men roamed their eyes over her. Searching for a sign that she had sold her soul to the devil.

What did they know of souls, these men who sat on bolsters all day, clothed in finery, and saw fit to condemn a woman to death?

I do not profess to know much of souls, myself. I am not a learned woman, other than in the ways my mother handed down to me, as her mother handed down to her. But I know goodness, evil, light, and dark.

And I know the devil.

I have seen him. I have seen his mark. His real mark.

I have seen these things. And so has Grace.

I dreamed of him, sometimes, in the dungeon. The devil. The form he takes when he appears.

I also dreamed of Grace.

Most of all, I dreamed of my mother, on that final night. Her last in this world. Her dry fingers in mine. The little rasping sounds of her breath, her skin so pale I could see the blue-green veins beneath it, like a network of rivers. Her parting words. "Remember your promise," she said. She has been gone these last three years, but the memory of her in her sickbed was as strong as if I had just lost her.

Time seemed changed by the trial. Whereas before, my days had been broken up by little rituals and milestones—milking the goat of a morning; picking berries in the afternoon; readying tonics for the sick in the evening—now there was just court and sleep. Fear and dreams.

The day after he questioned Doctor Smythson, the prosecutor called the Kirkby lad. Daniel.

We'd attended his birth, my mother and I. I couldn't have been more than six years old, had only seen animals birthed. Lambs in blue cauls. Kittens with milky eyes. Birds, hatching pink and scrawny. I had felt their fear, coming into the world with all its unknowns. Its dangers.

I did not know birthing babies was something humans did, too. I took my own existence for granted, and it was only after watching Daniel's mother push him out of her body that I learned my mother had made me with a man and pulled me from her like a root from the earth. I never found out who the man was. She refused to tell me. "That is not our way," she'd said. She hadn't known her own father either, she told me later.

As a babe, Daniel Kirkby had screamed so loud that I'd covered my ears. But in court he spoke with a quiet voice. He was solemn and wide-eyed when he took the oath. I saw him look towards me, then away, like a horse flinching from the whip. He feared me. My mother would have been sad to know this, having assured his safe passage into the world.

"How long have you worked at the Milburn farm, Daniel?"

"Just since last winter, sir."

"And what was the nature of the work you undertook?"

"Just helping, like. Whatever the master needed. Milking the cows, when Mistress Milburn could not."

His cheeks colored, at her name on his lips. His eyes flickered, roaming the gallery. I wondered if he was seeking her face.

"And were you working this past New Year's Day, in the year of our Lord 1619?"

"Yes, sir."

"Please could you tell the court the events of that day, as you can best recall them."

"I got up early, sir, when it was still dark. It's a long walk from our house to the Milburn farm so I set off in good time like I always did."

"And when you got there?"

"Everything was normal, sir. Same as before. I met John—Master Milburn—round the back, outside the barn."

"And did he seem well to you?"

"He seemed in good health, sir. John were always hale. I never known him to be ill or have funny turns, not while I worked there."

"And what happened after you arrived?"

"We milked the cows, then freed them from the barn so they would go out to the field."

"And how did the cows seem to you? Were they placid, docile? Or aggressive?"

"They were less keen than usual to get outside into the field, sir. It was a very cold morning. But they were calm."

"Did you ever know them to be aggressive in any way, while you worked for Milburn?"

"No, sir."

"I see. So, you and Master Milburn were out in the field, having just released the cows from the barn. Are you able to tell the court what happened next?"

"I was looking back to the barn, sir, thinking I ought to go and shut the gate. Then I heard the cows . . . they weren't making no sound I'd ever heard an animal make before. They was almost—shrieking, like. There was a bird—a crow, I think—swooping down from the sky. They were spooked by it, sir. Their eyes were back in their heads, their mouths were frothing. John was trying to calm them. He loved them, you see, those cows. Didn't want them to be scared."

At this the boy's voice broke. I saw his Adam's apple quiver as he gulped away tears. He was fifteen, a man. It would not do to cry, not in court, wearing the finest wool he was ever like to wear, seeing that his master got justice.

A brave little lad. I could see it was important to him, the getting of justice. I knew the value of it myself.

I wondered what he'd known, while he worked there. I knew Grace would have fed him, those mornings. She'd have fed the both of them, would have ladled steaming pottage into their bowls when they came in from seeing to the cows. The three of them would have sat round the table together, Grace looking down into her bowl, John looking at Daniel, wondering if he'd ever have his own boy to help him take the cows to the field.

I saw the muscles work in Daniel's jaw as he gritted his teeth to continue his tale.

"But the cows couldn't be calmed, no matter what John did. They dug at the ground with their hooves, eyes rolling, as if they were about to charge. Like they were bulls. And they did charge. They charged straight at John."

He paused. The air in the courtroom grew taut as a skin drum.

"It was loud, with the cows' hooves thundering and John shouting. He fell and I couldn't see him no more. The shouts turned to screams."

I looked down at Grace. Her head was still bowed. I saw some in the gallery watching her as Daniel Kirkby continued with his testimony.

"John became quiet. Then the cows stopped. As if nothing had ever happened. As if . . . as if . . ."

He turned his head to look at me. I could see in his face that he did not want to look at me, that he was forcing himself. But he kept his eyes on me while he spoke.

"As if a spell had been broken."

Gasps and cries rent the air. I didn't look at the gallery. I watched the spider, still spinning its web.

I didn't need to see the prosecutor to know the look he had on his face. I could hear the pleasure in his voice.

"Thank you, Master Kirkby. You have been very brave. Your king and our heavenly Father will be grateful for your service. I hope not to take up too much more of your time. Please could you tell the court what you saw next?"

"I saw the master's injuries, sir. They were . . . I still see them now, when I shut my eyes. I pray I never see anything like them again. Then Mistress Milburn came running out the door of the farmhouse. She kept asking what had happened, repeating herself again and again. Then I saw there was someone running towards us. It were the accused, Altha Weyward. She were yelling out the mistress's name. She flung her cloak on the master's body—for the sake of decency, she said—and told me to fetch Doctor Smythson from the village. I ran and did what she said, sir."

"Thank you, son. And was that the first time you saw the accused that day? You didn't see her—or anyone else—besides the Milburns, before the incident occurred? Did you see her muttering an incantation, inciting the cows to stampede their master?"

"No, sir. I didn't see her before then, that day. But I had a funny feeling that morning, before it happened, when we was taking the cows out to the field."

"And what was that?"

"I had a feeling of eyes on me. As if someone were watching, from the trees."

PART TWO

CHAPTER TWENTY

VIOLET

Violet studied her reflection as she dressed for dinner. She tried to work out if she looked different now that she had been kissed. But she was still the same old Violet—with maybe a new touch of redness around her mouth. She put a hand to her face. The skin there felt tender and sore, as if it had been scraped by sandpaper. She wondered if anyone else would notice.

She picked a stray twig out of her hair and combed it. The dark strands shimmered in the low light of the room, making her think of her mother.

She had the same dark hair.

Violet was reminded of the conversation she'd overheard between the servants when she was younger. What was the word Nanny Metcalfe had used for her mother? *Uncanny.*

What on earth did that mean? Her stomach churned as the awful image came back to her: her mother, wild and pale, trapped in a room. Mad.

Perhaps that was why everyone lied about what had happened to her. Although, when she came to think of it, Violet couldn't remember anyone ever *telling* her that her mother had died giving birth to Graham. Instead, Nanny Metcalfe and Mrs. Kirkby had said things like, "Your brother survived, thanks to Jesus" and "The doctor did his best."

Violet's fingers went to the pendant around her neck, the way they often did when she was worried, tracing the delicate *W*. Her head was beginning to ache: there was a tightness to her forehead and a thudding at her temple. She was still very thirsty after the kiss (how was it that something so wet could make one so parched?) and a little faint.

She had the queer feeling that she was looking at something so closely that she could not yet make out its full shape. Frederick's words echoed in her mind.

Your father would have to take her back to her room . . . Lock her in.

The gong rang for dinner, reverberating through the house like a call to battle. She looked in the mirror one last time, trying to ignore the throbbing in her skull. She was wearing the green dress again, same as last night. Suddenly, she noticed how short it was: her knees were perilously close to exposure. She couldn't decide if she looked like a child or a strumpet (*strumpet* was the word Violet had heard Mrs. Kirkby use to describe Penny after she'd kissed the apprentice gardener).

Violet tried to see the dining room through Frederick's eyes. It was a rather grand room, and in the candlelight the slight grubbiness that had set in since the start of the war was barely noticeable. The space was dominated by an enormous mahogany dining table that Father referred to—inexplicably—as the "Queen Anne." (*Had Queen Anne sat at it,* Violet wondered?) Long-dead Ayreses looked out from the gilt frames on the walls with a melancholy air, as if they regretted not being able to sample whatever meal was being served. A stuffed peacock—which Violet had secretly nicknamed Percy—perched atop a Georgian sideboard, once-glorious tail feathers hanging limp to the floor.

This evening, Mrs. Kirkby served a roast pheasant, which Father had shot a few days prior. Violet could see the bullet hole in the pheasant's neck, a dark smudge in the golden flesh. The sick feeling in her stomach returned. As she cut into her serving, she was horribly aware of poor Percy watching from the other side of the room. One day, when Violet was grown up and had become a biologist (or a botanist, or an entomologist), she would eat only vegetables.

There seemed to be little chance that Frederick shared such dietary aspirations, Violet noted as he tucked into his roast pheasant with relish. There was a hungry look to him, she thought, as he surveyed the things in the dining room: the Queen Anne, the musty old portraits, her. It didn't go away, even though he'd eaten rather a lot of pheasant already.

Father and Frederick were having a long conversation about the war. Violet was distracted, haunted by what Frederick had said about her mother, until Graham kicked her under the table. She set her mouth into a prim smile and tried to focus on what Father was saying.

"Can't say I'm a huge fan of General Eisenhower," he said. "Do we really need all this help from the Yanks?" He spat the last word out violently, as if he were still smarting from American independence.

"We need all the help we can get, Uncle," Frederick said. "Unless you want the Hun sitting here eating pheasant with your daughter. He'd make short work of both, I expect."

The wave of heat again. Violet wasn't exactly sure what Frederick meant, but she thought unaccountably of the pulsing swarm of mayflies, the roughness of Frederick's mouth on hers. Next to her, Graham was watching Father, his eyebrows raised.

But Father hadn't heard; Mrs. Kirkby had come to ask if they were ready for the pudding. Violet saw a flash of gold out of the corner of her eye. It looked as though Frederick had put something in his drink. They were drinking claret, like they always did at dinner. It was watered down, so that Graham and Violet could "get a taste for it." There was the Christmassy smell again. Violet remembered the word for the substance Mrs. Kirkby had deployed to make the Christmas pudding go up in blue flames. *Brandy.* That was it. It lived in a beautiful crystal decanter on Father's drinks trolley. Violet had never seen anyone drink it—Father preferred port after dinner.

She looked at Frederick more closely. There was a glassiness to his eyes, she saw, and his fingers shook when he reached for his claret.

Was he drunk? In the same way that she'd read about kissing long before she'd actually kissed someone, her reference points for drunkenness also came from literature—Falstaff being "drunk out of his five senses" at the start of *The Merry Wives of Windsor.* She'd read rather a lot of

Shakespeare—not that Father knew this, of course (he hadn't noticed that his *Complete Works* had been missing from its rightful place in the library for the past two years).

Frederick was now attacking the pudding—a rather pale spotted dick, doled out generously by Mrs. Kirkby—so the retention of at least one of his senses wasn't in doubt. Violet looked down at her bowl. The pudding glistened with fat. She ate the thin custard around it instead. Her headache was gathering strength, like a summer storm. "Good heavens," Father said. "Suet! Mrs. Kirkby must have been saving some up."

Violet couldn't remember Father commenting on Mrs. Kirkby's cooking before the war. She suspected that Father's war (against a scarcity of his favorite port, a shipment of which had been bombed crossing the Atlantic) was rather different to Frederick's.

Violet wondered if Frederick was thinking this, too, from the forceful way he clasped his goblet (part of a set given to the First Viscount by Elizabeth I, or so Father claimed).

"Delicious," he said, attacking the spotted dick once more. "Don't think I've had pudding that didn't come from a tin since 1939. My compliments to Mrs. Kirkby."

The conversation returned to the war. Frederick was telling Father about the sort of guns his regiment used ("Howitzers for tanks and Colts for close range") and Violet let her thoughts drift again as Mrs. Kirkby came to take away the plates. She could still hear the crickets chirping outside. Actually, it sounded like just one cricket—which made Violet feel rather sorry for it. Perhaps something had happened to its mate. Or perhaps there had never been a mate at all.

She wondered what it would be like, to live out one's days alone, without having someone to love and be loved by. She thought of the Virgin Queen again, the illustrious donor of the goblets. She had never married, of course. Perhaps no one would ever marry Violet, either. Father would be most put out by that. Miss Poole, too—Violet imagined her bemoaning the waste of a perfectly good trousseau.

Violet had never much liked the idea of being married. She would have been quite happy to pursue her ambitions alone, like Elizabeth I—though Violet's ambitions were rather more prosaic than victory against the Spanish and conversion of the nation to Anglicanism.

She thought, with powerful longing, of the giant moths and scorpions from Father's atlases. She pictured herself bending to stroke a scorpion's glittering head, the desert heat pressing against her skin . . . perhaps discovering a new species, being the first to decipher the secrets of its cells . . .

Might it be possible to have both things? Love *and* insects? Perhaps Frederick would fall in love with her, and then, once they were married, would be quite happy for her to become a world-traveling scientist. But even as these thoughts made her feel warm and light inside, doubt rolled in like a dark cloud.

She remembered the way that her heart had punched in her chest while Frederick kissed her. There was that feeling again, of being pulled by a tide. Her lungs tightened. She hadn't expected that love—if this was what she felt—to be so similar to fear.

Truthfully, she wasn't sure that anyone had ever loved her in her life, apart from Graham perhaps, in an irritable sort of way. Violet supposed that her mother must have loved her, but other than the faint memories triggered by the discovery of the handkerchief and feather—now somewhat tarnished by Frederick's story—it was impossible to imagine what this might have felt like.

It was hard to tell if Father loved her. Often, it seemed that all he cared about was whether or not he could mold her into something pretty and agreeable, a present to be given away to some other man.

Though Violet wondered if there wasn't another layer to her father's feelings about his daughter—sometimes, she thought she could see regret cloud his face when he looked at her. Perhaps it was because—according to Frederick, anyway—she looked so much like her mother.

Now, Father was pouring three glasses of port to take into the drawing room. Graham was staring at the third glass with an expression of mingled terror and pride.

She cleared her throat. Father looked up at her and frowned.

"Violet," he said, looking at her and then the grandfather clock opposite the door. "It's late. You should be getting to bed."

It was half past eight. Shafts of pink light patterned the staircase as Violet made her way back to her bedroom. As she passed the window on the second floor, she realized that she could no longer hear the chirp of the solitary cricket. Perhaps it had given up.

CHAPTER TWENTY-ONE

KATE

As the days grow warmer, Kate opens the windows and the doors, so that the cottage is filled with the scent of the garden. Sometimes, she sits for hours on Aunt Violet's sofa, enjoying the sun on her skin as she reads. The fresh air helps with the nausea that still pulses in her gut, and she finds the distant murmur of the beck soothing. Outside, the other-worldly plants look almost beautiful, the ragged stems curling towards the sky. She rests one hand on her stomach, thinking of her daughter, blooming inside.

Violet's bookshelves burst with tomes on science—insects, botany, even astronomy. One of them—a guide to local insect life called *Secrets of the Valley*—seems to have been written by Violet herself. Kate was relieved to find some fiction, too—even a few volumes of poetry.

Most of the novels are by female authors—Daphne du Maurier, Angela Carter, Virginia Woolf. In the last month, she has read *Rebecca, The Bloody Chamber, Orlando*. It's been a long time since she's derived such pleasure from it, from the stories spun of other people's dreams. Those last days at the library, before she left Simon, had felt furtive, dangerous; she'd flinched at the tick of the clock on the wall, at every shadow that fell over the page. She had thought, for a while, that she'd lost the magic of it: the ability to immerse herself in another time, another place. It had felt like forgetting to breathe.

But she needn't have worried. Now, worlds, characters, even sentences linger—burning like beacons in her brain. Reminding her that she's not alone.

She's just finished a slim novel called *Lolly Willowes* by Sylvia Townsend Warner, about a spinster who moves to the countryside to take up witchcraft. A stamp on the flyleaf reads *Kirkby's Books and Gifts, Crows Beck*. The bookshop next to the church. There is a handwritten message next to the stamp:

MADE ME THINK OF YOU! EMILY x

Looking through Violet's collection, Kate sees that some of the others bear the same stamp. There are no other books about witches—although she does find a collection of Sylvia Plath's poetry, dog-eared at a poem called "Witch Burning." Two lines have been circled in pencil:

Mother of beetles, only unclench your hand:
I'll fly through the candle's mouth like a singeless moth

She remembers what she'd overheard the receptionist hiss at the medical center. That one of the Weywards had been a witch.

Kirkby's Books and Gifts is a red-brick building attached to the village church, St. Mary's. Small and squat, it nestles close to the church, as if trying to hide behind it. A bell chimes as Kate opens the door, welcomed by the comforting smell of dust and old leather bindings. Original floorboards are almost hidden by brightly colored Turkish rugs, dusted here and there with glimmering strands of what seems to be cat hair.

"Hello," calls a voice, its owner hidden by a maze of bookshelves. Kate peers around a sparsely populated shelf labeled *St. Mary's History* and sees a woman in her fifties, standing behind a desk stacked high with new releases. The woman is wearing a sweet, woody perfume—patchouli oil. In her arms she cradles an enormous orange cat, which swats at the glasses that dangle from a chain around her neck.

"Get off," she says to the cat, who meows and leaps to the floor. And, to Kate: "Can I help you?"

There is something familiar about her, about the way her eyes crinkle as she smiles. The graying auburn curls. Kate flushes when she realizes: it's the same woman she saw at the greengrocer, all those weeks ago.

Could this be Emily?

"Are you all right, love?" the woman asks, when Kate doesn't answer.

"Yes, sorry." She wipes her sweaty palms on her trousers. "My name's Kate . . . Kate Ayres. I'm looking for Emily?"

"Oh!" The woman's smile widens. Kate is embarrassed to see a sheen of emotion in her eyes. "Violet's great-niece. I should have known—you have her eyes. I'm Emily—your great-aunt and I were friends. I'm so sorry for your loss. She was a wonderful woman."

"Oh, it's OK." She colors. "I mean—I didn't really know her. I didn't even know she had died until her lawyer contacted me—she left me her house."

"We should get together sometime," Emily says brightly. "Me and Mike—that's my husband—live out at Oakfield Farm. We'd love to have you round. Then I can tell you all about her."

"Oh," Kate falters. "That's really kind. Maybe I could let you know?"

"Of course."

There is a pause, and she feels Emily's eyes on her. She wishes, suddenly, that she was wearing something else: her T-shirt is cut too low, and her jeans stick uncomfortably to her thighs. Even her hair feels wrong. She lifts a self-conscious hand to the coarse, bleached strands of it.

"Anyway, is there anything else I can help you with?" Emily asks. "Book recommendations?"

"Actually," she says, "I was wondering if you had anything on local history. Or if . . ." She pauses, nerves ticking in her stomach. "You could tell me about the Weywards?"

"Ah," Emily grins. "Heard the rumors already, then?"

Kate thinks of the receptionist at the doctor's office, the word she had spat from her mouth as though it was something rotten.

Witch.

"Something like that, yeah."

"The villagers do like to gossip. Well . . . the story goes that a Weyward was tried as a witch back in the 1600s."

She thinks of the cross under the sycamore tree. Those carved letters. *RIP.*

"Really? What happened to her?"

"I don't know the details, I'm afraid, pet. But there was a lot of that going on around here then, sadly. Women being accused left, right, and center."

"Did Aunt Violet ever talk about them? About the Weywards?"

Emily pauses, frowns. She fiddles with the chain of her glasses, so that the lenses blink in the light.

"She didn't like to talk about her family much. I got the impression it was too painful. Something to do with leaving Orton Hall."

Kate thinks of the turrets she passed on the drive up, gilded by the dawn.

"Anyway," Emily blinks and turns to look up at the clock, which is shaped like a cat's face. One of its whiskers—the shorter one—hovers close to five. "I'll be closing up soon, I'm afraid, pet. Do come back another time, though, let me know how you get on. And the offer stands."

Kate feels heat rising in her cheeks as she says goodbye. There is something else she wants to ask, too, but she hasn't been able to work up the nerve. Her bank balance is dwindling rapidly—soon she'll be down to the emergency stash of notes hidden in her handbag. She'd developed a silly fantasy, when she'd found the note in Aunt Violet's copy of *Lolly Willowes*, that perhaps she could work here, in the bookshop. She'd almost convinced herself of it, that she could slip on that old professional persona the way one would a coat.

But now that she's standing here, her skin prickles with self-doubt. She hasn't worked for years—not since Simon made her quit after she tried to leave him the first time. Her memories of work seem so distant that they might have happened to someone else. Even at the time, she'd known the job wouldn't last. She didn't deserve it.

It was a silly fantasy. Nothing more.

Not ready to face the walk back to the cottage, Kate tries the front door of the church. It's locked. But the gate of the little graveyard is open, swinging on its hinges. She looks behind her to see if anyone is watching, and then slips inside.

The graveyard is bordered by high stone walls, green with moss and lichen. Ancient trees line the walls, their branches threatening to brush against the tops of the headstones.

She has been here before, she realizes with a start. Of course. Her grandfather's funeral. She remembers the other mourners, black as crows in their somber raincoats, the drone of the minister. And the *noise*.

There is a rustle of movement. She looks up; a dark shadow flits from one tree branch to another, and her heart jolts. She runs her fingers over the reassuring shape of the brooch in her pocket as she walks through the graveyard.

The headstones are a motley of different ages: some of them are new, sparkling granite, surrounded by tiny terra-cotta pots of bright flowers. Others are so worn by time and weather that the inscriptions are barely readable. She sees the same names again and again: *Kirkby, Metcalfe, Dinsdale, Bainbridge.* As if the same cast of actors has been brought out to play each generation of villagers.

She weaves her way through the lanes of headstones in search of her family. At first, she makes towards a gloomy-looking mausoleum in the center of the graveyard. It is ornately carved from marble, topped by a cross and a crouching bird of prey. But the marble is stained green with age, half covered by some creeping plant. The little door, set into the center of the tomb, is padlocked shut—to keep something in or out, she isn't sure. There is a sad bouquet of wilted lavender at the entrance. Kate, seeing a little card attached with moldering ribbon, crouches down to get a look, but the writing is blurred, illegible.

Eventually, she finds her relatives in the far corner, protected from the elements by the heavy boughs of a large elm. Graham, her grandfather, and Violet, his sister. Side by side, beneath a starry quilt of wildflowers. She crouches down next to the headstones to read their inscriptions. Graham is described as a loving husband and father. A loyal brother. There is a quote from Proverbs 17:17—*A friend loves at all times, and a brother is born for a time of adversity.*

Violet's headstone—a hunk of granite, still in its natural shape—is simpler. There is just her name, Violet Elizabeth Ayres, and the dates of her birth and death. And something else—faint, inscribed so delicately that she doesn't notice it straight away.

The letter *W*.

W for Weyward? There is something familiar about the look of it. A hot breeze blows through the graveyard, rustling the leaves of the trees.

She stays like that for a while, looking at Violet's headstone. Her great-aunt had left explicit instructions for it, according to the lawyer. She wonders who attended her funeral; she hadn't been able to go without rousing Simon's suspicion. Kate feels an ache of regret at not being there. She'll come back another day, she decides, with some flowers. Violet would have liked that, she's sure.

She gets to her feet and decides to see if she can find any Weyward graves. She wanders up and down the graveyard a few times, but sees none, though some of the headstones are blank from age. Perhaps a woman accused of witchcraft wouldn't have been buried in a church graveyard. It is—what's the word for it again?—*hallowed ground*. But surely, if the family does go back centuries, other Weywards must have lived and died in Crows Beck? If not in the graveyard, then where could they be buried?

A vague unease fills her as she thinks of the weathered cross under the sycamore tree. Could it—surely it *doesn't*—mark a human burial site?

She distracts herself by taking the scenic route home, the path that follows the beck, which is the color of burnt sugar in the afternoon light. She looks at the clumps of vegetation on the banks: ferns, nettle, a plant she doesn't know the name of with tiny buds of white flowers.

Something makes her look up at the sky; there is a dark shape against the pink clouds. A crow.

Later, Kate opens Aunt Violet's jewelry box.

In the dim light, she sees that the necklace is tangled. She lifts it out gently. She sits down on the bed, switching on the bedside lamp to take a closer look. She wonders how old the necklace is. It looks at least a century old, if not older: the gold is dull and tarnished. It feels cool in her palm, reassuring.

The engraving on the oval pendant is dark with grime and dust, but it is unmistakable: the same *W* that is carved onto Violet's headstone.

CHAPTER TWENTY-TWO

ALTHA

I feared that they all believed the Kirkby boy. The men and women in the gallery, but also the judges and the jurors, who were the ones that mattered.

They believed that I'd been there, that I had set John's own cows on him, as if I were some great puppeteer. As if I were God himself.

While I sat in the dock, still watching the spider, I thought back to that morning, the morning that John died. I'd woken with the light, as I always did. I looked out of the window and saw the sky was still pink and new. I remember I thought of beginnings, as I dressed and put on my boots. Then I set off on my walk. I always took a walk at that time, in the weeks leading up to the new year. It had become my habit.

It had been very cold that day, and I had walked through great banks of snow, which soaked my boots and the hem of my dress. My breath was like crystals in front of me. The valley was always at its most beautiful in the morning. I remember thinking that it was as if it had been made so on purpose, to remind us to keep living.

The cows looked almost majestic in the field: the gold dawn turning their flanks amber. The power in those flanks as they ran towards him; the muscle rippling. As if they were different animals entirely, and had spent their days chewing cud, biding their time until this moment of glory. The sharp cries of the crow reeling above had mingled with the men's shouts. I could feel the ground shake with their hooves from where I stood, under the trees at the edge of the field.

It was over quickly. The cows returned to their former selves, with only the white roll of an eye, the heave of a flank, to show what had gone before. And the body. John's body.

I saw Grace come out of the farmhouse. I gathered up my skirts and ran, the winter air sharp in my lungs. As I ran, I unfastened my cloak, so that I could cover the body. I didn't want her to see. The limbs like broken tools, the pulped face. I knew then that I would see that face, again and again, until I took my last breath.

They were dismissing the Kirkby boy now. His Adam's apple quivered as he walked down the aisle of the court, stiff in his new clothes. He did his master proud. On the way home—I imagine—he will go over each detail of the trial until it is polished and sparkling, ready to show to his parents, the other villagers. The prosecutor's questions. The ancient stone of Lancaster Castle; the soaring rafters of the courtroom. Grace, pretty in her white cap. And in the dock: Altha, the witch.

Witch. The word slithers from the mouth like a serpent, drips from the tongue as thick and black as tar. We never thought of ourselves as witches, my mother and I. For this was a word invented by men, a word that brings power to those who speak it, not those it describes. A word that builds gallows and pyres, turns breathing women into corpses.

No. It was not a word we ever used.

I did not know, for a long time, what my mother thought of our gifts. But I knew what was expected of me, from a young child. She named me Altha, after all. Not Alice, meaning noble woman, nor Agnes, lamb of God. Altha. Healer.

She taught me how to heal. And she taught me other things, too.

"They say that the first woman was born of man, Altha," she said to me once when I was a child, for this was what we had heard the rector say in church that Sunday. "That she came from his rib. But you must remember, my girl, that this is a lie."

It was not that long after we'd attended Daniel Kirkby's birth that she told me this. "Now you know the truth. Man is born of woman. Not the other way round." I asked her why Reverend Goode would lie about something like that.

"It comes from the Bible," she told me. "So the rector isn't the first to tell that lie. As for the reason: it is my belief that people lie when they are afraid."

I was confused.

"But what could Reverend Goode be afraid of?"

My mother smiled. "Us," she said. "Women."

But she was wrong. We were the ones who should have been afraid.

I sensed it in my marrow, much as my mother tried to shield me from it. There were strange happenings, in the years before she died. Long days and nights when she would be gone, having begged a horse from whichever family was in debt for our services. She would leave under cover of darkness, her crow flying ahead, its feathers stippled by moonlight. She would not tell me where she was going, only that if anyone were to ask, I was to say she was visiting relatives in Lancashire.

I knew that was not the truth, though. For we had no other relatives. Only each other.

One night, the autumn Grace's mother died, a couple came to our door. The air was chill with the threat of winter and I remember that the woman held a babe to her breast; though it was swaddled in many layers, its tiny fist was blue.

My mother set her face tight, and I had the impression she did not want to admit them to the cottage. But she could not leave them out in such conditions, especially with the babe in such a state. She bade me put a pot on the fire, and spoke to them in hushed tones, but even so there was no escaping their conversation in our little cottage.

The couple had traveled from a place called Clitheroe, in the south, and had walked for many days and nights. It was no wonder they looked as they did: their faces haggard, and the babe half starved when out of his swaddling clothes, for his mother's milk had dried up. They were heading to Scotland, they said, and thence across the seas to Ireland, where no one would know them.

The woman was a healer—though not in the way my mother was. She made the occasional poultice, that was all. But they feared this would not matter: two families had been rounded up, they said, near Pendle Hill, and tried for witchcraft. Nearly all of them had been hanged.

What names, my mother asked.

The Devices, they said. And the Whittles. More besides.

These names were unfamiliar to me, but my mother's face blanched at their mention.

Things changed after that.

The prosecutor called a second witness that day.

Reverend Goode himself. His black cassock flowed behind him as he walked towards the stand. It made me think of a bat's wings, and without thinking I smiled. Then, I heard the hum of voices rise in the gallery and remembered I was being watched. I kept my face still. I looked for the spider, but it was gone. Only its web remained, glinting and delicate. I wondered if it was an omen, if the spider could sense what was to come.

The rector took the oath. A thin man, his face was pale and pinched from years of sermons.

"Reverend," said the prosecutor, "would you be so good as to tell the court where you preach?"

"Certainly," said Reverend Goode. "I am the rector of St. Mary's church, Crows Beck."

"And how long have you held this post?"

"It will be thirty years this August."

"And in that time, have you been familiar with the Weyward family?"

"Yes—though I am not sure that *family* is the proper term."

"What do you mean, Reverend?"

"While I've been there, it has been just the two of them. The accused and her mother. Now only Altha remains, since Jennet passed some years ago."

"Has there never been a male member of the household?"

"None that I have been acquainted with. It appears that the girl was born out of wedlock."

"And did the Weywards attend services, Reverend?"

Reverend Goode paused.

"Yes," he said. "They came every Sunday, even in winter."

"And has the accused kept up her attendance, since her mother's death?"

"Yes," said Reverend Goode. "For this, at least, I cannot fault her."

I hated slinking into the back of the church, feeling the other villagers shrink away if I took the same pew. But I knew I had to go, as my mother and I had always done, to avoid being dragged before the church courts.

At Reverend Goode's last words, the prosecutor looked like a cat who'd been handed a dish of cream.

"'For this at least,' Reverend? What can you fault her on?"

"One hears things, in a small village," he said. "Like her mother, Altha tends the sick. Sometimes she has favorable results. She's nursed quite a few villagers back to health in her time."

"'Sometimes' she has good results? What of the other times?"

"Sometimes the patient has died."

I remembered the last death I'd witnessed, before John's. Ben Bainbridge's father, Jeremiah. He'd passed ninety winters, had been the oldest person in Crows Beck for two score years. His mind had died long before, leaving only his body behind. His eyes were blue and clouded, and I remember looking into them as I sat by his deathbed, wondering what he was seeing in the world beyond this life. He had said his wife's name with his last breath, his body shuddering like leaves in the wind. Old age, it was. And nothing more. There was nowt I could do but ease the pain of his lingering.

They could not pin that death on me. Not that one.

There had been others, too. Times when the patient's skin was so blanched with approaching death that I knew I could do little. The Merrywether woman, who'd died in childbed, her blood lapping at my wrists, the babe a mere knot of still flesh. These ones had been past my help.

I expected the rector to produce a litany of these deaths. But he did not. After all, he had stood at their gravesides and told their families that their loved one's passing was part of God's plan. It would not do well for him to say, now, having taken his sacred oath, that God had planned for them to be murdered by a witch.

"They did die, sometimes," he went on. "Though death awaits us all, along with reunification with our Father in Heaven, if we have lived well."

I felt the gallery grow restless. They were not here for a sermon. Someone coughed, another giggled. I saw one judge lean close to another, to murmur something.

The rector had the prosecutor in a bind now. But he needed the church to stand with him, on the matter of witchcraft.

He paced.

"Thank you, Reverend. And thank you for the great service you have done to your country and king, in coming forward to report this crime. For it was you, was it not, who wrote to me, informing me there was suspicion of a witch in Crows Beck? And that it was suspected that this witch had had a hand in the death of John Milburn?"

"Yes," said the rector slowly. "It was."

"Reverend," said the prosecutor. "Did you see the body of John Milburn?"

"I did. He was injured most grievously."

"And did you bring the accused to his corpse, to see if it bled anew at her touch?"

"No, sir."

"But, Reverend, would this not have been conclusive proof of murder? Why was this not done?"

"Master Milburn had already been buried, sir, by the time suspicion fell upon the accused. It was his widow's wish that he be laid to rest quickly, the sooner he could be reunited with his maker."

"Thank you for that explanation. And could you tell the court how it was that suspicion did fall on the accused? What caused you to make the report?"

"Someone in the parish spoke to me of their concerns. They were certain that an innocent life had been taken, through a wicked contract with the devil. They wanted to do their duty, by their Lord and maker."

"And who was that person?"

Reverend Goode took his time in telling the court who had brought suspicion on my name. Who had consigned me to sit on the cold, hard seat of the dock by day and dream of death by night.

"It was the deceased's father-in-law," he said finally. "William Metcalfe."

The courtroom grew loud, the whispers from the gallery like the drone of a hundred insects.

The prosecutor was finished with Reverend Goode. He climbed down from the stand slowly, and I saw his age in his faltering movements. The intimidating figure I remembered from childhood was diminished. Soon he too would start his journey from this world to the next. I wondered what he would find there.

I was taken back to the dungeons. Night had already fallen for me.

CHAPTER TWENTY-THREE

VIOLET

Frederick didn't come down for breakfast the next morning.

Violet was beginning to feel quite worried about him, until he emerged at luncheon, looking pale and green. He barely touched his food, taking only a delicate bite of Mrs. Kirkby's leftover rabbit pie before crossing his knife and fork on his plate.

"They finished off that whole bottle of port last night," Graham whispered to her, as they filed out of the dining room. A rough note in Graham's voice told Violet he was jealous. "Actually, I think *he* had more of it than Father did."

"Don't be so quick to judge," Violet hissed. "He's fighting a *war*. I imagine it's been utterly exhausting. I should think he's earned a glass or two of port."

They hung back and watched Father and Frederick go on ahead. Father had his hand resting on Frederick's shoulder ("Good thing, too, or he'd fall over," said Graham) and was pointing out various items of furniture in the entrance hall, as if he were some sort of sales merchant.

"That," said Father, motioning to a rather hulking side table, "is an original Jacobean. "Worth at least a thousand pounds. It was commissioned by our ancestor, the Third Viscount, in 1619. James I was on the throne then—though you knew that already, I expect, with your interest in history." Father beamed, and Graham rolled his eyes.

"Strange fellow, King James," said Frederick. "Rather fancied himself a bit of a witch-hunter. He wrote a book about it, did you know?"

Father's face darkened, and he moved away from Frederick before continuing the tour as if he hadn't heard.

"This clock," he said, gesturing to an ornate gold carriage clock carved with cherubs, "was my mother's, given to her by her aunt, the Duchess of Kent, for her twenty-first birthday . . ."

"Never told me any of that," Graham muttered. "Anyone would think *he* was the son and heir."

Later, as they played bowls on the lawn outside, Violet thought that Frederick must have forgotten his suggestion that they take a walk that evening. He had barely looked at her all day. Perhaps he had forgotten about the kiss, too. Or perhaps—worse—he regretted it. Maybe it hadn't been a very good kiss; maybe she'd done it wrong.

She was doing a terrible job of the lawn bowls. It was very warm, and her hairline was damp with sweat. Though she wasn't the only one—dark stains had appeared on Father's shirt, and Graham's face had flushed to match his hair. Even Cecil was subdued: curled up beneath the rhododendrons, pink tongue lolling from his mouth. He looked almost sweet.

Only Frederick seemed unbothered by the heat—she supposed he had got used to it, in Libya—and had perked up considerably since luncheon. He rolled his ball so that it hit the jack with a *plink* and grinned, white teeth flashing in his tanned face. She would have thought he looked perfectly at ease, if she hadn't noticed that his hand kept straying to the pocket of his trousers and patting something hidden there, as if it were a talisman.

"I'm going to go and ask Mrs. Kirkby for some lemonade," she said.

"Rather you than me," said Graham, watching his ball veer away from the jack and into a rose bush. Graham was afraid of all the servants, but especially Mrs. Kirkby, who had recently caught him divesting a roast chicken of its legs. She had ardently vowed to box his ears if he ever set foot inside her kitchen again.

"I'll come with you," said Frederick. "You might need help carrying the glasses."

Violet's stomach lurched.

"Thank you," she said, barely pausing to wait for him as she made her way to the house. Conscious of his eyes on her, Violet moved stiffly, as if she had forgotten the correct way of walking.

He caught up with her as they entered the cool of the house. She thought how quiet it was in the entrance hall. Although the doors had been flung open to let in the summer air, she couldn't even hear the bees buzzing outside. Frederick took a step closer to her. Blood rushed in her ears.

"I'm looking forward to our walk later," he said softly.

So he *had* remembered. Her pulse flared as he moved closer. Why was there this awful thrumming sensation in her veins? Sweat prickled in her armpits. She was merely excited at the prospect of asking him more questions about her mother, she told herself. That was why her heart was thudding. Suddenly, she worried that he would kiss her again. Did she—should she—*want* him to?

There was the sound of a door opening and closing and Frederick sprang back. They looked up to see Miss Poole at the top of the stairs, carrying a stack of French textbooks that Violet supposed she would have the joy of wading through at some point in the future.

"Good afternoon," said Miss Poole, curtsying as though Frederick were King George rather than her employer's nephew.

"How do you do," he said.

"We're just off to the kitchens for some lemonade," Violet said, but Miss Poole merely nodded, her eyes still trained on Frederick.

"I hope you enjoy your stay," she said to Frederick.

"I'm sure I will," he said, looking at Violet.

The lemonade was watery and sour from lack of sugar ("Anyone would think there wasn't a *war* on," Mrs. Kirkby had hissed, once Frederick was out of earshot).

When Father wasn't looking (Graham's lawn bowl technique required significant refinement), Frederick produced a golden flask from his pocket. Without asking, he unscrewed the cap and poured a generous amount of amber liquid into her glass.

"Is that—?"

"Brandy. Have you never had it? How innocent you are," he said. Something in his smile reminded her of the hungry way he had looked at the dining-room furnishings the night before.

"Drink up, quick," he said. "Before your father sees. I don't want him thinking I'm a bad influence."

The brandy was like fire going down her throat. She coughed, and Frederick roared with laughter.

Father made his way over to them, having given up his attempts to tell Graham how to aim his ball so that it hit the jack rather than Dinsdale's roses.

"What's so funny, Freddie?" he asked. It stung to hear the nickname on her father's lips. Father never called Violet and Graham anything other than—well, Violet and Graham.

"Your daughter is a very amusing young woman," said Frederick.

After a while, Father seemed to tire of lawn bowls, and instead had Mrs. Kirkby—who looked very disgruntled to have been torn away from the dinner preparations yet again—set folding chairs up on the lawn.

"The cheek of 'em," she could be heard muttering as she walked away. "Where they think their meals come from, I don't know . . . magicked up by fairies . . ."

"I'm afraid we're rather short on the ground with staff," Father told Frederick apologetically. "My butler went down on the HMS *Barham*."

"Poor old Rainham," said Violet, who had always liked the butler, a whiskery man with a penchant for colorful waistcoats. She'd once seen him carry a mouse—which had narrowly escaped Cecil's grasp—out into the garden, as delicately as if it were made of glass. It was very strange to think that he would never return to Orton Hall. His coat still hung on the hook at the servants' entrance as if he had merely gone for a stroll around the grounds.

Violet watched as Frederick drained the rest of his lemonade, before looking down into the empty glass. She saw his hand brush the pocket of his trousers and wished that Father hadn't mentioned the war.

The canvas of the chair creaked as she settled back into it. She considered fetching a book to read, but the brandy had made her mind heavy and slow. The sun was lovely and warm on her face and the world was a pleasant, green-gold blur. Both Graham and Father had fallen asleep and were snoring almost in unison. Violet thought she might just close her eyes for a moment. She heard the rasp of Frederick dragging his chair closer to hers. She shifted onto her side and opened one eye to see him watching her with that same hungry look. There was a hot, liquid feeling in her stomach.

She could hear a faint buzzing sound—a mayfly, she thought, or perhaps a midge.

"Ow." Violet sat up straight in her chair, her cheek throbbing with a sudden pain. Graham muttered in his sleep, but Father snored on, undisturbed. She pressed her fingers to her face: she could already feel the skin growing hot. Alarm flickered in her gut.

"Are you all right?" Frederick asked, leaning closer to her.

"Yes—thanks. Something bit me. A midge, I think."

"Ah. Damned things. I expect you're used to that, around here."

"Actually, I've never been bitten by one before."

He studied her for a moment. Opened his mouth, closed it again.

"I say—it's gone rather red," he said. "I think you need something cold on it."

She watched as he came closer. He picked up his lemonade glass and pressed it to her cheek, the cool shock of it blotting out the pain.

"There," he said softly. She could feel his breath, the rough edges of his fingertips.

They stayed like that for a moment, Violet's heart drumming furiously in her ears.

"Thank you," she said finally, and he took the glass away.

"This'll sort you out," he said, pulling the flask from his pocket and handing it over to her. Fingers shaking, she unscrewed the cap and lifted the flask to her lips. The brandy burned as much as before, but this time she didn't cough. She pictured it, a fireball glowing down her throat. *Dutch courage*, they called it in books, didn't they? She had a strange, portentous feeling that bravery would be required for whatever was going to happen next.

"Better?" he asked.

"Better."

"Do you know what," he said. "I think a walk could be just the ticket. Take the edge off the shock. What do you say? I'll protect you from the midges."

"You're right," she said. "Just the ticket."

She rose unsteadily, as if she were on the sloping deck of a ship. Frederick offered her his arm. She looked at Father and Graham, both of whom continued to snore. Graham would be disturbed to learn how much he looked like Father when he slept.

"We'll let these two catch up on their beauty sleep," said Frederick, steering her away.

CHAPTER TWENTY-FOUR

KATE

Kate was right.

She *is* having a girl. The female GP, Dr. Collins, confirmed it today, at her twenty-week scan. She gave Kate a printout of the sonogram: her daughter, cocooned safe inside her womb, iridescent fingers curled into fists.

"She looks like a fighter, this one," Dr. Collins said.

Now Kate sits on Aunt Violet's bed, caressing the photograph. The window is open and outside, a wood pigeon coos, the gentle notes carrying on the breeze. There's something she needs to do.

Her mother answers on the second ring.

"Kate?"

Her voice is muffled, concern driving away traces of sleep. What time is it there? The early hours of the morning. She should have checked. She is forgetting things, these days—lying down for a nap after putting on the kettle, waking with a start to its anguished whine. The tiredness makes her feel as if her bones have been sucked of their marrow.

"Are you OK? You haven't been returning my calls."

"I know," she says. "Sorry—I've been a bit distracted. Settling in, you know."

Her mother sighs into the phone.

"I've been so worried about you. I wish you'd tell me what's going on."

The saliva leaves her mouth.

"I need to . . ."

"Need to what?"

Her pulse beats a frenzied rhythm in her ears. She can't do it.

"I need to ask you something. About Dad's family."

"What is it?"

"Do you know who lives in Orton Hall now? Someone in the village said something about a viscount, but I don't know if he's related to us."

"Hmm. I think your father said he was a distant relative. There was that scandal, the disinheritance—but I don't really remember the details."

"So you don't know why they were disinherited? What the scandal actually was?"

"No, love. I'm sorry. I'm not even sure your father knew."

"That's OK. Um—one more thing . . ." She pauses, licks her lips. "Did Dad ever say anything about one of his ancestors being accused of witchcraft?"

"Witchcraft? No. Who told you that?"

"Just something I overheard," she says. "They seem to have had some funny ideas about Aunt Violet around here."

"Well, she was a bit of a strange woman," her mother says, but Kate can hear the smile in her voice.

Kate looks around her, at Violet's things. The shelves of books, the framed centipede glimmering on the wall. She thinks of the cape in the wardrobe, the dark glitter of its beads. Violet wouldn't be afraid, the way Kate is now.

She would tell the truth.

"Actually, Mum, I do have to tell you something." She takes a breath. The next words, when they leave her mouth, sound as if they've been spoken by someone else. "I'm pregnant."

"Oh my God." For a moment there is silence. "Does Simon know?"

"No."

"OK, that's good. And have you . . . decided what you're going to do?"

She knows about Simon, Kate realizes. *She's always known.*

The pain in her mother's voice sends a jolt of nausea to her gut. Sun flares bright through the window, blinding her.

She knows.

For a moment, she thinks she might be sick. Her eyes sting.

But she won't cry. Not today. She looks down at the sonogram, grips it tighter in her hand.

"I'm having it. Her. It's a girl, I found out today."

"A girl! Kate!"

She can hear her mother crying into the phone.

"Mum? Are you OK?"

"Sorry," her mother says. "I just—I wish we hadn't left, Kate. I should have stayed. And then maybe you wouldn't have met him . . . I should have been there."

"Mum. It's OK. It's not your fault."

But it's too late, the words are tumbling from her mother's mouth, as if she can undo the years of silence between them. "No, I knew something wasn't right. Quitting your job, losing touch with your friends . . . it was like you were becoming someone else. But he was always in the room, whenever we spoke on the phone . . . and then I didn't know if he was reading your messages, your emails . . . I didn't know what to do."

Kate can't bear this, her mother's guilt. It burns, like acid on her skin. She remembers the night she met Simon. The way she'd been pulled towards him, a moth kissing a flame.

Can't her mother see? It is no one's fault but her own.

"There was nothing you could have done, Mum."

"I'm your mother," she says. "I sensed it. I should have found a way."

For a moment, neither of them speak. The line crackles with distance.

"But I am happy," her mother says eventually, in a soft voice. "About the baby. As long as it's what you want."

Kate touches the photograph, tracing the bright bulb of her daughter's shape.

"It's what I want."

After they say goodbye, Kate takes her wallet out of her handbag. She wants to put the sonogram picture inside it, to keep it safe.

Now, it holds a Polaroid of her and Simon. Taken on holiday, in Venice. They are holding ice cream cones on the Ponte di Rialto. It had been a hot day: she remembers the fetid stink of the canal, the blisters that had formed on her feet from hours of walking. She looks happy in the picture—they both do. He has a smudge of ice cream on his lip.

The following day, he had yelled at her in the middle of St. Mark's Square. She can't remember why. Probably he didn't like something she'd said, or a particular way that she had looked at him. Later, in the hotel, he had hit her during sex, so hard that blood blisters formed on her thigh.

She crumples the Polaroid in her hand, then rips it to tiny shreds. They float to the floor, like snow.

The next day, Kate frowns as she walks. She zips up her rain-jacket; the day is muggy but overcast, the clouds swollen purple. It begins to spit. Already, the hedgerows glisten with water, tiny drops quivering like crystals on the wildflowers. Some she recognizes: frothy white pignut, the golden bells of cow wheat. She has been learning the names from a great botanical tome of Aunt Violet's.

She has to cross the fells to get to Orton Hall. The ground becomes steeper as she leaves the familiar comfort of the hedged paths for open fields. The gray sky suddenly seems both enormous and far too close.

Her calves burn, her sneakers slipping on the rocky trail. Her heart beats dizzyingly fast and her mouth feels dry. She's never much liked heights, or wide-open spaces. She touches the bee brooch for reassurance, and then, on impulse, takes it from the pocket of her jeans and pins it to her lapel like an amulet.

At the crest of the hill, she pauses, doubled over and panting for breath. She can see a dark pocket of woods ahead, next to an old railway line. According to the blurry map on the Motorola, Orton Hall is just behind the trees.

She reaches the bottom of the hill with relief. Stone walls rise on either side of her, the flint green with age and moss. Raindrops begin to fall in earnest as she enters the woods. The trees are tight and claustrophobic, and she can barely see the sky for the branches overhead. The winding trail is uneven and overgrown: greenery rustles as she walks, and a pale rabbit streaks away into the undergrowth.

The downpour grows heavier, and soon the leaves and tree trunks are shining wet. Kate pulls up her hood. She looks at her phone: she should be nearing the edge of the woods now. She walks a little faster. Something about the woods makes her feel uneasy: the cloying scent of damp earth, the snap of twigs around her. A shape flickers at the edge of her vision, shadow-black, a shiver of wings against leaves.

She turns around, scans the twisted canopy overhead. There is nothing, other than a brown and orange butterfly quivering on a leaf. She takes a deep, steadying breath and keeps walking.

The woods are so thick that she doesn't see Orton Hall until she is almost out of them. It rises up before her so suddenly that she gasps. She was not expecting this. She wonders if Emily was wrong about someone living here—the whole place looks as if it's been abandoned for years. Its stone is dull and faded, with great craters where the render has worn away. Thick ropes of ivy climb the turrets. Movement flutters on the roof, and she sees that the gutters are lined with birds' nests. As she approaches, she can't shake the feeling that she is being watched—but that could just be the huge, dark windows, staring down at her like eyes.

She walks through the weed-choked gardens to get to the imposing front door. There is no doorbell. She clangs the heavy iron knocker and waits.

Nothing. Kate shuffles her feet. The stone is slick with a patina of old leaves, the balustrades fissured with cracks. The whole place has an air of neglect, sadness, and she has just decided to leave when she hears the scrape and click of a bolt being drawn back. The door creaks open slowly, until she and a wispy old man in a tartan dressing gown are staring at each other in mutual surprise. The viscount. It's got to be him.

"Yes?" says the man in a thin, reedy voice. "What do you want?" His eyes narrow behind the clouded lenses of his glasses, and for a moment Kate can't think what to say.

"Hi," she begins. "I hope I haven't disturbed you—um—my name is Kate. I've just moved in around the corner. I'm doing some research into my family history, and I think some of my relatives used to live here . . ."

She trails off awkwardly. The man blinks and for a moment she wonders if he hasn't heard her, if he could be deaf. The whites of his green eyes are yellow, the lids pink and hairless.

He opens the door wider, and then turns, disappearing into the fathomless dark of the house. It takes her a while to realize that he means for her to come inside.

She watches the ragged hem of his dressing gown lick away from his feet as she follows him into a dim entrance hall. The only source of light comes from a dusty-looking lamp on a large side table. In its yellow pool, she can see that the table is stacked high with mail: old, gnawed-looking envelopes at the bottom, and plastic covered brochures at the top. The stack of mail rustles as they walk past, and Kate notices that the curling envelopes are covered with a strange, glittering film, like tiny particles of broken glass.

The other furniture in the room is covered in ragged dust sheets, as is a large painting on the wall, above a cavernous fireplace. Something glints on the mantelpiece, and Kate sees that it is an old carriage clock, swathed in cobwebs. Its hands are stopped; frozen forever at six o'clock.

Kate wonders how on earth the man can see as she follows him up a sweeping staircase. The large windows over the staircase are dark with filth and only let in a chink of light here and there. Kate squints to see the little man bobbing up the steps in front of her. For a moment, she stumbles and grips the banister, feeling grit under her palm. Peering at her hand, she sees it is the same glittering substance that covered the mail. It is not dust, she realizes with horror. Her palm is coated with the crystal flakes of wings. Insect wings.

With a jolt, Kate realizes that she has lost sight of him. There's the creak of a door opening somewhere. She reaches the top of the staircase, and, following the sound, turns left down the corridor.

There is a slender chink of orange light ahead, and her eyes adjust to make out the form of the old man standing outside a slightly open door, waiting for her. When she is a few paces away, he enters the room and she follows. As she crosses the threshold, fear leaps in her veins, for what she sees unsettles her even more than the rest of the house.

There are no wings to be found in this room, which would have been impressive, once. The space is dominated by a beautiful mahogany desk. A floor-to-ceiling window, largely hidden by rotting curtains, takes up much of the wall behind the desk. The rest of it is covered by a dark portrait of a bald man with an angry expression.

The desk itself is crowded with strange trinkets: mirrored boxes, an old compass. A globe, half of its sphere rotted away. Most startling is an elephant's enormous tusk, which she initially takes to be a human bone, yellow in the dull light.

There is a sour stink of flesh, and Kate quickly averts her eyes from a sort of nest in the corner of the room, made from blankets, rags, and even items of clothing. There's another smell, too: over-sweet and chemical, abrasive in her nostrils. Insect repellent. A hurricane lamp—of the kind she's only ever seen in old films, or antique shops—burns on the floor, giving the room its gauzy glow. Empty tins glint orange in the lamplight. He has been living here, she realizes. In this one room.

"They can't—couldn't—get in," the little man says, as if he has read her thoughts. "I made sure."

He gestures to the door, and Kate turns to see a roll of fabric nailed to it, another stretched across its hinges. Turning back, she realizes suddenly why the room is so dark: behind the frayed, rotted curtains, the windows have been boarded up.

The little man sits down at the desk, slowly lowering himself into a high-backed chair, its leather streaked with mold.

"Please," he says, gesturing to a small chair in front of the desk. Kate sits, and dust rises around her. She stifles a cough.

"What did you say your name was?" the man asks. Kate finds the contrast between his cut-glass accent and shabby appearance jarring—unsettling, even. She notices that his hands are shaking, that his gaze flickers repeatedly to the edges of the room. He's looking for them, she realizes. The insects. The skin on the nape of her neck prickles.

"Kate," she says, her unease growing. She wants to leave, to get away from this little man with his vacant stare and animal smell. "Kate Ayres." He leans forward, the papery skin of his forehead furrowed.

"Did you say *Ayres*?"

"Yes, my grandfather was Graham Ayres," she explains. "I think he used to live here, as a child. With his sister, Violet. Do you—are we . . . related?"

Kate isn't sure if she's imagining things, but his hands seem to shake harder at the mention of her great-aunt, the bony knuckles whitening.

"There were so many of them." He licks his lips, which are pale and cracked. His voice is so quiet that it takes her a moment to understand the words. He is looking past her, now, his eyes glazed with distance. "And then the swarm . . ."

What is he talking about?

"The swarm?"

"The male taking the female . . . and then the eggs, everywhere . . . covering every surface . . ."

Doubt nags at her. This man—whoever he is—clearly isn't well. The way he is talking, the way he is *living*—he needs help, rather than to be pestered with questions. He seems . . . traumatized.

But just as she rises in her chair, making to leave, his gaze fixes on her with a startling clarity.

"You had some questions for me?"

Perhaps he is more lucid than she thought. Really, she knows, she should leave—but she's walked all the way here, over the dizzying fells and through the woods. Surely there would be no harm in asking a question or two . . .

She takes a deep breath, trying not to think about the staleness of the air.

"I was wondering, actually—if you could tell me anything about my grandfather and his sister? They've both passed away, and so I don't have anyone to ask. My father is dead, too—and I . . . well, I was hoping you might be able to tell me a bit about them."

The man shakes his head vigorously, as if trying to dislodge her words from his ears.

"Terribly sorry," he says. "Memory isn't what it was."

Kate looks around the room. There are shelves stacked with old books, the spines cracked and dusty.

"Oh," she says, hearing the disappointment in her voice. "What about records? Would you have any I could look at? Family trees, birth certificates, that sort of thing? Letters?"

The man shakes his head again.

"Those are all farm records, tax ledgers," he says, seeing her look at the shelves. "Wouldn't be of help to you, I'm afraid. Everything else . . . gone. The insects . . ." He trembles.

"Oh. That's OK." Kate sits quietly for a moment. She feels a twinge of pity for him, all alone in this decrepit house, with only dead bugs and old ledgers for company. "What happened? With the insects, I mean. That must have been awful. I'm not such a fan of bugs, myself. Did you have to get an exterminator?"

The man's eyes become dark pools as he fixes them upon the space above Kate's head. When he speaks, even his voice has changed; the accent that sounded cold and hard moments ago is now tremulous, uncertain.

"I must give thanks," he says, his voice barely louder than a whisper. "The Lord answered my prayers. Last August, they all began to die—the sweetest sound, it was, their little bodies falling to the floor. Like rain on parched earth. It was then that I knew . . . she had released me at last."

"Sorry—what do you mean? Who had released you?"

She takes a deep breath as she waits for him to answer—the air is rank in her mouth. How can he stand it? She unzips her jacket, to alleviate the feeling of being choked.

Suddenly, the man jolts in his chair. He is staring at her, she realizes.

"Oh dear," she says, standing hurriedly. "Um—sir? Are you all right?"

He lifts his hand and points. Kate sees that his fingers are shaking again. The nails are yellow and curved, their undersides coated with grime.

"Where," he says, his breath coming in little ragged bursts, "did you get that?"

For a moment, Kate thinks he is pointing at Aunt Violet's old necklace, which she'd almost forgotten she was wearing. But then she realizes: he means the brooch, in the shape of a bee.

"This?" she says, touching it. "Sorry—it looks quite real, doesn't it? It's silly, really; I've carried it around since I was a child . . ."

The man rises out of the chair, his small frame trembling.

"Get. Out." The eyes are wide, the lips snarled away to reveal pale, desiccated gums.

"OK," says Kate, zipping up her jacket. "I'm so sorry for disturbing you. Really."

Kate fumbles her way down the corridor and the stairs, wincing at the crunch of the wings beneath her shoes. Shutting the heavy front door behind her, she gulps in the air, fresh with the scent of rain. It is coming down in sheets and she begins to run, forcing herself to look straight ahead. The leaves of the trees whisper in the downpour and she wishes she'd brought headphones to block out the eerie noise. The hill seems even steeper on the way back: the wind buffets her, knocking the hood from her head. Water runs into her eyes, so that the valley is a blur of green and gray.

Fear turns to frustration as she finally reaches the cottage. She is no closer to knowing anything about her family. No closer to knowing why Violet and Graham were disinherited, no closer to knowing what—or who—is buried in Violet's garden.

Kate sighs as she shuts the front door behind her. She turns on the shower, desperate to scrub away the memory and the grime of the house, with its blanket of tiny, broken wings. The dank, animal stench of the study. While she waits for the water to heat, she unpins her brooch, then holds it up to the light. The viscount must be very traumatized indeed to have had such a reaction to a mere replica of an insect.

She remembers the way his eyes danced from side to side, as if he were searching for movement in the corners of the room. She can still taste the acrid stink of insect repellent on her tongue.

If she closes her eyes, she can picture it.

The air shimmering with thousands of beating wings, the sound droning through the walls of the house, the little man cowering in his fetid nest inside the study . . . and then, the briefest moment of stillness, silence . . . before the rain of tiny bodies.

She had released me at last.

Once the bathroom fills with steam from the heat of the shower, Kate begins to undress. Unbuttoning her shirt, she shivers as her fingers brush against a pale, glimmering wing.

The words from "Witch Burning" come back to her.

Mother of beetles.

Who had released him? And from what?

CHAPTER TWENTY-FIVE

ALTHA

In the dungeons, I wished for parchment and ink. These words were already forming in my head, you see, and I wanted to set them down while I still could. So that something remained of me, after they cut my body down from the rope. Something other than the cottage, which would hold my things—things that belonged to my mother, and her mother before her—until someone came to clear them away.

But I had no parchment and ink then, of course—and even if they'd given me some, I'd have had no light to see my letters. My mother had taught me to read and write. She considered it as important a skill as knowing which herbs brought relief from which ailments. She taught me the alphabet just as she taught me the uses for marshmallow and foxglove. Just as she taught me the other things, of which I cannot yet speak.

Having no way of writing, back in the dungeons, I ordered things in my head. I was practicing, almost, in case what Reverend Goode said about the next life was true and I would soon see my mother again.

My mother. Her death weighed heavily upon me still, for she was another one of my failings.

Not long after the couple from Clitheroe came to see us, my

mother began to change. One night, as the moon rose outside—it was a young moon, I remember, just a pale scratch in the sky—she told me to put on my cloak. Then she took the crow, placing her gently in a covered basket. I asked her what she was doing, for we had raised the bird from a hatchling, just as we had its mother, both of whom carried the sign. She did not answer me, only had me follow her into the night. She did not speak until we came upon the oak trees that bordered one of the farms—the Milburn farm, where one day Grace would live, though I did not know this then. I was thinking of her that night, of how we used to climb those trees together, their gnarled branches cradling us. The memory sat heavily in my heart.

My mother knelt before the largest oak tree and coaxed the crow from its basket. No sooner was it on the ground than it took to the air, the moon catching on its feathers. It flew back to its usual spot on my mother's shoulder, but she pressed her cheek against its beak and shut her eyes, murmuring something that I could not hear. The crow gave an anguished cry, but it flew away to the upper branches of the oak, which were thronged black with its kind.

We walked back to the cottage. In the darkness, I could not see my mother's face, but from the sharp, shuddering sounds of her breath I knew that she wept.

She bade me stay indoors, after that, only leaving the cottage for church and for walks when darkness fell over the land. I began to prefer the winter months to the endless summer days, though I was hungry by this time. We had less coin now, and would have gone without meat if not for the kindness of the Bainbridges. My mother refused to take on new work; she would only see to those she trusted.

"It isn't safe," she said, her eyes shining large and frightened in her skull.

As the months went on, turning into years, she looked less and less like my mother. She grew thinner. Curled into herself, like a plant missing the sun. Her cheeks lost their bloom and her skin was tight on her bones. Still, we only left the cottage for church services. The villagers stared at us as we crossed the nave, my mother leaning against me, the two of us hobbling like some monstrous creature.

Some of them said we were cursed. For what we had done to Anna Metcalfe.

"We should go outside," I said, when my mother did not rise from her pallet for five days. "You need to feel the air, to listen to the wind in the trees. To hear birdsong."

For I had begun to suspect that nature, to us, was as much a life force as the very air we breathed. Without it, I feared my mother would die.

Sometimes, in my darkest moments, I wonder if she herself knew this—if she had decided that she would rather face that great, yawning unknown than continue our existence in the shadows.

"No," she said that day, her eyes blacker than I had ever seen them. She gripped my arm, her nails sharp on my flesh. "It isn't safe."

It was the sweating sickness that took her, in the end. Three years after my first blood. She had directed her treatment from her own sickbed, telling me which roots to crush, which herbs to apply, even when she could barely lift her head from the pallet. I did everything she asked of me, but soon she was more asleep than awake, the bedclothes damp around her as she murmured my name. I was frightened of her, her yellow face in the candlelight.

"Remember your promise," she said, her body arching with pain. "You cannot break it."

One morning, as dawn split the sky, she grew still. Then I knew she was gone. I thought of how she had named me. Altha. Healer. I had let her down.

I thought a lot of Grace, after my mother passed. She was the only other person I had ever loved. Now I had lost both of them.

Grace was married by then. William Metcalfe had arranged for his daughter to marry another yeoman—a dairy farmer, like himself. Grace had already played the role of farmer's wife since her mother passed, no doubt. I imagine she thought herself ready for marriage.

John Milburn was well thought of in the village. And handsome, too. They looked good together, at the wedding: she pale and pretty, and he with his dark hair shot with gold.

I wasn't invited, of course. But I found a place to watch, in a shaded lane where I could see the entrance of the church while remaining in shadow. It was a summer morning. The villagers threw wildflower petals over the couple as they crossed the nave. Grace had hawthorn flowers woven into her red hair. Pain closed my throat as I remembered the flower chains we'd made as girls. She'd loved to pretend at marriage, then—describing the face of her future husband as though she could conjure him with speech alone. I had been quiet in those moments. If I hoped for a future with anyone, it was with her.

She looked happy, hand in hand with her husband. Perhaps she was, then. Or perhaps I was standing too far away. A great many things look different from a distance. Truth is like ugliness: you need to be close to see it.

I would explain all of this to my mother when I saw her in the life that follows this one, I decided in the dungeon that night. I would tell her the ugliness. The truth.

The next day, the prosecutor called William Metcalfe. The years had not been kind to the man who walked down the aisle to take the box. Time and grief had made deep crags in his face. His hair hung in strings over his forehead. I felt his eyes on me when he took the oath, the hatred in his gaze like a brand on my skin.

The prosecutor smoothed his robes before he began the questioning. I wondered if this was the last witness. His last chance to prove my guilt.

"Master Metcalfe," he said. "Could you tell the court who first made this charge of witchcraft against the accused?"

"I did."

"Why?"

"Because she killed my son-in-law, sir."

"Were you a witness to your son-in-law's death, Master Metcalfe?"

"No."

"Then how can you be so sure of the accused's guilt?"

"Because of what happened before."

"What happened before?"

"She killed my wife."

I looked for Grace in the gallery. I wished the white cap would turn so that I could see her face. So that I could see some small sign that she didn't still believe her father, after all these years. After everything.

"Master Metcalfe, are you able to tell the court about your wife's death, and the accused's involvement in it?"

When Metcalfe spoke again, his voice had changed. The fire had gone out of it, the words cracking with pain.

"My wife—Anna—she fell ill with scarlatina. It were eight years ago. Grace were only thirteen. Doctor Smythson came out and applied some leeches. But my Anna didn't get better. I would have sent for the doctor again, but one night Grace slipped away. She returned with the accused and her mother. She was . . . friendly with the accused, at that age."

He stopped. I didn't want to look at him. I looked about the courtroom for something else to focus on. Nothing remained of the spider's web in the dock. I wondered if someone had brushed it away.

A fly hovered above the gallery. I kept my eyes on it as William Metcalfe continued.

"Altha's mother—Jennet—she was known around Crows Beck for her healing skills, at that time. And seeing as the girls were close . . . well, you can see why Grace saw fit to fetch them. She were only trying to save her mother. The first thing Jennet did when she arrived was pull the leeches off my Anna. Then she promised me she could save her. But she gave her something, some noxious draught, and then my Anna . . ."

Metcalfe paused, shuddering. His hand went to his throat, and I recalled the string of beads I had seen clutched in his fist the night his wife died. Only later had I realized they were rosary beads; that Grace's family were Papists.

I remembered the fear in his eyes when we came upon him at prayer. Perhaps he had worried that we would expose him. Or perhaps I was searching for another reason for his hatred of my mother and me, when the truth was simple: he believed us murderers.

"My Anna shook all over," he continued. "It were . . . unspeakable. And then she was gone. Jennet had killed her."

"And where was the accused, in all of this? Was she near your wife when she passed?"

"No. She were standing with my daughter. But . . . I know she helped her mother. And even if she didn't, you just have to look at her to see she's the spitting image of Jennet." The fire returned to his voice as he continued, growing louder and louder. "The spitting image of her. In image and in manner, too—it has been passed down, this rot, like a contagion, from mother to daughter . . . They're not like other women. Living without a man—it's unnatural. I wager that the mother took the devil for a lover, to beget a child . . . and now that child has done his will. You must cut her out, like bad flesh from meat! You must hang her!"

The gallery had been shocked into silence by Metcalfe's claims. A child born of the devil. I wished to scrub myself all over, to scrub away time with my skin and return to a place where I had never heard those words spoken about my mother and myself.

Metcalfe had stopped yelling. He was slumped forward in the stand, shoulders heaving with keening sobs, the likes of which I had never heard from a man before.

A guard came to lead him away. Just as he reached the doors, he turned back towards me.

"Damn you! I hope you rot in Hell like your whore of a mother!" The heavy doors closed and he was gone.

I had striven to show no emotion through the trial, but to hear my mother spoken of thus was too much. My eyes burned with the salt of the tears that ran down my face. Whispers rose in the courtroom. From the corner of my eye I saw that they were pointing at me, at my tears.

I put my face in my hands and cried. I kept my face hidden as the prosecutor spoke. It was clear from the testimony of Grace Milburn, Daniel Kirkby, and William Metcalfe that I was the devil's whore, he said, who had used my evil influence to goad innocent animals into trampling their master to death. I must be cut from society like a canker, he said, scoured from the earth like rot from wood. I had robbed my community of a good and honest man. I had robbed a woman of her loving husband. Her protector.

At this I raised my head and looked at him, staring until my eyes burned. I did not hide my face in my hands again.

CHAPTER TWENTY-SIX

VIOLET

"So," said Frederick. "Where are you taking me? Somewhere with shade, I hope—I'm absolutely roasting."

They were walking in the meadow at the very edge of the grounds. It was hilly, and at its crest they could see the green landscape below. Violet felt strangely light, as though her bones had filled with air. The sun was hot on the back of her neck. She should have brought a hat. Nanny Metcalfe would give her a telling off if she got sunburnt.

"There's the wood, down by the old railway line," she said, pointing to a dark seam of trees running through the fields. Technically that was public land, not part of the grounds, and she didn't think Father would like it if she went there. But he couldn't really object if she were chaperoned, she reasoned. Especially not if she were chaperoned by Frederick. Freddie.

The lemonade suddenly seemed like a long time ago.

"I'm parched," she said. She shut her eyes. Frederick was half carrying her to the woods now, her arm draped over his shoulders. Her body felt very heavy but Frederick walked on steadily, as if she weighed nothing. She felt the cool metal of the flask at her lips and gulped down more brandy, even though it was really water that she craved. Aside from her thirst, she felt quite pleasant. Was this what it was to be drunk?

She could smell the rich, damp scent of the wood. She opened her eyes. The sun was dappled by the trees, which were ancient and packed closely together. Frederick reached down and plucked a primrose flower, before putting it behind her ear. She didn't know how to tell him that she didn't believe in picking flowers. A butterfly took flight from a branch, orange circles on its wings like eyes.

"Scotch argus," she murmured.

"What?"

"The butterfly. That's what it's called."

Everything was growing dimmer. Violet opened her eyes and saw that they had come to a clearing in the woods, thickly carpeted by foxglove and dog's mercury. Through the trees, Violet saw blue irises and thought of Miss Poole. She wondered how long they had been away from the Hall. Perhaps someone would come and look for them.

Frederick was laying her down on the ground. She must be very drunk, she thought. Perhaps she had become too heavy for him to carry, and he was going to go back to the Hall for help. Father would be furious. Perhaps they could just leave her out here. She wouldn't mind. It was so pretty. She could hear a bird singing—a redstart.

Frederick was still there. She wondered why he hadn't set off for the Hall yet. He was getting down on the ground next to her—maybe he didn't feel well either? She could smell him—rich cologne, mingled with an animal scent of sweat. It was overpowering. The bite on her cheek was stinging rather painfully.

He was on top of her. She wanted to ask him what he was doing but her tongue was too clumsy to form the words, and then he was covering her mouth with his. He was very heavy; her lungs burned from lack of air. She tried to put her hands on his shoulders, to push him off, but they were pinned by her sides.

Violet felt his hand on her thigh, under her skirt, and then he was forcing her tights down. She heard them tear. They were silk; the only pair she had. He moved her legs apart and for a moment she was freed from his weight as he unbuckled his belt and undid his trousers. She gulped at the air, tried to speak, but then he was upon her again, his hand on her mouth, and there was a bright, searing pain between her legs. She felt the ground dig into her back harder as he moved, again and again. Still the pain continued, as if he were opening a wound inside her.

She could taste sweat and dirt on his hand. Her eyes watered. She looked up and tried to count the green leaves that filtered the sunlight but there were too many and she lost track of them. After a while—it felt like an entire life span, the years stretching on and mercilessly on, but afterwards she realized it couldn't have been more than five minutes—he cried out and grew still. It—whatever horrible thing it was—had ended.

Frederick rolled over onto his back, panting.

She could feel something wet trickling out of her. She put her hand between her legs and when she looked at it, it was sticky with blood and something else—something white, like the mucus from a snail.

The redstart was singing again, as if nothing had happened.

"We'd better get back," he said. "I say, you do look a bit of a fright. We'll tell your father that you had a tumble, shall we? Good thing your cousin was there to help you up."

She lay for a moment, winded, watching him push through the trees. Slowly, she pulled up her tights—she could hardly bear to touch her own skin—and crawled to her feet. Something glimmered in the greenery: looking down, she saw that her pendant appeared to be cracked into two halves, like rusted wings. It was this, rather than anything else, that brought the first hot pricks of tears to her eyes.

Her mother's necklace. He had broken it.

It looked like a smaller piece of the pendant had snapped off and fallen onto the ground. Picking it up, she realized it was a tiny key with jagged edges. It dawned on her that her mother's necklace wasn't a pendant at all, but a locket; with a hinge so small that she had never noticed it. The key shone brighter than the battered locket, as if it had not seen daylight for many years.

As Violet made her way through the woods, listening to the strange sound of her own breathing, she gripped the key tightly in her palm. Distantly, she wondered if her mother had been the last person to touch it. Even that thought gave her no comfort.

The deck chairs had been put away and Father and Graham had gone inside by the time they got back. The entrance hall was filled with the smell of whatever Mrs. Kirkby was cooking for supper—some kind of roast meat. It turned Violet's stomach.

"I think I'll go and lie down before dinner," she said. Her brain felt like it was swimming, and her speech sounded slurred and thick.

"Good idea," said Frederick. "Shattered, myself. You've rather worn me out. I trust you enjoyed yourself?"

She made for the stairs, swallowing the bile that coursed up her throat. The colors from the stained-glass windows, backlit by the afternoon sun, were impossibly bright, streaking the parquetry as though with blood. Her head thudded and she gripped the handrail for support. The staircase seemed longer and steeper than usual, as if the Hall had turned into some nightmarish inverse of itself.

Once she was in the safety of her bedroom, she tried to wash away the strange, sticky substance at the old enamel washstand. Then, she changed into her nightgown. She bundled the soiled underwear and the ripped tights into a ball and hid them between the mattress and the bed frame. She thought of the silk slip she'd made for her trousseau, intended for her wedding night—useless now.

Before she got into bed, she took the feather—Morg's feather, as she thought of it—from its hiding place between the pages of the Brothers Grimm. She placed it gently on her pillow, next to her mother's locket and the tiny key. She stared at them, the blue-black of the feather blurring into gold as her vision swam with tears.

When the gong rang for dinner, she squeezed her eyes shut. The room seemed to be shifting, like a carousel at a fair. She must have slept, because the next thing she knew, Nanny Metcalfe was calling her name, holding a tray of tea and toast.

"Sorry," she said, sitting up and quickly sweeping her treasures under the coverlet. "I don't feel at all well."

"The heat," said Nanny Metcalfe. "I'd say you've gone and given yourself sunstroke. Should've had your hat on. Lots of water and a bit of food, followed by a good long sleep, and you'll be right as rain in the morning."

Violet nodded weakly.

"Frederick was asking after you," said Nanny Metcalfe. "Came down to the servants' sitting room, after he'd had his supper. Wanted to know if I'd look in on you. Nice young chap, isn't he?"

"Yes," Violet said. "Very nice." She could still smell the sour tang of his sweat.

"What's that you've got in your hair?" Nanny Metcalfe reached out and pulled something from behind Violet's ear. It was the primrose flower that Frederick had given her.

"Very pretty," said Nanny Metcalfe. "But be careful you don't ruin the sheets with such things. Flowers leave stains, you know."

She slept without dreaming, and when she woke with the birds, her whole body felt stiff and painful.

She dressed slowly. In the mirror, she looked pale and sallow, as if she were an invalid in a book. She almost wished that she were an invalid (was there a way of becoming one?) and could stay in her room for the rest of the day. Then she would never have to see Frederick again.

The dining room was rich with the smell of breakfast. Father was hidden behind *The Times* ("*Kentucky* sunk near Malta" the front page blared) and Graham was forking food into his mouth over a Dickens novel. Scrambled eggs congealed in their dish, a lurid yellow. A plate of bacon rashers (the last remains of Jemima, Violet thought grimly) looked like flayed skin.

Frederick wasn't there. Gradually, the hammering in her heart slowed.

She sat shakily at the table.

"Nice walk with Freddie yesterday?" said Father from behind his newspaper. Violet flinched.

"Yes, thank you," she said, because what else could she say? Even if she knew the words for what had happened, Father could never know. He would think it was her fault somehow, she knew. Perhaps it had been her fault? *I trust you enjoyed yourself?* He must have thought she wanted him to do it. She thought she might be sick. How could she face him?

"He's gone back to London, by the way," said Father. "Took the early train this morning. Ran him down to the station myself. He said to tell you goodbye, Violet."

"Oh," she said, not knowing what she should feel—relief? Sadness? She remembered the primrose flower, with its crushed petals.

"A fine young man," Father said. "Rather reminds me of myself at that age. I do hope he makes it through the war."

Graham rolled his eyes at her. She tried to smile at him, but her cheeks felt as though they were made of India rubber.

"What happened to you?" Graham asked her. For a moment she thought that he could see—that everyone could see—the shameful memory that lay coiled inside her, like something rotting.

"Nothing," she said quickly.

"I mean, what happened to your face? There's a big red mark on it."

"Oh." She had forgotten all about the bite. "Something got me—a midge, I think."

Father turned a page of his newspaper, apparently uninterested.

"Ha," said Graham. "But they never sting you! Whereas I can never get the bloody things off me. Maybe they got sick of me and thought they'd sample something new."

"Language, Graham," said Father.

"Who knows," said Violet. "Maybe they did."

CHAPTER TWENTY-SEVEN

KATE

Two hundred pounds.

Kate counts again, just to be sure. Her bank account is empty, so she's down to her last clump of notes, still hidden in the lining of her handbag. She needs to make this last, until she finds a job. Several times, now, she has walked past Kirkby's Books and Gifts in the village. But she couldn't bring herself to go in.

But she has to do *something* . . . there is food to buy, and utility bills to pay—fat brown envelopes have begun to appear through Aunt Violet's letterbox, the most recent marked *URGENT* in angry red letters.

Later, a book in Aunt Violet's collection catches her eye: *The British Gardener.*

Looking out of the kitchen window at the garden, she feels a twinge of doubt. It is so overgrown and filled with the oddest of plants: great green trumpets reach skyward, vying for space with hairy stems, purple buds nodding on their leaves. She's not sure she's up to this. But a baby needs nutrients, vitamins. From vegetables, green things, like the ones that crowd Aunt Violet's garden.

And so she has to try.

It is a hot day, almost midsummer. In the bedroom, she peels off her jeans and top—both of which are starting to become uncomfortably tight—in favor of a pair of canvas dungarees she finds in the wardrobe. She dons one of Aunt Violet's hats—a straw behemoth with a tawny feather tucked into the band. In the cupboard under the sink there are gardening gloves, and leaning against the back of the house, a spade.

With *The British Gardener* tucked under her arm, she takes a deep breath and ventures outside.

She touches the smooth shape of the brooch in her pocket, reflecting that she's breaking the only rule she's ever set for herself. But it's hard to feel threatened by the plants and flowers golden with the sun, the clean gurgle of the beck. She even enjoys listening to the birds—wishes she could identify each species from its song, the way she used to when she was a child.

A caw, throaty and almost human, sends a cold needle down her spine.

She looks up. Her heart beats a little faster when she sees the crow, observing her from the highest branch of the sycamore. For a moment she is still, fearing that sudden movements will bring a rain of claws and feathers. But the bird just shifts on the branch, the sun coating its wings with an oil-slick sheen.

Blinking away the memories, she resists the urge to touch the brooch in her pocket. Focus. She must focus on the task at hand.

Guided by the pictures in Aunt Violet's gardening book, she learns that the green trumpets are rhubarb, the hairy-stemmed plant wild carrot. These, she digs from the ground, marveling at the delicate stems of the rhubarb, the pale, gnarled carrots. She can make soups, salads. Hunger gnaws at her; the craving for food borne from the earth so intense she is almost giddy with it. She looks down at the carrot she grips in her hand. Part of her wants to eat it now—to suck the soil from it, feel the freshness burst into her mouth as she crunches down, hard. She needs this, she realizes. The baby needs this.

She breathes deeply, places the carrot into her basket.

There are herbs, too, she sees: sage, rosemary, mint. These she also collects. She leaves behind other strange plants that don't seem to feature in the book: under the sycamore tree she finds a long-stemmed bush with yellow buds, like clusters of tiny stars.

After a while, she has an urge to remove the gloves, to feel the soil against her skin. She pushes her fingers deep into the earth, relishing its softness. The smell of it is intoxicating: its mineral tang reminds her of the taste that still coats her tongue when she wakes every morning.

She feels something brush against the scar on her forearm. Turning, she sees it is a damselfly, the same insect she saw down by the beck when she first arrived. It trembles there for a moment; then, as she watches, it flutters to her stomach.

There is a surge inside her—a fizzing warmth in her gut, her veins. Rising into her throat.

For a moment she thinks it's morning sickness, worries she might vomit, faint. She bends over, on her hands and knees in the dirt, lets the blood rush to her head.

She feels a tickling sensation against her hand, different from the silky touch of soil. Looking down, she sees the pink glimmer of a worm—and then another, and another. As she watches, spellbound, other insects emerge from the earth, glowing like jewels in the summer sun. The copper glint of a beetle's shell. The pale, segmented bodies of larvae. There is a buzzing in her ears, and she's not sure if it's from the roar of her pulse or the bees that have begun to circle nearby.

They're getting closer. It's as if something—as if *Kate*—is drawing them. A beetle climbs her wrist, a worm brushes against the bare skin of her knee, a bee lands on her earlobe. She is gasping, now, overwhelmed by the heat that blooms in her chest, surges up her throat. Her vision blurs like snow, then goes dark.

When she wakes, the day is cooler, the sun hidden behind clouds. Her mouth tastes of earth, and her body, sprawled on the ground, feels heavy, wrung out. Hazily, she watches the crow take flight from the sycamore, wings blotting out the sun. Blades of grass itch against her skin, and she flinches, remembering the insects. She scrambles to her feet, brushing the dirt from her clothes, fingers searching for the creatures that surely crawling over her neck, in her hair.

But there is nothing.

Looking down, she sees that the earth is still: just an empty, velvet mound where she has dug up the soil. No worms, no beetles, no larvae. She can't even hear any bees.

Did she imagine it? Hallucinate?

But something catches at the edge of her vision—a glitter of wings. The damselfly she saw earlier, before she blacked out. She watches as it flits towards the sycamore, dancing over the gnarled trunk, the little wooden cross, before disappearing from view.

Then she knows. She didn't imagine it. It was real.

A memory hovers, clouded and uncertain, like something seen from a distance. Early childhood. Sun on her face, the brush of wings on her palm, that feeling in her chest . . . She squeezes her eyes shut, tries to pull it closer, but she can't bring it into focus. Somehow, though, she is left with the odd sense that this has happened before.

The villagers' gossip echoes in her mind. One word, ringing louder than the rest.

Witch.

She has to know the truth.

About the Weywards. About herself.

The next day, Kate sets off to Lancaster. The drive reminds her of the night she left London. The road snaking through the hills, stretching endlessly out before her. She feels the familiar rise of fear in her gullet as she speeds along with the other cars. Her blood beats hard in her veins. Her blood, but the baby's blood, too—the Weyward blood—and the thought makes her feel stronger, grip the steering wheel hard, determined. She can do this.

She's never been to Lancaster before. It's quaint and pretty, with its neat white buildings and cobblestones. But something about the throng of crowds—she is almost swallowed up by a gaggle of tourists—unsettles her. There's a sharp taste in her mouth, a sour coating that she recognizes as the precursor to an anxiety attack. She's surprised to feel relief when she catches sight of the River Lune flashing silver in the distance, the hazy mountains beyond.

She finds the council office easily enough: a large, imposing building hulking on the city's main street.

Inside, the air is crisp and still, and Kate gathers herself together, joins a winding queue to speak to the man at the desk. Her appointment is at 2 P.M. She'd thought the Cumbria County Council Archives might hold some information, but the curt woman she'd spoken to on the phone explained that Lancashire Council holds the records of local witch trials, given the trials took place at Lancaster Castle.

Eventually, she is ushered to another waiting room, and then summoned to a cubicle, where she takes a seat opposite a thin, middle-aged man, shoulders dusted with dandruff.

A manila folder rests on the desk in front of him. Nerves flicker at the thought of what might be inside. She shuts her eyes briefly, thinking of how much she spent on gas to get here . . . *Please, let it be worth it. Let him have found something.*

The man offers a perfunctory greeting before detailing the results. She watches as his tongue flicks out to moisten his lips before he talks, like a frog catching flies.

"I've only found four records about a Weyward," he explains. "Three of them I had to pull from the Cumbrian archives. Let's start with those, shall we?"

He opens the file, takes out two documents.

"Both of these records concern an Elizabeth Ayres, née Weyward."

Kate nods.

"Yes—my great-grandmother, I think."

"We have a record here of her marriage to a Rupert Ayres in August 1925."

Kate nods again. She knows this already.

"And a death certificate. From September 1927."

She leans across the table, heart pounding.

"What does it say? How did she die?"

"The cause of death is quite vague—'shock and blood loss,' it says. Childbirth, perhaps? Quite common in those days, of course, though unusual that it hasn't been explicitly referenced. The certificate was made out by a Doctor Radcliffe, place of death listed as Orton Hall, near Crows Beck."

"I think my grandfather was born that year. Maybe she died giving birth to him?"

Something else the man said snags in her brain.

Doctor Radcliffe.

With a start, she thinks of the doctor in the village, who performed her first ultrasound. His liver-flecked hands, cold on her skin. He'd mentioned inheriting the practice from his father, hadn't he?

How strange, to think that his father might have been present for Elizabeth's death. For her own grandfather's birth. Though she supposes that is the way of small villages—of rural life. She remembers the weathered headstones in the graveyard. The same names, again and again. And yet not a single Weyward. If it weren't for the cottage, it would be easy to imagine they'd never existed; that they were merely the stuff of local legend.

She turns her attention back to the man across from her. How is it that he has only found four records? Can that really be all there is?

"Next, we have a death certificate for an Elinor Weyward. Died aged sixty-three, in 1938. Liver cancer. Given a pauper's funeral."

"A pauper's funeral? What does that mean?"

The man frowned. "It means that there was no one to cover funeral expenses. She would have been buried in an unmarked grave."

Kate feels a throb of pain that this woman—her relative—had been so neglected in death. And yet she'd had family living just a few miles away, at Orton Hall.

The man takes the last sheet of paper from his file. She notices that the skin of his hands is moist, with a pearlescent webbing between the fingers. Again, she thinks of frogs.

"This last one is much older," he explains. "One result for the surname Weyward in the records of the assizes for the Northern Circuit, from 1619. An Altha Weyward, aged twenty-one, indicted for witchcraft and tried at Lancaster Castle."

Her heart jumps. Prickles sweep her skin, like the tracings of phantom insects.

So the rumors are true.

"Was she found guilty?" she asks, her mouth dry. "Executed?"

The man frowns.

"I'm afraid we don't have that information," he says. "We only have the record of the indictment—not the outcome of the trial. Sorry not to be of more help."

"Do you know," Kate begins, thinking of the cross under the sycamore tree, "where she would have been buried? If . . . if she had been executed, I mean."

"Again . . . that's not something we know. There aren't records. At least, not anymore."

"And—there's really nothing else? No other records of the Weywards between 1619 and 1925? For three hundred years?"

The man shakes his head. "Nothing I could find. But official registration of births, deaths, and marriages only began in 1837. And a lot of parish records haven't survived. So it was quite easy to fall through the cracks—especially if you were from a poorer family."

Kate thanks him, trying to ward off the disappointment that spreads through her. She's not sure what she expected, really. That it would be easy to draw her family's history from the murk of the past, the way she'd somehow drawn insects from the soil. That doing so would help her understand herself.

But at least she isn't leaving empty-handed.

On her way out of the building, she turns the fragment over and over in her mind, as if it is some precious heirloom.

Altha Weyward. Aged twenty-one. 1619. Tried for witchcraft.

Altha. A strange name. Soft and yet powerful. Like an incantation.

On the drive home, the afternoon sun settles pink on the hills. The landscape is so ancient—the sweeping meadows, the rocky crags. The slate-colored tarns. Altha Weyward—whoever she was—would have looked out at these same hills, once.

Kate has an image of a young woman, wan-faced in the dawn, dragged to a pyre, or gallows . . . She shudders, pushes it from her mind.

Twenty-one. Almost ten years younger than she is now. She remembers herself at that age—tense and watchful, the spark of her childhood long snuffed out. But she'd been free, really, in comparison to the women who had come before her. She thinks of Elizabeth, her great-grandmother, dying in childbirth, and one hand goes automatically to her stomach. The twenty-first century afforded a degree of protection. But it hadn't protected her from Simon. She remembers his face; his expressions fluid, mercurial. How he'd look at her sometimes, as tenderly as he had in those early days, when she'd believed in their love. When the slightest touch of his hand on hers was enough to set her pulse thrumming. But then she'd do something—say something—he didn't like, and the look would sour into disgust. The scar on her arm throbs.

All those years. Caught in a brutal dance, with steps she never knew how to follow.

Perhaps things haven't changed so much, after all.

It was quite easy to fall through the cracks, the man at the archives had said. But wasn't it also possible that Kate's ancestors—the Weywards—had wanted to hide, given what had happened to Altha? After all, it was Elizabeth's marriage to Rupert that had earned her a place in the record books. A relationship with a man.

I must have you.

Kate knows better than anyone how dangerous men can be.

The thought sparks fury in her. She's not sure if it's a new feeling, or if it was always there, smothered by fear. But now it burns bright in her blood. Fury. For herself. And for the women that came before.

Things will be different for her daughter. She'll make sure of it.

And that means she has to be brave.

It is 3 P.M. Kate doesn't have long until Kirkby's Books and Gifts closes for the day.

She stands in Aunt Violet's chilly bathroom, looking at herself in the mirror. Sunlight falls across her body, washed green by the creeping ivy on the outside of the cottage.

It's been a long time since she looked at herself properly. For years, she hasn't been able to bear the sight of her own nakedness. All of those evenings, molding her flesh into whichever lingerie Simon wanted her to wear. Lying back and letting him arrange her limbs how he liked. She had become a vessel. Nothing more.

Perhaps this was why she had hated the idea of being pregnant before, when she still lived with him. She already felt like a means to an end.

But. She hadn't known it would be like this.

Now, in the mirror, Kate assesses herself. The strong lines of her limbs, the new spread of her hips. Her belly, with its growing curve. Her breasts amaze her—the darkening of the nipples, the veins that glow blue and bright beneath her skin. The mole on her breastbone has darkened, too: ruby deepening to crimson.

Even her skin is different—it is smoother, thicker. As if she is armored.

Armored and ready, to protect her daughter.

The force of it—this love that surges in her veins—shocks her. As does the searing clarity that she will do anything, whatever is necessary, to keep her child safe.

Unbidden, the day of the accident flashes in her mind. Her father's hand on her shoulder, rough and desperate, pushing her out of the way of the oncoming car. Had he felt this way, too?

She blinks the memory away, refocuses her gaze on the woman in the mirror. A woman she can barely recognize as herself.

She looks—and feels—powerful.

There's only one thing she wants to change.

Aunt Violet's kitchen scissors are next to the sink. Kate lifts them to her head and begins to snip, smiling as coils of bleached, brassy hair fall to the ground. By the time she is finished, only the roots remain, bristling from her scalp like a dark halo.

She dresses before she leaves.

Not in her old clothes, the things that Simon chose for her. Those, she leaves behind.

Instead, she dons a pair of Violet's linen trousers and a loose tunic of green silk, embroidered with a delicate pattern of leaves. Last, the straw hat with the feather. The walk to the village is peaceful, and she tests her growing knowledge of the local plant life—there, by the side of the road curl green fronds of stinging nettle; from the hedgerows peer creamy spouts of meadowsweet. Silver flashes amongst the green: the silky strands of old-man's beard. She breathes deeply, inhaling the scent.

She is passing under the oaks when she feels a dark shape fall across her body, hears a guttural cry. But there is no needle of ice, this time. Instead, a whisper of the feeling she'd had in the garden, when the insects had brushed against her skin, returns. Movement in her chest, like the unfurling of wings.

Come on, she tells herself. *You can do this.*

She keeps walking.

Emily slumps forward over the counter, flanked by stacks of books. Her graying curls quiver as she scribbles in a ledger. A ceiling fan putters, ruffling the pages of the books.

"Hello," Emily looks up at the sound of the door chime. "How can I—"

For a moment, she looks a little pale, before she recovers herself and smiles.

"Kate! Sorry," she says. "It's just that—I didn't realize before, how much you look like her. Like Violet. How are you getting on?"

"I'm good, thank you. Actually, I was wondering," says Kate, the confidence of her tone surprising her, "if you needed an assistant."

CHAPTER TWENTY-EIGHT

ALTHA

That night in the dungeon was the longest of my life. The next day, I knew, the jurors would decide my fate. I knew that I would be hanged—that evening, or the following day. They would take me to the moor. One of the guards told me. I comforted myself with this, with the thought that at least then I'd see the sky, hear the birds. One last time. I wondered if anyone would come to watch—whether there would be a crowd, thronging below the scaffold, hungry for the sight of my body twisting on a rope. Satan's bride dispatched back to Hell.

Perhaps they would be right to hang me.

I thought of the promise I had made to my mother. The promise I had broken. I had failed to live up to her name for me. I had not been able to save her. For this, and the broken promise, guilt weighted my heart like an anchor.

But to be hanged for the death of John Milburn . . . that was a different matter.

I do not know if I slept at all that night. Images appeared before me, looming in the dim of the cell. My mother's face, her features bloated by death. A crow, black wings cutting the sky. Anna Metcalfe writhing on her deathbed. And John Milburn, or what had remained of him. His ruined face, dark and wet as spoiled fruit.

When they unlocked my door the next day, I felt as if I had already begun my passage from this world into the next. I seemed to be seeing everything through a haze.

Shadows haunted the edges of my vision. The veil was lifting, I thought. The veil between this world and the next. Soon I would be with my mother. I hoped she would understand what I had done, and why.

There seemed to be more people in the gallery than ever: as they led me to the dock, the courtroom swelled with jeers and booing. I looked at the faces of the judges, set into heavy creases of thought. The jurors, blank-eyed in their dark garb. Only the juror with the square jaw looked me in the eye. I was not proud this time; I searched his face, hungry for some clue as to what would become of me. Then he looked away and a chill took hold of my heart. Perhaps he did not want to look upon a woman condemned.

I sought Grace in the crowd. Her cap shone white, pristine. She was sitting with her father, her head bowed. I willed her to turn, so that I could see her face—the face that haunted my dreams—one last time. But she did not.

One of the judges spoke.

"The accused, Altha Weyward, has been charged with murdering Master John Milburn by witchcraft. The alleged crime took place on 1 January, in the year of our Lord 1619.

"Witchcraft is a grave scourge on this land, and our king, His Royal Highness James I, has charged us with fighting against its insidious evil. We must be wary of it in all aspects of our lives. The devil has long fingers and a loud voice, which reaches us all with sweet entreaties.

"As we know, our womenfolk in particular are at great risk from the devil's temptation, being weak in both mind and spirit. We must protect them from this evil influence, and where we find it has already taken root, tear it from the earth.

"We have heard the evidence against the accused. It has been established that Master Milburn was trampled to death by his cows.

Neither witness to John Milburn's death has given evidence to suggest that the accused uttered any incantation to compel the animals to behave in this manner.

"Indeed, Daniel Kirkby described how a crow tormented the animals and drove them into a frenzy. We know that crows are common in this part of the land, and that they can be violent in their interactions with other animals and humans alike.

"The accused was not brought to touch the corpse; and thus we cannot know if it would have bled at her touch. The court, aided by the good Doctor Smythson, has examined the accused's body for the witch's mark.

"None was found.

"Having heard this evidence, I ask the gentlemen of the jury to deliver their verdict, bearing in mind their duty to God and their consciences."

A hush fell over the court as the foreman stood. My breath caught in my chest. It did not matter what the judge had said. I could see the gallows. Could feel the noose rough against my neck. I thought of all the other women who had been put to death before me, the fate my mother had tried to shield me from. The women of North Berwick. Of Pendle Hill. Soon I would join them. I was sure of it.

"Of the charge of murder by witchcraft," he said, "we find the accused . . . not guilty."

Then, I was floating. Dreaming. I could hear the condemnation from the gallery, but it seemed to be sounding from miles away. My body was weightless, as though I were in water. I looked for Grace. Next to her, William Metcalfe had his head in his hands. So he did not see it. He did not see Grace look up at me. He did not see the expression on her face.

CHAPTER TWENTY-NINE

VIOLET

V iolet spent the weeks after Frederick departed in her room.

"Lovesick," she heard Nanny Metcalfe say to Graham one morning, who had come to ask if she'd seen his biology textbook.

"Over *whom?*" she heard him hiss. Then, louder, for her benefit: "Bloody hell, Violet, not you, too."

Later that day, he'd pushed a note under her door that read:

FORGET ABOUT THE OLD GIT. YOU'RE AS BAD AS
FATHER, PINING FOR HIS LAPDOG!

Violet didn't write back.

She had decided that it would be easier to forget about what had happened in the woods if she never spoke of it to anyone. But it wasn't. At night, she dreamed of Frederick, forcing his way inside her while the trees loomed overhead, spinning in circles. It was as if he had left a spore of himself in her brain, which was now multiplying and spreading through her neurons. She felt *infected*. She remembered the sticky substance he had left dribbling out of her.

This was the thing she wanted to forget most of all. Whenever she thought of it, something tugged at her brain, threatening to form a connection. It—the sticky thing—had reminded her of a word she had read in Graham's biology textbook. *Spermatophore*. It was the substance that male insects used to fertilize the eggs of female insects. She refused to think about it further. She couldn't bring herself to find the section of the textbook that covered it; she had hidden it under her mattress, along with the soiled underwear and stockings.

Most of the time, Violet lay cocooned in blankets, quite cold although it was past midsummer by now. She didn't feel right in her body—the room continued to spin even when she wasn't having nightmares, and there was a heaviness to her limbs, as if her bones had been threaded through with lead. She had a constant urge to bathe, to slough off the tainted skin in hope of finding a new, clean layer beneath.

She could still hear properly: starlings in the morning, the chirp of crickets in the evening. But there was a new edge of pain to these sounds, one that she hadn't noticed before: an owlet in search of its mother, a bat lamenting its broken wing, a bee in its death throes.

Sometimes, it all seemed too much to bear, suffering weighting the air like gravity, pressing down on her skin. It was as if the sparkle had gone from life, as if the apple had withered and rotted.

At first, she managed to draw comfort from her mother's things. The silky, speckled strands of Morg's feather, the locket with the delicate *W*, the tiny key that had lain hidden inside it for years. But what was the key *for*? There were no longer any locked rooms in the Hall. She began to wonder if Frederick had lied about her mother—about that white-faced, desperate woman, needing to be locked away. She could almost believe that he had made it up, if it weren't for the word scratched into the wainscoting. *Weyward*.

Crouching next to it one night, when the Hall was silent save for the mice that rustled in the walls, she wondered whether her mother had used the key to gouge those letters into the paint. She couldn't bear to think of her like that. Instead, she tried desperately to conjure up the memories that had been triggered by the handkerchief: the scent of lavender, the dark fall of hair, the warm embrace . . . sometimes she even thought she could remember Morg, appraising her with a beady, glittering eye . . .

She didn't even know where her mother was buried. When she was younger, she had spent long afternoons carefully examining the crooked headstones in the grounds next to the old chapel they no longer used. She had knelt in cold soil, gently brushing away green threads of lichen, to no avail. The graves all belonged to long-dead Ayreses; even the most recently departed had been in the ground for a century.

Perhaps she was buried in the village graveyard. That was where she had been from, wasn't it? Violet thought about running away, running to Crows Beck and looking for her mother's grave. But what would that solve? She would still be dead.

And Violet would still be alone. Alone with what had happened, that day in the woods.

There was only one way to escape Frederick's pollution of her mind, her body. Her very cells.

Violet wasn't sure she believed in Heaven or Hell (though she doubted they'd let her into the former, after Frederick had sullied her so). She was a lover of science, after all. She knew that when she died, her body would be broken down by worms and other insects, and then she'd provide nutrients for the life-sustaining plants aboveground. She thought of her beech tree. She'd rather like to be buried under it, to give it sustenance. And while the tree fed from her, she would feel . . . nothing. Oblivion. She imagined the nothingness, as heavy and dark as a blanket, or the night sky. Her mind and body would cease to exist, along with the spores Frederick had left behind. She would be free.

She spent the long days planning. She settled on dusk, her favorite time of the day, when the sky was the color of violets—her namesake—and the crickets sang. She would leave with the light.

In the summer, as far north as they were, the days stretched on until almost midnight, which meant that everyone was asleep at the time she had chosen. She put on her favorite green dress and brushed her hair in front of the looking glass one last time. The bite on her cheek had faded to a silvery pink semicircle, like a crescent moon.

Her bedroom was amber and gold with the sun setting through the windows. Violet opened them and looked out, savoring the last sight of her valley. She could see the wood from here, a dark scar on the soft green hills. She looked down. She was very high up—about thirty feet, she thought. She wondered who would find her in the morning. She imagined her body, crumpled like the petals of the primrose flower. Violet had left a note on the window seat, asking to be buried under the beech tree.

She climbed up onto the windowsill and felt the cool evening air on her face. Breathed it in deeply, one last time. Just as she prepared to propel herself forward into that empty horizon, she felt something brush her hand. It was a damselfly, its diaphanous wings golden with the sun. Just like the one that Graham had given her, all those weeks ago.

There was a knocking on the door, and then Graham—whom Violet had thought was asleep—burst in.

"Honestly, Violet, you can't keep taking my things without ask—Jesus, what the devil are you doing up there? One wrong move and you'd be splattered all over the garden."

"Sorry," said Violet, scrambling down from the windowsill and scrunching the note into her pocket. "Was just—looking out at the view. You can see the railway line from here, did you know?" Graham loved trains.

"No, Violet, despite living in this house all my life I did not know that the second-floor windows offered views of the Carlisle to Lancaster line. Honestly, what's got into you lately? Thought I was going to have to put another damned insect in a jar for you." He shuddered. She looked down at her hand, but the damselfly was gone.

"I'm fine. Just—rather tired."

"*Please* tell me you're not heartbroken over bloody *cousin Frederick*. Or I suppose he's probably Freddie to you, isn't he? *Darling* Freddie. What did you talk about on your walks together? More rubbish about his hunting prowess? I must say, I wouldn't have expected you to fall for such a crashing bore."

"It's nothing to do with Frederick," said Violet, too quickly.

Graham looked at her for a moment, raising one pale red eyebrow.

"If you say so. Glad to see the back of *darling Freddie*, myself. Reminded me of a chap in the year above at Harrow. Similar air of arrogance.

Expelled last autumn for getting a girl pregnant. One of the professor's daughters. She had the baby in a convent, poor thing."

"Really," Violet said, feigning disinterest. *Spermatophore*, she thought. "How awful for her."

"Indeed," said Graham. "Anyway, you've got to be careful of chaps like that. He didn't try anything with you, did he? That day we played lawn bowls—Father and I fell asleep and when we woke up you were both gone. Father seemed quite pleased about it, actually."

"Nothing happened," said Violet. "We just went for a walk. I showed him the woods."

"Hmm. So long as that's *all* you showed him. Look—anyway, it's really late. I was waiting for Nanny Metcalfe to give up her post so that I could come and get my biology book back. You do have it, don't you? I'm supposed to have wrapped my head around the subphyla of anthropods by the end of the summer. Running out of time."

"Arthropods, you mean. The ones with exoskeletons."

"Ugh. Yes, those. Well—anyway, can I have it back?"

Violet thought of the book, wedged under her mattress along with her bloodied undergarments.

"Lost it. Sorry."

"*Lost* it? How the blooming hell do you lose a *textbook*?"

"Dropped it in the beck."

"Can you imagine the look on the science master's face when I tell him that? Sorry, sir, don't have my textbook—my feckless sister *dropped it in a stream*. Well, that is just capital, thank you, Violet. Now I'll have to send off for another one. It'll probably arrive after I'm back at bloody Harrow. Thanks *a lot*." He left, slamming the door behind him.

Once the sound of Graham's footsteps had faded down the corridor, Violet tried to think what to do about the note. She couldn't very well burn it. Nanny Metcalfe was bound to smell smoke—she had the nose of a bloodhound—and then there would be questions. And, anyway, she hadn't completely decided whether or not she would still need it. But then she thought of the damselfly and her stomach ached with guilt over Graham. Could she really leave him all alone with Father?

She retrieved the Brothers Grimm book from next to her bed, opening it to stash the note inside. Before she fell asleep, she thought of her mother again. If Violet died, she would never learn the truth. She carefully placed Morg's feather next to her face on the pillow, hoping she would dream of her mother. Instead, she dreamed of Frederick, of what had happened in the woods. In the dream, she looked down at her pale body and saw the flesh of her stomach darken, felt it give way under her fingers. Mayflies swarmed around her, wings glistening as they ducked and weaved in their endless, brutal dance.

She woke the next morning to the strong smell of kippers wafting from a tray borne by Nanny Metcalfe.

"Get these down you," she said. "Nanny's orders." The fish was yellow and puckered, like the carcass she had once seen of a slow-worm, mummified in the summer heat.

She struggled to sit up and took the tray. Her stomach churned and she shuddered at the memory of the dream.

"Are you all right, Violet?" Nanny asked.

"Fine, thank you," she said, bringing a forkful of fish to her mouth. She chewed slowly, and even after she swallowed, the gelatinous sensation lingered on her tongue and on the roof of her mouth.

She managed one more mouthful. Then, the roiling in her stomach intensified, and the room shifted again. She felt a gathering inside her, something pushing up from her stomach and into her throat, the acid sweet in her mouth.

She vomited. Again, and again.

Afterwards, when Nanny Metcalfe had sponged the flecks of vomit from her mouth and helped her change into a clean nightgown, they sat in silence for a while. A crow screamed outside. Violet could see it through the window, a black comma in the blue sky.

Eventually, Nanny Metcalfe spoke.

"I think we'd better call the doctor," she said.

CHAPTER THIRTY

KATE

Time passes more quickly, now that Kate's days are filled by her shifts at the bookshop.

She finds the work soothing—sorting through the boxes of donations, stamping them with the label gun. Mostly, the shop sells Mills & Boon novels ("Beggars can't be choosers," Emily says); though occasionally Kate will unearth a first edition Austen or Alcott. These are displayed in the window, so that their gilt-embossed covers spark in the sun.

She and her boss settle into a comfortable routine, the older woman often bringing her cups of tea and plates of biscuits, chattering easily about her husband, Mike, about growing up in Crows Beck. Emily is impressed by Kate's affinity with her ginger tomcat, Toffee, who—she swears—despises all humans (Emily's own hands are often patterned with scratches from his eager ministrations).

Kate is due in December. She hopes for snow for the birth. Often, alone in the cottage, she tests names out loud, tasting them on her tongue. Holly, perhaps—a nod to the season. Or maybe Robyn. Though nothing feels quite right, yet.

It is early autumn when she feels the first kick. She is out in the garden, pulling up clumps of tansy from beneath the sycamore—quite a poisonous plant, she's learned, despite its bright yellow flowers—and listening to the trees murmur in the wind. She gasps at a sudden fluttering movement inside her womb—a liquid feeling that makes her think of quicksilver, or the pale minnows darting in the beck.

Her daughter.

By November, her skin is stretched tight as a drum over her stomach. None of her old clothes fit—she raids Aunt Violet's wardrobe for loose smocks and tunics, draping herself in pashmina shawls and a battered mackintosh. As it has grown, her hair has become unruly—she'd forgotten its tendency to curl, in all those years of expensive hair treatments. The back is a sort of mullet, now, but Kate doesn't care. She doesn't even brush it, these days—just lets it fall in dark waves to her ears.

Simon wouldn't recognize her.

"Are you in touch with him?" asks Emily. "The baby's father, I mean."

Kate has invited her over for Bonfire Night; they have built a small pyre in the center of the garden and sit in front of it on camp chairs, gripping mugs of hot chocolate. Kate breathes deeply, savoring the scent of woodsmoke. Above them, the sky is thick with stars.

"No," she says. "I haven't spoken to him for months. It's . . . better that way. For the baby. He . . . isn't a good person."

Emily nods. She reaches over, squeezes Kate's hand.

"I'm here, you know," she says, taking her hand away. "If you ever want to talk about anything, you just say the word."

"Thank you."

Kate's throat narrows. She stares into the fire, watching sparks dance gold into the night. For a while, neither of the women speak. The only sounds are the hiss and crack of the flames and, somewhere, an owl.

She wonders if Emily has guessed the truth. It could be obvious, she supposes, from the way that she flinches when her phone rings, her refusal to talk about her old life in London. About why she left.

But she can't bring herself to say the words. Not yet. She doesn't want to risk the delicate threads of their friendship. It's been so long since she's spent time with another woman. She hasn't seen her university friends for years.

The last time was the wedding she and Simon went to, in Oxfordshire. Five years ago now, not long after she'd left her job. Her friend Becky was getting married. She remembers the dress she wore—that Simon picked out for her—pink, the color of broken flesh, the color of the scar on her arm. Gold heels she couldn't walk in. She'd sat across from Simon at the reception, laughed too loudly at the feeble jokes of the man next to her. It was an open bar; Simon was drunk. But he was watching. He was always watching. One of her friends saw him push her into the taxi before the speeches, the practiced way his hand gripped the back of her neck. He wouldn't let her take their calls, afterwards. In the end, her friends had stopped trying.

"I wish Violet were still here," Emily says eventually. "She'd be gutted to be missing this. To be missing you."

"What was she like?"

"Sorry," Emily shuffles her chair closer to the fire. "I always forget you didn't really know her, you remind me of her so much. She was . . . odd. In the best way. I used to think that she had no fear—the things she did when she was younger! She climbed to Mount Everest base camp once, she told me. To make a study of the Himalayan jumping spider. Crazy woman." She shakes her head, laughing. "You have her spirit."

"I wish," Kate grins.

"You do. It takes strength what you've done—starting again. She had to do the same."

They fall into silence.

"She never told you what happened? My mum said she was disinherited, that there was some sort of scandal."

"No. Like I said . . . I think it was too painful for her. So your mum had no idea what it was? This scandal?"

"No. My dad might have known, but he died when I was a kid."

"Oh, I'm sorry."

"It's OK." She has been thinking of the accident more and more lately, her perception of it shifting now that she carries a child of her own. A child she would do anything to protect. Even if that meant sacrificing herself, the way her father had done.

Sometimes, lately, she can almost believe that maybe—just maybe—it wasn't her fault. That she isn't a monster after all. But then she'll remember—the blood, slick and glossy on the road. The bee brooch, forever tarnished, in her hand.

"I had a baby, once, you know," Emily says softly, in a strange echo of her thoughts. Looking over at her, Kate sees tears shine in her eyes. "Stillborn. She'd be about your age, if she'd lived."

"I'm so sorry."

"It's all right. We all have our cross to bear."

After Emily leaves, Kate sits for a while, watching the fire.

As she stares into the leaping orange flames, resolve hardens in her. She won't repeat the mistakes of the past. Things will be different, this time. *She* is different. And she is never going back to him.

She fetches her duffel bag from the bedroom, struggling slightly under its weight.

In the garden, she unzips it, pulling out clothes—the clothes she used to wear, for Simon. The skintight jeans, the clingy tops. Even the lingerie she'd been wearing when she left: red lace, a diamante heart quivering between the cups of the bra. She throws the lumpy shape of them onto the fire, watching as the flames burn brighter. An effigy of the past, melting away. Shreds of lace float into the air, like petals.

She stands for a while, watching. One hand resting on her belly, where her daughter swims safe inside.

December.

The days begin white and glittering with snow—on the roof, the branches of the sycamore, where a robin has taken up residence. It reminds Kate of Robin Redbreast from *The Secret Garden*—for so many years, her only safe portal to the natural world. Only now does she truly understand her favorite passage, memorized since childhood:

"Everything is made out of magic, leaves and trees, flowers and birds, badgers and foxes and squirrels and people. So it must be all around us."

Often, before she leaves for work, she stands outside to watch the sun catch on the white-frosted plants, searching for the robin's red breast. A spot of color against the stark morning. Sometimes, while she watches it flutter, she feels a tugging inside her womb, as if her daughter is responding to its song, anxious to breach the membrane between her mother's body and the outside world.

The robin is not alone in the garden. Starlings skip over the snow, the winter sun varnishing their necks. At the front of the cottage, fieldfares—distinctive with their tawny feathers—chatter in the hedgerows. And of course, crows. So many that they form their own dark canopy of the sycamore, hooded figures watching. One bears the same white markings on its feathers as the crow that startled her in the fireplace when she arrived at the cottage. She is growing braver—testing herself each day by moving closer and closer to the tree. This morning, she presses her palm against its ice-crusted bark, and warmth swells in her chest.

Later, Kate is at the bookshop, thinking about this and smiling. She sips coffee from a leopard-print mug of Emily's. It's a little after ten, and she wants to get through five boxes by lunchtime.

It's been seven months since she left. Sometimes she feels as if she's always lived in Weyward Cottage; always had this routine of waking with the sun, then either spending time in the garden or walking leisurely into the village for her shifts at the bookshop. Even some of the locals seem to be starting to accept her. According to Emily, they treat her with the same slightly baffled acceptance they reserved for Aunt Violet.

Other times, it's harder to forget what happened.

Her phone rang last night at 2 A.M., its blue flare jolting her gut. A number she didn't recognize. She knows it wasn't him calling. It's impossible: he doesn't know about the Motorola, doesn't have the number for it. But it doesn't stop her from running through scenarios in her mind as she sorts through boxes of books, worry ticking inside her.

Thank God he doesn't know about the baby.

"Oh, Kate?" Emily walks into the storeroom, a welcome interruption. She crouches next to a stack of weathered-looking boxes under the window. "Someone dropped this off yesterday . . . I think you might find it interesting." She grunts as she lifts a box from the top of the pile and plonks it down in front of Kate.

"What is it?"

"Take a look," says Emily, beaming at her. "You can keep what's inside, of course. Yours by right, really."

At first, Kate thinks she has misread the label, scrawled hastily over the top of the box in pen. She checks again, but there is no mistaking it.

Orton Hall.

CHAPTER THIRTY-ONE

ALTHA

Outside the castle, it was a bright day. The light seared my eyes so that the streets and buildings of Lancaster looked white as pearls. For a moment I wondered whether they had actually hanged me, whether this was Heaven. Or Hell.

I staggered towards the road out of the town, keeping my head bent in case anyone should recognize me. Everywhere, I jostled through crowds, the warm press of bodies making me sweat and panic.

"Have you heard the news?" one woman said to another. "Queen Anne has died!"

A man shouted; another woman uttered a prayer for the queen's soul. The babble of voices rose in pitch, and the crowd pushed and heaved. My thoughts swam. In a wild moment, I had the thought that it should have been me who died, that there had been some great error, my life saved instead of hers.

My heart froze at the feel of a rough hand on my shoulder. I turned, fearing it was someone from the gallery come to right the jury's wrongs, to set me back on the path to death. But it was one of the jurors. The square-jawed man with the pitying eyes.

I saw for the first time the richness of his clothing: both his cape and doublet were embroidered with silver thread. Standing in front of him in my crude gown, I felt every bit the pauper I was.

For a while, neither of us spoke as the crowd flowed around us.

"My wife," he said eventually, slowly, as if it pained him to speak the words. "She nearly died in childbed, delivering our son. A wise woman in our village saved both their lives. Beatrice, she was called. I said nothing, when they accused her. She was hanged."

He took a velvet pouch from his breeches and pressed it into my hands, before melting away into the throng.

I looked inside the pouch and saw gold coins. I understood, then, that I had this man—or the woman who saved his family—to thank for my life.

On the road, I found a peddler traveling by donkey and cart. He would take me back to my village, he said, for one of the gold coins. I should have been wary of him, a strange man in the dark, but I reasoned that even if he killed me it would be a quick death compared to the long one I faced on the road, without food or shelter.

The peddler gave me some ale and a sweetmeat. Then he put me in his cart, amongst his wares, which were soft shawls and blankets. Nestled amongst them, I felt almost as if I, too, were an exotic ware from some distant land, spun from foreign cloth. I tried to stay awake but the blankets were warm and comfortable and the motion of the cart gentle and rocking, as I imagined the ocean to be.

When I woke next, we were half a mile from Crows Beck.

I knew when I saw the gate swinging on its hinges that the villagers had been at the cottage. Those who broke bread with William Metcalfe, who mourned John Milburn.

The shutters had been torn from the window and lay in a splintered, ruined heap.

The front door was dented, the lock broken. Inside, shards of glass sparkled on the floor like fallen stars, and I had to be careful where I stepped. The smell of herbs and fruit hung rotten in the air and I realized they had broken my precious jars of salves and tinctures.

I lay down on my pallet, which was slashed so that tufts of straw poked through. I slept. When I woke at dawn it was to a sea of broken things.

It took me the better part of two days to put the cottage to rights. Mercifully, they had left my dear goat unharmed, though my absence meant that her ribs now showed clearly through her hide and, when I put my hand to her, she bleated in fear. "All will be well," I murmured as I led her inside, though I was not at all sure that it would.

One of the chickens had died, but the other had lived. I could still have eggs for my breakfast, and milk from the goat. I made nettle soup and dandelion tea from the plants in the garden. They hadn't got to the vegetable plot, either, so I pulled beets and carrots from the earth and ate and pickled them. They were small, misshapen things, hard with frost and forced from the soil before their time.

I broke up one of the chairs and used this for firewood. The cottage was very cold, with the shutters gone from the windows, and I ripped one of Mother's old gowns in two and used it to block the draft from getting in.

When I had done all this, I was ready.

I took down the parchment, quill, and inkhorn from the hiding place in the attic, thankful that it had not been discovered.

Then I sat at the table and began to write.

I have been writing for three days and three nights now, pausing only to make fires and food, and to check on the animals. I do not want to sleep until I have finished.

They could come back, you see. The villagers. They could drag me through the village square, in protest against the verdict, and hang me themselves. Or they could find another crime to accuse me of.

So I must write what has happened while I still breathe. Perhaps I will go away from here when I have finished. I do not yet know. The thought of traveling on the open road frightens me. And I cannot bear to leave the cottage behind. I wish I were a snail, and the cottage my shell that I carried with me everywhere. Then I would be safe.

It is hard to write the next part of my story. So hard that, even though it happened first—before I was arrested, tried, and acquitted—I come to write it last. My heart has shrunk away from it until now.

But I promised to set things down as they happened and this I will do. The act of it brings me comfort. Perhaps if someone reads this, if someone speaks my name after my body has rotted in the earth, I will live on.

I am trying to think of where the beginning is. Who decides where things begin and end? I do not know if time moves in a straight line, or a circle. Here, the years do not pass so much as loop back on themselves: winter becomes spring becomes summer becomes autumn becomes winter again. Sometimes I think that all of time is happening at once. So you could say that this story begins now, as I sit down to write it, or you could say that it began when the first Weyward woman was born, so many moons ago.

Or you could say it began a twelvemonth ago today.

Last winter was a cold one, stretching its fingers well into spring. On this particular night early in 1618, there was a storm, and so when I heard the pounding, I thought it was only the wind at the door. But the goat, whom I keep near me in the winter months, looked up with eyes of liquid fear.

A high female voice called my name.

When you have grown up with someone, as close as sisters, you come to know her voice even better than your own. Even if you have not heard it call your name for seven years.

So I knew before I opened the door and saw her, standing there with shadows ringing her eyes, that it was Grace.

CHAPTER THIRTY-TWO

VIOLET

The doctor's hands were cold on Violet's abdomen.

"Hmm," he said. Violet could see white specks of dandruff clinging to his brilliantine hair. He turned to Nanny Metcalfe, who hovered next to Violet like an anxious moth, her hands wrung red.

"Are her menses regular?" he asked.

Menses? Whatever were those? Violet wondered if the doctor had meant her *mens*, Latin for mind. Well, that certainly wasn't regular. Far from it. For instance, although she knew that it was the doctor who was touching her, not Frederick, and that she was lying comfortable and safe in her bed rather than in the woods, her heart fluttered in her throat. The smell of brandy and crushed flowers returned and she fought the impulse to retch. She wanted desperately for the doctor to take his hands away, for him to stop poking and prodding at her stomach. It was taking all her willpower not to scream.

"Oh, yes," said Nanny Metcalfe, flushing. "Always on the fifteenth, like clockwork."

Violet thought of the clots and clumps of blood that came out of her every month, accompanied by days of cramping pain. So that was what he meant. She'd never heard the medical term for it before—Nanny Metcalfe always referred to it as *her curse*. It had barely occurred to Violet that it was something that happened to other girls, too. Last month was the first time it had let her alone in years. She hadn't missed it one bit.

Nanny Metcalfe was frowning at her.

"She didn't ask me for any rags last month, mind," she was saying to the doctor. Violet wished they would stop talking about her as if she weren't lying right there. Her cheeks grew hot at the mention of these private subjects to a complete stranger.

"Hmm," said the doctor again. There was more prodding, and then he asked a question so bizarre that Violet thought she must have misheard.

"Is she intact?"

Violet thought of the pictures from Father's newspaper, of soldiers wounded in the war, arms ending at elbows or legs ending at the knee.

"As far as I know, Doctor," said Nanny Metcalfe. There was a slight quaver to her voice, as if she were afraid.

Then, without warning, the doctor had slid his fingers between her legs, to that place that had felt like a bruise since the day in the woods. She winced from pain and shock.

"She is not," he said, looking at her with mild disgust. Nanny Metcalfe gasped, clapping her hands to her mouth. Violet felt cold shame spreading through her. Somehow, he had known exactly what had happened between her and Frederick, almost as if he had looked inside her brain.

The doctor had her urinate into a humiliatingly clear vial, which he held up to the light and inspected briefly before putting it in the pocket of his jacket. Violet turned her face away.

"I'll telephone in a few days with the results," he said.

Nanny Metcalfe nodded, barely able to force out a "Good day, Doctor," as he went down the stairs. They sat together in silence as they listened to Father's study door opening, a low murmur of conversation, followed by the heavy clink of the front door and the sputter of the doctor's motorcar.

A moment of stillness hung in the air, like a raindrop threatening to fall from a leaf. Then there was a great crash, and the sound of glass breaking. A high-pitched whine from Cecil. Later, Nanny Metcalfe would report that Father was so angry that he had swept the Jacobean side table in the hall clear of its ornaments in one fluid movement.

"What have you done?" said Nanny Metcalfe, who had still not explained to Violet what was happening. But she didn't need to, not really.

Violet thought of the word that had lingered on the edge of her consciousness for weeks, no matter how hard she tried not to think about it. *Spermatophore.*

Violet barely slept, for fear of dreaming about the woods. About Frederick. She passed the days between the doctor's visit and his telephone call in a fog, halfway between sleep and wakefulness. She tried her hardest not to succumb to her drooping eyelids and heavy limbs, but often she found herself in a terrifying kaleidoscope of dreams: Frederick on top of her, under a tree-veined sky; her stomach distended and dark, rotting from the inside out. Mayflies, pulsing all around.

Not even Morg's feather brought her any solace.

Graham and the servants had been told that she was ill again, with the same "condition of the nerves" that had kept her bedbound earlier. Only Father and Nanny Metcalfe knew the truth.

When the telephone rang, five days after the doctor's visit, Violet lay under the coverlet and waited for Nanny Metcalfe to come and tell her the news. But the footsteps that sounded up the stairs and down the corridor were too heavy to belong to Nanny Metcalfe.

Father opened the door. Violet sat up in bed, wondering if her appearance would shock him. He had not been to see her in weeks, and she had lost a lot of weight from the constant vomiting. Her bones felt sharp in her face; her eyes were shadowed by lack of sleep. Perhaps he would ask her how she was feeling.

He looked at her for a moment with an expression of distaste, as though she were a piece of spoiled food on his plate.

"I have spoken to Doctor Radcliffe," he said, his voice chill with fury. "He has informed me that you are with child, and have been for several weeks."

Violet's pulse flickered. She thought she might faint.

"What do you have to say for yourself?" he asked, taking a step closer. The anger made his face larger and redder, so that his blue eyes almost disappeared. A blood vessel on his cheek was swollen and purple, like a fattened slug. Violet wondered if it would burst.

"Nothing," she said softly.

"Nothing? *Nothing?* Who do you think you are, the bloody Virgin Mary?"

She had never heard him speak like this before.

"No," she said.

"Who is the father?" he asked, though surely he must have known all along. For whom else could it be? She remembered what Graham had said, about when he and Father had woken from their nap that day to find Violet and Frederick gone. *Father seemed quite pleased.*

"Cousin Frederick," she said.

He turned on his heel and slammed her bedroom door behind him, sending dust motes flying. For a moment they hung suspended in the shaft of sunlight from the window, reminding Violet of the midges she had seen with Frederick, the day he had kissed her. She had thought they looked like fairy dust.

What a child she had been.

That day, Nanny Metcalfe came into her bedroom with a large, worn-looking suitcase that Violet had never seen before. She had never been anywhere, had never had need of a suitcase. Without looking at her, Nanny Metcalfe began piling things into it.

"Am I going somewhere?" Violet asked, though she wasn't particularly interested. Everything had felt muted and colorless since the doctor's visit. She knew that she was heading inexorably towards something, something terrible, and there was little point in resisting. She thought of the dreams, the flesh of her stomach dark and soft beneath her fingers. Rotten.

"Your father will explain," said Nanny Metcalfe. "The others think you're going to a sanatorium in Windermere, for your nerves. You're not to tell them different."

Violet added nothing to the suitcase, apart from Morg's feather, which she wrapped carefully in an old scarf. Everything else—her books, her green dress, her sketching things—she left behind. She didn't even take Goldie the spider—Nanny Metcalfe had agreed to release him into the garden when Father wasn't looking.

Graham and the other servants were lined up in the hall to say farewell. Nanny Metcalfe had dressed her in one of Father's old trench coats and a wide-brimmed hat, to hide the weight she'd lost and the shadows in her face. Violet felt like a scarecrow, and she saw Graham blanch when she appeared on the staircase.

Miss Poole and Mrs. Kirkby said goodbye and told her to get well soon. Graham said nothing, watching in shocked silence as Father took her by the elbow and marched her out of the front door to where his Daimler waited in the drive. Violet had never been in Father's motorcar before. The chrome-green exterior reminded her of the shiny casing of a pupa. Perhaps she would emerge from it a butterfly and fly away, miles and miles away, to a place where she would be safe and free. One could dream.

There was a lingering smell of cologne. It occurred to Violet that the last occupant of the passenger seat, where she was sitting now, must have been Frederick. The thought of it made her want to open the door and hurl herself out onto the road. Instead she just looked out of the window, at Orton Hall disappearing behind them.

"Where are we going?" Violet asked. Father didn't answer. Rain began to splatter on the roof of the car in fat, loud drops. Father turned a dial and mechanical arms unfolded themselves across the windshield to wipe the rain away. For a while, there was no sound in the car but their rhythmic scraping.

They drove through the gates, rising up on either side of the car like omens. Violet wondered if she would feel something when she left the estate, having spent her whole life inside its bounds, but she felt nothing. Father cleared his throat.

"I have written to Frederick," he said, keeping his eyes on the road. "I have told him of your condition and asked him to marry you."

Violet watched a bird rise and fall with the wind. Father's words seemed to come from a place very far away. She wondered if she hadn't imagined them; if she hadn't imagined everything that had happened since the afternoon they had played bowls on the lawn. Perhaps she was still asleep in her canvas chair, the sun warm on her face and the brandy warm in her belly. *Wake up*, she thought.

"Marry me?" she said. "Why?" What had any of this to do with marriage, she wondered. She had thought that couples wed when they were in love. There had been nothing of love that afternoon in the woods.

"It is the decent thing," he said. "For the child. And for the family."

The child. The spore that was growing in her stomach, feeding from her like a parasite. She hadn't thought of it as a child.

"But I don't want to marry him," she said softly. Father ignored her, looking ahead at the road.

"I *won't* marry him," she said, louder this time. Still he ignored her.

Outside, the sky grew dark and knotted with clouds. There was a storm coming, she could feel it on her skin. She watched the sudden glow of lightning. The rain grew heavier, blurring the window so that she could barely see out of it. Then, the car slowed and shuddered before coming to a halt. She tried to remember how long they had been driving. Less than ten minutes, she thought—surely that wasn't long enough to get to Windermere?

Father opened his door and Violet breathed in the fragrant smell of wet earth. He collected her case from the trunk and then opened the door for her to get out. She drew her coat around her and pulled the brim of her hat down against the rain. Squinting ahead, she could see a low, squat cottage, overgrown with vegetation, the stone dull and wet. The windows were cobwebbed and dark.

Father rummaged for the keys in his overcoat. Now that they were closer, Violet saw that there were letters carved into the stone above the door. *Weyward*.

She rubbed the rain from her eyes, in case she was seeing things. But there it was. It looked like it had been carved a very long time ago: the first slant of the *W* was faint, and the other letters were green with lichen.

"Father? Where are we?"

He ignored her.

Violet was gripped by the sudden fear that Frederick would be in the cottage, waiting for her . . . but when Father unlocked the heavy green door and she saw the dim corridor beyond, it was clear that there was no one there.

Father lit a match, piercing the blackness.

Inside, the dark rooms had a sunken look, as if they were trying to disappear into the earth. The ceiling was so low that Father, who was not a tall man, had to stoop.

There were only two rooms: the largest one, at the back of the cottage, had an ancient-looking stove and a cavernous fireplace. The other, two single beds and a battered old bureau. There was a scrabbling sound in the roof: mice, Violet thought. At least she wouldn't be totally alone.

"You will stay here until Frederick next has leave and can return for the ceremony," said Father. "I'll come to check on you every few days with provisions. For now, you'll find some tins and a dozen or so eggs in the kitchen. Perhaps the solitude will help you reflect on your sins."

He paused before looking at her, his features twisted with disgust. "Frederick told me he had intended to ask for your hand, that he wanted to wait until after the wedding but you . . . wouldn't take no for an answer."

Her cheeks burned as the memory of the woods came back to her.

Father was still talking.

"I have been foolhardy," he said. "I should have known. You are your mother's daughter, after all." He turned away, as though he could no longer bear the sight of her.

"My mother? Please—where are we? What is this place?" Violet asked as he walked towards the door. He stood at its threshold, his hand on the doorknob, and for a while she thought he would simply leave without responding.

"It belonged to her, actually," he said. "Your mother." He slammed the door behind him, so hard that the little house shook.

PART THREE

CHAPTER THIRTY-THREE

KATE

K ate stares at the writing on the box for a long time.
Orton Hall.

The cardboard is mildewed and lifting at the edges. One side looks as though it has been eaten by something. She remembers the glittering remains of the insects at Orton Hall and shudders. She isn't sure she can even bring herself to touch the cardboard, but she is conscious of Emily watching her, eyes bright with anticipation.

She takes a deep breath. Then she opens the box.

Dust clouds the air, catching in her throat. She coughs as she peers inside.

All the books are very old, and some are in better condition than others. She pulls out a copy of *An Encyclopedia of Gardening.* Its green cover is faded and swirled with mold. She shakes it, and crushed insect wings fall out, glimmering like pearls in the light.

"Ugh," says Emily, reeling backwards. "That'll be the infestation Mike mentioned. He's been up at the Hall, helping to clear it out. He thought I might want the books. The viscount's been moved to a care home, over in Beckside. He was in quite a state, apparently. Poor man. Hold on—I'll get a dustpan."

Emily bustles out of the storeroom, and Kate pulls the next book out of the box.

It's a rather dense-looking tome titled *Introduction to Biology*. One of the pages is folded down, and Kate shudders at the unsettlingly graphic diagrams of insect reproduction.

There are some fiction titles, too: a dog-eared copy of *The Adventures of Sherlock Holmes. The Complete Works of Shakespeare.* She wonders whom they belonged to. If they could have belonged to Graham or Violet.

There's one last book in there. Kate fishes it out. It is very handsome—it looks as though it could be more valuable than all the others. She should tell Emily, she knows; ask her what sort of price it could fetch. But for some reason she doesn't want anyone else to see it. She wants to keep it for herself.

She runs her fingers over the front cover. The book is bound in soft red leather, the title embossed in gilt:

Children's and Household Tales

The Brothers Grimm

The Brothers Grimm. She'd had her own copy as a child, she remembers—though her newer edition had been titled *Grimms' Fairy Tales*. Some of the stories, she recalls, had been rather frightening, the characters—no matter how innocent and pure—meeting grisly ends. Hansel and Gretel, eaten by a witch. Good preparation for the real world, she supposes.

Could the book be a first edition? She opens it, looking for a publication date on the first page.

A crumple of yellowed paper falls onto her lap. Unfurling it, she sees it's a handwritten letter, but before she has time to read it, Emily opens the storeroom door, dustpan and broom in hand.

She slips the letter into the pocket of her jacket before Emily can see.

Toffee creeps in, climbing over her, his claws digging into her legs. He settles into her lap and begins purring. The baby kicks in response.

"I think she likes you," she says to the cat.

"And he's smitten with the pair of you," Emily laughs. Her feathered earrings quiver as she bends down to sweep up the wings. "I can only get him to purr by leaving the room. What have you got there?"

"Fairy tales," says Kate quietly.

"I wonder if it belonged to Violet," Emily says. "Though it's odd, isn't it—that she didn't take her things with her, when she moved out of the Big House."

"Yes," Kate says, struggling to reconcile what she knows of Aunt Violet—her love of green dresses, the insect drawings, the strange collection of artifacts under her bed—with dark and horrible Orton Hall. She can't picture her ever having lived there. "Perhaps she left in a hurry?"

Emily brings her a plate of chocolate digestives before heading back to the front of the shop to deal with a customer. Though she desperately wants to, Kate doesn't dare open the letter in her pocket. She doesn't want to risk Emily coming back and seeing it. It feels private, somehow. Secret.

At half past three, after they've closed up for the day, Emily offers her a lift home.

"You shouldn't be carrying heavy things, you know," she says. "Not now, in your condition."

Kate looks down at her stomach, swaddled in layers of wool. She eases herself into an old coat of Violet's, pulls a green velvet beret over her head.

"I'll be fine," she says. "Anyway, I want to see the snow." It's funny, now, to think of her early walks into the village, back when she'd first arrived at Crows Beck. How she'd flinched at the rustle of leaves, startled by a sparrow. Now, her amble home is something to look forward to, something to savor. She loves noticing the little seasonal changes of the landscape—how now, in winter, the trees reach bare and graceful towards the sky, the hedgerows are jeweled red with rowan berries.

She hoists the box onto her hip and pushes open the door, leaving behind the musty warmth of the bookshop. Outside, she inhales the wintry air, savoring its crispness. The cold prickles her cheeks, and she grins at the sight of the village: the buildings half hidden under great lips of snow, windows glowing orange. Someone has strung Christmas lights from the streetlamps, and as the sun sets pink in the sky, they twinkle into life.

For the first time in years, she has been looking forward to Christmas—her daughter is due a few days before. With only weeks to go, she can feel her body preparing for the birth: her breasts have swelled, and she's begun to notice streaks of golden fluid on the inside of her bra. Colostrum, Dr. Collins calls it.

Even her senses seem to have sharpened; sometimes, she thinks she can hear the most incredible sounds: the *click* of a beetle's antennae on the ground, the whirr of a moth's wings. A bird clamping its beak around a worm. It's strange, how she feels attuned to things happening at such a great distance, and yet all the while her child's heartbeat thrums in her ears.

But now, as she walks home, the countryside is still and silent, muffled by snow. It is *so* still, in a way that unsettles her; she has the sense that the land, and the creatures in it, are waiting for something. As she strides on, the only sounds are her own footsteps crunching in the snow and the rustle of the letter in her pocket. The letter. Something about it doesn't feel right. Foreboding creeps across her skin, setting the hairs on end.

When she does get home, she is almost afraid to look at it. She takes her time lighting the fire, boiling water for her tea, chopping vegetables for the stew that she'll prepare later.

Finally, everything is done. She can no longer put it off.

She sits down at the kitchen table and unfurls the piece of paper.

The note is very yellow, almost translucent in places. Lined, as though it was torn from a school exercise book. There is no date.

Dear Father, Graham, Nanny Metcalfe, Mrs. Kirkby, and Miss
*   Poole,*

I am very sorry about what I have done, especially to whomever it
was who found me.

*   Father, I know that you think taking one's own life to be a mor-*
tal sin, and that you will be shocked—and perhaps ashamed—by
what I have done. But please understand that I truly felt I had no
other choice after what happened.

*   I know you all—Father especially—think very highly of my cousin,*
Frederick Ayres. But please believe me when I tell you that he is not
the man you think he is. I know he seems charming and chivalrous—
like a knight from a fairy tale, with his dark hair and green
eyes. But something has happened—something terrible and wrong.

*I do not quite have the words for it; just that I am plagued by mem-
ories of it, night and day. Perhaps it is my fault; perhaps I should
have done something to prevent it, though I do not know what. In
any case, I cannot see how I can continue in this fashion.*

*Graham, I am sorry that I was not a better sister to you. Nanny
Metcalfe, I am sorry if I have been a difficult charge. Mrs. Kirkby,
I am sorry about the time I said your roast beef tasted like a shoe.
Miss Poole, I am sorry for all the times I made fun of your singing
voice.*

My best wishes to you all, and my deepest apologies once again,
    Violet

*PS If it isn't too much trouble, I should like to be buried under the
beech tree in the garden. Perhaps you could also ask Dinsdale to
plant some flowers above my grave. Something bright and colorful
that will attract bees and other insects. Any flowers will do, so long
as they aren't primroses.*

Kate reads the letter again.

I am plagued by memories of it.

She shuts her eyes, touches her arm, where the skin is smooth and pink.
Sometimes, Kate would wake in the night to Simon's insistent mouth on
her neck, to the feel of him inside her. As if she had forfeited the rights to
her own body the day they'd met.

She understands, she thinks, what happened to Aunt Violet.

Obviously, she hadn't gone through with the suicide attempt—somehow,
Violet had left home and found the strength to live the academic, adventur-
ous life that awaited her. To break free from her past.

Kate wonders if Violet ever told anyone, in the end. She knows what it's
like, wanting to tell, to no longer be alone with the awful, secret knowledge,
poisoning your cells like a disease. Wanting to speak but being choked into
silence by the shame of it.

As she rereads Violet's words, something else leaps out at her.

His green eyes.

She thinks back to her visit to Orton Hall, to meeting the old viscount. He had green eyes, too. Her spine tingles with revulsion at the memory—his fetid, animal stink, the yellow curls of his nails.

Fingers shaking, she unlocks her phone and taps *Frederick Ayres* into Google.

The first result is an article from the local paper, dated five years ago.

FLY INFESTATION BUGS VISCOUNT

Local exterminators have struggled to remove thousands of mayflies from Orton Hall, the seat of the Viscount Kendall.

According to residents in nearby Crows Beck, the infestation has plagued the Hall for decades, worsening in recent years.

"Every pest control company in the valley has had a go," said a source. "Insecticides, LED traps, the works. But they won't budge."

Mayflies are most common in the summer, when the females can lay up to three thousand eggs. The insects normally frequent aquatic environments and rarely infest dwellings.

Lord Frederick Ayres, the Tenth Viscount Kendall, has lived in Orton Hall since succeeding his uncle to the title in the 1940s. He served as an officer in the Eighth Army in World War II and saw action in North Africa.

Viscount Kendall has not been seen in public for some years and could not be reached for comment.

Her stomach drops.

There's a photograph with the article. A young man in military uniform, handsome features blurred by time. But she can see him there—just—in the firm line of the jaw, the deep-set eyes. It is the same stooped, haunted man she met at the Hall.

Frederick is the viscount.

What kind of father would disinherit his children in favor of a man who had *raped* one of them? Surely, he can't have known. For a moment, Kate allows herself to consider a worse possibility: that Violet had told her father about the rape, and that he simply . . . hadn't believed her.

Outside, an owl hoots mournfully. Kate feels a surge of sadness for her great-aunt, this woman she can barely remember. They'd had more in common than she realized.

She goes to the sink for a glass of water, gulping it down as if it can flush away her memories. She stays there for a moment, looking out at the snowy garden, flaming with sunset. Violet's garden.

Despite everything that happened to her, her great-aunt had built an independent life for herself. She may have never married and had a family of her own, but she had her cottage, her garden. Her career.

Now Kate, too, has built her own life.

And she won't let anyone take it away from her.

CHAPTER THIRTY-FOUR

ALTHA

Grace and I stood looking at each other for a long time before she spoke. It was the first time she had looked at me directly in seven years. Since we were thirteen, I had only ever seen her from afar: in church, or shopping on market day. She had always passed her eyes over me as if I were not there.

"Will you not invite me in?" she asked.

"Prithee, wait," I said, before shutting the door. Hurrying, I herded the goat into the garden, my mother's warning ringing in my ears.

When this was done, I opened the door and moved aside to let Grace through. I noticed she walked slowly, as if she were a much older woman. She sat heavily at the table. She kept her cloak on, even though it was soaked from the gale outside.

"Would you care for some food?" I asked.

She nodded, so I cut a slice of bread for her, and some cheese, and sat down opposite her. As she ate, her cap shifted, and I saw a dark shadow on her cheek. I thought perhaps it was cast by the flicker of the candle on the table. Still she did not say anything until she finished eating.

"I heard about your mother," she said. "Now we are both orphans."

"You have your father," I said.

"My father," she said, "hasn't looked at me properly since I was thirteen years old, though I kept house for him and brought up my brothers and sisters until I left home."

"Well, you have your husband."

She laughed. It was a dry sound, like the crackling of flames. She did not laugh like this before, when we were children, I remember thinking. She'd had a sweet laugh then, sweeter than the hymns we sang in church, sweeter even than birdsong.

"You will have to tell me what it's like, sometime," I said. "Being a wife."

"I haven't come here for idle talk," she said sharply. "I'm here on business. To purchase something from you."

One small white hand went to the pocket of her kirtle, and I heard the clink of coins.

"Oh," I said. My face flushed, and a tide of pain rose in my throat. I had been stupid to think she had wanted things to be as they were before, after all these years. After everything that had happened.

"I am with child," she said, turning her head away. Her voice was very quiet; her face hidden by the cap.

"What joyful tidings," I said. I remembered how much she had spoken of wanting to grow up and have a babe of her own when we were children. When I was very young, I had told her, horrified, of Daniel Kirkby's birth: his mother grunting and glistening all over with sweat, the child sliding out of her in a rush of slime and blood. Grace, who had seen her brothers and sisters born, laughed at my ignorance. "That is just the way of things," she had said. "You'll learn yourself one day."

There had been rumors of a pregnancy around the village in the months after she married, and when I saw her in church, I had noticed a swell beneath her dress, a plumpness to her face. But no child ever came. I did not know if she had lost the baby, or if there had never been one. Either way, she must be very happy now, I thought, to be so blessed.

She did not say anything for a moment. When she spoke again, I was sure I must have misheard her.

"I need something," she said slowly, as if she were reluctant for the words to leave her mouth, "that will make it go away."

"Go away? Morning sickness, you mean? I can see to that. I can make a tonic with balm, to settle the stomach—"

"You misunderstand me," she said. "I meant the child. I need . . . I need something to make the child go away."

Her words hung heavy in the air. Neither of us spoke for a moment. I heard the pop and hiss of the fire, the drum of rain on the roof. These sounds swelled in my ears, as if they could take away what she had said.

"Has the baby quickened?" I asked.

"Yes."

"Grace," I said. "Are you quite sure? What you are asking of me . . . it is a sin. And a crime. If anyone were to discover it . . ."

"It will die anyway." She said this as coolly as if she were commenting on the yield of the harvest or the turn of the weather. "You would be doing it a kindness."

"Grace," I said. "Even if I knew how . . ."

"You must know," she said. "Your mother would have known. Look through her things. There's certain to have been a village girl or two who came to her for help after some indiscretion or other. Besides . . ." She paused. "She was good at taking life, wasn't she?"

The memory of that terrible night swam before me. Anna, still and lifeless while Grace sobbed.

"Grace. Your mother would have died anyway, had we not come. She was too ill by then . . . the fever was so strong. And the leeches . . ."

Her head turned sharply back towards me. In the candlelight, her eyes were bright—with tears or fury, I did not know.

"I do not wish to speak of it," she said. "Just tell me if you can help me or not. If you ever loved me as your friend . . . then you will do this thing for me. And you will ask me no more questions."

All the moisture had gone from my mouth. I felt giddy, as though the room had lurched to one side and taken me with it.

"I will try," I said softly. "But I cannot promise that it will work."

"Aye, then. I will return in one week. Will that give you enough time?"

"Yes."

She rose from the table. "I must be going. I have left John asleep. He does not normally wake until dawn, after so much ale. But I cannot risk him rousing to see that I am gone."

I myself slept a poor night after she left. I thought for a long time, wondering what I had agreed to. All for the love of someone who—and I knew in my heart that this was true—still blamed me for her mother's death. Still hated me.

How it pained me, to hear that hate in her voice. My mind ran over her speech, remembering the coldness of it, and my eyes burned with tears. As children, we had learned each other before we could speak. I had once known the meaning of her raised brow, the curve of her mouth, as though they were words in a book. Now she was a stranger.

The following morning was calm and sunny, and as I listened to the robins sing, I wondered if I hadn't dreamed up Grace's visit. Then I went into the other room and I saw the second mug and plate and knew it had been real. Grace really had come. She really had asked this terrible thing of me. She wanted me to atone for one wrong by committing another.

I would look through my mother's papers as she had suggested, I decided. If there was no recipe for the kind of draught that Grace wanted, then I could tell her that I could not do it, did not know how.

I opened the bureau that had been my grandmother's—the handle inscribed with a *W*, much finer than anything else we owned. She had been given it by the First Viscount Kendall for nursing his son through milk fever. It was where my mother and I stored all our notes and recipes, our cures and remedies, for relieving ailments and suffering. My mother always kept the drawers locked and wore the key around her neck. She gave it to me before she died, bade me do the same.

"To save things getting into the wrong hands," she said.

I riffled through handwritten recipes for all manner of salves and tinctures: elderflower for fever, belladonna for gout, agrimony for back pain and headache. And then I saw it, in my mother's fine hand.

For bringing on the menses
Crush together three handfuls tansy petals
Steep in water for five days before administration

My heart sank. I had no excuse, now.

I could not be sure that it would work if the baby had quickened. Perhaps I could strengthen the dose of tansy, I thought. Just slightly, so that it would still be safe.

I caught myself. Did I even want it to work? Why would Grace want to harm an innocent babe, which had not yet had its chance at life?

I remembered her eyes, glittering and hard with fury and pain. "You would be doing it a kindness," she had said.

Perhaps I was too quick to judge. I had never felt a child grow in my womb, only to lose it in childbed. I remembered the Merry-wether woman I had attended to and the small, dead coil of flesh she had labored over for hours. Had given her life for.

What if Grace carried the baby to term and bringing it forth killed her? What if Grace were to die for the sake of a child that would never open its eyes, never take its first breath?

I couldn't lose her. She may still hate me, blame me. But it didn't change the love I felt for my friend then, and always would. I had to keep her safe.

I waited until nightfall to gather the tight yellow buds of the tansy from the garden. It was still a time when villagers came to my door frequently enough in the daylight, to seek treatment for some complaint or other. I did not want anyone to know what I was doing.

I liked being in the garden. It was where I felt my mother's presence most strongly: in the furred leaves of the plants she had tended; the strong, tall sycamore she had loved; the creatures that rustled in the undergrowth. I felt as if she were still there, watching over me. I wondered what my mother would make of Grace's visit.

I knew my mother had felt a great deal of guilt over Anna Metcalfe's death. She never liked to speak of it afterwards. I could see that the end of my friendship with Grace pained her. She was afraid to leave me, friendless and alone in the world, I think. As I write this and think of everything that has happened, I know she was right to be afraid.

When I had got enough tansy, I went inside and crushed it with our old mortar and pestle. I added the water and put the mixture in a covered bowl to steep. I hid it in the attic in case I had visitors over the next five days.

Its scent was so strong—like fouled mint—that I could still smell it when I laid my head on my pallet for sleep.

CHAPTER THIRTY-FIVE

VIOLET

Her mother. This house belonged to her mother. Violet touched her necklace, tracing the *W* engraved on the pendant.

The Weywards. Her mother's family, she could be sure of it now.

Violet looked around the dingy room for some record of them. There was barely anything to suggest it had ever been lived in at all. She sat down at the creaky kitchen table, which was covered with a thick patina of dust. She wiped some away with her finger and coughed. Underneath, the wood was scored and gouged, as if someone had taken a knife to it. The roof was leaking, and the far wall of the kitchen shone with rain. She was cold and it was dark. There was no clock anywhere in the house, and the small square of violet sky visible through the filmy window gave no clue as to the time.

She looked at the provisions that Father had left. Tinned peas, corned beef hash, sardines. One of the eggs still had a soft curl of feather clinging to it. The eggs made her think of *spermatophore* and she pushed them to one side, stomach queasy. She ate some peas, cold from the tin. She struggled to light an ancient-looking candle with one of the matches Father had left behind, flinching at the small blue flame. She sat for a long time, watching the wax bubble and melt.

It was strange to imagine her mother living here. It was a hovel, Violet thought. Like something from a fairy tale without a happy ending. She walked over to the small door that led to the back garden and opened it, sheltering the candle flame from the wind. The garden—if it could be called that—was wild and rampant: strange-looking plants shivered in the rain. A large sycamore loomed over the house, and Violet could see nests in its upper branches, the glimmer of black feathers. Crows. She felt their eyes on her, watching. Assessing.

She shut the door, letting darkness fall. She took the candle into the next room and sat on one of the beds. It gave a great creak of protest. In the bedroom, the air was thick from dust and it moved through her lungs like molasses. She lay down on the bed and watched the candle throw shadows onto the wall. Violet felt tears well up in her eyes. She was here, in her mother's house, closer to her than she had been in years, and yet she had never felt so alone in her life. She shut her eyes and waited for sleep. When it came, it was blank and dreamless.

Violet was woken by a wave of nausea. She retched into a basin she found next to the bed. Her head pulsed with pain and her mouth was dry and sour. She needed water. The candle had long since gone out, and the room was very dark. She drew back the threadbare curtains to look outside. The windowpane seemed to have thickened from years of grime, so that the outside world was just a murk of brown. She tried to open it, but the latch had rusted shut.

She felt her way into the next room, fumbling on the kitchen table for the box of matches. She knocked one of the tins onto the floor and it rolled to the other side. Violet lit a candle and left it on the table before going outside.

The garden was red with dawn, and she could hear the chatter of thrushes and wood pigeons. The wind whispered through the leaves of the sycamore and Violet detected another layer of sound—the gurgle of the beck. She could see it from here, shining in the morning sun; the garden sloped down to it. The same beck that curved through the valley and around the fells, all the way to Orton Hall. Connecting Violet to this place—to her mother—without her even knowing.

There was no tap in the cottage, but Violet saw an old water pump outside, like the one in the kitchen garden at the Hall. The pump was green and stiff with age, and she struggled to work the handle, the way she'd seen Dinsdale do. The first drops of water that trickled out were brown, but eventually she had a clear stream flowing, which she cupped in her hands and splashed at her face. She got a bucket from inside and filled it to the brim. The bucket was very heavy and she half dragged it back indoors, sloshing water over the sides.

Here, she paused, thinking of the pails of scalding water she'd watched Penny lug up the stairs, face pink from steam. She needed to heat the water. She lit the stove with a match, before fetching a dusty pan from a hook on the wall. She would bathe, then wash the windows, try to get some light in.

Violet saw that Father hadn't left her any soap. She supposed he thought it was appropriate that she sit here in squalor. *Reflect on your sins*, he had said. She didn't want to think about her sins, about the woods, Frederick, *spermatophore*. She wanted to scrub the house and her body until both were shiny and new.

Perhaps she could find some soap somewhere. The bigger room had very little in the way of storage, or, indeed, furniture at all; it was bare, other than the stove and the table and chair. She remembered the bureau in the other room.

Lifting the candle to it, she could see that it would have been a fine piece, once, before time and dirt had eaten away at it. Much of it was covered in grime, but the bits of wood she could see were warm and rich, the handles a heavy brass beneath the dirt. It was far nicer than the battered old table in the kitchen, almost as if it didn't belong in the house. She tried one of the drawers, but it was locked. The other, too. She frowned. She hadn't seen a key anywhere. Father had taken the front door key with him, she remembered. She had heard it turn in the lock.

In the kitchen, she stripped—taking care not to look down at her body, the places Frederick and the doctor had touched—and scrubbed herself as best she could with a wet handkerchief. Once she was dressed, she set about wiping down the table and the windows. Soon her handkerchief—a present from Miss Poole, she remembered, rather guiltily—was brown and stiff with dirt.

The rooms were a little brighter now that she had cleaned the windows. No matter what she did, she couldn't get the one in the bedroom to open, but she flung the kitchen window wide, letting in the smells and sounds of the garden. She opened a tin of beans and ate it outside, feeling the warmth of the sun on her face. The garden was loud with bees and swallows, and the occasional caw of a crow from the sycamore tree. Violet thought she heard a note of approval in the crow's voice, as though it had assessed her favorably. It made her feel a little less alone.

She could do something about the garden, she thought. She could see that it would have been neat and ordered, once: there were recognizable patches of violets, mint. It was waist-high with helleborine now, the crimson heads nodding in the breeze.

Her mother had sat in this garden, perhaps exactly where Violet was sitting now. It was obvious to Violet that her mother had been very poor— especially compared to Father. Was that why he was so secretive about her? Was he ashamed? Violet remembered what Frederick had said. That her mother had *bewitched* her father.

Bewitched. Everything she knew about witches came from books, and none of it was good. The witch who ate Hansel and Gretel, for instance. The three witches in *Macbeth*, raising the wind and the seas. But what about the witch in "The Robber Bridegroom"? She had helped the heroine escape. Anyway, she was being ridiculous. Witches weren't real. Her mother hadn't been some sort of evil hag, brewing potions in a cauldron and zipping about on a broomstick.

Still, there had to be something of her mother's somewhere in the house. Inside, Violet tried the old bureau in the bedroom again. She hadn't noticed before, but each handle was carved with a *W*. She pulled her necklace out from under her dress and held it up against the bureau to check. No, she hadn't imagined it . . . the exact same *W* as the one carved on her mother's locket. Barely breathing, she opened the locket and put the tiny gold key into the lock. It stuck, and for a moment Violet thought it must have snapped off inside. She turned it gently again, and felt the mechanism give way with a soft click. She opened the first drawer, which was empty. The second drawer was filled with paper, old enough that it was almost transparent, the writing so faded that she could not make it out. A scrap of newsprint had been daubed with what looked like a hastily scrawled shopping list. *Flour*, it read, *kidneys, milk thistle.*

There was an invitation to a jumble sale at St. Mary's, dated September 1920. A crumpled letter from the Beckside branch of the Women's Institute asking for volunteers to make socks and stockings for "our boys abroad." Violet looked at the date: 1916.

Something familiar caught her eye at the top of the pile. A bundle of thick, creamy paper stood out from the other scraps and tatters. The Ayres coat of arms: a gilded osprey, suspended in flight. Father's writing paper.

They were letters, from Father to a woman named Elizabeth Weyward. *E. W.* Lizzie, he called her.

Violet's mother. It had to be. Her hands were shaking.

I have not slept this past week for thoughts of you, read one missive. It then beseeched Lizzie to *be brave, for the sake of our union.* The paper was thin with creases, as if it had been continually folded and unfolded, read and reread.

Another letter, jumbled in with the rest of the pack, stood out. It was not written in her father's elegant, Etonian script. Instead, the writing was rushed and slapdash, at one point almost veering off the page.

Ma

I am sorry it has taken so long to write but I have not been able to get out a message to you. I've had nothing to write with but today Rupert has gone out hunting—the butler Rainham, who takes pity on me, has brought me some paper and ink. He has said he will take you this note on his way to Lancaster to purchase new clothes for Rupert.

It has taken me too long but I see that you were right. I should never have left home. For some time, Rupert has not let me go outside and now I am to be locked in my room.

How I hate this room. It is small, like a cage, with walls painted yellow as tansy flowers. It makes me think of the tansy tea we used to prepare for the village women, and it pains me to think that Violet will not know the cures and treatments that have been our way for hundreds of years. When I shut my eyes, all I see is that bright yellow, reminding me of what I have forsaken. My past, and my daughter's future.

I miss her so, Ma. They will bring the babe to me so that he can feed, but they have not let me see Violet in days. I hear her cries echoing through those yellow walls.

My only comfort was Morg, but I told her to go, Ma—this is no life for a bird. All I have left now is one of her feathers. Though I do not like to look at it.

It reminds me of what I did. What Rupert made me do.

I should have listened to you, that day we argued down by the beck. "He takes you for a dog that he can train to eat from his hand," you said.

I thought he loved me for myself. But you were right. To him I am but an animal, like those he hunts and puts on display.

That was another thing you told me. That if a man saw my gifts for what they truly were, he would only use them for his own ends. I told myself I was doing it for her, for Violet. As you guessed, she had already quickened in my belly, then. I began to dream of her, grown into a dark-haired beauty, but alone and bleeding in our cottage. Whether from sickness or injury I did not know, but it was clear: my daughter would not survive a life of poverty such as the one I could give her. In my terror, I told Rupert of the dream and asked him what would become of our child. His parents would never acknowledge her, he said. He would be ruined if he married me, being only a second son, with no title to smooth his path in the world. And worse—his parents already knew. They knew about the child we'd made together that night in the woods, when only the moon saw my fear and heard my cries. They planned to drive us—the last Weyward women—away from Crows Beck, he said. From our home, where our forebears have lived for centuries.

But, he said, I had the power to give us all a chance of happiness. He would have his title, and my daughter would have a life of safety, riches. Acceptance.

I liked the idea of that. I was never strong like you, Ma. The things the villagers said, the looks they gave us—I never could stand it. I yearned for a life free from stares and whispers.

And so I did the terrible thing he asked.

I lay in wait, hidden by gorse and heather, as dusk spread over the fells. Morg dug her claws into my shoulder. I heard them before I saw them—the whinnying of the horses, the clatter of hooves. I waited until they were close enough to the edge of the hill, where the ground cut away sharply into a ravine. When Morg took flight, I shut my eyes, opening them only when the screams had stopped, when all that remained was the twisted shape of the carriage on the rocks below, the spokes of one wheel still spinning. Something sparkled on the ground near my feet—a pocket watch, a family heirloom that Rupert had spoken of with great envy. Its face was cracked and sharp, so that when I picked it up, drops of blood welled along my finger.

I stood for a while, looking. Ignoring the horror in my heart.

I thought I was like Altha, our fearless ancestor, that our deeds linked us across time. I thought I was good and brave, made strong by her blood.

But I was wrong.

We took three lives that day, Morg and I. I told myself that they deserved it—Rupert's parents, his older brother, too— that they had been cruel to the man I loved; that they would hurt you, hurt my child, without remorse. But truthfully, Ma, I didn't know them—or what they might have done—at all. Rupert has lied about so many things. I suspect now that his parents never knew of our child, never planned to drive us from our home.

I wish I had seen it before—that his words held as much truth as a fairy story. That he never loved me at all.

Sometimes I wonder if he planned this from the first. He'd been watching me, he said, even before we danced at the May Day Festival. He saw how I was special, and wanted me for his wife. I believed him, from the way he looked at me. A blaze in his eyes that I took for love.

But I am familiar with that look, now. It is the same way he looks at a gun dog or a rifle, a mere instrument to deliver his wants.

I do not ask, or expect, forgiveness. I write this because I want you to know the truth. And I am running out of time to do so. The doctor is coming; Rupert says I am to have a new treatment. I do not know if I will survive it. Shut in this tiny room, and without even Morg's presence to sustain me, I grow weaker each day.

I take a strange comfort from this—have almost willed it. For I am become like a rifle without bullets, and useless in his schemes. I will never harm another for his sake.

Ma, I beg of you, please be there for the babe—and for Violet. Keep our legacy safe for her.

I hope she has your strength.

All my love,
Lizzie

Heart pounding, Violet riffled through the rest of the pack, searching for more of her mother's handwriting. But the remaining letters were from Father, to a woman whose name she did not recognize.

1 September 1927
Dear Elinor,

Thank you for your letter to Lizzie, which I am afraid she was not well enough to receive, her health having declined significantly in recent weeks.

I have discussed your request to visit with Doctor Radcliffe. Given the marked decline in Lizzie's physical and mental state, Doctor Radcliffe does not feel a visit would be appropriate at the present time.

Elinor, your daughter has become—there is no other word for it—hysterical. She has conspired to bring that ghastly crow into the house—Morg, she calls it, ridiculous name—and speaks to it as if it is human. This is, I suppose, exactly the kind of behavior you encouraged in her. Violet may be a lost cause. She has already begun to mimic her mother; befriending flies and spiders, for heaven's sake. But I will not have this madness infect my son. My heir.

And it is not good for Lizzie, Elinor. It is not good for Lizzie to tear around the house in such a state, engaging in such fantasies. Last week she told me she could predict the weather—or rather, that Morg, that foul bird, could. I live in, I am ashamed to say, constant dread of her.

I do fear—and Doctor Radcliffe shares my concerns—that, should she lose her remaining grip on reality, she will pose an even greater danger to herself. And to the children.

In fact—and I shudder to even relate this incident to you— the housekeeper came upon her attempting to climb out of her window, which a feckless maid had neglected to lock. Most horrifyingly, she was carrying the baby. She put the life of my son—my heir, Elinor—in danger.

Fortunately, Doctor Radcliffe was able to come at once. Given the recent developments, he has suggested a treatment that may help: hysterectomy, removal of the womb. It may seem an extreme course of action, but the doctor is of the view that it is warranted in such rare circumstances, when the state of the sexual organs begins to pollute the mind.

It is my fervent hope that Doctor Radcliffe's treatment will be effective in returning Lizzie's sanity. I shall keep you abreast of developments.

Yours sincerely,
Rupert Ayres, Ninth Viscount Kendall

———

10 September 1927
Elinor,

Your unannounced visit yesterday was most irregular.

I regret that Rainham was unable to admit you to the Hall, but I was tied up dealing with some urgent correspondence relating to the estate.

As I think Rainham explained to you, Lizzie is currently preparing for treatment. You need have no concerns for her well-being: Doctor Radcliffe and his small team of highly trained attendants have installed themselves at the Hall in readiness for the surgery.

Doctor Radcliffe has the utmost confidence that the treatment will work. We must allow the good doctor to do his work in peace.

In the meantime I ask that you refrain from engaging in further correspondence. I will let you know when there is news.

Yours
Rupert Ayres, Ninth Viscount Kendall

———

25 September 1927
Dear Elinor,

It is with sincere regret that I write to inform you of Elizabeth's death.

She departed this earthly realm in the early hours of this morning. Doctor Radcliffe believes that a weakened heart was the culprit, no doubt exacerbated by the strain of her recent delusions.

While I am sure that Doctor Radcliffe used his best endeavors to save her, I gather that by the time it became clear that something was amiss, it was too late.

I have made arrangements for her to be interred in the Ayres family mausoleum at St. Mary's church next Tuesday.

I trust that will be satisfactory.

Yours,
Rupert Ayres, Ninth Viscount Kendall

———

30 September 1927
Elinor,

Given your display on Tuesday, I think it best that you have no
further relationship with the children. It is my priority that they
recover as quickly as possible from this regrettable episode. As such
I think it best that they are not subjected to discussion of Elizabeth;
Doctor Radcliffe's view is that this would do more harm than good.

And as for your absurd request to take Elizabeth's remains to
your slum of a cottage for burial—I can't imagine that you ever
thought I could agree to such a thing. Elizabeth was my wife and
it is thus appropriate that she be interred in the Ayres family plot.

However, I will do as you ask and give Violet the necklace you
are so concerned with—I can make arrangements for Rainham to
collect it next week. I may need to revisit this decision, should you
attempt to contact me again.

Yours,
Rupert Ayres, Ninth Viscount Kendall

———

Violet's cheeks were wet with tears.

Now she knew the truth. Her mother had not—as she'd been led to believe—died giving birth to Graham. She had died because a doctor—the same doctor who had slid his cold fingers inside Violet—had *mutilated* her. Killed her.

She reread Lizzie's letter, tracing the loops and curves of her mother's handwriting. At first, she didn't understand the section about the carriage, but then she remembered. Her grandparents and an uncle had died, not long before her parents' marriage.

Coach accident, it was. Very sudden.

All that remained was the twisted shape of the carriage.

Had her mother somehow been responsible? The letter made no reference to anything that might be used to engineer an accident—Violet pictured a trap hidden in the gorse, something to make the horses spook. But Lizzie had written only of Morg.

In any case, it was Father who was to blame. Who had—her stomach turned at the thought—wished for his own family members to die. She thought of the broken pocket watch she'd found in Father's desk. She wondered if it had belonged to Edward—that was the name of the uncle who had been killed, she remembered. The eldest of the three Ayres sons. That must have been why Father wanted him out of the way. With his parents and older brother deceased, he would have been free to inherit the title of viscount, and Orton Hall.

His greatest conquest of all.

Her mother must have been the only person who knew of his guilt. And so he had locked her away—pretended she was mad—to cover up what he had done.

She hadn't even been allowed to see her own mother, Violet's grandmother. What had become of Elinor? Violet supposed she must have died, which would explain why Father owned the cottage. But where were their things—Elinor's, and Lizzie's? If not for the contents of the bureau, one might think they had never existed in the first place.

The last sentence of her mother's letter came back to her.

Keep our legacy safe.

What had she meant by "legacy"?

Blinking away her tears, Violet riffled through the remaining sheaves of paper in the second drawer, sending dust sparkling into the air. At the bottom of the drawer was a thick book, clumsily bound in calfskin and mottled with age. Her heart skipped a beat. The parchment was worn, barely readable. She had to squint to make out the writing: the hand was tight and cramped, the ink faded. She held it up to her candle to get a better look. There was a name . . . Altha, the ancestor her mother had spoken of in her letter.

Her fingers traced the first line.

Ten days they'd held me there. Ten days, with only the stink of my own flesh for company . . .

CHAPTER THIRTY-SIX

KATE

Kate is sitting on the floor in the bedroom when her phone rings. She has been making a mobile for the baby, using treasures she's collected on her walks around the area. An oak leaf of translucent amber; the shiny whorl of a snail's abandoned shell. The white-speckled crow's feather she found in the mug on the kitchen windowsill when she first arrived. All of these things she threads onto fishing wire attached to a frame made of twigs, tied together with green ribbon.

Her phone is in the kitchen, and she's been sitting for so long that her foot has fallen asleep. She stumbles down the corridor. By the time she reaches the other room, she's missed the call, but the ringing starts up again, the vibrations harsh against the wooden table.

"Hi, Mum," she answers.

"Darling. How are you?"

"Good—I'm just finishing up the mobile, the one I was telling you about the other day."

"It sounds beautiful. How are you getting on with it all? Have you got everything you need?"

The cottage is crammed with baby paraphernalia: the kitchen table hidden under piles of tiny vests and muslin squares, soft as gossamer. Emily has given her a Moses crib and a car seat, donated by a niece.

"I think so. Everything but a buggy."

She sighs. She's looked everywhere for one online, but even the most basic model costs hundreds of pounds. And she can't find a secondhand one advertised nearby: not even Emily's niece has been able to help, having sold hers years ago.

Perhaps she should buy one of those slings, strap the baby to her front. Maybe she could even make one. At least that way she'll be able to take her out for walks. Show her the beck, now frozen under a sheen of ice. The trees with their white coats of snow.

"You know, I've been thinking," her mother is saying. "Perhaps I could buy you one. As a sort of early Christmas present."

"Mum. You don't have to do that. You're already spending so much money on flights . . ."

Her mother is coming in two weeks, so that she can be with Kate for the birth. It will be the first time they have seen each other in years.

"But I want to. Please, let me."

"I don't want you going to any hassle."

"Well, how about I just transfer you some money? And then you can pick one yourself."

"Are you sure?"

"Positive."

"Thanks, Mum."

"I love you, Kate."

She blinks away the sting of tears. When did they last say this to each other? Not since Kate was a teenager. It was her fault: she never said it back. She couldn't bear the weight of it, this love she didn't deserve. But now the words are there, familiar shapes in her mouth.

"I love you, too, Mum."

The buggy she picks is green, with a segmented hood that reminds her of a caterpillar. She smiles at the thought of her daughter nestled inside. Though part of her wishes she could stay for longer, warm and safe in her womb.

Sharing everything, even the blood that beats in their veins. And yet, she can't wait to hold her in her arms, breathe her scent, stroke her tiny fingers.

She cradles her stomach with one hand as she orders the buggy. Taps in her address, the number of her new debit card. Her email address, for the receipt.

She smiles when the purchase is complete. The kettle is singing, and she is slow as she moves towards it, her body curving under the weight of her stomach.

As she sips her tea, she looks out of the window, watching the crows in the sycamore tree. Their dark, liquid movements against the white snow.

Her mug slips from her hands, smashes onto the floor.

The email.

She'd used her old email address. The one linked to her iPhone.

Simon has her iPhone. He's going to see it.

She scrabbles for the Motorola, blood roaring. Her fingers shake as she opens a new browser, brings up Gmail.

Please God, no.

The page won't load. She refreshes it, again and again.

Finally, it loads. There's the confirmation email—it's got her address, her new phone number, everything. Even a graphic of a smiling baby.

She deletes it. Stands for a moment, a chill spreading through her veins.

If he's seen this . . . then he knows about the baby.

And he knows where to find her.

Leaning over the kitchen sink, she splashes water onto her face. The icy shock of it calms her.

How long did the email sit in her inbox—three minutes? It's—what—Tuesday, 2 p.m. The middle of the workday. He won't have seen it. She's caught it in time.

It's OK. He doesn't know where she is.

She looks down.

"Don't worry," she says to her stomach. "I won't let him anywhere near you."

———

Outside, there's that same, unsettling stillness from the previous night. She doesn't like the look of the clouds—the way they hang low and gray in the sky. There is something ominous about it.

She sweats under her layers as she heaves herself into the car. The seat is as far back as it can go, her hands barely reaching the steering wheel.

Her heart races as she turns onto the A66, passing the snow-blanketed fields. In the distance, the peaks of the mountains spark silver.

She takes a deep breath, tries to calm herself. She is safe. The baby is safe.

For now, she just needs to focus on driving.

She's going to see Frederick at his nursing home in Beckside. Really, she's not sure what she expects: he barely made any sense last time she saw him, all those months ago at Orton Hall. Guilt twinges in her stomach at the memory. She should have told someone—those dead insects everywhere, the room he'd been living in with its animal scent . . . and Frederick himself. She shudders at the memory of those eyes. At their emptiness. And yet. She can't quite bring herself to pity him.

Violet's words come back to her.

I am plagued by memories of it.

She has an image of him barricaded in that festering study while insects swarm outside, undulating through the corridors of the Hall like one great, glistening snake.

And the strange thing he said to her, just before she left.

She had released me at last.

There had been thousands and thousands of the things, according to the newspaper article. *The insects normally frequent aquatic environments and rarely infest dwellings.* This wasn't some natural phenomenon.

A plague for a plague.

Kate thinks she knows what happened. But she needs to be sure.

The nursing home—Ivy Gate—doesn't exactly live up to its name. The imposing iron gate is devoid of all greenery. Even from a distance, the buildings have an institutional look—something about the slate gray stone, the narrowness of the windows.

241

"Ivy Gate," a curt voice answers the intercom at the entrance.

"Hello," she says. "I'm . . . I'm here to see a relative—Frederick Ayres?"

"Better be quick about it," says the voice, with an impatient sigh. "Visiting hours are coming to a close."

She is directed to the common room—or, according to a sign on the door, the "Scafell Room"—which is decorated in insipid peach; landscapes on the walls the only nod to its alpine name. Kate's stomach turns at the smell—a combination of cooking oil, bleach, and, faintly, urine. Frederick is in the corner, huddled in a wheelchair far away from the other residents. As she approaches, she realizes that he is asleep: his head lolls to one side, eyeballs flickering beneath almost translucent lids.

For a moment, she wonders if she should just leave, come back some other time. But, she knows, there may not be another time—the baby will be here soon, passing into the world just as Frederick is fading out of it.

This could be her only chance to get some answers.

She lowers herself into the chair next to his, leans forward.

"Hello?" she says softly. "Frederick?"

Slowly, his eyes open. At first, they look clouded, unfocused, but then they widen in horror. She touches the lapel of her jacket, remembering his previous reaction to the bee brooch—but it's not there, it's in her pocket. Then she realizes. He's looking at her necklace. Aunt Violet's necklace.

He arches back in her chair and—Kate's heart stops—screams.

"Get away!" he shrieks, spittle flying towards her. "You're supposed to be gone!"

An orderly comes running—young, cheeks bright with acne, peach scrubs loose on his thin frame.

"There, there, Freddie, old mate," he says. "Let's take you back to your room." He glares at Kate as he steers Frederick's wheelchair into the corridor.

"What'd you do, to upset him like that?" The orderly throws over his shoulder.

"I—nothing," she says, still stunned by Frederick's outburst.

"Hold on, are you that woman he's always talking about? Valerie or something?"

"Violet?"

"That's right. Look, I don't know what happened between you two, but he's not stopped going on about you since he got here. What are you, his granddaughter?"

"No, I—"

"So you're not even family. Honestly, miss, I think you should go. It's Saturday. Visiting hours end at 4 P.M. anyway."

Kate can hear the orderly reassuring Frederick as he is wheeled away.

"You're all right, mate. Just a little scare."

"But it was her." She hears him take a great, shuddering breath. "She's the one who sent them. The one who sent the insects."

Fresh snow begins to fall as Kate drives home from Ivy Gate.

She's so distracted that she stalls the car twice. Luckily, there's barely any traffic in the valley. Both times, before she manages to get the car started again, panic snakes its way up through her body, gaining intensity as it passes through her stomach, her heart, her throat.

He thinks Violet was responsible for the infestation.

She remembers something else he said, when she went to Orton Hall. That the insects had died last August.

Just like Violet.

It is snowing harder now, the air so thick with it that she can barely see the road. The radio sputters with static, and she turns up the sound to catch the weather forecast. "Heavy snowfall . . ." a man is saying. "Disruption while traveling . . ." The signal is lost.

In her gut, panic blooms. She shouldn't have come. What if she's put the baby in danger?

She is driving past the woods, the trees sugared with ice. The woods. Where she'd felt such unease, before her unsettling visit to Orton Hall. Fear bubbles in her chest, the steering wheel suddenly slick under her hands. She remembers the claustrophobia of those tightly packed trees, the way they'd blocked out the light.

Kate forces herself to look straight ahead, at the reflective lines of the road curving ahead of her, away from the wood, disappearing into a haze of white. The wind roars. She needs to turn the fog lights on so that she can see better, but in her terror, she can't remember how. Her fingers slip and fumble on the wheel and the dashboard, and she takes her eyes off the road briefly. There. She's found the button. She lifts her eyes back to the road and the twin beams illuminate the remains of an animal—matted, bloodied fur; pale limbs—strewn across the road. The blood impossibly bright against the snow.

She screams. She loses control of the wheel. The car careens forward, and the noise of the trees scraping against the roof and smacking the windshield is deafening.

Everything goes white.

Kate's heart pounds in her chest. It takes her a moment to realize that she has crashed into the woods, that the front seat of the car is littered with ice, with glass from the windshield.

The wind howls through the jagged edges of the windshield. Kate shivers. She is so cold.

Oh God. *The baby.*

She places her hands over her stomach, willing her child to show her some sign of life.

Please. Kick. Let me know you're OK.

But there is nothing.

She needs to get help. Wincing at a bolt of pain in her shoulder, she twists to reach for her phone on the passenger seat. *Please God, don't let it be broken.*

She exhales with relief when she sees that the screen is intact. Relief turns to horror when, unlocking it, she sees only one bar of reception; it flickers for a moment, then disappears.

Shit.

She thinks she's about five miles from the cottage; the road loops around the fells in long, lazy circles, adding extra distance. The direct route, across the fells, is shorter. Two miles, no more, she thinks.

At this hour, while the light dims in the sky, the woods seem so black and thick that it feels as if the car has been swallowed up by a beast and has come to rest in its rib cage. She imagines the dark stretch of trees, a spine running across the land.

She could wait by the side of the road, see if someone drives past. Then she remembers how quiet it is here, how she hasn't seen a single other car for the entire journey back from Ivy Gate. And no one is going to take to the roads in a blizzard. She could be waiting till morning. It's already so cold in the car with the broken windshield. People die of exposure in situations like this, don't they?

She doesn't have a choice. If she wants to get home before night falls, she'll have to walk.

She pushes the car door open, scraping against branches, gasping as the cold hits her.

Snowflakes sting her face as she makes her way back to the road, stumbling over icy tree roots and clogs of mud. The road is dusted white. There is the body of the animal—it is a hare, she sees now—splayed out and flattened. She can't take the road, not unless she wants to risk sharing its fate.

She turns back to the woods, the leaves hissing with the wind.

There's only one way home.

CHAPTER THIRTY-SEVEN

ALTHA

When five days had passed, I collected the mixture from the attic and strained it. As I bottled it, I saw that it was a clear amber color, like the waters of the beck.

Two nights later, Grace came, as she had said she would. I remember it was a clear night, and the moon hung bright in the sky. This time, Grace wore a shawl wound tight around her neck and chin, so that only her eyes were visible, flashing beneath her cap.

She would not come in.

"Are you quite well?" I asked, for she was a strange sight, with her face half covered like a bandit.

"Yes," she said, her voice muffled by the shawl. "Do you have the tincture?"

"It will be painful," I said as I gave it to her. "It will bring on cramps and blood. And with the blood, the beginnings of the babe. Will you tell John it is a miscarriage?"

"I will burn the remains. John cannot know," she said. "How soon will it take effect?"

"In a matter of hours, I should think," I said. "But I cannot be sure."

"Thank you. I will take it tomorrow night, while he is at the alehouse. His sleep is restless tonight—I must be getting back quickly."

She turned to go.

"Will you—will you let me know that you are well?" I asked. "That it has worked?"

"I will try to come another night and tell you."

She walked away quickly, taking care to open the gate so that it did not creak, although there was no one around for miles.

I passed the next days and nights in a state of distraction. In the evenings, I flinched at the slightest of sounds, then lay restless on my pallet until the night sky paled with dawn.

On the Wednesday, Mary Dinsdale, the baker's wife, came to see me about a cut on her hand.

"Have you heard the news from the village?" she asked, as I dressed the wound with honey.

My heart jolted. I was sure she was going to tell me that Grace had died, but it was just that the Merrywether widower was engaged to be married.

The following night, there was a knock on my door.

It was Grace. This time, her face was uncovered—she wasn't even wearing her cap—and when I raised my candle, I flinched at the sight of it. The skin around her right eye was swollen pink and shiny, her bottom lip bruised and torn. There was a smear of blood on her chin, and bright flecks of it on her collar. I noticed faint yellow marks on her neck.

I led her inside and she sat slowly at the table. I put a pot of water on the fire and gathered some rags so that I could clean the cut on her lip and soothe the swelling of her eye. When the water had warmed, I combined it with ground cloves and sage for a poultice. Once this was ready I knelt next to her and applied it to her wounds, as gently as I could.

"Grace. What has happened?" I said quietly.

"I took the draught last night," she said, her eyes on the floor. "As soon as he had set off for the alehouse. Some nights when he drinks, he comes home early and falls asleep by the kitchen fire. Other times, he is out much later, and when he comes home he is . . . without his senses.

"It would have been easier if he had come home early and fallen asleep until morning. I could have stayed up in the bedchamber and, when it was over, burned my shift. I have two others so perhaps he would not have noticed. I would have just needed to take care not to bloody the bedclothes.

"But he didn't come home. Not for hours. The pain was so much worse than I thought it would be, so early. You should have warned me. It felt as if the babe was gripping at me from the inside, fighting the draught . . . so much pain caused by such a small thing. When it came out, it didn't even look like a baby at all, or anything living that I have ever seen. Just a mass of flesh, like something one might buy from the butcher . . ." She was crying now.

"I was getting ready to throw it on the fire when he returned. I thought that maybe he would be too drunk to know what he was looking at. But he was not. I told him that I had lost it—I had hidden the tincture bottle—and he was angry. As I knew he would be. He hit me, as you can see. Though compared to the other times, he was almost merciful."

She laughed that dry, crackling laugh again, but her eyes shone with tears.

"Grace," I said. "Do you mean to say that he has—he has been even rougher with you than this?"

"Oh, yes," she said. "After I labored—twice—and gave him a blue corpse instead of a bonny, bouncing son."

I was silent. She looked up and saw the shock in my face.

"I made sure no one knew I was pregnant, the second time," she said. "I tightened my stays over the bump and, when I got bigger, took care to see as few people as I could. In case it happened again. Then—afterwards—Doctor Smythson was sworn to secrecy. John didn't want anyone to know that his wife had a poison womb."

"I am so sorry, Grace. I wish you had come to me. Perhaps I could have helped."

She laughed again.

"There's no helping it," she said. "Doctor Smythson says he cannot find the reason. But it makes sense to me—God could not mean for a living child to be brought into the world by such an ugly act."

She looked away, staring into the fire.

"That is why I came to you," she said. "I thought that if it happened again—if this baby were dead like the others—he might kill me."

I didn't know what to say. I looked at her as she watched the fire. Without her cap, I could see that her hair, which had been bright as poppies when we were young, had darkened into a deep auburn.

"I am sorry about the baby," she said softly. "It was innocent. I tried not to let it get to that stage. Each night, after he—after he has been in me, I wait until he has fallen asleep and take care to wash away his seed. But it was not enough."

"It is not your fault," I said. I knew the words sounded hollow. Really, I did not know how to bring her comfort. I had never lain with a man. In church, the rector said that the physical union between a husband and wife was sacred and holy. There was nothing sacred about what Grace had described.

"I do not want to talk anymore," she said. "I am tired. May I sleep here?"

"Of course," I said, reaching over to take her hand in mine. She flinched at my touch and her grasp was limp, defeated.

We lay curled together on my pallet like kittens. On the pillow, my dark hair mingled with her reddish strands. I could tell from the rhythm of her breathing that she was close to sleep. I drank in the smell of her—milk and tallow—as if I could keep it with me always.

I remembered, then, a sun-warmed day from childhood. We had been very small, so small that we were not allowed to wander far alone. My mother had been watching us, but we crept out of the garden when her back was turned and followed the beck all the way to a green meadow, bright and soft with wildflowers. Weary from play, we had curled up together on the grass. There, with the bees droning gently and the air sweet with pollen, we had fallen asleep in each other's arms.

I thought of the bruises on my friend's skin and tears wet my cheeks.

"Grace," I whispered. "There could be another way."

I wasn't sure that she heard what I said next, but I felt her hand reach for mine in the darkness.

When I woke the next morning, she was gone.

CHAPTER THIRTY-EIGHT

VIOLET

Violet was roused by the sound of footsteps. She had stayed up until dawn reading Altha Weyward's manuscript. The candle had burned right down, leaving a moon of wax on the floor. She felt as if something had shifted inside her. As if she had been told something about herself that she had always known. One by one, memories fell into place, revealing their true form. The day of the bees. The *click* of Goldie's pincers in her ear. The way she had felt the first time she had touched Morg's feather.

Her legacy.

Father was in the kitchen, bearing provisions and a tight expression. Violet felt as if she were seeing him clearly for the first time in her life.

The treasured picture of her parents' wedding day—their faces shining with love, the air bright with flower petals—dissolved.

He had never loved her mother. Not properly.

Deep down, Violet had known this all along. She'd only let herself be fooled by the fact that he'd held on to those things of her mother's—the feather and the handkerchief—since her death.

But she had been wrong. They weren't treasured mementos of a beloved wife much mourned. They were trophies. Like the tusk, the ibex head . . . even Percy the peacock.

Her mother had been little better than a fox, to be discarded after the hunt, broken and bloodied.

251

She remembered the look on her father's face the day of the bees, when his cane split her palm in two. At the time she had thought it was fury. But now she knew better. It was fear. All along, he'd recognized that she was her mother's daughter, had known what she was capable of. That was why he had hidden her away, forbidden her from learning about Elizabeth and Elinor. About who she really was.

And as for Father himself?

He was a murderer.

Violet watched him as he lined new tins up on the table. It was a warm day, and his forehead was pearled with sweat. The blood vessel on his cheek had burst into a red spider's web. He spoke and Violet watched his jowls tremble.

"Frederick has sent a telegram," he said. "He has agreed to marry you. He has been granted a week of leave in September. We'll have the wedding breakfast at the Hall. You'll be able to stay for a while, afterwards. The engagement will be announced in *The Times* next week."

Violet said nothing. The sight of him was making her ill. He was her only surviving parent, but she would have been happy never to see him again for as long as she lived.

Thankfully, after delivering the news, Father didn't linger. He left without saying goodbye. She closed her eyes in relief at the sound of the key turning in the lock.

Now she could think.

She pictured a life with Frederick. The memory of the woods—the crushed primrose flower, the searing pain—came back to her.

I trust you enjoyed yourself?

She wouldn't—*couldn't*—marry him. Perhaps she wouldn't have to, she thought desperately. Perhaps he would die in the war. But Violet had the awful feeling that he'd survive, like a cockroach clinging to the underside of a rock. Meanwhile, his spore would continue to grow inside her. The thought of his flesh mingled with her own made her want to retch. And then, once it—the child, though she refused to think of it in those terms— had slithered out of her and into the world, Frederick would come to claim them both.

What would become of her then? She thought of her mother, who had married the man who swooned over her dark eyes and bloodred lips. Who had ended up alone in a locked room, scratching her name into a wall so that there would be some evidence that she had existed, before suffering a gruesome, painful death.

Violet would not let that happen to her.

The child was the only reason for Frederick to marry her, surely. *That* was his obligation and interest, the rope that tied them together. A noose, shackling her from the inside.

Violet saw things clearly now. She had to cut the rope.

The manuscript. *Bringing on the menses. Menses.* The same strange word that Doctor Radcliffe had used for her monthly blood.

Outside, the garden shimmered with heat. She waded through the helleborine, its flowers leaving crimson smears on her dress. The air hummed with insects, the sun catching on the wings of a damselfly. Violet smiled, remembering the words from her mother's letter.

Walls painted yellow as tansy flowers.

It was as if she was reaching out to her from beyond the grave, guiding her.

She found the plant under the sycamore, bobbing with yellow flowers, each one comprised of tiny buds clustered together like a beetle's eggs.

It had worked for Grace. There was no reason why it wouldn't work for her, too.

CHAPTER THIRTY-NINE

KATE

Kate draws her hood over her head as she steps into the woods. Here, the wind is quieter; the close-knit trees arching around to protect her from the elements.

But still she shivers, panting with fear—her breath a white cloud in front of her.

The silence is unnerving. She can hear nothing but the blizzard. Suddenly, she longs for the sight of an owl, or a robin—even the flutter of a moth. Anything but this white, deadened world.

Snowflakes swirl around her, landing in icy bursts on her exposed skin. She wishes she had some gloves. Instead, she draws the sleeves of her sweater down over her hands, winds her scarf around her nose and mouth. Her eyes water from the cold.

There is a crack in one of her boots—an old pair of Aunt Violet's that she's been meaning to get resoled—and now the snow seeps in, drenching her foot.

She pushes through the trees, all the while forcing herself not to think about the baby, about the stillness in her womb. She has to get to the village. She has to get help.

After a while, the trees all begin to look the same, with their branches quivering under matching lips of snow. She is no longer sure which is the right direction. A ladder of pink fungus creeps up a tree trunk in a way that looks horribly familiar, and she is seized by the fear that she has passed it before.

Is she walking in circles? Awful images flood her mind: her body, curled on the forest floor, barely visible under its shroud of snow. Her child frozen inside her, tiny bones calcifying in her womb. She stumbles over a tree root and cries out, her voice dying in the wind.

Something answers.

At first she thinks she must be dreaming, like a lost traveler hallucinating a mirage in the desert.

Then she hears it again. A bird, calling.

It's real.

She looks up, breathing hard as she scans the canopy of trees. Something shimmers. A liquid eye. Blue-black feathers, dusted white.

A crow.

Panic flickers, but fades.

Something else is there, closer than ever, on the other side of her fear. That strange warmth she felt in Aunt Violet's garden, when the insects rose from the earth. She pushes through her panic, breaches the wall to find the light, the spark she holds inside.

It reaches her veins, hums in her blood. Her nerves—in her ear canals, in the pads of her fingers, even the surface of her tongue—pulse and glow.

The knowledge comes from deep within her, some hidden place she has long buried.

If she wants to live, she has to follow the crow.

After a while, she sees a grayness ahead of her, feels wind on her face. The woods are almost like a tunnel, she thinks. A tunnel of trees. She is coming to the end of it.

Up ahead, there is a gap in the trunks. Beyond it, she can see the steep rise of the hill, like the haunches of an enormous animal, furred pale with snow. Crouched and waiting.

She has done it. She has made it through the woods.

———

On the hill, she feels so exposed that she almost wishes for the claustro-phobia of the woods. The wind whips her face and takes the sound from her ears. Her lips and nose sting with the cold.

The crow is still there. Flying above her in blue-black loops. She can barely hear its guttural call above the rush of the wind in her ears.

At the crest of the hill, she can see the orange glimmer of the vil-lage below. Coming down is easier: she is sheltered from the wind, now. Her hands and face feel raw, and a blister throbs on one heel. But the snow is gentle on her face. And she is almost back at the cottage. Almost home.

She looks up. The clouds have parted to reveal a smattering of stars, bright in the dusk. She watches the crow and feels no fear—instead, she is struck by its beauty as it glides away, the light gray on its feathers.

She has been afraid of crows since the day of her father's death. Since she saw the velvet flash of wings, dark in the summer sky.

Since the day she became a monster.

But she *isn't* a monster, and never was. She was a child—just nine years old—with nothing in her heart but love and wonder. For the birds that made arrows in the sky, for the pink coils of earthworms in the soil, for the bees that hummed through the summer. Her throat aches as she reaches into her pocket, fingers closing around the bee brooch. She holds it up to the night and it is as radiant as the stars. Almost as if it had never been damaged at all.

She remembers the strength in her father's hands, pushing her to safety. The last time he ever touched her. He died for her, the same way she would die for her child. Hot tears stream down her cheeks. She isn't sure who they are for—the little girl who watched her father die, or the woman who spent twenty long years blaming herself for his death.

"It wasn't my fault," she says out loud, acknowledging the truth of it for the first time. "It was an accident."

The crow wheels right, disappearing into the distance, one final cry echoing.

"The baby's fine," says Dr. Collins later, her open features creasing into a smile. She is crouched by Kate's stomach, listening intently to her stethoscope.

"Are you sure?" asks Kate. She hasn't felt her daughter move since the car accident, since stumbling into the GP surgery, shivering from cold. The awful image rears up again—her child frozen in the womb, tiny fingers curled closed.

"Here, have a listen," says the doctor, passing her the stethoscope.

There it is, the thrum of her child's heartbeat. Relief floods her body; tears burn behind her eyes.

"Like I said before," says Dr. Collins, "this one's a fighter."

"Are you sure you'll be OK until your mother gets here?" Emily is loitering in the doorway of the cottage. Her husband, Mike, waiting in the car, beeps the horn.

It is a bright day; the snow-topped hedges sparkle in the sun. Kate watches as a waxwing forages for rowan berries, its crest quivering. It chirps as it is joined by its mate. Starlings sweep overhead, making shapes in the sky.

"Positive. Thanks so much for everything." Emily has stocked the fridge with all the food Kate could possibly need—microwaveable meals, bread, milk. She's brought diapers and a blow-up mattress for Kate's mother to sleep on. She and her husband even arranged for her car to be towed to a garage in Beckside. Kate doesn't know how to thank them enough.

"All right, well, you just let me know as soon as anything happens! Soon as there's even the hint of a contraction, I want to know about it!" Emily gets into her car and waves goodbye, and Kate feels a pang of sadness for her friend, as she remembers what Emily said to her on Bonfire Night.

I had a baby, once.

She still can't quite believe that she—they—escaped the accident unscathed. Each day since, she's braced herself for crisis: for pain in her gut, blooms of blood on her underwear. But everything has been fine; the baby is moving again, wriggling and fluttering inside her. In the evenings, Kate watches the surface of her stomach ripple, marveling at a tiny foot protruding here, a little hand there.

That she will soon hold her child in her arms feels nothing short of miraculous. Kate wonders what color her eyes will be, after they've changed from newborn blue. What she'll smell like.

Her mother's flight leaves tomorrow. Once she arrives, she'll get the train from London, then hire a car so that they'll be able to get to the hospital when the baby comes.

She only has one more day to herself. As she drifts around the cottage, aimlessly touching surfaces, picking things up and putting them down again, she wonders what her mother will make of it. Of the framed sketches of insects, the centipede preserved behind glass. Of the corner of the bedroom she's prepared for the baby; the secondhand cot, draped with Violet's old shawls for blankets. The handmade mobile, twirling with leaves and feathers, the glittering bee brooch now the centerpiece.

And of Kate herself—her cropped hair, the strange outfits she pulls together from her great-aunt's wardrobe. Today she has thrown the beaded cape around her shoulders—the twinkling of its beads reminds her of the time she met Aunt Violet. It helps her feel ready to bring her daughter into the world. Ready to protect her, at all costs. She will be strong, just like Violet was.

You remind me of her so much, Emily had said. *You have her spirit.*

Kate touches the *W* pendant around her neck. She thinks of the insects that rose from the soil of Aunt Violet's garden. The birds that have flocked to the cottage since her arrival, as if to greet her. Even now, she can hear the hoarse cries of crows from the sycamore, where they throng its snow-covered branches, darkest jet against white. She thinks of her experience in the woods. That humming feeling in her blood; the crow that led her home.

She thinks, also, of the things she's heard about Violet: of her fearlessness; her love of insects and other creatures. The infestation at Orton Hall.

Mother of beetles.

And of Altha Weyward, tried for witchcraft. Kate still doesn't know what became of her—whether she was executed, where she was buried.

But she's been leaving sprigs of mistletoe and ivy by the cross under the sycamore tree. Just in case.

In the evening, Kate is heating one of Emily's meals—homemade tomato soup—when the phone rings. She rushes to get it—thinking it's her mother, maybe, or Emily. Or someone from the doctor's office, calling to check up on her.

"Hello?"

For a moment, Kate hears nothing—only her blood ringing in her ears. Then, that voice. The one she wishes she could forget.

"I've found you."

Simon.

CHAPTER FORTY

ALTHA

G race did not come to the cottage again. I saw her only from a distance, at church, where her husband sat close to her, afterwards holding her arm tight as if he had her on a yoke. Her face was empty under her cap, and if she felt my eyes on her, she did not look up. At least I knew she was alive.

Winter softened into spring, and I counted the days to May Day Eve, when I thought I might have a chance to speak to Grace.

When my mother was alive, we kept our own May Day Eve custom rather than attending the village bonfire. We spent the last days of April gathering moss from the banks of the beck and making a soft, green bed on our doorstep, for the faeries to dance on. Then we lit our own small bonfire and burned offerings of bread and cheese to bless the fields.

When I was a child, I asked my mother why we could not attend the celebrations in the village, where I knew there was music, dancing, and feasting around a towering bonfire on the green.

"May Day Eve is a pagan festival," she said. "It is un-Christian."

"But everyone else from the village attends," I said. "And they are all Christian, are they not?"

"They do not need to be careful like we do," she said.

"Why do we need to be careful?" I asked.

"We are not like the others."

Since my mother's death, I had kept up our tradition. But this was to be the first big village festival since the end of winter, and I wondered if Grace would be there. I needed to know if she was safe and well.

I could smell the smoke from the bonfire as I set off from the cottage. I could see it, too, an orange glow in the distance. When I got to the green, the villagers were dancing in rings around the flame, which threw sparks high into the air with each offering. The night was loud with song and the hiss of burning wood.

The heady smell of ale hung in the air, and many of the villagers looked drunk, their eyes sliding over me as I approached. I looked for Grace but couldn't see her, or her husband. Adam Bainbridge, the butcher's son, grabbed my hands and pulled me into the fray. Around and around we went, until everything became a blur of orange and black. I was beginning to melt into it, to enjoy the crush and heat of other bodies around mine, the feeling of being a part of something bigger than myself.

And then I saw her. A girl, standing alone on the green, shadows dancing over her body. Dressed only in a shift, thighs black with blood. In the dark I could not make out her face, nor the color of her hair, but it was Grace—I was sure of it.

I pushed through the ring of bodies to reach her.

"Grace?" I called.

I was too late. She was gone.

I turned back to the dancing villagers. None of them had seen her, I could tell.

I felt my eyes water, whether from the smoke or tears I did not know. I wanted to go home. I set off towards the cottage when I heard footsteps behind me. I turned to see it was Adam Bainbridge, who had danced with me around the bonfire.

"Where are you going?" he asked.

"Home," I said. "I am not much one for festivals. Good night."

"Not all of us believe it, Altha," he said softly. "You do not need to hide yourself away."

"Believe what?" I asked.

"What they say about you and your mother."

Shame crept up my throat, and I hurried away. I felt relieved as I turned from the light of the bonfire, as the darkness cloaked me from the eyes of the villagers. As I walked on, I listened to the night sounds—the hoot of an owl, the scratching of mice and voles—and felt my breathing slow. I could see well enough—it was a full moon, like it had been the night that Grace had stayed at the cottage.

Grace. She had not really been there, at the bonfire, I knew.

"Sight is a funny thing," my mother used to say. "Sometimes it shows us what is before our eyes. But sometimes it shows us what has already happened, or will yet come to pass."

I barely slept all night, and I rose and dressed as soon as the sky lightened. I made my way to the Milburn farm, and by the time I got there, dawn was breaking over the valley, turning the hills a soft pink.

I kept my distance, lingering under the oak trees on the boundary of the farm—the same place where my mother had released her pet crow, all those years before—so that I would not be seen. I could see the farmhouse now, but not well: there was a slight slope to the earth, which hid some of it away. I needed to be higher.

I bunched my skirts around my waist and began to climb the largest oak—a great, twisted thing that stretched high into the sky as though seeking God. I hadn't climbed a tree since I was a child with Grace, but my hands and feet remembered how to find holds in the curves and knots of the branches. I climbed so high that I could see the sleek forms of crows in the branches, then went no further. I wondered if one of them was the same bird that my mother had cast out. I searched their dark feathers for the sign but could not see it.

Now I could see the farmhouse well, and the cow barn next to it. I watched John leave the farmhouse and open the barn so that the cows spilled out onto the field. I counted a score of them, far more than any other farm in the area, as far as I knew. No doubt some had been Metcalfe cows and had come with Grace as her dowry. I wondered if John would ever beat one of his cows the way he beat his wife.

After a while, I saw Grace come out from the farmhouse, carrying a pail of water and laundry. I felt relief course through me. She was alive. I watched her squat on the ground and scrub the laundry, and, when she was done, hang it on the rope that stretched between the farmhouse and the barn. The white smallclothes shone gold in the early sun. I wondered if she had been washing blood from them.

I saw John cross the field to approach her. She turned her head to him and then looked away, and there was something in the set of her body that made me think of a dog waiting for a kick from its master. I saw him speak to her and they went inside together, she with her head bowed.

I remained for a while, in the tree, watching the farmhouse, but neither of them came out again. The day was growing warmer and brighter. I climbed down, in case someone from the village happened to be passing and looked up to see me.

As I walked home, I wondered what my vision at the bonfire had meant. There had been so much blood, the darkness an open maw between her legs. Had Grace been pregnant again, and miscarried? Or was she pregnant still? I remembered what she had said to me: "If this baby were dead like the others, he might kill me."

May became June, and the days lengthened. The sun lit up the sky for hours, so that I slept and woke in daylight. While I went about my daily tasks, and when I laid my head to rest at night, I thought of Grace. She and John still came to church, and after the sermon, while John spoke to the other villagers, she kept her eyes on the ground. I wondered what she was thinking, if she was well.

I couldn't send a message, for Grace did not know her letters and would not be able to read it. I had thought about walking to the Milburn farm again—to do what, exactly, I did not know—but I was too worried about being seen, now that the nights were so brief. I dared not ask the villagers, who came to my door seeking fixes for hay fever and midge bites, what news they had of John Milburn's wife. The rift between us was well known in Crows Beck. It would raise many an eyebrow for me to ask after her now. They might guess that she had sought my help. I did not dare give her husband another reason to hurt her.

Her husband. I had not known it was possible to hate another person so much. My mother had taught me that each person deserves love, but I will not deny that I would have happily seen Grace a widow, even then.

I remembered with shame how I had thought Grace and John looked well together on their wedding day. How little I understood of anything then.

I had thought that I knew a great deal of people, just because I knew how to dress their wounds and cool their fevers. But I knew nothing of what went on between a husband and wife, the act that made a woman swell with child. I knew nothing of men, other than what my mother had told me. I was always shocked, as a girl, when a man came and sought my mother's treatment. By his size, his deep voice, his meaty hands. The smell that hung about him. Sweat and power.

The leaves darkened and began to fall. A chill returned to the air. One day, I had gone to the market square for meat and bread, when I saw a woman stooped over a table of pig hearts, a red curl escaping from her cap. Grace.

I could not approach her there, in the village square, in front of everyone. I hung back as she had Adam Bainbridge wrap up two pig hearts in cloth, then put them in a woven bag that she slung from her shoulder. I myself bought some bread, watching her from the corner of my eye. Then I followed her, a few paces behind, as she set off down the road to Milburn farm. The trees either side of the road looked stark without their leaves, which glistened red underfoot, wet from weeks of rain. I watched as Grace drew her woolen shawl more tightly around her shoulders.

I was beginning to wonder if she could not hear my footsteps behind her, for she did not turn around. But once we could see the Milburn farmhouse ahead through the trees, she turned.

"Why are you following me?" she asked. More of her red hair had escaped from her cap, and beneath it her face was pale as milk.

"I have not seen you, other than from a distance, for six moons," I said. "I saw you in the village square and . . . I wanted to make sure that you are well. There is no one else on the road, you can speak freely."

At my last words she laughed, but her eyes were blank.

"I am well," she said.

"Are you—have there been . . ."

"I have not been with child again, if that is what you want to know. Not for John's lack of trying."

Her eyes darkened. I took a step closer, to see if there were bruises on her face, like before.

"You will not see any marks on me," she said, as if she had read my thoughts. "Since the last time . . . Mary Dinsdale asked about my lip, after church. Now he takes care to spare my face."

"Have you thought any more on what I said that night?" I asked. She was silent for a while. When she spoke, she looked not at me but up at the sky.

"A man of John's age and health does not just fall down and die, Altha," she said. "Doctor Smythson will know poison when he sees it. Hemlock, nightshade—they will know you had a part in it.

There's no one else in the village who understands plants the way you do. They will hang you. They will hang us both. I do not much care whether I live or die, but I cannot have another death on my conscience. Not even yours."

With these last words, she turned to leave.

"Wait," I said. "Please. I cannot bear to know that you are suffering . . . I could think of something, a way that we would not be discovered . . ."

"I shall speak no more of it," she called over her shoulder. "Go home, Altha. And stay away from me."

I did not go home right away, as she had asked. I watched as her small frame disappeared into the trees. Some time later, a plume of smoke rose from the Milburn farmhouse. I shivered. The day was growing colder, and icy drops of rain began to fall on my face and neck. I walked on, until I reached the oak tree I had climbed to watch the farmhouse. I would not climb it today. The crows sat like watchmen in the upper branches of the tree, and their sharp cries of pain could have been my own.

CHAPTER FORTY-ONE

VIOLET

Five days. Violet worried that she would lose track of the times the sun dipped in the sky and rose again. Here, in the cottage, time followed different rules. There was no gong for dinner, no Miss Poole demanding she conjugate ten French verbs in as many minutes. She spent most of her days in the garden, listening to the birds and the insects, until the sun glowed red on the leaves of the plants.

She could almost imagine that she was already free.

Almost.

At night, she slept with Morg's feather gripped tight in her hand, dreaming of her mother.

Her mother. *Elizabeth Weyward.* She who had given Violet her middle name. Her legacy. She whispered the name out loud, as if it were a spell. It made her feel strong, steeled her for what she had to do next.

On the fifth day, the wind roared and sucked at the cottage, bending the branches of the sycamore so that the leaves looked like they were dancing.

Violet strained the mixture in the kitchen. She used two empty tins to separate the golden liquid from the sodden petals with their smell of rot. She waited until she was in bed to drink it. It was strong and acrid, stinging the back of her throat. Her eyes watered. She lay down and listened to the wind shake the walls of the cottage, waiting for the pain to come.

Gradually, she felt a pulling inside her. It started out like the cramps that came with her monthly curse, dull and pulsing, but soon grew stronger. It was as though there was something inside her, tugging and contorting her innards into strange shapes. Violet tried to find a rhythm to it, to breathe through it as though she were sailing a boat through a churning sea, but there was none. The pain was overwhelming now. The window rattled, and Violet heard the crack of a branch hitting the roof. There was a rushing inside her, a breaking free, and then a great flood.

She marveled that such a bright color could come from her own body. It was like magic, she thought. The blood was still coming: her legs were slick with it. She shut her eyes, reached the crest of the wave. Then she fell.

CHAPTER FORTY-TWO

KATE

Her heart thuds in her chest, fluttering like a trapped moth.

He can't have found her. It isn't possible. Unless—

The email.

Her phone lights up with messages, one after the other.

I'll see you soon.

Very soon.

For a while, she is still; a black hole yawns inside her, swallowing her ability to move, to think . . . then she feels the baby kick.

Everything becomes hyperreal: the sun setting on the snow outside, staining the garden red, the screams of the crows in the sycamore. Her blood, rushing through her veins. All of her senses engaged, heightened.

Quickly, she draws the curtains, bolts the doors, frantically trying to think what to do next. Curtains and locks won't be much use, she knows. Simon will just break a window. If only she had the car. Without it, she's trapped—an insect, quivering and exposed in a spider's web.

She can call the police; call Emily. Ask if she can come and get her. But she might not make it in time. . . . It's Sunday, meaning Emily's at home, at her farm an hour's drive away . . .

The attic. She'll need to hide. She presses a hand to her forehead as she tries to work out what to take with her. She grabs a bottle of water and some fruit and shoves them into her handbag. Her phone, too, so she can call the police. Candles and matches, so she doesn't run the phone battery down using it as a light.

She unlocks the back door again to get the ladder, from where it leans against the back of the house, covered in snow. She tries to lift it, sweat breaking out at her temples as she staggers under its weight.

She heaves the ladder onto its side, dragging it into the house. It is heavy and cobwebbed; a spider trembles on one rusted rung. Grunting, she positions it under the trapdoor and climbs up as quickly as she can, her palms slipping on the rungs.

Once she's at the top, she stares into the dark abyss of the attic. The trapdoor is so small—she hasn't been up here for months. Will she even fit, with her pregnant belly?

Doubt twinges in her gut. She has to try. There's nowhere else she can hide.

At first, she tries to climb into the attic the same way she did before, but her arms aren't strong enough to lift her swollen body through the gap. She shifts position, tries climbing in backwards. The ladder rattles beneath her, and for a moment she fears it will clatter to the floor. She heaves herself in, gasping at a sharp pain in the palm of her hand.

She's cut herself. But she's done it, she's inside the attic.

Kate's heart begins to slow again. But then: the crunch of car tires on gravel outside. She freezes, heart galloping, hands growing slippery with blood and sweat. There's a knock on the door.

God, she should have just called Emily first. Or gone to stay with her in the first place. Simon would never have found her there.

"Kate?" At the sound of his voice, her heart drops into her stomach. "I know you're in there. I just want to talk. Please, let me in." The doorknob rattles, and she hears the creak of old wood as Simon throws his weight against the front door.

The door. She forgot to lock the back door after getting the ladder.

She has to stay hidden. But—fuck, the ladder. He'll see it as soon as he gets in, smack bang in the hallway, like an arrow pointing up to her hiding spot. Why didn't she think of this? Idiot. The panic fizzes in her

chest, threatening to overwhelm her. She closes her eyes and forces herself
to breathe in and out, slowly . . .

Think. Think. She opens her eyes. He's knocking again, harder this time,
punctuated by the thud of his bodyweight against the door. She'll have to
pull the ladder up inside the attic. It's the only option. She switches on the
torch of her phone. The old bureau is behind her. She hooks one leg around
it to anchor herself, praying that Simon won't hear, then shifts onto her side,
before lowering her upper body through the trapdoor.

The blood rushes to her head, pounding like the sea. She grabs the
ladder and pulls, wincing at the pain in her hand. *Come on, Kate. Come on.*
Half the ladder is inside the attic now. Thank God there's so much room
in here. She scoots as far back into the attic as she can, tugging hard on
the ladder. She can hear Simon pacing outside, occasionally pausing. She
imagines him peering through the windows, looking for her.

Kate wonders how many seconds she has until he makes his way to the
back of the house and tries the door. Five; ten if she's lucky. Her arms burn,
and there's a scraping sound as she finally pulls the rest of the ladder inside.
She yanks the trapdoor shut just in time to hear the back door swing open.

CHAPTER FORTY-THREE

VIOLET

Violet was in the beech tree, looking down at the valley. Far below, the beck glinted like a golden thread. She could see the wood, a bruise on the land. Then air rushed at her. She was flying—away, far away.

The dream faded, and Violet swam up to consciousness. Outside, the wind had died down to a low whistle. The blankets were sodden with blood.

I began to dream of her, grown into a dark-haired beauty, but alone and bleeding in our cottage.

This was the fate her mother had foreseen. The fate her mother had done everything—had laid down her life—to alter. All in vain.

The candle was still burning, the flame quivering blue. Violet was cold, so very cold.

She lifted the candle and pushed back the covers.

It had worked.

There was nothing of Frederick inside her anymore. She was free.

It took her a long time to stand up. Her legs felt weak, and the room kept slipping in and out of focus. She was so tired. Perhaps she should lie back down and sleep, she thought. Close her eyes and return to the beech tree, feel the sun and wind on her face. But the *thing*, the thing that had come from Frederick—she had to get rid of it.

She felt her way into the other room, gripping the cool stone of the wall. She needed water, food. Her fingers shook as she cupped water from the bucket and drank. It took an age to open one of the tins of Spam. Her hand slipped and the metal sliced into her palm, the blood welling up in bright drops. Her head buzzed and she sat down at the table heavily. The blood on her nightdress was beginning to crust and darken into brown peaks and swirls, like a map.

The Spam gleamed pale and wet in the tin. It made her think of the spore. She pushed it away. The wind had picked up again and she sat for a while, listening. The wind had a peculiar high pitch to it, almost like a human voice. *Violet*, it seemed to say. *Violet*.

CHAPTER FORTY-FOUR

KATE

Kate puts her hand to her mouth, tasting blood.

Below her, the floorboards creak as Simon stalks through the cottage.

"Kate?" he calls. "I know you're in here. Come on, Kate, you can't hide from me."

She can hear him opening cupboards then slamming them shut again. There is the crash of porcelain on wood from the kitchen. He swears loudly.

She listens to the click of the back door opening. He's looking for her in the garden again. Kate takes the opportunity to light some candles, fingers trembling. The shapes of the attic emerge under the orange glow of the guttering flames. The bureau. The shelves, with their glass jars of insects. Being surrounded by Aunt Violet's things makes her feel a little bit stronger.

She needs the police. She pulls her phone from her pocket and dials 999, listening for the sound of him coming back into the house. The reception in the attic is patchy and the connection drops out after the first ring.

Swearing under her breath, she tries again.

"Emergency, which service do you require?"

She opens her mouth to speak. The back door clicks again.

"Hello? Which service do you require?"

The footsteps are in the hallway now. They stop. She hangs up the phone. There is no sound other than the beat of her heart in her ears. Kate thinks he must be directly beneath her. She is gulping at the air now, her breathing fast and ragged. What if he can hear it?

He must be looking at the trapdoor. Wondering what it leads to. Wondering if it leads to her. Tears sting her eyes as she remembers all the times he's hurt her. She touches the scar on her arm. All those years she's lost. Six years of cowering from him, of letting him tell her she is stupid, incompetent. Worthless. The fear is replaced by a hot bolt of fury.

He's not going to hurt her again. He's not. She won't let him.

And she won't let him anywhere *near* her child.

The footsteps start again. She hears him walk into the sitting room. There's a faint creak as he settles onto the sofa. She can picture him, staring at the window, waiting for her to come home.

Kate shifts position, slowly and carefully. She looks at her phone: the reception bar flickers. She needs to get help—she should have dialed 999 as soon as she saw those messages, but her mind was too blurred by panic, by the need to hide. And now it's too late for her to call. He'll hear her, and discover her hiding spot.

She wipes her bloodied hand on her trousers, then types out a quick text to Emily.

Please can you call police. Abusive ex-boyfriend at cottage. Hiding in attic.

Kate holds her breath.

Message failed to send.

She tries to re-send it, greeted again and again by that cold, impersonal sentence.

She's on her own.

There must be something in the attic she can use to defend herself. Something she can use as a weapon. If only she'd thought to grab the fire poker from the sitting room.

She lifts one of the candles and looks around, searching for a crowbar, a hockey stick . . . anything.

The candlelight passes over the bureau, catching on its golden handles.

She sees something that she didn't notice before.

She crawls to the bureau, as slowly and quietly as she can, sucking in her breath.

There is a *W* carved onto the handle of the locked drawer.

She pulls the necklace out from under her shirt, slips it off. The engravings match.

Kate runs her fingers over the pendant. There is a tiny bump at the bottom of the pendant, barely visible. She presses it, holding her breath. Nothing happens.

She presses it again.

This time, the pendant springs open with a snap. Not a pendant after all. A locket. Inside is a rolled piece of paper. She lifts it out carefully, revealing the small golden key.

The paper looks white and fresh, as if it has been placed there recently. She unrolls it, heart thumping in her chest.

The handwriting has changed: become more refined, elegant, but still she recognizes the spidery loops from the note she found in the Brothers Grimm book.

Aunt Violet.

I hope she can help you as she helped me. That is all it says. No reference to who the mysterious "she" might be. But as she carefully turns the key in the lock, Kate thinks that she knows already.

She eases the drawer out, little by little, terrified that it will creak and alert Simon to her presence. She doesn't breathe until the drawer is open enough for her to see inside.

A book.

She lifts it out of the drawer, inhaling the scent of age and must. As she holds the book in her hands, she hears the first drops of rain fall on the roof.

The leather cover is worn and soft. It looks old. Centuries old.

She opens it. The paper—it isn't paper, she sees now, but parchment—is delicate. Diaphanous, like an insect's wings.

The writing is faded and cramped, so that at first it is illegible. She holds the candle closer, watches the words form. Her heart beats faster as she reads the first line.

"Ten days they'd held me there . . ."

CHAPTER FORTY-FIVE

ALTHA

I have not written this last day. Yesterday, I came to my parchment and ink, but the words could not come.

Last night, I dreamed of my mother, her words as she lay on her deathbed. Then, I dreamed that I was back in the dungeon at Lancaster, the shadow of death hanging over me. When I woke safe in my bed to the morning birdsong, I nearly cried with relief. Then I wrapped myself in my shawl and sat down to write.

To tell the story, as it really happened, I must put things down on this page that my mother would not have wanted me to. Things that she told me were not to be spoken of, with anyone, or they would risk our exposure. I must speak of the promise I made, and how I broke it.

I have decided that I will lock these papers away and see to it that they are not read until I have left this earth and joined my mother in the next life. Perhaps I will leave them to my daughter. I like the thought of that: a long line of Weyward women, stretching after me. For the first child born to a Weyward is always female, my mother told me. That is why she only had me, just as her mother only had her. There are enough men in the world already, she used to say.

I was fourteen, still weak from my first blood, when she told me what it really meant to be a Weyward. It was autumn, a twelvemonth since the couple had come in the middle of the night, since my mother had cast out her crow. Even longer since that last, precious summer with Grace.

My mother and I had been walking in the woods at dusk, gathering mushrooms, when we came across a rabbit in a trap. Its poor body was torn and bloodied, but it was still alive, the eyes flickering with pain. I knelt down, muddying the dress that my mother had laundered only the previous day, and brushed my little fingers against its flank. Its fur felt wet, the heartbeat faint and slow under its skin. I could feel that it feared death, but also welcomed it. The end to suffering. The natural way of things.

My mother looked about her, scanning the dark shapes of the trees as if to be sure we were alone. Then, she crouched next to me and put her hand over mine.

"Be at peace," she said. I felt the heartbeat fade beneath our fingers, watched the light flicker from the eyes. The rabbit was gone, freed from this world. It had nothing to fear of traps and hunters now.

We walked home in silence. Already then, she was weakening: her back, which had always been straight, was curving inwards, her long plait of hair was dry as grass. I took her arm and rested it on my shoulders, so that I might support her weight.

When we were home, and night was falling over our garden outside, she sat me at the table while the stew warmed on the fire. I have set down the words she then spoke to me as best as I can recall them, though the memory grows dimmer with each passing year.

She said that there was something I needed to learn, now that I had passed into womanhood. But I must not speak of it to anyone.

I had nodded, hungry at the thought of sharing a secret with my mother. At the thought of understanding at last the pull I felt inside me, the golden thread that seemed to connect me to the spiders that climbed the walls of our cottage, the moths and damselflies that fluttered in the garden. To the crows that my mother had raised for as long as I could remember, the gleam of their eyes in the dark chasing away my childhood nightmares.

I had nature in my heart, she said. Like she did, and her mother before her. There was something about us—the Weyward women—that bonded us more tightly with the natural world. We can feel it, she said, the same way we feel rage, sorrow, or joy. The animals, the birds, the plants—they let us in, recognizing us as one of their own. That is why roots and leaves yield so easily under our fingers, to form tonics that bring comfort and healing. That is why animals welcome our embrace. Why the crows—the ones who carry the sign—watch over us and do our bidding, why their touch brings our abilities into sharpest relief. Our ancestors—the women who walked these paths before us, before there were words for who they were—did not lie in the barren soil of the churchyard, encased in rotting wood. Instead, the Weyward bones rested in the woods, in the fells, where our flesh fed plants and flowers, where trees wrapped their roots around our skeletons. We did not need stone-masons to carve our names into rock as proof we had existed.

All we needed was to be returned to the wild.

This wildness inside gives us our name. It was men who marked us so, in the time when language was but a shoot curling from the earth. Weyward, they called us, when we would not submit, would not bend to their will. But we learned to wear the name with pride.

For it has always been a gift, she said. Until now.

She told me of other women, across the land—like those the couple from Clitheroe had spoken of, the Devices and the Whittles—who had died for having such gifts. Or for simply being suspected of having them. The Weyward women had lived safely in Crows Beck these last hundred years, and in that time had healed its people. We had brought them into the world and held their hands as they left it. We could use our ability to heal without attracting too much suspicion. The people were grateful for this gift.

But our other gift—the bond we have with all creatures—is far more dangerous, she told me. Women had perished—in flames, or at the rope—for keeping close company with animals, whom jealous men labeled "familiars." This was why she had to banish her crow, the bird that had shared our home for so many years. Her voice cracked as she spoke of it.

And so she made me promise: I was not to use this gift, this wildness inside. I could use my healing skills to put food in my belly, but I must stay away from living creatures, from moths and spiders and crows. Doing otherwise would risk my life.

Perhaps one day, she said, there would be a safer time. When women could walk the earth, shining bright with power, and yet live. But until then I should keep my gift hidden, move through only the darkest corners of the world, like a beetle through soil.

And if I did this, I may survive. Long enough to carry on the line, to take a man's seed from him and no more. Not his name, nor his love, which could put me at risk of discovery.

I had not known, then, what she meant by seed; I had thought a seed was something to be put in the ground, rather than inside a woman. I imagined the next Weyward girl, who would one day grow inside me, blooming into life.

When my mother lay dying three years later, on that awful night when our few candles were no match for the darkness that stole into the room, she reminded me of my promise with her last breath.

I had heeded her words for so long. But after speaking to Grace that day after the market, I felt the first desire to disobey them. The first desire to break my promise.

CHAPTER FORTY-SIX

VIOLET

"Violet!" said the voice again. It really did sound like a human voice. Violet wondered if she were hallucinating; surely it was dangerous to lose so much blood. There was a tapping sound. She looked up. She saw—or at least, she thought she saw—a face at the window. Pale and moonlike, with a shock of ginger hair.

She opened the back door, and Graham was silhouetted against the garden. Behind him the helleborine rippled in the wind, a dark red sea.

"Christ," Graham was saying. He was looking down at her nightgown, at the black stain that bloomed between her legs. Violet wanted to scuttle away from him and hide, as if she were an animal in its death throes. Graham kept talking but she had a hard time understanding the words. She could see his mouth moving and knew that sounds were coming out of it, but they seemed to float away before she could catch them, like the downy husk of a dandelion.

Graham was inside the cottage.

"For the love of God, Violet," he said. "Sit down."

He picked up a candle from the table and walked towards the bedroom, his face grim in the flickering light.

"Don't," she said weakly, but it was too late.

"Jesus Christ," she heard him say again.

There was a rustling sound, and Graham reappeared, holding the bundle of bloodied sheets away from him. His white face looked guilty, as though he were carrying something dead. He *was* carrying something dead, Violet remembered.

"I don't want to look at it," she said.

"We'll have to bury it," said Graham. He stood for a moment, watching her. "I found your note," he said. "I was in your room, looking for my biology book. It was poking out of that book of fairy tales you used to love."

"The Brothers Grimm," she said softly.

Graham nodded. "Then Father told me that you and Frederick were engaged. After reading about . . . after I read the note, I knew that you didn't want to marry him. I was going to visit you in Windermere—in the sanatorium—to check if you were all right. But then I heard Father on the telephone in his study last night . . . he was talking to Doctor Radcliffe about you. Then . . . he gave him this address, so this afternoon I told Father I was going for a walk . . . and I came here instead."

He looked around as he spoke, taking in the dim, low-ceilinged room. "God knows what this place is," he said.

Violet said nothing, but there was a twist of dread in her stomach. Father speaking to Doctor Radcliffe . . . giving him this address . . . she knew that wasn't good, but she couldn't think why it was so bad, exactly. Her brain felt thick, sluglike, the same way it had felt that afternoon in the woods with Frederick, after all that brandy. Before he—

"What happened to the baby, Violet?" Graham's voice was low. "Did you take something? Something to make the baby go away?"

"*Bring on the menses,*" Violet said.

"Violet, are you listening to me? You have to tell me if you took something. Doctor Radcliffe is coming here, today. He's meeting Father here. They could arrive any minute. If you did take something . . . you need to tell me. We've got to get rid of the evidence. It's a crime, Violet. They could put you away for life."

The dread in her stomach again.

"Tansy petals," she said. "Steep in water for five days before administration . . ."

"Right," said Graham. He put the bundled bedsheets down on the floor and went back into the bedroom. The door burst open and the wind roared through it, unfurling the bundle to reveal a gleam of pale flesh. Violet was gripped by the awful fear that the spore would reanimate and slither up inside her again. She couldn't bear it. She turned around to face the wall.

Graham returned, holding the tin that she'd prepared the tansy mixture in. She could smell it, dank and cloying. He took the tin and the bundle outside. Violet heard the first hiss of rain on the roof, and watched it trickle down from the hole in the ceiling. She wanted to get up, to stand in the garden and let the rain wash her clean, but she was too tired to move. Her head lolled forward onto her chest. Darkness lapped at her.

When Graham came back inside, his hair was wet and mud was splattered across his clothes.

"I've buried it," he said. "The child." He brushed the dirt from his hands as he spoke, not looking at her.

"Thank you," she said, though she wished he wouldn't refer to it as a "child." He nodded.

He brought her a pan of water and a rag, along with a fresh nightgown from the suitcase in the bedroom.

"I'll let you clean yourself up," he said, walking out of the room. "Call me when you're decent."

I've buried the child.

Violet wondered if she would ever be decent again.

She wobbled to her feet and took off her soiled nightgown. The blood had glued it to her legs so that removing it felt like peeling away a layer of skin. Her vision slid and she gripped the back of the chair. She dabbed at her thighs with the rag and watched the blood run in watery rivulets down her legs, staining the floor. Outside, under the sound of the wind shearing through the trees, she thought she heard a crow squawk. Then, the sputter of an engine. A car.

"Violet," Graham called. "Quick. Get dressed. They're here."

CHAPTER FORTY-SEVEN

KATE

K ate has been in the attic for hours.

There have been moments of silence, when she has allowed herself to wonder if Simon has given up waiting for her and left. But then: the menacingly slow progress of his footsteps down the corridor. Of course he hasn't given up. He is never going to let her go. Never going to let *them* go.

These are the worst moments, when the fear recedes only to close its cold fist around her heart again. But as Kate turns the fragile pages of Altha's manuscript, as she reads a story that is centuries old but echoes her own life so closely, rage unfurls inside her.

The rain still falls, drumming loud on the roof, like a battle call. She has finished reading the manuscript. She knows the truth. About Altha Weyward. About Aunt Violet, too. About herself; and her child.

The truth. She can feel it spreading molten through her body, hardening her bones.

This wildness inside gives us our name.

All those years of feeling different. Separate. Now she knows why.

The rain grows heavier. There is something not quite right about the sound—rather than the rhythmic patter of water, it is erratic and heavy. *Plop. Plop. Plop.* As though hundreds of solid objects are landing on the roof. There's a scraping noise, too. At first, Kate thinks it is the wind, a tree branch scraping the tiles. She focuses. Not scraping, *scrabbling*. Claws.

The flapping of wings. Kate can feel them there, a frenzied, swelling mass. Birds.

Of course. The crow has been there, ever since she arrived. In the fireplace. Watching from the hedgerow, the sycamore tree. The same crow led her through the woods after the accident. The crow that carries the sign.

She is no longer afraid. Not of the birds and not of Simon.

She thinks of all the times he has hurt her, has used her unwilling flesh as if it were there for his pleasure. Has made her feel small and worthless.

But she isn't.

Her blood glows warm; her nerve endings tingle. In the dark, her vision becomes clearer, sharper; sounds feel as if they are coming from inside her very skull.

The birds on the roof begin to chirrup and squawk. Kate imagines their bodies covering the house in one undulating, feathered mass.

She thanks them, welcomes them. Puts her hand on her stomach.

I am ready. We *are ready.*

Simon cries out downstairs and she knows that he has seen them, too.

It is now, she knows. Now or never.

She opens the trapdoor.

CHAPTER FORTY-EIGHT

ALTHA

I was busy, those last months of 1618. As the leaves turned red, so too did the sky, for a great comet appeared, chasing the stars like a streak of blood. My mother had often read the stars, and I wondered what she would say if she could see the red sky, if it would have told her what was coming.

Autumn gave way to winter, and the village was struck by fever. It seemed half of the villagers sent for the physician, and the other half—the ones who had not the coin to offer up their flesh to leeches—sent for me. In each fever-bright face—the eyes glassy with pain, the spots of fire in the cheeks—I saw Anna Metcalfe. I saw my mother.

A mistake could cost my life.

And so I stayed up working half the nights, either cooling a patient's brow at their bedside or toiling in the cottage, preparing tonics and tinctures for the next day. My fingers smelled always of feverfew, as though it had seeped into the fabric of my skin from so much chopping and crushing. Each night I was so exhausted that I fell asleep as soon as I laid my head on the pallet. I did not even dream.

Neither Grace nor her husband fell ill, as far as I knew, but if they had, they would have sent for Doctor Smythson. They both attended church each Sunday, and though the pews were near empty that winter, with so many ill, I kept my distance and sat as far behind as I could. During the sermon I let Reverend Goode's voice fade to a low hum, the words running into each other, and watched Grace's red curls quiver as she bent her head in prayer.

I wondered, then, if Grace still kept the old ways, like her father. If she prayed to Mary for deliverance. Though I doubted the Virgin—who had been spared the feel of a man's flesh on hers—could deliver Grace from her husband.

She looked the same as always. The face white and distant, the head bowed. No marks on her that I could see, but I remembered what she had said. That he was taking care not to harm her face. I could not bear to think what lay under her shift. I remembered my vision, at the bonfire on May Day Eve. The blood.

The fever that gripped the village burned itself out by advent, and though snow lay thick as cream on the ground, the church was full on Christmas morning. The villagers sat in the pews, with the ice on their hats and cloaks making them look like floured loaves. In my usual spot at the back, I craned my neck to see Grace. But she was not sitting next to John. I scanned the pews. She was not there at all.

All through Reverend Goode's sermon, I wondered why she had not come. Had she caught the fever? After the service, John stood with the Dinsdales and threw his head back and laughed at something Stephen Dinsdale said. He did not have the worried look of a man whose wife was ill, I thought. But perhaps that was to be expected. After all, from what I knew, Grace's value to him was in her ability to bear him a child, and in this she had failed thus far. Perhaps he would be quite happy for her to wither away and die, giving him an excuse to marry a woman who could give him a son to carry on the Milburn name.

I stood as close as I dared in the churchyard, in case John said something that hinted at Grace's condition. But I heard nothing: the villagers were merry with the promise of the festivities to come, and the churchyard was loud with chatter. After a time, people trailed off, bundling themselves more tightly in their cloaks and hats, wishing each other a happy Christmas. I felt sad, thinking of the feasts and laughter they would enjoy with their families, while I sat alone in my cottage. I watched as John turned to go and heard Mary Dinsdale ask that he pass on her best wishes to his wife.

"Thank you," he said. "No doubt she'll be on her feet by the morrow. Well, she'll have to be, seeing as the cows need milking." He laughed, a harsh, cranking sound like the jaws of a plow, and bid them merry Christmas.

I walked home through white fields, under trees as bare as bones. I thought on John's words, and the winter wind numbed my face and chilled my heart.

The next morning, I woke to such silence that I wondered if I had lost my hearing. Looking out of the window, I saw that snow had fallen so heavily in the night that the whole world was muffled by it. No birds had sung that morning and the sun, though weak and gray, was already high in the sky.

I hoped that the villagers would remain tucked up and warm inside their houses, perhaps still sleeping off the previous night's merriment. I hoped that no one would see me as I set off into that still, white world.

As I walked through the snow, my feet cold in my boots and my hands raw in my gloves, my stomach twisted with fear. Whatever he had done to her, I thought, it must have been very grave if she was not fit to be seen in public on Christmas Day.

When I first came upon the Milburn farm, I thought that I was lost, or that it had vanished. Then, I heard the cows mooing in the barn, complaining of the cold, and I realized that a great lip of snow covered the roof of the farmhouse. I tried to climb the oak tree to get a better view, but my hands and feet could not find purchase, the trunk was so slick with ice. Then, I saw the dark figure of a man make his way from the white mound of the farmhouse. Even from a distance, there was no mistaking his long, flowing robes and the leather case he carried in his hand.

Doctor Smythson.

I spent the last days of December rising before the sun, when the valley was thick with darkness and silence. As the sky grayed around the edges, I made my way to Milburn farm, where I climbed the oak and sat high in its branches. I might have been another of the crows, who welcomed me silently with their glittering eyes. One of them settled next to me, its feathers brushing my cloak. Together we watched the farmhouse.

I watched candlelight flicker orange through the shutters. I watched the back door open as John left the farmhouse and walked to the barn to milk the cows. I heard their low protest as his rough fingers pinched at their udders, and the fear grew in me. Milking had been Grace's job. John took the cows to the fields, which were dark and swollen with melted snow. Some days, the Kirkby lad came. I did not see Grace. The winter sky grew light, and then pink became icy blue. Still she did not leave the farmhouse: not to wash the clothes, not to fetch water from the well or make her way to the market.

Five days passed thus. Then, as the sixth day dawned, I watched as the back door opened and Grace emerged in John's stead. I saw her make her way to the barn for the milking, moving slowly, her body curved over itself with pain. I saw her stagger, and then sink to her knees and retch. I pressed my hand to my mouth as I saw the door open again. John came out, walking quickly towards his wife, who knelt in the frozen mud.

In spite of all I knew of the man, some innocent part of me expected him to offer his wife some kindness, to take her hand in his and tenderly raise her to her feet. Instead, I saw him tear off her cap and twist his fingers into her hair. In the dull light, her curls were the color of old blood. John pulled her to her feet by her hair, and her sharp cry of pain sent a shiver through the morning. Around me, the crows shifted uneasily on the branches.

Tears froze on my cheeks as I watched him haul her into the barn, as if she were no better than a piece of waste. It had been one thing to hear her speak of his rough treatment of her. It was quite another to see it. Fury flowed through my blood like fire.

The next morning, New Year's Eve, Adam Bainbridge delivered me a gift for the new year. He had wrapped a small piece of ham in a cloth.

"There's something else," he said, after I thanked him. "I stopped by the Milburn farm first this morning, to deliver my gift. John Milburn has long kept us in veal, you see, and my father bid me to take a token of our gratitude this new year." He paused, as though the act had made him uncomfortable. He knows, I thought. He knows how John treats her.

"John was in the field, so it was Mistress Milburn who answered the door. Grace. She asked if I planned to give any other gifts that day. I said I was taking a gift to you, next, for the care you showed my grandfather when he passed this year. She bid me give you this."

He pressed a bundle of cloth into my hands. I didn't dare open it in front of Adam, and pretended the gift was a surprise—as far as the villagers knew, Grace had not uttered a kind word to me in public for seven years.

He looked at me for a moment, as if he had wanted to ask me a question but thought better of it.

"Well, happy New Year, Altha," he said. "Blessings be upon you."

He touched his cap and left.

I watched him disappear down the path, then went inside. Once I had shut the door behind me, I unwrapped the bundle. It was a fragrant, golden orb—an orange, I realized. I had only ever heard them spoken of, the fruit is so rare and precious. An expensive gift. The smell of it was sharp in my nostrils, mingled with another, woodier scent. Clove. I pulled at the clove; it was rough against my fingers. I saw that it had not been secured with a simple piece of twig, but a figure fashioned from twigs and twine. It was crude and looked hastily made, but I could see what she had intended it to be. The figure of a woman, with a curl of twine around her waist. A baby.

Grace was pregnant again. And she was asking for my help.

That night, I dreamed again of my mother, as she had been on her deathbed. Her features were waxen, and the pale lips barely moved as she spoke.

"Altha," she said. "Remember your promise . . . you cannot break your promise . . . it is not safe. You must keep your gift hidden . . ."

I woke with a jolt and the dream fell away. I pushed my mother's face from my mind. A sound had woken me, I realized. I heard it again. A cry that throbbed in the quiet. A crow. I looked outside. Night was only just beginning to lift from the valley. It was time.

I dressed quickly. In the looking glass, my hair shone bright as feathers. With my black cloak fastened around my shoulders, I looked as dark and powerful as if I were a crow myself.

CHAPTER FORTY-NINE

VIOLET

The key turned in the lock. Violet pulled her nightdress on hurriedly, dizzy from the effort. She sat back down. The darkness was there still, at the edges of her vision. Perhaps it would be easiest to give into it, she thought. To let it take her away, before Father and Doctor Radcliffe did.

The creak of the front door, and then the wind roared into the cottage. She heard Father's voice, raised above the storm.

"Graham? What are *you* doing here?"

"Father—I can explain—"

"Where is the girl?" She recognized Doctor Radcliffe's voice, cold and clinical.

They were in the room, the rain glittering on their overcoats. Violet looked down at the floor, stained pink with her blood.

"She's lost the baby," Graham said quietly.

Father didn't ask him how he knew about the baby. Violet felt his eyes on her and looked up. There was no concern, no tenderness in his gaze. His mouth curled in disgust.

"I'll need to examine her," said Doctor Radcliffe. "Take her to the bedroom and have her lie down."

Graham slung Violet's arm around his shoulders and lifted her to her feet. Neither Father nor Doctor Radcliffe made any effort to help. Violet closed her eyes, and imagined she was in the beech tree, feeling the summer breeze on her face. In the bedroom, the small window flared bright and the air crackled with electricity. A thunderclap. God moving his furniture, Nanny Metcalfe used to say. Nanny Metcalfe. She would be ashamed, Violet knew. God, too, perhaps. She had committed a sin.

After she lay down, Doctor Radcliffe asked Graham and Father to turn around, before lifting the skirt of her nightdress. His nostrils flared at the smell of blood. It hung in the air, sweet and metallic. Looking down, Violet saw that her thighs were ringed red, like the inside of a tree trunk. She suddenly felt very old, as if she'd lived a hundred years instead of sixteen.

"Can you explain what happened?" Doctor Radcliffe asked. It was the first time either he or Father had addressed her directly.

"I felt a cramping, this morning," she said. "Like I get with my monthly curse, but stronger . . ."

"I found her as it was starting," Graham interjected, still staring at the wall. "She began losing blood not long after I arrived. And then, with the blood . . . it . . ."

"The baby," said Doctor Radcliffe.

"Yes, the baby . . . the baby came out . . . there was so much blood . . ." Graham retched, and Violet knew that he, too, was thinking of that mottled twist of flesh. The spore, the rot.

Violet felt tears sting her eyes, blurring her vision so that Doctor Radcliffe's face swam before her.

"Is that what happened?" he asked her. "You did not do anything to bring about this miscarriage? You didn't take anything?"

"No, I didn't," Violet said softly, the tears wet on her cheeks. The darkness was there again, and she rolled towards it. Fragments of conversation drifted towards her as she fell, the air rushing at her.

"Lost a lot of blood," Doctor Radcliffe was saying. "A week of bed rest, at least. Plenty of fluids, too."

"Can you be sure, Doctor?" Father asked. "Can you be sure she didn't bring it on herself?"

"No," Doctor Radcliffe said. "We have only her word for that. And the boy's."

She was flying now, the wind singing on her skin. She slept.

Graham was there when she woke up, sitting on the bed opposite, watching her. Everything was quiet and still. The candle had burned down to the wick. She could hear a fly outside, buzzing past the window.

"They've gone," Graham said, seeing that she was awake. "They left last night. You've been asleep since. Father said I could stay with you. He had to keep up appearances in front of Doctor Radcliffe, I suppose."

Violet sat up. Her body felt hollow and light.

"They'll be back in a week, to see how you've recovered. Father's writing to Frederick. I expect the wedding's off."

The feeling of lightness again. She heard a redstart sing and smiled. It was a beautiful sound.

"I don't think Father believed us," said Graham.

Violet nodded. "It doesn't matter," she said. "As long as Doctor Radcliffe did."

"I suppose you're right," he said. "Father would hardly go to the police of his own accord. The scandal."

They were quiet for a moment. Violet watched a thin ray of sun dance on the wall.

"Do you know what this place is, Violet?"

"Yes. It was our mother's house," she said. "Her name was Elizabeth. Elizabeth Weyward."

Graham was quiet. It took Violet a moment to realize that he was crying, his hunched shoulders shaking, his face hidden in his hands. She hadn't seen him cry since before he left for boarding school, years ago.

"Graham?"

"I thought . . ." He took a deep, steadying breath. "I thought you were going to die, too. Just like she did. Our—our mother."

They had never spoken of her before.

"That's why you hate me, isn't it?" Graham lifted his face from his hands

294

as he spoke. His pale skin was mottled with tears. "Because I—because I killed her."

"What do you mean?"

"She died having me."

"She didn't."

"Don't, Violet. I know. Father told me years ago."

"He lied," she said. And then she told him the truth—about what Father and Doctor Radcliffe had done to their mother. About the grandmother who had tried to reach them, the grandmother they had never known.

"So you mustn't think it's your fault anymore," she said, afterwards. "And you mustn't think I hate you. You're my brother. We're family."

She touched her necklace as she spoke. The locket was warm against her fingers. She felt stronger, knowing that the key was safe inside. She considered telling him the rest: about Altha's manuscript, locked away in the drawer. After all, the Weywards were Graham's family, too.

But Graham was—or would soon become—a man. A good man, but a man all the same. It wouldn't be right, she knew.

"How did you know to use the—what was it?"

"Tansy." She paused. "Just something I read somewhere," she said.

Graham stayed with her for a week. He helped her mend the latch on the window of her bedroom, so that she could breathe clean air every night. Together they scrubbed her blood from the floor of the kitchen, until the wood glowed rich and brown. The cottage looked good as new.

There was a carrot plant in the garden, tangled up with the helleborine—though the carrots were misshapen and pale, unlike any she had seen before. There was rhubarb, too; she pulled the stems delicately from the soil, careful not to disturb the worms that lived nearby.

They ate the carrots with the eggs Father had brought. They no longer turned her stomach, now that the spore was gone.

Graham found a rusted axe in the attic. He chopped the branches that had been felled by the storm into firewood.

"To keep you warm in winter," he said. They both knew she would never return to Orton Hall. Not after everything that had happened.

Graham used some of the wood to fashion a small cross and drove it into the soil where he had buried the spore, down by the beck. Violet thought about asking him to take it down, but she didn't.

Father came back, with Doctor Radcliffe.

"She seems to have recovered well," Doctor Radcliffe said to Father. "You can have her brought home, if you wish."

Doctor Radcliffe left, and it was just Father, Graham, and Violet in the cottage. They were silent as they listened to the sputter of Doctor Radcliffe's car engine.

"I am sure you understand," Father began, looking past Violet at the wall, "that I cannot allow you back into my house after what you have done. I have arranged for you to be taken to a finishing school in Scotland. You will stay there for two years, and after that I will decide what is to be done with you."

Violet heard Graham clear his throat.

"No," she said, before her brother could open his mouth to speak. "That won't be acceptable, I'm afraid, Father."

His jowls slackened with shock. He looked as if she had slapped him.

"I beg your pardon?"

"I won't be going to Scotland. In fact, I won't be going anywhere. I'm staying right here." As she spoke, Violet became aware of a strange simmering sensation, as though electricity was humming beneath her skin. Images flashed in her mind—a crow cutting through the air, wings glittering with snow; the spokes of a wheel spinning. Briefly, she closed her eyes, focusing on the feeling until she could almost see it, glinting gold inside her.

"That is not for you to decide," said Father. The window was open, and a bee flitted about the room, wings a silver blur. It flew near Father's cheek and he jerked away from it.

"It's been decided." She stood up straight, her dark eyes boring into Father's watery ones. He blinked. The bee hovered about his face, dancing away from his hands, and she saw sweat break out on his nose. Soon it was joined by another, and then another and another, until it seemed like Father—shouting and swearing—had been engulfed in a cloud of tawny, glistening bodies.

"I think it would be best if you left now, Father," said Violet softly. "After all, as you said, I'm my mother's daughter."

"Graham?" Violet smiled at the note of panic in Father's voice.

"I'm staying, too," said Graham, folding his arms across his chest.

Violet heard Father's shallow, rasping breaths. Several of the bees were dangerously close to his mouth now.

"The front door key, please, Father," she said. It landed on the wooden floor with a dull clank.

"Thank you," she called, as Father, pursued by the bees, slammed the door behind him.

Violet held out her hand, and a lone bee came to rest on her palm.

"You're not afraid, are you?" she asked, turning to Graham. "They won't hurt you this time."

"I know," said Graham.

He put his arm around her. They stood still for a moment, listening to the car rumble away.

CHAPTER FIFTY

KATE

In the corridor, Kate can hear what sounds like hailstones hitting the windows. But they are not hailstones, she sees, looking through the doorway at her bedroom window; they are *beaks*.

Outside, illuminated by the moon, are hundreds of birds. She sees the gunmetal sheen of a crow's feathers, the yellow glare of an owl. A robin's red breast. Their bodies writhe and flutter against the glass. Snow falls around them, drifting to the ground. Their cries echo in her ears. They are here, she knows, because of her.

The door to the sitting room is slightly ajar. Simon is yelling frantically. He can't hear her as she approaches, cloaked by the sound of the birds.

She pushes open the door. Simon is standing in the center of the room, facing the window. The poker quivers in one white-knuckled hand. She is still for a moment, watching the muscles of his back tense beneath the fine wool of his sweater. The skin on the nape of his neck is goose-pimpled with fear.

Birds clamor at the window. Kate can see cracks begin to form in the glass, glinting silver like the thread of a spider's web. There's a scratching sound coming from the chimney.

"Simon," she says. He doesn't hear her.

"Simon," she says again, louder this time, trying to keep the fear from her voice.

His blond hair flashes as he turns around.

Her heart knocks in her chest. The handsome features are sharp with anger, the lips snarling away from the teeth. The shock on his face at the first sight of her. How different she must look to him, she thinks, with her huge belly and cropped hair, Aunt Violet's beaded cape around her shoulders. Then his eyes narrow, glittering with rage.

"*You*," he hisses.

Kate takes a gulp of air as he moves towards her. She tries to shift her body away from him, back to the doorway, but he is too quick.

He shoves her into the wall, so hard that plaster dust drifts into the air like the snow outside.

"You thought you could leave?" he shouts, spittle landing on her face. "You thought you could leave *with my child*?"

The poker clatters to the floor, and then his hand is around her neck, squeezing, crushing, like a vise.

Horror settles into her stomach, cold and hard.

Thoughts spark and die in her brain. The colors in the room look brighter, even as her vision grows hazy at the edges. She sees the flecks of gold in his blue irises. The whites of his eyes, with their red tracing of veins. His breath is hot and sour in her face.

So this is it, she thinks, as her lungs burn from lack of oxygen. The end. Even if he lets her live—for the sake of the child, he might—it will not be a life, but a cell. She thinks, suddenly, of the jail in the village: the cold gray stone, darkness closing over her.

He is saying something now, but she can barely hear him above the tapping on the windows and the scrabbling on the roof.

He says it again, louder and closer, tightening his grip on her throat. Aunt Violet's necklace is digging into her neck.

"You are nothing," he says, the words tolling in her skull, "without me."

The panic is rising. Except it isn't panic, Kate knows now. It never was. The feeling of something trying to get out. Rage, hot and bright in her chest. Not panic. Power.

No. She is not nothing.

She is a Weyward. And she carries another Weyward inside her. She gathers herself together, every cell blazing, and thinks: *Now*.

The window breaks, a waterfall of sharp sounds. The room grows dark with feathered bodies, shooting through the broken window, the fireplace.

Beaks, claws, and eyes flashing. Feathers brushing her skin. Simon yells, his hand loosening on her throat.

She sucks in the air, falling to her knees, one hand cradling her stomach. Something touches her foot, and she sees a dark tide of spiders spreading across the floor. Birds continue to stream through the window. Insects, too: the azure flicker of damselflies, moths with orange eyes on their wings. Tiny, gossamer mayflies. Bees in a ferocious golden swarm.

She feels something sharp on her shoulder, its claws digging into her flesh. She looks up at blue-black feathers, streaked with white. A crow. The same crow that has watched over her since she arrived. Tears fill her eyes, and she knows in that moment that she is not alone in the cottage. Altha is there, in the spiders that dance across the floor. Violet is there, in the mayflies that glisten and undulate like some great silver snake. And all the other Weyward women, from the first of the line, are there, too.

They have always been with her, and always will be.

Simon is curled on the floor, screaming. She can barely see him for the birds, swarming and pecking, their wings quivering; the insects forming patterns on his skin. His face is covered by the tawny wings of a sparrow hawk; a flock of starlings have landed on his chest, their crowns shimmering purple. A brown fieldfare nips at his ear, a spider circles his throat.

Feathers swirl in the air—small and white, gold and tapered. Opaline black.

She lifts her arm—the pink scar catching the light—and the creatures draw back. Dark drops splatter on the floor.

Simon's hands, crisscrossed with red gashes, are pressed against his eyes. Slowly, he removes them, and she sees the pink flesh, oozing blood, where the left eye should be. He cowers as she stands tall above him, the crow on her shoulder.

"Get out," she says.

The creatures leave after Simon.

Kate's hair moves in the wind created by their wings. The insects first, then the birds. As if by agreement.

She looks at the floor. It is strewn with glass, feathers, and snow glittering like jewels. It is the most beautiful thing she has ever seen.

Only the crow remains. It loiters on the windowsill, head cocked to one side. Unsure of whether to leave her.

There is the growl of an engine outside, the slamming of car doors.

The doorbell rings, then the door shakes with frantic knocking.

"Police, open up!"

"Kate? Are you in there?" She hears the fear in Emily's voice. Emily. Kate smiles. Her friend.

"We're going to force the door," says the police officer. "Stand back!"

The crow turns to her one last time. Kate watches as it takes flight, rising above the moon into the night sky. Free.

CHAPTER FIFTY-ONE

ALTHA

For a moment, I forgot where I was when I opened my eyes this morning. I had to pinch myself, to make sure that I was safe, that the dungeon and the courtroom really do lie in the past, along with that cold winter morning where ice glittered on the trees.

But the sun shone, bright as gold, through my window. I could smell spring on the air: the garden is crowded with daffodils and bluebells now. Even as I write, lambs are being born wet and bewildered, nuzzling at their mothers to get back to that dark, warm place where nothing can hurt them.

Sometimes, I remember that day so clearly that I think it is happening now, that all my life is happening at once and all I can do to take refuge from it is crawl under the bedclothes and sob. I am like a lamb, wishing for a warm place where nothing can hurt me. Wishing for my mother.

My mother. I hope she would have understood. Perhaps it would have been better to be guilty in their eyes, to have swung from the rope even, so long as I could be innocent in hers.

I do not want to write what happened next, but I must.

I moved quickly through that frozen morning. The sky was already pink through the trees, so I had to hurry. I felt something pulse in me, but I do not think it was fear. I could see my breath before me, could feel frost falling into my hair from the trees above, but I did not feel cold. I thought of what I had seen John do to Grace and the blood grew hot in my veins, warming me.

When I reached the oak tree, I saw that great skirts of ice hung from its branches and its trunk had hardened with frost. It would be slippery, I thought, preparing myself for struggle. But my feet found purchase easily, almost as if the tree were helping me up, and before I knew it, I was perched up high with the crows, their wings frosted with ice crystals. And then I saw it. My mother's crow. It carried the sign—the tracing of white across its feathers, as though it had been stroked by magic fingers. The same marks that my mother said had appeared on the first crow, when it was touched by the first of our line, before the words to describe either existed.

Tears pricked my eyes and I was certain, then, that what I planned to do was right. The crow came to rest on my shoulder, its scaly claws sharp through my cloak.

Together we watched the farm. I felt the coolness of its beak against my ear and I knew that it understood what I was asking of it.

The fields were green and white with snow. A dark spiral of smoke rose from the chimney into the sky. I watched as the door opened and John came out. As he walked to the barn, a small figure moved in his shadow and I realized it was Daniel Kirkby. I had forgotten that he worked at the farm some mornings. I would have a witness, now. But in that moment, knowing not what lay ahead, I did not care. I did not care if the whole world saw me do what I was going to do next.

John opened the barn and the cows came out. They were already agitated; they did not like the cramped fug of the barn, but nor did they like the feel of the winter air, sharp on their flanks. I watched their tails swing and their shoulders ripple, hide gleaming in the morning sun.

It was time.

The crow took flight, wings slicing through the air. I could feel the frozen wood of the oak tree beneath me, but I could also feel the wind singing through the crow's feathers as it dived down into the field. I saw the eyes of the cows grow white and wide, I saw the fear collecting in froth at their nostrils. Their hooves stamped the frozen ground as the crow flew near, looping around and around with sharp beak and claws, stoking them as one would a fire.

I saw it up close: the new sweat that froze on a flank, the white roll of an eye, John's face as death bore down on him. And I saw it from afar: the cows a golden stampede, the body crumpling beneath them. The fields: green, white, and red.

Then it was over. The morning quiet returned, and I could hear Daniel Kirkby panting in shock, and the soft gurgle of John's blood into the snow. The crow had returned to its friends in the branches, barely pausing to look at me. I climbed down the tree quickly, in time to hear the creak of the farmhouse door and then Grace screaming.

I ran towards the sound, my boots slipping on the frosted grass, and as I got closer I could smell the body. The sweet meaty stink of blood, of guts and other inside things: things that were not meant to be exposed to the world. Half of the face was gone, disappeared into a red maw. I threw my cloak over it to spare Grace the sight. As I neared the farmhouse, I saw her sink to her knees screaming, again and again. The Kirkby boy stood off to the side, his fists pressed to his eyes as if he wanted to scrub away what they had seen.

I told the Kirkby boy to fetch the doctor and he ran in the direction of the village. I went to Grace. Her breath was sour and I saw that she had vomited down the front of her dress. I brushed a brown smear of it from her cheek and pulled her to me.

"It's over," I said, leading her inside. "He's gone."

She shook as she sat at the kitchen table, and her skin had a gray tinge to it. I fixed her tea, to calm her. The fire had gone out and the water took an age to boil in the pot. Once the bubbles rose to the surface I put my face over the steam, breathing it in as if it could cleanse me of my sins.

I made the tea and sat down with her at the table. She did not touch the cup. Her eyes stared ahead as if she were still in the field, looking at his body. I reached my hand across the table towards her, and left it there. After a time, she put her hand on mine. The sleeve of her dress fell back and I saw the bruises on her wrist, as purple as summer fruit.

We sat like that until Daniel Kirkby returned with Doctor Smythson: her clammy hand on my cool one.

So I have set it down, as I promised to. The truth. I will let whoever reads this when I am gone decide whether I am innocent or guilty. Whether what I did was murder, or justice. Until then, I will lock these words away in the bureau and keep the key around my neck. To save them falling into the wrong hands.

Yesterday, Adam Bainbridge came to the cottage, bearing a leg of mutton wrapped in muslin. I led him inside, where I asked him to give me something else. Not his name, nor his love. I remembered my mother's lesson, in this respect, at least.

He was gentle, but I was afraid. As my body opened to take his seed, I shut my eyes and thought of Grace. Of the hot hand that had gripped mine as we ran over the fells, that last innocent summer. Of the way her red hair had spread across my pallet, of her milk and tallow scent. Of the relief that shone out of her face when I was acquitted.

When it was over, I lay curled on my side, wondering if it had taken, if a child flowered inside me already. I would name her for my friend, I decided. For my love.

I have not seen Grace since the trial. I do not know how she fares and I do not know when I will see her again. Perhaps, one day, it will be safe for her to visit me. Safe for me to take her in my arms and stroke her pretty hair, breathe in her precious smell.

Until then, all I can do is imagine her. Looking out at the same blue sky I see through my window now. Feeling the breeze on her neck and tasting the sweet air. Free.

Free as the crows that made their home in the sycamore tree, waiting for my return. The marked one eats out of my hand now, the way she did for my mother once.

My mother. I think she would understand what I have done. What I had to do. Perhaps she would even be proud. Proud that I am her daughter.

I am proud, too. Much as I shy away from it, the hard truth in my heart is that I am proud of what I have done.

And so I will not flee, I have decided. Not even if the villagers come, seeking justice. They cannot make me leave my home.

They do not frighten me.

After all, I am a Weyward, and wild inside.

CHAPTER FIFTY-TWO

VIOLET

Graham stayed until September, when he went back to Harrow. Father had written to say that he would pay for the remainder of Graham's schooling, but after that he was on his own. The letter didn't mention Violet. It was as if Father had decided that she had never existed.

"I'm not sure about leaving you here," Graham said before he set off on the long walk to the bus station. There had been frost that morning, sparkling on the sycamore tree. The first sign of winter's approach. "Will you be all right, all by yourself?"

"I'll be grand," said Violet. She planned to spend the day in the garden, sowing seeds she had been given by the village greengrocer. She had thought about asking Graham to cut down the helleborine but in the end she decided to leave it. It was a good source of pollen for the bees, she thought. There seemed to be even more insects in the garden than ever, now: their constant thrum lulled her to sleep each night, an arthropod lullaby.

"See you at Christmas," Graham waved as he set off down the lane. "I'll bring you some new books!"

As she shut the front door, she wondered whether anyone had found the biology textbook she had hidden under her bed back at Orton Hall, along with the bloodied clothes from the woods.

She still dreamed about Frederick. The dull weight of him on top of her, squeezing out her breath. All of that blood, seeping out of her.

She would wake up and stare at the ceiling, a line from Altha's manuscript echoing in her head.

The first child born to a Weyward is always female.

She had killed her daughter. The next Weyward girl. Violet knew, then, that she would never have her own baby. She would never teach her daughter about insects, birds, and flowers. About what it meant to be a Weyward.

"But you weren't supposed to be born yet," she would whisper into the darkness, thinking of the tiny curl of bones buried under the sycamore tree. "You were meant to come later, when I was ready."

It was all because of Frederick, and what he did to her. What he made her do. That sun-spangled afternoon in the woods, the trees circling above. Blood, staining her thighs pink.

He had taken away her choice. Her future.

For that, she would never forgive him.

The problem was that she wasn't sure she could forgive herself, either.

Another letter arrived in November. Addressed to Violet, this time. According to the back of the envelope, it had been sent from Orton Hall. She didn't recognize the handwriting.

Violet's heart thudded as she unfolded the letter and saw the name at the bottom. It was from Frederick.

He was on bereavement leave, he wrote. Father was dead. A heart attack while hunting. Before his death, he had declared that neither Graham nor Violet were his biological children. Father had managed to produce documents—no doubt falsified—demonstrating that he was in Southern Rhodesia at the time of Graham's conception. Violet, he said, had been conceived before her parents' marriage, and so could not be proved to be his daughter.

Gripping the letter in her hands, she wished that it were indeed true—that none of Father's blood ran through her veins, that her cells weren't ghosts of his own. Tears blurred her vision, and the rest of the letter swam before her eyes.

Father had left everything to Frederick, who was now the Tenth Viscount Kendall. Enclosed with the letter was a deed, transferring Weyward Cottage into Violet's name. At this, her tears gave way to fury. She was tempted, for a moment, to throw the letter in the fire.

Did Frederick really think a piece of paper could make up for what he did to her?

And anyway, Weyward Cottage wasn't his to *give*. It was Violet's, and always had been—before she even knew it existed. Frederick couldn't lay claim to the land any more than Father had.

In the days after the letter, sadness stole like a shadow into the cottage. But Violet wasn't mourning Father—how could she, after what he had done? It was her mother and grandmother that she longed for. She hadn't known either of them, not really, and yet she felt their loss as keenly as a missing limb. For she had managed to confirm her suspicion: Elinor had died. Cancer, the villagers said. Only four years ago. She had lain alone on her deathbed, the grandchildren she'd never met just a few miles away.

Graham visited at Christmas, and they said goodbye to their mother and grandmother together. Back in the summer, Violet had dried a bouquet of lavender, and it was this that they placed on the Ayres family mausoleum, a spot of brightness in the snow. Violet hated to think of her mother encased in that cold stone. Even worse was the thought of her grandmother, buried in an unmarked pauper's grave.

She preferred to think of Lizzie and Elinor in the garden that they had loved. In the fells, the beck.

She preferred not to think of Father at all.

"Frederick has offered me an allowance until I finish university," Graham said later. "I'm not going to take it, though. My form master thinks I could get a scholarship. Law at Oxford or Cambridge. Durham, maybe. It'd be nice to stay up north. Besides, I don't want his money."

"It's not really Frederick's money though, is it?" said Violet. "It's—" She couldn't bring herself to say her father's name. "It should be yours."

"All the same." There was a crackling sound as Graham put another log on the fire. It was snowing outside. In the moonlight, the drifting flakes looked like falling stars. The garden was still and muffled; the insects quiet. Violet knew that some insects hibernated in winter—*diapause*, it was called.

Last week, she had crouched next to the wooden cross and looked at the beck, which glittered with a thin layer of ice. Underneath the surface, she knew, thousands of tiny, glowing spheres clung to twigs and pebbles. Mayfly eggs. Frozen until the warmer months, when they would continue to grow, cells splitting and changing into nymphs and then, when they were ready, rising up into an undulating, breeding swarm.

It had given her an idea.

The next night had been a full moon. She'd climbed the sycamore tree in the garden, the moonlight silver on the branches, until she could see for miles all around. In the distance, she could just make out the fells, crouched below the star-studded sky. Beyond, she knew, was Orton Hall. Frederick. She closed her eyes and pictured him sleeping in Father's bedchamber. Then, she focused as hard as she could, until her whole body pulsed with energy. There it was again, that gold glint. It had always been there, she now realized, shimmering under her skin, brightening every cell of her body. She just hadn't known how to use it.

In the summer, it would begin. She pictured the Hall, her father's things—his precious furniture, scarred and black with rot, the globe on his desk eaten away. The air shimmering with insects, in a swarm that grew and grew each year, until there was no escaping it.

And Frederick. Trapped there alone.

He would never forget what he had done.

"Oh! Almost forgot. Presents," Graham was saying, unbuckling his school rucksack. "All the way from Harrow library."

"Did you steal these?" she asked, as he handed her two heavy books: a great tome on insects, and another on botany.

"They haven't been borrowed since before the war," he said. "No one is going to miss them. Trust me."

"Thank you," she said. They sat in silence for a moment, listening to the logs spitting on the fire.

"Have you thought any more about what you might do?" Graham asked. A couple of the villagers had paid her to help with their farm animals. One of them kept bees, and was aghast when she insisted on tending to the hive without a beekeeping suit. So far, she'd been able to make enough to keep herself in bread and milk. Winter would be difficult, though. The greengrocer was looking for a shop girl. She'd thought about applying. Her dreams of becoming an entomologist seemed very distant indeed.

"A little," she said, fingering the cover of the book on insects. *From Arthropods to Arachnids*, it was called.

"Don't worry," said Graham. "Once I'm a rich lawyer, I'll pay for you to learn all about your blasted bugs. Promise."

Violet laughed.

"In the meantime, I'll put the kettle on," she said. She went over to light the stove, pausing to look out of the small window. A crow was watching her from the sycamore, the moon lighting on the white feathers in its coat. It made her think of Morg.

She smiled.

Somehow, she felt certain that everything would be all right.

CHAPTER FIFTY-THREE

KATE

Kate looks out at the garden while she waits for her mother to arrive. The winter sun gilds the branches of the sycamore tree. The tree is like its own village, Kate is learning. Home to robins, finches, blackbirds, and redwings.

And, of course, the crows—a comforting presence, with their familiar dark capes. The one with the speckled feathers often comes to the window to accept some tidbit from the kitchen. At those moments, when she feels the glossy beak nudge against her palm, Kate has the overwhelming feeling that she is exactly where she is supposed to be.

The sycamore hosts insects, too, although many of them have burrowed away from the cold, sheltering in the ridged cracks of the sycamore's trunk, the warm soil beneath its roots.

She is still for a moment, listening. It is strange, to think she's spent all her life cringing away from nature. From who she really is. It is as if she had been in hiding—like the insects—dormant and docile, until she came to Weyward Cottage.

There could be others like her, in need of waking.

She told me of other women, across the land, Altha had written. *The Devices and the Whittles.*

Perhaps one day, after the baby is born, Kate will find them. She will go south, to Pendle Hill, where the land curves up to meet the sky. Where women were ripped from their homes, centuries ago. Perhaps something has survived, in the dark, hidden places where men dare not look. But for now, she is grateful—for her mother, for Emily.

And for Violet.

Snowflakes are falling onto the little wooden cross underneath the sycamore. She isn't sure what is buried there, though she has a suspicion the grave is more recent than she originally thought.

She thinks of Altha's friend, Grace. And of Violet's note. *I hope she can help you as she helped me.* Some secrets, she's decided, can stay just that— secret.

Kate feels the locket under her shirt, warm against her skin. The key is safe inside, along with a small curl of a feather that she retrieved from the floor that night, spangled with broken glass.

The police arrested Simon in London, charging him with assault. There is to be a hearing next year, at the courthouse in Lancaster. The police have warned her that even if he's found guilty, Simon could be out in two years. Sooner, probably, with good behavior. She is working on a victim personal statement for the trial, though she dislikes that label. She is not a victim, but a survivor.

"Are you worried he'll come back here? When he gets out?" Emily asked her.

Kate had thought of how he looked that night, clutching his ruined face while feathers swirled in the air. Powerless, once she had robbed him of his only weapon: her fear.

"No," she had told Emily. "He can't hurt me anymore."

Tires crunch on snow. Then, the soft chime of the doorbell.

Her mother is smaller than she remembers: there are creases around her eyes and her hair is threaded with silver. She is wearing a striped beanie Kate gave her one Christmas years ago, when she was a teenager. Along with her luggage she holds a bouquet of pink roses, crisp from the airport.

There is a moment when neither of them speak. Her eyes go to the wreath of bruises at Kate's throat, the dome of her stomach.

Together, they begin to cry.

Two days later. The first, searing clench of her womb.

"I can't do this," she gasps, curled on her side. "I can't."

"Yes," says her mother, as she calls for an ambulance. "You can."

And then, she is doing it. Her muscles tensing, her blood surging.

There is the warm flood of her waters breaking, then the contractions—bright waves of pain. She has the feeling, as she crouches on her hands and knees in Aunt Violet's kitchen, that the animal part of her brain has taken over.

Her daughter moves quickly through her body, ready to leave the dark sea of the womb behind. Ready to feel sunlight, to hear birdsong. As she slips in and out of lucidity, her body humming with pain and power, Kate thinks of these things, and more, that she will show her daughter. The crows that call from the sycamore tree. The insects that skim the surface of the beck. The world and all its wild ways.

The next Weyward girl is born on Aunt Violet's floor, the same floor that sparkled with snow and feathers and broken glass, in a rush of blood and mucus.

She smells of the earth, of damp leaves and rich clods of soil, of rain, of the beck's iron tang.

Kate cries as she touches the tiny fingers, the silky strands of hair. The glowing curve of her cheek. Her eyes, dark as a crow's. The cottage is loud with her cries. With life.

Kate names her Violet.

Violet Altha.

EPILOGUE

August 2018

Violet switched off the television in her bedroom. She'd been watching a David Attenborough program on the BBC. A rerun. *Life in the Undergrowth*, it was called. This episode had been about insect mating rituals. Not her favorite topic, really. The act always seemed quite brutal, even in the insect world. She decided to read instead. She still had a stack of *New Scientist* magazines sitting on her bedside table, gathering dust.

First, she really had to open the window, get some air in. The cottage was absolutely boiling in hot weather—and yet Graham had still been on at her to get the windows double-glazed. Fat chance of *that*. She could already barely hear a damn thing when they were shut.

Poor Graham. He'd been dead for nearly twenty years now. Heart attack, like their father. She supposed all those long hours of writing affidavits in an airless, high-rise office hadn't helped. She was always telling him he needed more nature in his life.

She remembered the bee brooch—gold, the wings set with crystals—he had given her before she went off to university to take her first degree in biology. She had been nervous, fearing that, at the age of twenty-six, she'd be too different to fit in with the other students.

But, as Graham said when he handed her the brooch in its pretty green box, perhaps being different wasn't such a bad thing after all. Perhaps it was something to be proud of.

At first, the prospect of being away from Weyward Cottage terrified her; she'd taken a room in a ladies' boardinghouse run by a formidable woman by the name of Basset ("Her bite's even worse than her bark," the residents used to joke) who charged her thirty shillings a week for a damp room with an unreliable tap. She would lie awake in her rickety single bed, listening to the pipes groan in the wall, and clasp the brooch tight in her hand, imagining she was in her garden, watching bees dance through the helleborine.

Later, she took the brooch with her everywhere. This way, no matter where she was—in Botswana, tracking the Transvaal thick-tailed scorpion, or in the Khao Sok rain forest in Thailand studying Atlas moths—she was never far from home.

She opened the window, a task that seemed to take an inordinately long time. Afterwards, Violet's arms shook from the effort. They really were quite pathetic, now. She still got a shock, sometimes, when she looked in the mirror. With her thin, weedy limbs and her stooped back, she rather resembled a praying mantis.

She heaved herself back into bed. She looked for her reading glasses, which she normally left perched on top of the tower of reading material on her bedside table. They weren't there. Damn. The girl from the council must have moved them. It was ridiculous, really—Violet didn't need some stranger in her house, fetching her cups of tea and wanting to tidy up. Last week, she'd asked if she might help "Mrs. Ayres" out by cleaning out the attic.

"Absolutely *not*," Violet had barked, touching the necklace under her shirt.

No reading tonight, then. Well, that was all right. She might just look out of the window. It was half past nine, but the sun was only just beginning to sink in the sky, turning the clouds rosy. She could hear the birds, singing at the top of the sycamore. The insects, too: crickets, bumblebees. They made her think of Kate, Graham's granddaughter. Her great-niece.

She remembered the first time she saw Kate, at Graham's funeral. Violet had been so consumed by grief that she was barely aware of Graham's son and his wife, their little daughter. She'd have been about six, then. A tiny thing, with watchful eyes under her mop of dark hair. There was something familiar about her; the coltish legs, the sharp angles of her face. The prim white socks streaked with mud, the leaf quivering in her hair.

Even then she didn't see it.

Violet had long accepted that the Weyward line would end with her death. The only daughter she would ever have—or the feeble beginnings of her—lay buried under the sycamore tree. Frederick was paying for what he had done—she felt a dark flush of delight every time she thought of him at Orton Hall, besieged by mayflies—but she couldn't change what really mattered. The line that had continued for centuries, flowing as surely as the gold waters of the beck, was coming to an end. And there was nothing Violet could do about it.

But after the wake, Graham's son, Henry, and his wife had come to Violet's for tea. Henry was so like Graham: even the way he leaned forward as he listened to her, face furrowed with concentration. He enjoyed her story about traveling to India in the 1960s, to undertake a field study of Asian giant hornets (she still held the record for the only person who had held one without being stung).

She'd rather forgotten about the child, who was playing outside, until she heard her murmuring through the window.

"There you go," the girl was saying. "See, told you I wouldn't bite."

Who on earth was she talking to? Violet opened the window and poked her head out. Kate was sitting cross-legged in the garden, looking down at something she was holding in her hand. A bumblebee.

Violet felt tears spring to her eyes, a lightness in her chest. She had been wrong, for all these years. Later, when neither Henry nor his wife were looking, she had unpinned the bee brooch from her kaftan and pressed it into the girl's hand.

"Our little secret," she'd said, staring into the wide, dark eyes that matched her own.

Violet liked to think that one day it would lead Kate back to the cottage. To who she really was.

317

After everyone left and the cottage was quiet again, Violet sat by her window, gazing out at her garden. Joy twisted into pain as she thought of the young girl she had been when she had first arrived here: motherless and afraid, thighs bright with blood. She looked at the cross under the sycamore tree, now crooked with age.

She let it go. The guilt that had grown, like a weed around her heart.

Two years after Graham's death, Violet had woken from a terrifying nightmare. Her heart drummed in her chest and her skin was filmed with sweat. She clutched desperately at the dream, but only fragments remained: the red streak of a car approaching her nephew and his daughter, a scream tearing the air. A man, tall and lion-haired, eyes slitted with rage.

A man who wanted to hurt Kate.

The old words, traced by her fingers countless times, hummed in her blood.

Sight is a funny thing. Sometimes it shows us what is before our eyes. But sometimes it shows us what has already happened, or will yet come to pass.

It was as if Altha was speaking to her across centuries. Telling her that Kate was in danger.

It was 2 A.M.—dawn just a hint of silver at the horizon—but Violet got up and dressed immediately. She drove through the morning, all the way down to London, accompanied by one of the crows—the one that carried the sign—flying ahead like a lodestar.

She reached East Finchley, where her nephew and his family lived, just before 8 A.M. No one answered the door when she rang the bell.

Violet got back in the car, for the first time wondering if it hadn't been a little mad, tearing across the country like this. But then she thought of the cross under the sycamore. She had already lost her daughter. Kate was her second chance—she couldn't let anything happen to her.

Where were they? It was a Thursday. Of course—on the way to school.

She parked near the house and sent the crow ahead, to be her eyes and ears in the sky. Her heart thudded with relief when the bird found her nephew and his little girl a few streets away, approaching a zebra crossing. But then she saw a car turning onto the street and ice brushed her spine.

It was the same red car from her dream.

Henry and Kate were already crossing the road. The car was getting closer.

Violet had to do something.

She closed her eyes, focusing on the gold glint she'd discovered inside herself, all those years ago.

As the crow called to her great-niece, Violet felt its cry in every beat of her heart, in every cell. Her only hope was that Kate did, too. She had to pull her away from that car, from the cruel-faced man she was certain was inside.

At first it seemed like it would work. The girl stopped and turned, gazing at the trees overhanging the road. But the car wasn't slowing down.

Get off the road. Hurry!

The crow took flight, and Violet saw Henry run back to his daughter. She saw him shout, then shove Kate out of the way. Rubber sang on metal as the driver hit the brakes.

But it was too late.

The sun lit on Henry's face for one brief moment, before his body crumpled underneath the car. The trees and the road swam together, a blur of green, white, and red.

After the peal of the sirens had died away, Violet started the engine and drove back to Cumbria. For the whole journey back, the accident played itself across her vision, again and again. Henry, risking his life to keep his daughter safe.

He was a good man, not like Violet's own father.

Even if Violet hadn't been there, he would have done anything to defend his child. He would have kept her away from the cruel-faced man. But Violet had never imagined such a possibility, that a father could be capable of such love.

So she interfered, and in trying to save Kate had instead put Henry in harm's way.

And now he was dead.

A strange animal keening filled her ears. It took her a moment to realize that it was the sound of her own weeping.

Violet didn't go to Henry's funeral. How could she face his wife and daughter, after what she had done?

The years rolled on, and it was easier not to put pen to paper, not to pick up the phone. Violet comforted herself by picturing her great-niece growing up. She imagined the skinny child maturing into a young woman, with the dark hair and glittering eyes of her forebears. A strong young woman, Violet told herself, in spite of her loss—reaching for life the way a plant reaches for the sun.

She'll be eleven now, starting secondary school.

Eighteen. Headed to university. Science, perhaps, like me. Or English, if she likes to read.

She still dreamed of the cruel-faced man, the driver of the car. Perhaps, she told herself, she really *had* spared the girl a fate worse than the loss of her father. Perhaps she *had* been right to intervene.

Henry had loved his daughter. Maybe he'd have understood what Violet had done.

Recently, Violet had had the disturbing realization that she was old. In fact—both her parents having died relatively young—she was the oldest person she'd ever known. (Apart, of course, from Frederick. He really was like a cockroach clinging to the underside of a rock.) Her skin and muscles seemed to be loosening from her bones, preparing to abandon ship. Before falling asleep each night, in that strange half-light between waking and dreaming, she had begun to wonder if she would still be there come morning.

Like a once bright fire burning to embers, her life was coming to an end.

She was running out of time to see her great-niece.

She'd hired a private investigator to track Kate down. He'd found an address, and Violet had been so thrilled that she'd braved the long drive down to London the next day. It was raining, and as the countryside passed in a green blur, her heart ached at the thought of a similar journey made so many years before.

But this would be different. A happy occasion.

She imagined embracing her great-niece, admiring the life she'd created. (A brilliant career, a beautiful home—filled with plants and animals, perhaps children, a kind man to share her bed. Two crickets, singing in harmony.) Sunshine broke through the clouds, making crystals of the raindrops on her windshield. She touched the locket under her shirt and her heart swelled.

But her excitement faltered as she pulled up outside Kate's address. A block of apartments.

Later, Violet would pinpoint this as the moment she knew something was very wrong. How could Kate be happy in this soot-stained place, the air warm with rubbish and exhaust? There wasn't a single note of birdsong, a single blade of grass.

But she hobbled carefully out of the car, forcing a smile.

A happy occasion.

"Hello—is Kate here?" There was something familiar about the man who answered the door. He wore an expensive-looking bathrobe, and Violet flushed at the realization that she'd interrupted her great-niece on a Sunday. Was this man her husband, boyfriend? She looked at him more closely. His hair was a tawny sort of gold, rather like a lion's pelt. His narrowed eyes were faintly pink, as if he'd had too much to drink the previous evening.

"No. There's no Kate living here," he said, though the set of his mouth told Violet he was lying. There was something cold in his voice. It made her think of Frederick.

She began to apologize, flustered—but he shut the door before she could get the words out.

Later, in the car, Violet realized why he looked familiar.

He was the cruel-faced man from her dream long ago, with the golden hair and livid eyes.

The world fell away as she realized.

She'd glimpsed *two* events from Kate's future, not one—the car accident that killed her father and then, many years later, the meeting of this man. The man who wanted to—perhaps already had—hurt her.

Just like her mother before her, Violet had thought she could change the course of the future as easily as tearing out the pages of a book. She'd thought she could save her great-niece.

She'd been wrong.

She hadn't saved Kate from anything.

But Violet was determined to make things right, while she still had breath in her body.

The day after her trip to London, she made an appointment to see a lawyer. It was past time she made a will.

At the lawyer's office, she remembered the bee brooch she had given to Kate when she was small. Perhaps Kate had lost it; perhaps she didn't even remember Violet—the eccentric old woman she'd met only once. The woman who had disappeared from her life, all those years ago.

But now Violet could make amends. She would give Kate her legacy.

She would give her a new life. Away from him.

"When the time comes," she instructed her lawyer. "Make sure you speak to my great-niece directly."

The light was fading outside. She squinted at her watch; it was half past ten already. Who knew where the last hour had gone. Time was funny like that, Violet thought. Speeding up and slowing down at the strangest of moments. Sometimes, she had the odd sensation that her whole life was happening at once.

Violet took off her necklace and put it on the bedside table. She rolled over onto her side, facing the window. The sun was disappearing behind the sycamore tree now, turning the garden red and gold. She closed her eyes and listened to the chatter of the crows. She was so tired. Darkness pulled at her, gentle as a lover.

She felt something brush her hand and opened her eyes. It was a damselfly, its wings fiery with the sunset. How pretty.

Her eyelids drooped. But something was tugging at her, keeping her awake.

Sighing, she sat up in bed. Reaching over to the bedside table, she tore a piece of paper out from her notebook. She hesitated for a while, thinking of what to write. Best keep it simple, she thought. To the point.

She scrawled the sentence down quickly, then rolled up the paper and put it inside the locket of her necklace.

She stowed the necklace safely in her jewelry box. Just in case.

*The connections between and among women
are the most feared, the most problematic,
and the most potentially transforming force
on the planet.*

Adrienne Rich

ACKNOWLEDGMENTS

When I was seventeen, finishing my final year of high school, my English teacher took me aside. "Whatever you do," she said, eyes bright with passion, "promise me you'll keep writing."

Mrs. Halliday, I've kept my promise. Thank you so much for nurturing my love of stories. I've taken the liberty of naming one of my characters in your honor. I hope you don't mind.

Felicity Blunt, my brilliant agent: your email changed my life. Thank you for making this a better novel, and for making me a better writer. Much gratitude to everyone else at Curtis Brown—particularly foreign rights marvels, Jake Smith-Bosanquet and Tanja Goossens. Thank you also to Sarah Harvey and Caoimhe White. Many thanks also to Rosie Pierce for your endless support and patience.

Alexandra Machinist, my US agent—I'll never forget that incredible phone call in March 2021. Thank you so much for your support.

Carla Josephson and Sarah Cantin: I couldn't have wished for better editors. I so treasure our working relationship and the magic you've worked on this novel. It has been an absolute joy.

Thank you to everyone at Borough Press and St. Martin's. I have been privileged to have such incredible teams on both sides of the pond. So many talented people have worked so hard on *Weyward*. At Borough Press, a huge thank-you to my lovely publicist, Amber Ivatt, and to Sara Shea,

ACKNOWLEDGMENTS

Maddy Marshall, Izzy Coburn, Sarah Munro, and Alice Gomer in sales and marketing. Thank you to Claire Ward for the stunning UK jacket design. Thank you also to Andrew Davis for the incredible ARC design and book trailer.

At St Martin's, I'm particularly grateful to Jennifer Enderlin, Liza Senz, Anne Marie Tallberg, Drue VanDuker, and Sallie Lotz. Thank you also to my incredible marketing and publicity team: Katie Bassel, Marissa Sangiacomo, and Kejana Ayala. Thank you to Tom Thompson and Kim Ludlam for the beautiful ARC design and graphics. In production, thank you to Lizz Blaise, Kiffin Steurer, Lena Shekhter, and Jen Edwards. Thank you so much to Michael Storrings for my gorgeous US jacket design.

I'm also very grateful to my excellent copy editors, Amber Burlinson and Lani Meyer.

I'm hugely grateful to everyone at Curtis Brown Creative, but especially Suzannah Dunn, my incredible tutor; Anna Davis; Jennifer Kerslake; Jack Hadley; and Katie Smart. And, of course, my lovely fellow students—thank you for your wonderful feedback and support.

Thank you to Krishan Coupland, whose encouraging comments on a very early draft of this novel inspired me to keep going.

I've been lucky in that I've been surrounded by those who believed in me from a very young age. My parents and stepparents—thank you for investing countless hours into my love of reading and writing.

My mum, Jo. You inspire me every day with your strength and resilience. I'm a feminist because of you. Thank you so much for supporting me every step of the way. And, of course, for reading (and discussing) this novel so many times. I don't know what I'd do without you.

Brian, I couldn't imagine a more supportive stepfather. Thanks for all your help and encouragement over the years.

My dad, Nigel—thanks for instilling me with your strong sense of justice, and with your determination. And, of course, thank you for reading this book!

Otilie, my stepmother (and another early reader!). Thank you for all your support, and for introducing me to some of the novels that inspired this one—including, particularly, *The Blind Assassin* and *Alias Grace* by Margaret Atwood.

My sister, Katie—you have always been my rock. Thank you for getting me through the bad times. The next one's for you.

My brothers. Oliver—thank you so much for reading this novel. I can't wait to see what you do with your own love of writing. Adrian—thank you for your faith in me, and for always making me laugh.

My grandparents Barry and Carmel. Your book-filled home is my sanctuary. Grandpa, thank you for your sharp wit (and your red pen). I'm thrilled to be following in your footsteps. Nana, thank you for your brilliant stories and your constant encouragement.

My grandparents John and Barbara—I wish you could have read this book.

My step-grandmother, Emőke. You've always inspired me so much. Thank you.

To Mike and Mary—I can't ever thank you enough for welcoming me into your beautiful home in Cumbria, where the first draft of this novel was written. Thank you for sheltering me during a pandemic and comforting me when I was so far from my family in Australia.

Ed—the first reader of this novel. I couldn't have written a single word without your love and support.

Clare, Michael, and Alex—thank you for the runs together, the wine, and the laughter.

My wonderful friends. I feel fortunate to know you all. But I must make special mention of Gemma Doswell and Ally Wilkes, brilliant writers themselves. Thank you for your incredible feedback—and your patience during a few panic attacks!

There was a time in my life when the writing of this novel—or indeed of any novel—seemed very much in doubt. I owe huge thanks to the medical staff who treated me after my stroke in 2017. To the doctors and nurses of the Moorfields Eye Hospital, Royal London Hospital, University College Hospital London, and St. Barts Hospital: you have my endless admiration and gratitude.